Twelve Motives For Murder

Download the Audiobook for the full immersive experience!

Twelve Motives For Murder

Fiona Sherlock

HODDERstudio

First published in Great Britain in 2020 by Hodder Studio
An imprint of Hodder & Stoughton Ltd
An Hachette UK company

This paperback edition published in 2021

5

A CIP catalogue record for this title is available from the British Library

B format ISBN 9781529360011
eBook ISBN 9781529360035

Typeset by Hewer Text UK Ltd, Edinburgh
Printed and bound in Great Britain by Clays Ltd, Elcograf S.p.A.

Hodder & Stoughton policy is to use papers that are natural, renewable
and recyclable products and made from wood grown in sustainable
forests. The logging and manufacturing processes are expected to
conform to the environmental regulations of the country of origin.

Hodder & Stoughton Ltd
Carmelite House
50 Victoria Embankment
London EC4Y 0DZ

www.hodder-studio.co.uk

To my darling little boy, Arthur x

The Characters

Jonty Caswell Jones

- Age: 45

Coffee merchant Jonty can't stand the taste of the beverage he sells, preferring tea, like most Englishmen! It's not the only secret he's keeping to maintain a facade. No matter where he travels on business, his heart remains in the greeny-blue waters of Lake Como. This Christmas, something feels amiss.

Catherine Caswell-Jones AKA Kate

- Age: 45
- Relationship to victim: wife

It doesn't take much to keep Catherine happy. As long as she gets her way, that is. Friction with her mother-in-law may bubble to the surface, but she's about the only person Catherine can't control. Retired from her war nurse duties, Catherine is a socialite. She can't abide by laziness.

Matilda Caswell-Jones

Age: 69
Relationship to victim: mother
The original Caswell-Jones matriarch, Matilda, has never been interested in domesticity. She prefers to collect exciting people, making her son feel like the odd one out at his own dinner table. She shows little

affection to anyone but her granddaughter, Polly. Matilda will go to any lengths to protect the honourable name of the Caswell-Jones.

Thomas Caswell-Jones

- Age: 21
- Relationship to victim: son

The heir to the Caswell-Jones estate, banker Thomas, does not attempt to hide the money lust running through his veins. Making a scene is his currency to get what he wants. He dreads his father cutting him out of the will. So consumed by greed, he may well take matters into his own hands.

Polly Caswell-Jones

- Age: 19
- Relationship to victim: eldest daughter

Polly is an art student who makes a keen study of life. The surrealism she enjoys on the canvas seems to echo in her own family. Only granny can keep her in check. But she's keen to distance herself from them and from outmoded ways of thinking. Polly wants her freedom and just can't wait any longer.

Flora Caswell-Jones

- Age: 17
- Relationship to victim: youngest daughter

The baby of the Caswell-Jones family, fair-haired Flora, is not as innocent as she seems. Academically brilliant, she will no longer accept being schooled. Flora is desperate to be treated as an adult; her reckless behaviour is erratic. Her father dare not tell her what to do, for she won't be happy until she's won him over.

Sally Lansdowne de Groot

- Age: 45
- Relationship to victim: ex-fiancée and best friend's wife

After jilting Jonty weeks before their wedding, Sally remained close to the victim by marrying his best friend. A wealthy businesswoman in her own right, she despises being introduced as Ludlow's wife. She seeks distraction from her faltering marriage, but appearances matter to Sally. Just as she is ruthless in business, she will do what she must to keep secrets buried.

Ludlow Lansdowne de Groot

- Age: 46
- Relationship to victim: best friend

Ludlow and Jonty are two friends more bound by decades of shared misdeeds than filial love. Jonty ignores his friend's outrageous flirtations with women and risky business practices. An avaricious stockbroker, Ludlow truly believes that everyone has their price and does not accept rejection in any form. Has Jonty outshone his old pal for the last time?

Nikolai Ivanov

- Age: 50
- Relationship to victim: friend of mother

Diminished from ballet star to ballet teacher, Nikolai is one of Matilda's 'collectable' friends. His friendship allows him access to the finer things in life, although he does not allow anyone to make him feel lesser. He has not always enjoyed a comfortable life and does not wish to return to hard times.

Francis Heath

- Age: 21
- Relationship to victim: friends with son

Writer and philosopher Francis has made a career from observing people. However, he detests when any attention is focused on him. A methodical thinker, Francis enjoys orchestrating circumstances to make the Caswell-Jones squirm. Can this family tragedy tug on his heartstrings?

Peter Smythson

- Age: 29
- Relationship to victim: Godson

Peter is the youngest son of a close family friend. An Olympic skier, spending Christmas with the Caswell-Jones family helps him remember his British roots. But he cannot let go of the anger at claiming only a bronze medal. Wondering where his life went wrong, Peter takes solace in midnight boat trips. Who knows what he's really doing?

Argento di Silva

- Age: 51
- Relationship to victim: paid friend

Eagle-eyed opportunist, Milanese native Argento has found a way to solve all of the problems in Jonty's life. Valet, lawyer, cook and alleged friend, Argento wields immense influence over Jonty, a fact which does not go unnoticed by his family. Despite his hatred for

Christmas and bad tailoring, he maintains a chummy disposition to get what he really wants.

Elizabeth Chalice

- Age: 36
- Relationship to victim: wartime colleague of wife

An unabashed hedonist, investigator Elizabeth Chalice likes her cigarettes like her men: strong. She's made her life mission on smoking out lying, manipulative criminals, so when old friend Catherine asks for her help, she has more than one point to prove. As a single woman living in Italy, she must do what she can to survive.

Margaret Horton

- Age: 47
- Relationship to victim: best friends with the wife

This lady who lunches has constructed her entire world on being a satellite of Catherine Caswell-Jones and her brood. A constant draw on the attentions of her hostess, Margaret does not welcome the return of Jonty. She hates just how much of Catherine's time he takes up.

Elizabeth's Introduction

ELIZABETH:

We are a selfish species. I remain dismayed at the motives for the murders I investigate. Revenge is one dish best served cold, but even in hot-tempered attacks, the killer's empathy for the victim is nothing but ice. They are cold. Heartless. From trivial annoyances between acquaintances to long and drawn-out family wars. Here, we have the murder of Jonty Caswell-Jones. I am Elizabeth Chalice, private detective and scrutineer. Are you taking notes? I must always journal my findings to keep the facts straight. Truth is clearer to me when written on paper.

So. Let us begin. It is Christmas day, 1953. After returning to my Milanese pensione following a fine Christmas dinner at the British Bankers' League, I was surprised when the call came through from none other than Catherine Caswell-Jones. Catherine, the victim's wife, is of course much too well bred to ever seem embarrassed about making such a call, but I could hear a light tremor in her voice as she settled on the word murder.

The December wind rattled around my ankles in the back seat of the black Fiat as the lights of the lakeside villa came into view. Deep in the rutted hills of the Italian countryside, I remembered how badly behaved I used to be coming here in years gone by. I am still badly behaved, just not here. I had spent some dazzlingly glamorous Christmases here. But the invitations dried up after a case went badly. I had not heard from the Caswell-Jones family in over five years until Catherine's call ... Of course, I am intrigued.

Meet the Victim

ELIZABETH:

I suppose I had better give you a little background on our victim, hadn't I? Luckily for you, I knew the man fairly well once upon a time. Poor Jonty Caswell-Jones. Born Jonathan Caswell-Jones, at the family estate in 1908. Jonty was a talented orator. An officer in the Fifth Berkshire Division during the war, he now ran the family business – he was a coffee merchant. Now, I can tell you Jonty was a good sort, prone to anxiety on matters of form and manners, but without a doubt he was a good friend and family man. On the phone, Catherine told me, with a quiver in her voice, that she had found him slumped over his desk with a sliver of blood trailing from his motionless mouth.

It was approaching eight o'clock when I arrived at Villa Janus. Catherine's daughter Polly opened the hefty mahogany door; the soft curl of her brunette hair sat expensively undisturbed by the increasing wind. The entrance hall was as tall as a church. Catherine and the rest of the family had congregated in the drawing room.

The hospitality I would have once received is greatly diminished – everyone knows there is a killer in their midst. Biting their nails and wringing their tissues ... the Caswell-Jones family and their eclectic Christmas house-party guests. What hidden agendas and past grievances will our investigations uncover? The voyeur in me is always thrilled by this part. Let us meet the suspects, starting with the Caswell-Jones family.

MEET THE SUSPECTS

CATHERINE CASWELL-JONES:

Thank you for coming. Elizabeth may have mentioned this already, but my name is Catherine; my *friends* call me Kate. It is my husband, my Jonty, who has been murdered. My dear man, Jonty. We've spent so many happy Christmases here, at Villa Janus, it is just horrifying to think that something as terrible as this could have happened. But, as always, I must thank Elizabeth for coming. It has been quite some time since we last saw her here. I must say, I do admire her bravery in returning. But, if she can get to the bottom of this, I'm sure we can put our past behind us. My dear, dear Jonty – he did not deserve to die so young. I cannot believe he is gone. And he's left us all, heartbroken, behind . . .

(The phone rings and Catherine answers it in the background.)

THOMAS CASWELL-JONES:

Right. I am Thomas, Thomas Caswell-Jones. The eldest child of Jonty and Catherine, who you have just met. My mother has never really been one to exaggerate . . . so her reaction here is so strange . . . We are *all* very sad father is dead, but really, it was nothing more than a tragic, untimely heart attack. As the eldest son, I really feel I must step in here and set the record straight. It's ludicrous forcing us to go along with this charade, with this bloody fraud. I cannot trust Elizabeth – we all heard what happened with that child . . . that case. She's not up to the job, and I highly doubt having her here is going to help anyone. There is simply no crime to investigate here – we all loved our father—

POLLY CASWELL-JONES:

Oh, do shut up, Thomas. Speak for yourself. Hello there. I'm Polly. Thomas's sister. I am not disappointed the old trout, my father, is dead, but I did not do it. Everyone here . . . they are all such phonies. If Mother says so, then I'm *certain* father was murdered by someone here. Goodness knows we all have a motive. You have quite the task on your hands, unpacking the minds of this motley collection of charlatans. I'm an artist, you know? And take it from me . . . I know only too well how art can imitate life, and I *fear* the dreaded portrait of this family that will be uncovered.

MATILDA CASWELL-JONES:

(Sternly) Polly! What a thing to say. *(To the reader)* Thank you for coming. I am sure you know me, but in case it is useful for your records, I am Matilda Caswell-Jones. Mother of the deceased. Both my boys are dead now – first my dear, dear William, now my only other child, gone. I must know what happened. I still don't understand why the official authorities aren't looking further into the matter, but we must remember the importance of keeping this terrible incident to ourselves. Elizabeth has a job on her hands, but I know Elizabeth well . . . haven't seen her in five years, but a woman like that never changes. I'm positive she will be keen to keep this discreet, too . . . Thank goodness. If Catherine and Polly's strange suspicions about Jonty's death are correct, the killer is here amongst us . . .

FLORA CASWELL-JONES:

(Sobbing) Granny, stop, please. Daddy is dead, and it is Christmas Day. This isn't how it's supposed to go. Let's not all fight. Oh, hello there. I'm sorry. I'm Flora Caswell-Jones. The youngest daughter of the Caswell-Jones family. I must apologise – we're in shock. This is rather horrible, absolutely unbelieveable. But I can make sure my family allow Lizzie – Elizabeth – to do her job and get to the bottom of it all. Mama, Granny, if you don't mind, I might take myself off. I'm feeling terribly panicked.

MARGARET HORTON:

Ah, Elizabeth is back . . . I am Margaret Horton. Kate – Catherine – is my oldest friend, and my cousin, and I'm godmother to those poor children, too. I'm very much a part of the family, as you can see. Poor old Jonty, it's truly tragic that he is no longer with us. But I must agree with Thomas, this obsession with murder . . . it's not healthy for anyone. Yes, he was a bit of a knave, but the chap had a dickie heart, and it stopped. Anyway, just for the record, I certainly didn't kill Jonty. Much as I might have liked to at times *(chuckles)*. Oh, sorry, not very funny, is it?

LUDLOW LANSDOWNE DE GROOT:

(Snidely) (To Margaret) Oh, you're here for them all right, Margaret, for them and the will reading. *(To the reader)* I am Ludlow Lansdowne de Groot, best friend of Jonty Caswell-Jones, successful stockbroker and godfather to Thomas . . . Don't be fooled by Margaret. You should know that while she might quickly claim she's innocent, she has always leeched off Jonty, acting as the old maid. Jonathan was my *best* friend, my oldest confidant. I am bereft at his untimely death. I'm sure he's up with Saint Peter quaffing a 1928 Pomerol, having a jolly good laugh at the trail of destruction. As Thomas's godfather, it is my duty to ensure he receives all that is owed to him without question. I welcome our detective, Elizabeth, questionable though her past experience may be. If she's any good, she'll put this whole murder business to bed without delaying things for Thomas. Am I right, my lady wife?

SALLY LANSDOWNE DE GROOT:

Quite, Ludlow. *(To the reader)* I'm Sally Lansdowne de Groot, Ludlow's wife. Jonty and I were cut from the same cloth. Born within six months of each other and raised in the very same town. I have known him longer than anyone else here, apart from you, Matilda. I can't quite take it in that he's dead. Bloody hell. Who could have done this? Anyway, you must know that this needs to be wrapped up quickly. I need to be back in London for New Year's

Eve, and do not intend for the entire Christmas break to be spoiled. Jonty would not have wanted that either. Of course, it goes without saying that I am completely innocent of any wrongdoing, but I am certain this little investigation will uncover some not-so-well-hidden secrets.

FRANCIS HEATH (WRITER):

Hello there . . . Let me introduce myself, shall I? If no one else is going to introduce me. I'm Francis Heath. I'm a friend of Thomas's and a friend of truth – I welcome any interrogation of reality. I'm a writer, you know? I see you've got a notebook at the ready. Memory is such a slippery thing, isn't it? But I am certain the old chap was killed. From my own observations, I don't think anyone here really likes each other. I'm a philosopher, I'm perceptive . . . I know, for example, that Elizabeth doesn't like our hostess, Kate, even though I'm sure they pretended to be friends during the war. Kate has already mentioned how *well* they got on during that time. But who am I to judge? I don't even really like Thomas, *(chuckles)* I just wanted to come for Christmas. And look at this place . . . who wouldn't? I'm sure I'm not the only one. Ah! Here's Peter . . . someone else you should meet. Did you know, Peter here was written into the victim's will only last year—

PETER SMYTHSON (SKIER):

Jesus, Frank, have some respect, will you? A man is dead. A good man. *(To the reader)* Yes, I am Peter. Peter Smythson. I have known Jonty my entire life, and witnessed nothing but a loving family man, a champion of commerce, and an advocate for those . . . who need it. We knew each other very well – I'm a skier, you see, an Olympic champion actually. Jonty Caswell-Jones has always supported me in my career and has treated me like his own son, too. He was a kind man, and I am happy to be interviewed to help find his killer. In my view, anyone who stands in the way of justice is as guilty as the murderer.

NIKOLAI IVANOV (DANCER):

Don't forget me. Your eleventh suspect. Are you keeping track of all these names? I hope you're writing them down somewhere! Ah, your notebook. Yes. Very good. Well, here, I am Nikolai Ivanov. You may or may not recognise my frame as that of a dancer . . . I trained in the Bolshoi Ballet. I have known Matilda, Jonty's mother, for quite some time, but, although I have been to Janus before, you should note that this is my first Christmas here. And certainly, it is not one I was expecting. To be frank, I have seen many murders. I can tell you that this is not one. Even the most skilled assassin in the Russian army could not conduct such an immaculate crime scene. There's not a sign that this is murder. As people have said, he had a weak heart. I expect that is what got him in the end.

CATHERINE:

Excuse me! Someone is on the phone for you, reader.

ARGENTO DI SILVA:

(Over the telephone) Hello there. Can you hear me? Yes, yes, I am Argento di Silva. I work for the family, but I am also a close friend. My dear pal Jonty is dead, and I am heartbroken I didn't get to say goodbye! I am on my way back now, and as soon as I arrive at Villa Janus I will help you find the killer. As the family's lawyer and now assistant, I can help provide any documents you might need. I will be there first thing in the morning with Jonathan's will.

ELIZABETH:

Now. I trust you have met all the suspects? We have twelve suspects . . . and twelve motives for murder. Why, you ask, am I including Argento, who wasn't even here when Jonty was murdered? A-ha . . . you'll have to wait and see. Now . . . keep an eye out for any strange behaviour, any suspicious answers to my questions, any inconsistencies in their own stories and others . . . be alert. There's a killer here, and we've got to find them.

Anyway, for now, where should I start my investigation, do you think? Half of the witnesses don't even believe it was murder. We should bear that in mind. Will their opinions change over the course of the interview? Or are they here to hide something from us? I have heard briefly what the constables have said about the crime scene – not a spot of anything suspicious, apparently. This leads me to believe it's a silent but deadly killer ... poison. Shall we see if my hunch is right?

EPISODE 1

Catherine Caswell-Jones

ELIZABETH:

Now, interviews. Suspects. Let's get going. There will be twelve interviews in total, for we must interview Argento once he arrives. Please do take note of each one in turn, if you can. Where shall we start? Naturally, I should begin with Catherine herself. After all, she is the person who called me here, the one who found Jonty's body, and, helpfully, she is the person here I know the best – she even lets me call her Kate. Once upon a time, we were friends. But I am not here for friendship, not today. I need to know one thing: what would motivate a wife to kill her husband?

Here we go. She sees me beckoning her into the elaborately corniced drawing room to begin. She is as perfectly put together as ever, not a hair out of place. There isn't a sweat patch or mark on her immaculate wool pencil dress. It's a wonderful claret, as red as the bow on the front door wreath.

CATHERINE CASWELL-JONES:

Elizabeth, I'm so pleased to be able to talk with you. Frankly and openly. I know on the phone you wanted to know his movements before I found him. I've been thinking long and hard about it, trying to get every detail right. After dinner, he just stormed off. I must say, it wasn't like Jonty, really, to go off in a sulk like that. I had noticed at dinner there was some tension between him and Ludlow. I had been too distracted orchestrating the various courses. It wasn't until halfway through the soup that I noticed Ludlow had completely turned his back on Jonty's end of the table. It was very rude. Jonty, I'm sure, would have hated it.

(Pause as tears catch her)

I'm sorry, Elizabeth, it's just, I used to love spying down towards the end of the dinner table to see what was going on. I would save it up as ammunition to tease Jonty with at night. To think I will never— (Her voice breaks up)

ELIZABETH:

Take your time, Kate, you've had quite the shock. I'm very grateful to you for thinking of all this detail. Can you remember who was sitting beside Jonty at the table?

CATHERINE:

(*Composing herself*) Matilda on his right; Sally – Ludlow's wife – was on his left. Ludlow is a man who *cares* about etiquette. It shocked me to see that he had turned his back on Jonty – they're so close, you know? – but I was perhaps even more surprised to see his back turned against his best friend's mother, Matilda. Ludlow would never normally be so impolite. This behaviour continued throughout the main course and into the *secondi* – we tend to do a mixture of British and Italian courses for Christmas, you may remember; this time it was roast turkey followed by a wild boar ragù.

ELIZABETH:

Yes, yes, that sounds delicious. Can you take me back to Jonty? So, he was sitting between his mother and Sally. Presumably Ludlow's rudeness was clear to all the guests. Did your husband seem put out by Ludlow's behaviour?

CATHERINE:

You know how much Jonty hated any conflict. All these years he's spent mediating between his mother and me because of that very fact. He just hated Ludlow's disruption, I could tell. The way he was smiling, but with dead eyes – like he was putting it on. There was something bothering him, clearly. But then again there seemed to have been something bothering him all week. Before we arrived on the twenty-third, the children and I hadn't seen him since September, when he left for the South American tour. I was shocked when he opened the door to me and the girls, he looked so wan. Unhealthy. I wondered if he was ill. But today Jonty seemed . . . I don't know . . . they have been friends since Stowe . . . Jonty always looked up to him and Ludlow didn't appreciate his friendship . . . it always seemed so one-sided. It has always upset me. Maybe today was the day Jonty realised it for himself . . . Oh, Elizabeth – how rude of me. Would you like a light for your cigarette?

ELIZABETH:

My cigarette is clutched between my teeth. My not-so-subtle hint . . . I'm sorry, I should have told you, my investigative brain doesn't quite work without some nicotine. But it has proved a good distraction technique, too . . . While Kate rustles around the marble-topped sideboard for matches, I must tell you what I know of Ludlow. He proved himself quite the cad to me in those first Christmases I spent at Villa Janus. I must file away my prejudice against him for the purpose of this situation.

A broad man, over six feet three, Ludlow's sheer physicality could have divided the dinner guests, causing a rift among the table perhaps. Kate has never worked very hard to disguise her dislike of Ludlow, that much was obvious even when I first met her during the war. I have always wondered whether her haughtiness towards Ludlow was out of concern for her husband.

CATHERINE:

Here you go. Well, where was I? Yes, it was always Ludlow this and Ludlow that, Ludlow hosts the grand garden party, is next in line for a peerage, Ludlow gets Thomas, our eldest, the job at Banc Le Bennet . . . Jonty followed him around like a lapdog. It was disgusting to see. *(Suddenly distracted)* Oh, look. Someone's out on the lake. It does look so beautiful at this time. So peaceful. It almost makes me forget . . .

ELIZABETH:

What? *(Slight pause)* Why is the skier chap – Peter Smythson, is it? – why is he taking a speedboat out in the middle of the night?

CATHERINE:

Thinking, I expect. Apparently his father was the same. Terrific fishermen, the two of them. Peter has been out there the past three nights. He just drives out so far, and comes back in.

ELIZABETH:

Ah . . . I see. Smythson . . . Smythson . . . Is his mother American?

CATHERINE:

Yes! How did you know that? He's an *Olympic* skier, you know? We've known him since he was a child. He's from three villages over in England.

ELIZABETH:

I can tell because of the little stars and stripes on his lapel. But Smythson is a British name. So that leaves an American parent to meet the citizenship requirement.

CATHERINE:

How in God's name can you see, let alone deduce all of that?

ELIZABETH:

That's why I'm here, isn't it? I noticed his lapel earlier when we met in the hallway. But sailing out on the lake in the middle of the night? It really is most peculiar behaviour, *especially* after a murder. But in my experience the strangest of actions are often the most readily explained. Nonetheless, it will need to be investigated, I'd better take note. *(Slight pause)* Now. Sorry, we got distracted. This view you have here . . . it's a wonder anyone gets anything done, isn't it?

What did I mean to ask you? Ah, yes. Today I saw the six hefty trunks and an array of suitcases at the bottom of your sweeping staircase with Ludlow's and Sally's initials. Were they arriving or preparing to leave, Kate? Is there anything you need to tell me about your Jonty and Sally?

CATHERINE:

(Laughing) Ha-ha. Ah, yes. The star-crossed lovers.

ELIZABETH:

I have always been amazed, during my stays here, that it never seemed to bother you. Jonty and Sally having once been engaged. And she was *always* around.

CATHERINE:

Elizabeth . . . there has never been anything to worry about. He married *me* in the end, didn't he? Sally is *completely* self-absorbed, of course, but it makes her easier to deal with. She's a very clever businesswoman and makes a good role model for Flora and Polly. I don't mind having her here. It's Matilda who can't stand it these days. Of course, she blames Jonty for not managing to sustain the interests of highly marriageable Sally. Such a slight would *never* have happened to William, Jonty's golden-boy brother. You know how Matilda is forever comparing the two? And who can compete with a dead man forever placed on a pedestal? I can't imagine how difficult it has been for Jonty to always feel like his mother would have happily traded which son died in the war . . . *(Gasping)* Elizabeth! Now that I mention it, one thing really did strike me as strange this year. Matilda took a decidedly back seat on this year's guest selection for Christmas. The inevitables aside, it's not like her to leave it to me. It really is very odd.

ELIZABETH:

Old age has begun to take its toll, perhaps? Maybe she felt she needed a rest.

CATHERINE:

Oh no, I don't think we are that lucky. I heard them arguing last night, on Christmas Eve – Matilda and Jonty, that is. She always insists someone walks her to her room at night, and of course Jonty is so *desperate* for her approval, the inheritance, everything, he just obliges . . . Well anyway, here's what happened: she's upstairs, directly over this room but at the back, overlooking the Orangery, and we hear a terrific banging, and the two of them just *shouting* at each other. In all the years I've known Jonty, I have never heard him raise his voice to that woman. Matilda used to tear shreds off him – but not so much in recent years. The argument, and Jonty's response . . . it was unusual.

ELIZABETH:

That must have been shocking for you all. Does Matilda speak about William often? And in front of Jonty?

CATHERINE:

I think her singular joy in life is recounting the life and times of William Henry Caswell-Jones. The right and true heir of Avonlea Hall. And yes, always in front of Jonty. That's part of her pleasure.

ELIZABETH:

So with William gone, and now Jonty, who is the heir now?

CATHERINE:

Well, it should be my eldest, Thomas . . . *(Growing angry)* Besides, why do you even need to know that? Jonty's not even cold out there . . . I haven't had time to think about—

ELIZABETH:

Oh dear, Kate, I'm sorry. I didn't mean anything by it. It's only . . . it's just for my investigation. Do you want to take a break? You must be heartbroken.

CATHERINE:

I'm sorry, I didn't mean to . . . Yes, I am heartbroken, but I am also still in shock, so I've been trying to capitalise on that. I want to lay things out for you before I really fall apart. Elizabeth, I know someone in this house killed Jonty. There is a murderer here, right now. I need you to find them.

ELIZABETH:

Here . . . someone is coming. A pair of hard-soled shoes heralds another Caswell-Jones into the room.

CATHERINE:

Polly, whatever is the matter—

POLLY:

Mother, there's been a theft . . . someone has stolen my notebook, you know, the one with the drawings?

ELIZABETH:

I would expect Kate to laugh at the absurdity of a missing notebook at a time like this when her husband, Polly's father, has just been murdered. Instead, a shadow of panic crosses her brow. Yes, she composes herself quickly, but not quickly enough. Clearly, this trivial news seriously disturbs her. There's something in the notebook she doesn't want anyone else to see, or notice. Polly, of course, is simply ignoring my presence, wholly consumed by her own distress.

CATHERINE:

Sorry, Elizabeth, that break might be a good idea after all. I need some coffee. Would you like some?

ELIZABETH:

I agree and watch mother and daughter leave in a forced show of calm. The room still smells of lily of the valley perfume, Matilda's signature scent, and cigarettes. Although I am sure I detected a hint of guilty sweat from the earlier congregation, too. Kate originally wanted me to contain them all here, in one room, but I prefer to let them roam. What they do with their freedom will be far more telling than keeping them cooped up. Kate is my chief suspect, despite her protestations and tears. It has not gone unnoticed, Kate's tiptoeing around my questions. Have you noticed it, too? She hasn't responded about the suitcases . . . skilfully sidelined . . . but I will give her time. I have nursed men back from the brink of death with Kate, through those wartime experiences . . . well, she was once a good friend to me – I know her well. But I need to be firm, direct, for we all know it is usually the person closest to the victim who has the most to gain from their murder. And Kate was jolly quick to change the subject from Sally and Jonty's engagement, despite the fact that she said herself it hardly bothers her now, almost thirty years later. Plus, while Matilda is the grand dame of the Caswell-Jones family, I suspect that Kate has since secretly superseded her dreadful mother-in-law as the true matriarch. Matilda isn't so happy to see me here ... have you noticed? In the past, Matilda has always found my presence acceptable, so long as I offered the dual benefits of socialite gossip and medical knowledge. Now I'm here for a very different reason, to investigate her son's murder, I can sense I am not so welcome.

I settle back into the armchair. The golden-panelled drawing-room is illuminated by the dark waters of the lake. I have the peculiar sensation of being in the centre of a raindrop about to break the water's meniscus. My thighs are sticky from the travel, and the lining of my dress is stuck to my nylons as I peer into the winter dark. The distant lights of Bellagio are twinkling, tapering to tiny communes across the lake edge. The console behind the sofa looks rather empty; I remember years ago Catherine had travelled with framed photographs to put around the villa. Not now, it seems. But there is a bunch of little dolls. Four of them in rag dresses with bright red lips. They are from South America, I'm not certain if they are Peruvian, or perhaps made by the Tarahumara tribe in Mexico. They do look out of place.

Kate and Polly are gone quite a while, but now Kate returns alone with a rattling tray. She pours coffee into squat espresso cups, the crema dribbling down the porcelain edge. Her hand shakes. I wonder what they spoke about. I wish you could be a fly on the wall for me. The whole situation smells off to me. A notebook. Why on earth is it so important? When I arrived, Polly had not been uncontrollably upset. She'd seemed tired, certainly, a little snarky and rude, too – but not upset. But then, ever since I've known that child, she's always been good at hiding her feelings. However, it seems to me she is considerably more distressed by this, her missing notebook, than she is by her father's murder.

CATHERINE:

Sorry that took so long, I had to make the coffee myself.

ELIZABETH:

Polly seemed quite upset. Is she okay?

CATHERINE:

She's always been rather disorganised. She's managed to misplace her art portfolio.

ELIZABETH:

It must be terribly important to her.

CATHERINE:

It's everything to her, the poor child. I'm sure it will turn up. Polly will be fine, you remember how wretched it is to be that age.

ELIZABETH:

All too well. Tell me, are those little dolls Flora's?

CATHERINE:

(Confused) What? Oh, these dolls, from the Andes, I believe. Can you imagine a girl of seventeen *still* collecting them? Jonty used to always bring home bits and bobs for the children, arrow heads, baskets, all sorts. There are shelves and shelves of curios at home in England. I insisted he stop.

ELIZABETH:

So, where did they come from?

CATHERINE:

Peter, our neighbour must have brought them for Flora. They are spooky little things, aren't they? Oh dear, you don't seem to be enjoying the coffee, Elizabeth.

ELIZABETH:

It's quite lovely.

CATHERINE:

It's far too strong. I'm sorry. Argento hasn't arrived yet.

ELIZABETH:

Please don't worry. Remind me, who is Argento again?

CATHERINE:

Argento di Silva. He called earlier. Poor chap. Used to be our
Italian lawyer but got himself into a bit of a scandal . . . We have
him here to help out – he looks after the house, helps us with various other things, and he's terribly passionate about cooking, so he
usually caters for us, too. It means he can make a little money. He
has joined us for dinner the past few years. We're all awfully fond of
him. His mother lives in Milan and hasn't been well – that's where
he is at the moment – but he should be here shortly. He actually
has some important papers for us all . . . it might be useful for you
to see, too. Speaking of important papers . . .

ELIZABETH:

*I spot Kate's eyes fly to the chequebook sitting on her desk. I prepare
myself for the awkward conversation that may follow – it is hard to get
paid in my line of work, so the cultivation and maintenance of friend-
ships with those much wealthier than me takes up much of my time. It
makes me feel cheap, but alas, it is essential.*

CATHERINE:

Before we get back to it, I wanted to raise the matter of your fee.

ELIZABETH:

I have known you for years, Kate, I don't expect payment.

CATHERINE:

Please, I insist. I'd rather we settle the matter now. Sterling or lira?

*(Scratching of a pen on paper – sound of Elizabeth writing down a
figure)*

ELIZABETH:

Here you go.

CATHERINE:

Very well.

(Scratching of a pen on paper – sound of Catherine writing the cheque)

CATHERINE:

The reason we are hiring *you*, of course, is that we want to keep this private, a family matter. For now, anyway. Until we know where we are with things. Are you sure you understand?

ELIZABETH:

Of course. I understand. Remind me again, how and when did you find Jonty's body?

CATHERINE:

It was just after four o'clock. I knew the time because I was waiting for the limoncello cake to cook in the oven . . . It had been in there for almost half an hour and was still cold; I was worried it would be dried out. Jonty came to tell me he had something urgent to do and to call him when the next course was served. I asked what could possibly be urgent on Christmas Day. But he just walked off in a huff. I stoked up the coals a bit and put the cake back in. I'll admit the lunch was poorly organised without Argento; they were all getting restless. I went in to top up the glasses and saw three more empty chairs. Polly, Ludlow and the writer chap had disappeared. Matilda was bent over the table completely incapacitated by alcohol. It was very unlike her to be that rude . . . she must have had quite a bit to drink. In all the years I've known her she has never been prone to drinking like that, especially in front of so many guests. I spotted Polly out on the patio and signalled for her to come back. Instead, she turned around to light a cigarette. When I went out to drag the child back in, I saw there were tears in her eyes. She wouldn't admit it, but that young chap, the writer . . . I think something is going on between them . . .

ELIZABETH:

I'm sorry to push, I know this is hard, but can you tell me about . . . about the body, Kate?

CATHERINE:

Yes, well, when I got to Jonty's study to call him for food . . . the door was shut firm, which was the first sign that something was not right. Jonty didn't like to close his office door. When I opened it, well, there he was. Lying flat across the desk – almost exactly like Matilda had been at the lunch table. You know, I thought at first that's what he was doing, making a joke because she had been so drunk – but I realised he hadn't seen her like that, and the way his eyes just focused into the corner . . . He was still warm. *(Pause for a guttural sob)* Ididtrytoresuscitatehim. . .butIknew,therewasnopulse—

ELIZABETH:

Oh, Kate. I'm so sorry. Can you tell me what you did next?

CATHERINE:

I must have let out a wail. The children came running. I know they're grown, but, well, I didn't want them to see . . . But it was too late. Thomas came in first – his face was red, like he had been shouting. Tears still rimmed Polly's eyes – she looked forlorn. I tried to get them out. Flora appeared quite a while later, thank God – I wouldn't want her scarred, she's still so young, only seventeen – not quite a young woman yet. Thomas called the doctor, he came quickly. Hmm. I hadn't thought about who called the undertaker, but it is important. Now I think about it, Thomas must have called the undertaker, too, as they arrived together from Bellagio. Within thirty minutes. Anyway, the undertaker was a small man with a thin moustache. I remember he said to me in slightly broken English: 'The dead do not know it is Christmas.' It was like a dream . . . but at some point, when they were wrapping him up to take him off, I realised I should have called the police. Thomas objected, accused me of dramatics . . . but I went ahead. I know they would need to preserve the evidence . . . and moving the body had already disrupted things. The officers looked around – two local chaps – they sighed and commiserated but shrugged it off as one of those things . . . Thomas, I'm sure, encouraged them to think I was mad.

His Italian is quite good. Better than mine. Margaret had to translate for me.

ELIZABETH:

(Sternly) So why am I here, Kate? If the local police said there is no crime?

CATHERINE:

Elizabeth, they weren't going to get a detective involved. They just wanted to get back to their Christmas lunch. They certainly didn't look likely to disturb a superior officer for some mad woman claiming her husband was murdered. After all, there wasn't a mark on the body . . . But I just know. I *know* Jonty was murdered. You're a detective, Elizabeth, I'm sure you know the importance of following your intuition.

ELIZABETH:

Of course, but he *did* have a heart condition, didn't he?

CATHERINE:

Yes, that's true. But, well, there's something else. I didn't even try to explain it to the investigator, but a few months ago, when Jonty was at home in Berkshire, he was very on edge. Screaming at me and the children . . . refusing to answer the telephone. One night I overheard him crying in the study. Not that I'm one to pry . . . but I needed to find out what was the matter with him. I went into the study and found a letter in the wastebasket.

ELIZABETH:

What did it say?

(Catherine shuffles around)

CATHERINE:

Here, read it for yourself. I brought it here with me as I wanted to ask Jonty about it. I thought he might be more relaxed here.

ELIZABETH:

Very well. Thank you. *(Reads aloud) Jonathan, watch where you are stepping, there are loose rocks and steep cliffs. You don't want to lose your footing, or worse, get pushed. (To Catherine)* It's typed – not signed, there's a brown mark here, it looks like—

CATHERINE:

It's tea, it had been spilt all over the bin.

ELIZABETH:

Who do you think sent it?

CATHERINE:

Heaven knows! Jonty is a coffee trader, after all – with all that travel, he meets hundreds of people a year. The reference to the cliffs, I wondered if it was a metaphor or if it was referring to something directly. For ages, I could not narrow it down to any situation . . . but then I remembered Villa Janus, this villa. All along the eastern edge is a loose cliff. Do you remember it?

ELIZABETH:

I remember we used to jump off it in the middle of the summer. But falling from it wouldn't cause death, would it?

CATHERINE:

Perhaps not in the summer, but that water is freezing right now. A few seconds would shock the system, for someone like Jonty.

ELIZABETH:

A shock big enough to cause a heart attack . . .

CATHERINE:

Exactly.

ELIZABETH:

So he had an enemy, who perhaps knew of his heart disease. But that isn't how he died – and the fact is, he did have a weak heart. I need to ask you again, Kate, *why* are you so certain that he was murdered, and didn't just die of natural causes, a very likely heart attack in a man with chronic and ongoing heart issues? You must have a suspect in mind. Who do you think killed your husband, Kate?

CATHERINE:

If you want my honest opinion, Elizabeth, I wouldn't put it past any of them.

ELIZABETH:

That is a chilling thing to say, Kate. But you need to be honest with me. You are so certain he was murdered. Do you have one single suspect in mind?

CATHERINE:

This is difficult for a mother to say. I *never* want it to get back to him, and it's one of the reasons I knew I could only trust you with this – for you know this family better than most. But, Elizabeth, I believe Thomas killed my husband.

(Pause)

He is capable of anything. He was so keen for the police not to get involved, and he has never got along with his father. It was the main reason I tried so hard to get him out of the country as soon as he finished university. They fought all the time. Thomas wanted to become more involved in the estate, the company, but Jonty would *not* let him. Thomas has been *so* different lately. He has always been difficult – I'm sure you remember from your stays here, years ago – but recently it's as if he has been possessed by . . . some sort of evil. Ludlow thinks I'm crazy, too, of course; he does not believe it's murder, and he'd *never* suspect Thomas, but . . . out of everyone here, Thomas posed the biggest threat to Jonty.

ELIZABETH:

How old is Thomas now?

CATHERINE:

Twenty-one. But don't let his youth fool you. There was an incident . . . in school. He must have been about twelve. Thomas claimed it was a horse-riding accident. They were going for a morning out on the gallops, him and this other chap. They get split from the rest of the group on the way back, then Thomas arrives back at school with this chap's body across his lap on the horse, with the other horse following behind. Says the horse reared on the friend and crushed his skull. It was *Ludlow* who convinced the headmaster to let it all go. I've never trusted either of them since that day. We all knew there was something not quite right about it.

ELIZABETH:

So Ludlow and Thomas are close?

CATHERINE:

Very. Ludlow and Sally have no children, so Ludlow takes his role as godfather very seriously. I had been glad of their relationship, if I'm honest. Jonty came back from the war a totally different person. He had no real interest in Thomas. Or the rest of us. Jonty just never seemed to get over William's death, or the shadow William left behind.

ELIZABETH:

His brother, William, what happened to him? I heard once that he was in a prisoner-of-war camp.

CATHERINE:

That's right. Vincigliata Castle. Near Florence. Lots of high-ranking officers. William died in the camp. Dysentery, I think, not that Jonty ever wanted to speak about it. They were unspeakably lucky, to find each other in there, to have that time together. Matilda always said the wrong son came home, you know, when they were arguing.

ELIZABETH:

I can only imagine that made for a difficult relationship.

CATHERINE:

To say the least.

ELIZABETH:

And how did you and Jonty cope during the war?

CATHERINE:

It was hard. We saw each other four times in six years. Not that that was unusual, even for officers, but each meeting just became more awkward. I'm sure you know much of this, but he was stationed at Aldershot initially, then went to France, then was captured in 1943 and taken off to the camp. The children were lucky – they stayed in Berkshire with Matilda, though they won't remember much. Flora was only a toddler when it started. But the war – it changed us all, didn't it? Tell me, do you ever think about that night?

ELIZABETH:

What . . . You don't mean . . .?

CATHERINE:

Yes, you know.

ELIZABETH:

All the time, Kate. But you and I both know that fellow deserved it.

CATHERINE:

It's taken me a long time to shed the fear, Elizabeth. You know, anytime some official sort turns up at the door, people recording statistics or that sort of thing. I worry it will come back to me.

ELIZABETH:

What he did to that girl, it ruined her life.

CATHERINE:

But it's not for us to decide, is it? Judge, jury and executioner.

ELIZABETH:

I doubt anything would have happened to him otherwise. He was a Captain or some other high rank.

CATHERINE:

We got a good dark night, I suppose . . . *(Snide laugh!)* You know, Elizabeth, I am sorry that we stopped, you know, having you here. I noticed after you came the first time – I realised how much your presence brought back to me the shame. Seeing your face just reminded me of that night.

ELIZABETH:

I know I am not here to discuss what happened all those years ago, but do you think – and I'm not going to leave until I've got to the bottom of this – do you think you could be reliving what happened to that chap now, and that's why you're so jolly certain Jonty was killed?

CATHERINE:

(Sharply) I want an investigator, Elizabeth, not a psychiatrist.

ELIZABETH:

Look, Kate. It is coming up to ten, I am an *investigator* and I really want to interview as many people as possible before bed tonight, so I will want to revisit some things with you. A few last things and then I'll wrap it up. I need you to be honest with me. Any affairs? You or Jonty.

CATHERINE:

Me, no, haven't the time or the inclination. Jonty, probably. His great tours take him away for a while, to all sorts of interesting places. I'm no fool. I know how the world works.

ELIZABETH:

What sort of travel is it that he does?

CATHERINE:

The winter tour, which he's just come back from. It's a public relations exercise mostly. He visits the brokers who haven't ordered enough coffee this year. Tells them what innovations and improvements to the coffee planting and harvesting and processing have taken place. Presents expensive cigars and Scotches, generally wines and dines them.

ELIZABETH:

Where did he go?

CATHERINE:

Buenos Aires, New York, Montreal, sometimes to the plantations themselves – the largest is in Guatemala.

ELIZABETH:

I would like full details of his trip. Can you ask his secretary or assistant to send it to me?

CATHERINE:

I may be able to convince her to go into the office, but it is Christmas Day, Elizabeth. I'm not even sure she's at home or near a telephone. There are some notes in his study – you might be best placed to look in there.

ELIZABETH:

Fine. One last thing. And please don't take offence.

CATHERINE:

I can't promise that.

ELIZABETH:

I know this chap Argento was meant to be here, but you have no other help for this trip, no one to clean?

CATHERINE:

My family have spent their whole lives being pampered with staff. I wanted them to realise, you know, how important the cooks, the cleaners all are. I wanted them to see that they can't always expect to be waited on hand and foot. They take things for granted, but times have changed. They needed to realise that. Jonty is – was – the worst of them all. He was slovenly, and I wanted more than anything to teach him a lesson. Of course, you're right, even with

Argento here there wouldn't be a full dinner service, no housekeeping. But they need to learn, Elizabeth. It's about time they realised the world does not revolve around them . . .

ELIZABETH:

Without waiting for further interrogation, Catherine Caswell-Jones leaves me alone in this room. So, what do you think? Do you believe her? Kate is certain her husband has been murdered by one of their guests, and, in her view, his own son, but that does not discount her as a suspect in my mind. Wives have been known to kill their husbands for the most trifling of reasons. And no staff, what could that possibly be about? Surely the family could spare a few lira for some help. Now, throughout my interview with his widow, a woman I nursed with during the war, a woman who invited me into her home as a friend – I watched for signs of guilt. I am very aware that she avoided some of my questions. She was leading me to certain areas of inquiry, wasn't she? But for what purpose? While there is something bothering her that I can't quite identify, in the end, what can we note down as her only clear motive for murdering Jonty? The fact that she hated how slovenly he was? How very . . . unconvincing. Not quite what I've been looking for . . .

EPISODE 2
POLLY CASWELL-JONES

ELIZABETH:

I can't trust the time on the carriage clock in here. Not that Catherine Caswell-Jones wishes anyone to know it, but Villa Janus is rented. So who winds the clocks? I know it's not the Caswell-Joneses. This villa is usually a place where time stops. It creates a particular problem for an investigator like me, when the clock can't be trusted. Modern clocks will work fine, but in this warehouse of antiques, must each timepiece be inspected? Checking against my own wristwatch, this gold rococo number displays the same time as my own wristwatch: ten-thirty on Christmas Night. So far, I have interviewed one suspect in the murder of Jonty Caswell-Jones, and what did we think? Did the wife do it? If his wife is a woman passed over, their eldest daughter – an artist repressed by her family – is a woman scorned. That notebook likely holds more than some sketches. Could there be a link with the writer fellow?

Polly's eyes were red when I last saw her – I know she's always been one to hide her emotions, hiding behind this stern exterior, rather spikey sometimes – she'd never admit it to me, but despite her words, I am sure her father's sudden death has rattled her . . . she will have felt something: anger, grief or even relief . . . perhaps. He may not have been a permanent fixture in her life, given that he was away so often, but he was a prominent one – from what I know, he was often dictating her life. She wears her hair in the same style as her mother but is far from a picture of health. Her chin is flagged by light bulges of flesh. The emerald-green skirt can barely zip up, the catch left undone as she tries to disguise it with a peplum and loose blouse. Well. Shall we find out some more from the woman herself?

POLLY:

My turn is it, Elizabeth? Has Mother brought you completely up to date on poor Daddy's demise? Did Mother tell you about the ridiculous showdown on the veranda? Giuseppe, the little undertaker chap – and these two clownlike police officers. Mother wouldn't let them put his body in the truck . . . so there he was, on the stretcher. The sun was setting, it was this gaudy orange colour, like how you'd picture the skies during the unfolding of the long-lauded rapture . . . He would have appreciated that, you know? Father enjoyed watching Mother get herself in tricky situations. They had a sort of loving contempt for one another.

ELIZABETH:

Quite the scene, I imagine. Tell me, Polly, were your parents happily married?

POLLY:

(Laughs) They were *successfully* married, I think that's how they would both refer to it. I'm not sure how much love came into things. They didn't see much of one another, really. Father travels – travelled – so much and even when he was at home in Berkshire, Mother would find reasons not to be there. But they put on a good show when they needed to, for Christmas, the annual garden party.

ELIZABETH:

Why is she so convinced he was murdered?

POLLY:

Oh, you know Mother. She's such a very *proper* sort of woman, so she must have some strong evidence. Catherine Caswell-Jones is not prone to hyperbole. Her conviction has me convinced.

ELIZABETH:

Do you think she could be trying to detract attention from herself? Could she have murdered your father?

POLLY:

Do you mean she's double-bluffing us? If she murdered him, *surely* she would want father to go off in Giuseppe's little van? Anyway, I know my mother is no killer.

ELIZABETH:

If you could make up your own mind, without taking into account your mother's steadfast belief, would you say your father was murdered?

POLLY:

Well, I'm not sure I personally would say murder . . . but someone had a blazing row with him after he left the table, before – well, you know. Right before he died. I can't quite believe I'm saying that about my own father. Anyway, everyone here knew that he had a heart condition . . . that's why he drank tea, you know? Even though coffee was his life, it was too much for his old ticker. Ironic, really.

ELIZABETH:

This is immediately before he died . . .?

POLLY:

Yes, earlier on today, right in the middle of Christmas lunch. Mother was taking quite some time with the cake . . . the air was so stuffy in that room, so I had to get some air. Maybe twenty minutes before Mother found him. I could hear the vibration of the two voices, Daddy and this other chap . . . it sounded like a *strong* discussion – but then things really lifted up a notch. I could hear a bang, sort of a slap-bang, as if something was thrown against the wall. As I said, this was before Mother found him and let out that almighty shriek . . . it was as if she cleaved a chink between this world and the next.

ELIZABETH:

How poetic you are, my dear.

POLLY:

I try. But anyway, I couldn't recognise the other voice, or hear exactly what they were saying. But whoever it was knew for certain that Daddy had heart trouble. You see, last night, when we all arrived for Christmas Eve drinks, Daddy was on tremendously good form, keeping our limoncellos topped up and cracking jokes. But he made a real point of reminding us all of his weak heart, strangely. He told us specifically 'not to sneak up behind him', et cetera. Whoever he was rowing with today could have used it against him.

ELIZABETH:

How do you know he had a row with somebody?

POLLY:

When I was outside, that's when I heard shouting from his office. He liked fresh air, so his window was open, even in the middle of winter. The sound travelled easily.

ELIZABETH:

It's just over there, beside the Orangery?

POLLY:

Yes, I was the other end of the patio, but I could still hear . . . it was definitely a chap's voice. Really going at it. I even heard poor Papa say, 'Over my dead body,' at some point. Then it all went quiet.

ELIZABETH:

Were you alone out there?

POLLY:

Yes. Completely alone.

ELIZABETH:

Polly readjusts her seat. The cold December air is beginning to invade the room, as the last tendrils of heat fade from the fire. I know Polly's assertion that her mother could never be a killer is not true. I cannot bear to linger further on the details of that night, in what seems like another lifetime ago . . . But of course, Polly likely knows so little about it. I know her mother better than she expects.

I reach for some firewood, knotted together in the basket, and I shake the wood loose. You see, at times, I like to slow an interview down – it can help when a suspect uses this time to overthink, and sometimes they start to open up, too . . . This young woman is identical to her mother; she has the same eyes, the same smile, and large lips, which she's now chewing nervously, catching the loose bits of skin between her teeth . . . My trick is working a treat. I can see her arms pulled protectively around her waist. A dark purple shadow has settled itself heavily around

her eyes. She is exhausted, but it is caused by more than one late night.
Polly Caswell-Jones is either very unwell or she hasn't slept properly in
months. At her age, what might cause her to lose so much sleep?

I stamp out the sparks that have splintered across the elaborate
Persian rug of the drawing room. Mud from the streets of Milan is
caught under my heel, reminding me of what a long day it has been –
with ten more suspects to interview, it is far from over yet. Polly yawns,
drawing tears to the edges of her eyes. She stares into the indigo dark
that hangs around the intricate cornicing. The ceiling in this room must
be twenty feet tall, we are enveloped in a golden orb of light from the
banker's lamp between us. Polly's demeanour shifts, her eyes conducting
a full examination of her cuticles. Her nails are stubby, broken, another
indicator of the young woman's poor health.

POLLY:

Elizabeth, are we nearly done here? I really am very tired.

ELIZABETH:

Just a little longer. How's university going?

POLLY:

What's that got to do with anything?

ELIZABETH:

Fine arts, in York, isn't it? And a masters on the cards, too? It must
be wonderful to come to such beautiful surroundings.

POLLY:

Pfft. I'm not so keen on the theory; it's rather dense, you know? But
my parents didn't believe in unleashing an eighteen-year-old on the
world to 'be an artist'. Not desirable in a debutante either, apparently. So here we are. After hanging on for the past two years by a
thread, I am on course to fail.

ELIZABETH:

Have you spoken to them about it?

POLLY:

There's nothing to say on the matter, according to father. He gave me two choices. Finish York or find a husband. Or else he'd cut me off.

ELIZABETH:

That's three choices. Which one will you take?

POLLY:

(Laughing) The penniless artist has a nice ring to it.

ELIZABETH:

Did your father know your plan?

POLLY:

I'm sure he had an idea. But it's hardly worthy of patricide. I didn't kill him.

ELIZABETH:

What happened with your notebook? Did you find it in the end?

POLLY:

It got . . . damaged. Some of my work is not acceptable for a girl in my position.

ELIZABETH:

Such as?

POLLY:

Oh, don't be coy, an unmarried woman like you, living over here independently. You're a woman of the world. You know what I mean.

ELIZABETH:

I am not unmarried. I'm widowed.

POLLY:

Sorry for your troubles, but you know what I mean. My sketches featured some rather . . . spicy images of the human form.

ELIZABETH:

Good Lord. I can't see your mother welcoming those all right. Did she know they were in the notebook?

POLLY:

Mother didn't see them, I don't think. I had been sketching the family, for a series of portraits. She was very excited about it when I told her, keen to see the sketches of her and father. She was very protective over my artwork – she didn't want anyone else to judge me the way father had done. Anyway, the notebook turned up back in my room – very peculiar, a few pages had been ripped out. I can't quite remember what was on those pages.

ELIZABETH:

Who would have done that?

POLLY:

Flora, perhaps Thomas. My siblings are very spiteful, you know? Getting upset would only play into their hands. In the end, it's only a few sketches.

ELIZABETH:

I see. Right. Tell me about last night. From what I remember of my time at Villa Janus, Christmas Eve is always the gala night. Is that right? And Christmas lunch is far more relaxed.

POLLY:

Yes, the Christmas Eve Ball. A Caswell-Jones tradition. Joyfully implemented by old Matilda and rigorously enforced by Mother. Dinner and dancing, cards and smoking, you know how it goes.

ELIZABETH:

How did everyone seem?

POLLY:

It was all business as usual until dinner. It was jolly lovely to be here, it always is, you know. No matter what else has gone on throughout the year, when I see the orange turrets across the lake

– well, it is home, I suppose, for the holidays, as they say in the States. Mother did a great job with the nativity, and there must have been fifty candles around the dinner table. Even Thomas arrived in time to join in a toast, still in his travelling clothes. There was a terrific sense of togetherness. Thomas usually lives in London, you see, but had been travelling in America, so came directly from New York. He deplores dressing for dinner anyway, but Granny insisted he smarten himself up. She really was quite unhappy with him. Sally and Ludlow arrived late; she was frazzled. You could hear her screeching at him throughout the house – there was such an echo from their room, the Marble Room. The atmosphere changed dramatically at that point. The food was wonderful – the juiciest oranges for dessert. Frankie, the dark horse – the writer, you know? Well, he had sourced an expensive bottle of Sauternes and we all knocked it back, but then Nikolai knocked it off the table. It was an accident – he had been helping Margaret up from the table. Then Nikolai told us all that he saw Frankie steal the bottle from Sally's bag. Their luggage was splayed all over the entrance hall. Frankie made a horrid fuss of the thing, swore he brought the wine himself – he was certainly not philosophical about it. It all got quite heated – Nikolai was very angry, too! He hates to see any sort of injustice.

ELIZABETH:

What did Sally have to say about it?

POLLY:

Nothing – she just seemed bemused at the coincidence that they would both bring the same wine. She didn't seem too bothered. Afterwards I noticed Frankie slink off with Thomas somewhere. Thankfully, Flora managed to rescue the night – she had us all dancing to that chap Dean Martin.

ELIZABETH:

That sounds more like the Villa Janus events I remember . . . Who were you dancing with?

POLLY:

Oh, I see what you're doing, Elizabeth. You're trying to see who my love interest is. Nobody here, let me tell you that.

ELIZABETH:

Just answer me, Polly. Who were you dancing with?

POLLY:

Granny mostly, but then she objected and insisted on pairing us up. I took turns with all the chaps, apart from Father. He's a terrible dancer, always standing on my dress – you know he's so short . . . I mean, he *was* so short. *(Tone becomes mournful)* Gosh, it's so terribly easy to forget. He is gone, that's it, he's not coming back.

ELIZABETH:

I know, Polly. Do take your time. But I must ask, how did you finish the night?

POLLY:

I left at about midnight, but everyone was still there, the chaps jolly well tucking into the Scotch, Daddy's good Scotch, which he usually saves for his clients. There were two tables of bridge. But I did notice something strange. It is most inconvenient that Mother refused to have the Conte family here to help us. I had to poke under the stairs for some candles. Anyway, I found a candlestick, and heard Sally laughing. Thomas was there . . . his jacket off. It looked like he was having quite the time with Sally. They must have been kissing. She was drunk, after her earlier episode. He can be such a devious little fox. I figured it was harmless enough.

ELIZABETH:

Did they realise you saw them?

POLLY:

(Dismissive) They heard something, they paused and looked across the marble floor in my direction, but I managed to stay in the shadows. After that they parted ways. I love those moments – I enjoy

scratching the scabs of life's dark little moments. I am an artist, after all. Or at least I can be, now that father isn't here to stop me. Granny promised to help me, too.

ELIZABETH:

How is she? I was surprised to hear about such an upstanding woman, asleep, conked out at the table at lunch—

POLLY:

None of us is perfect, Elizabeth. She had a little too much to drink. She usually doesn't imbibe at all and the wine was a strong Cabernet. She is in perfect health. You know it was actually *her* idea to call you?

ELIZABETH:

But your mother—

POLLY:

My mother loathes to admit it, but she knows Granny is very often correct about these things. Granny wanted it all kept in the family. Maybe she thinks Mother is crackers and doesn't want her embarrassed. But you can be damn sure it's to guard the family name. Nothing matters to Matilda Caswell-Jones as much as appearances. You of all people know that . . . it's one of the reasons you stopped getting invited, of course.

ELIZABETH:

Thank you for that, Polly. Your grandmother is very fond of you. If I remember correctly, she used to let you sleep in her room when you were a little girl?

POLLY:

She used to call me the pretty fairy she never had. Everyone knows I am Granny's favourite, but these days I wonder if it's only because I remind her of Uncle Will.

ELIZABETH:

Do you remember him?

POLLY:

No, I was seven the last time he was at Avonlea, our home in Little Bedford, Berkshire. By all accounts he sounds like a jolly fellow, not that father ever discussed him. Some people said that they looked like twins. It was strange that he never spoke of him to us. But now, with both him and my father gone, I suppose Thomas is the heir to the family fortune. I'm lucky Granny favours me so.

ELIZABETH:

Why do you think she prefers you?

POLLY:

Thomas makes no effort with her. Granny is quite a hands-on person, for her age, you know? She still hunts, makes jams, mends clothes. A bit like me, you know. And Thomas is not very well adjusted to being around other people.

ELIZABETH:

How do you mean?

POLLY:

There was an incident in Thomas's office, that's why he got sent abroad by the bank. Threw a kettle of boiling water on some poor secretary because she brought him Assam instead of Ceylon. Nothing was ever done about it, of course. Ludlow settled something with his employer, the girl was given some money and it was all hushed up.

ELIZABETH:

Good Lord, when did this happen?

POLLY:

About a year ago. And when we were teenagers—

ELIZABETH:

He arranged for a horse to kick—

POLLY:

No, no, not that, that was quite the trouble, too, but before that, he poisoned the groundskeeper's dog. Ground up glass and fed it to him. The creature hadn't done a *thing* to him – it was just because he didn't like the look of it. An Irish wolfhound. I remember him howling in agony before he bled to death. And Thomas told me what he had done, like he was proud of it – but I was too scared to tell anyone else at the time. I don't think anything can be done. He covers up his dark side so well.

(A knock at the door)

ELIZABETH:

Come in.

(Matilda enters)

POLLY:

Granny, why are you still up?

MATILDA:

Elizabeth, you have kept my granddaughter here for far too long. She had no involvement in her father's death. She needs to rest.

ELIZABETH:

Matilda, we are nearly finished here.

MATILDA:

If you ask me, you need to take a look at that Sally. She has *plenty* of secrets to hide. You make sure you finish up soon, Polly needs to sleep. She's just lost her father, for heaven's sake.

(Door closes)

ELIZABETH:

Your grandmother cares a great deal about you.

POLLY:

Everyone says that, even little Flora. I know I'm her favourite, but really she loves us all the same.

ELIZABETH:

Did Matilda play a large part in your upbringing?

POLLY:

Well, during our childhood, Granny didn't have much to do with us, really. We stayed in the gate lodge, as the house itself was requisitioned by the War Office – we were so close to Bletchley, so they used it to put up visiting dignitaries – so Granny was often too busy doing her charity rounds in the country. Or maybe she was preoccupied by fear that the soldiers might break some of her valuables – the Sargents, and those other nice pieces of art. Granny didn't really give a jot about us. Not until after Uncle Will died. Then she was leading the charge with baking and this, that and the other. She was so privileged, she had never experienced the loss of anyone before. Her parents, even her husband, Grandad, all died of old age. When Uncle Willie died, it was as if she lost something she never realised she had in the first place.

ELIZABETH:

How has she been today? Since . . . Jonty's death.

POLLY:

She must have a sore head now! All that wine she put away during lunch. I mean, she's making all the right noises, like a grieving mother should, but I don't know how she *actually* feels. Her greatest sin is pride, and the importance she places on how things look – it can get in the way.

ELIZABETH:

Should I rule her out as a suspect? Someone like that could do anything to maintain the public image of the family, surely?

POLLY:

Oh, Elizabeth, Granny wouldn't get her hands dirty, I can guarantee you that – and bad and all as she is . . . firstly, she had no opportunity – she was face-down in her sage and clementine gnocchi at the time, wasn't she? Means: she hasn't a clue about science or medicine, so I'm not sure she'd be able to concoct a murder without leaving a mark . . . And motive: there's no real way father's death would benefit her. In fact, it makes all our situations that bit more precarious. There will be a large tax bill – God knows what will need to be sold. If you ask me, Granny is the last person who would hurt father. And by the way, how do you suppose he *was* killed? He looked so serene.

ELIZABETH:

I'm afraid I can't tell you just yet how I believe your father was killed. But with regards to your grandmother, I agree, I am inclined to hold Occam's razor until there's sufficient evidence to dispense with it. Do you think Sally could have killed your father?

POLLY:

Sally Lansdowne de Groot. You know that's not her real name? She's quite the master of disguise, you know? *(Chuckles)*

ELIZABETH:

I believe she was born as Sarah Chandler.

POLLY:

Almost. That was her first married name, not her birth surname.

ELIZABETH:

Hmm, I didn't realise that. What is it?

POLLY:

O'Callaghan. Her father was Irish. She has quite the commercial mind. All those potato peelers add up. Father once told me she's made more money than Ludlow.

ELIZABETH:

Her company, Mother Brown's Kitchen Conveniences, it is rather successful. I know how it feels not to be taken seriously.

POLLY:

Don't we all? Mother, too. That wheedling little undertaker ignored Mother . . . Thomas was so against this suggestion of murder, and the undertaker knew immediately who he wanted to obey. Eventually after mother pleaded with them, they agreed to wait for the police officers.

ELIZABETH:

Tell me, what did the police officers do when they arrived? Did they speak English?

POLLY:

Not really. I mean, the smaller fellow had the basics of 'Go away'. Thomas spoke to them a bit, but they mostly heard from Mother – Margaret translated. I have an ear for Italian; it sounded about right. Anyway, she showed them to father's study, to where he was found. They took a statement from Mother, Thomas and Ludlow.

ELIZABETH:

Did Margaret translate them all?

POLLY:

Yes, except for Thomas, who's fairly good at languages. But, what are you writing down there?

ELIZABETH:

Don't get too excited, my dear, I am just making notes, not drawing up anyone's arrest warrant. I always need to get the facts down, you know, to work them out. There's another layer of truth that reveals itself in ink and print. The signification of language by these shapes we call letters makes things objective. And there are twelve of you, my dear, if we include Argento – I couldn't quite keep that all in the old noggin, now, could I?

POLLY:

You don't really think we are all as likely as each other to have killed father?

ELIZABETH:

I don't, no. However, it would be too easy to just discount this person and discount the other without any proper facts.

POLLY:

You seriously think Flora and Grandmother are as suspect as – as – Nikolai and . . . and Frankie?

ELIZABETH:

Francis, he's a writer, a philosopher, yes, do you know him well?

POLLY:

Well enough, Thomas picked him up at university. He doesn't really like Thomas at all, he just wanted to come here for Christmas. The world could benefit from more honesty like that. Goodness knows the Caswell-Joneses would be in a very different position if we did that. And you know what, Thomas doesn't even really mind that Frankie doesn't like him. He's a creepy sort of fellow, Frankie, don't get me wrong. I – well, his company unnerves me. You know how piercing his eyes are? The pupils are tiny, like thin little dots. It makes him look like a snake, or one of those little lizards that crawl on the rocks out there. *(Yawn)* Now, do you mind if we leave it there?

ELIZABETH:

Just a few more minutes. Tell me, when did you first fall in love with Peter Smythson?

POLLY:

(Laughing) You can't be serious.

ELIZABETH:

Would your grandmother approve of the match?

POLLY:

Please. Where on earth has this come from? I've known Peter my *whole* life. I might have loved him when I was seven. And I've always stood proudly as a friend of his family. But there is no match. Peter will make a terrific match for one girl, but not for me. I've always admired Peter . . . he has had to work hard to get to where he is.

ELIZABETH:

Tell me more about him.

POLLY:

We've known his family for years, he lived close to us as children. His mother's American, of course. Typical story, merchant family, they are very wealthy. It's just the colour of her skin some people are bothered about.

ELIZABETH:

But not you?

POLLY:

Never. Look, what has this got to do with anything? He loves to ski, we're family friends, why wouldn't he come to Como with us?

ELIZABETH:

How many gold medals has he won?

POLLY:

Bit of a sore subject, he won three bronze medals. *(Pause)* Peter was in *awe* of Father, he would never have hurt him.

ELIZABETH:

Now, you won't like this, but I saw his behaviour earlier when I arrived, I could see it in a split second – I'm watching you all, it's my role here. Peter was sweating, his nails gripping into his flesh. Not a killer's reaction, mind. Most killers can assume a much calmer veneer. Peter is addicted to—

POLLY:

As I said, Elizabeth, Peter has worked hard to get to where he is.

ELIZABETH:

Polly, no. I believe cocaine is his poison. And where would he get it? Who could possibly source the highest grade directly from the source in Colombia? Someone who travels for business regularly? Someone looking to resurrect their failing business?

POLLY:

You've got that all wrong, Elizabeth. I must warn you, I'm going along with this charade investigation for Mother's sake. As much as I deplored father, I won't have you sully his name, *or* Peter's, with these sorts of accusations.

ELIZABETH:

Right-o, right-o. I wouldn't be doing my job here if I didn't ask difficult questions of you. Nikolai is an interesting fellow, too.

POLLY:

Typical Granny, she loves to collect all sorts of people. She's been encouraging me to look *his* way for marriage, if you can believe that.

ELIZABETH:

Really? He must be forty.

POLLY:

A benefit, in old Tilly's book. She claims an older man would *cherish* a young woman in ways a young chap would not. Grandad was almost thirty years older than her, you know?

ELIZABETH:

I gather you're not interested in Nikolai in such a manner then.

POLLY:

Oh no. He's been lurking around for the past few Christmases. The truth is, he scares me. He's . . . well, he's *fearless*. On the one hand he's this elegant ballet dancer, but . . . once we went hare-trapping together. Nikolai took one little bunny and snapped its neck with his bare hands. Even worse, he tore the creature's fur from its body with his teeth. It was disgusting. I couldn't possibly think of him in any sort of romantic sense after seeing that. In fact, you should take a look at him. He has this glint behind his eyes. I'm almost sure he's killed more people here than anyone else. In fact, something rather strange did happen this morning. We were gathered at the crèche, in the great hall, saying some Christmas prayers. Nikolai had his head bowed. I thought he was flying through a Russian Orthodox prayer. He spoke to himself so intensely, it was as if he were battling his own demons there and then. Right beside ordinary old English Margaret.

ELIZABETH:

Margaret, your godmother? Splendid in florals, matron of the manor, Margaret?

POLLY:

Yes. I did have quite a giggle, but she's quite the polyglot. I think she speaks over seven languages! English, French, Italian, Russian obviously, Spanish presumably, and Arabic perhaps? Father used to have her come and translate if his non-English-speaking clients came to London. I did wonder what on earth she had to discuss with Nikolai at that precise moment. And why was it so important that they had to speak in a language the rest of us couldn't understand . . .?

ELIZABETH:

Very interesting. Thank you, Polly. Now, who else here speaks Italian?

POLLY:

Mother has only a few words; Thomas, Flora and I can all give it a stab; perhaps Frankie, too – I know he read Latin at Oxford . . . Father pretended he couldn't, but he always seemed to know what we were talking about.

ELIZABETH:

Why are there no staff here?

POLLY:

Mother says it is to teach us a lesson. But I reckon something happened when she was here in the summer. She came alone with Flora. None of the usual gang . . . it hardly seemed worth opening the place up, but there you are. Antonia and Matteo Balliano have been looking after us since before the war. We played with their children, used to give them presents at Christmas. In fact, I might go down to the village tomorrow and speak to them. I can't imagine us staying around here in our own filth for the next week.

ELIZABETH:

The next week? I assumed you would be returning home as soon as you could.

POLLY:

I imagine we're going to be burying father here. He spent almost as much time here as anywhere else . . . many of our friends live nearby. With this weather, I can't imagine how we could take him back to Blighty.

ELIZABETH:

Quite. Now, Polly, thank you for answering my questions. You may go.

POLLY:

(Sickly sweet in tone) Oh, Elizabeth, don't tell me what I may or may not do, after you've sat here insulting my family and my friends. We all know you're not perfect yourself, are you? Answer me this, do you feel bad about defrauding that poor child's family?

ELIZABETH:

I did not defraud anyone, Polly. If you think I did anything but my best to find little Lorenzo then you're not the young woman you appear to be.

POLLY:

We shall see. Goodnight, Elizabeth.

ELIZABETH:

I watch Polly's shapely heels rap across the floor. They are rather high, but my eye is drawn to the tear in her stockings just under her left knee on the back of her leg. It's clearly no trouble for her to source silk stockings, but they are the old-fashioned type, with a seam up the leg. Not very modern for a young woman to wear. Polly slams the door after her. The incident with the Conte child is obviously playing on everyone's mind, but I must take care not to be thrown off the scent by Polly's comment — I know she's trying to rattle me, in much the same way as I tried to rattle her about both Peter and Nikolai. I still very much suspect her in the death of her father, don't you? But why would a daughter murder her own flesh and blood? Revenge for stealing her dreams, perhaps? Polly is a broken woman, and I strongly suspect she blames her late father for the state she is in.

With Matilda's intrusion I have not properly attended to the fire, and the kindling has burned to dust. There's a damp cardigan hanging here. Who could have left it there? It's Peregrine, rather an expensive make to hang so precariously near the dusty fireplace. I can't imagine Sally or Matilda wearing something like this. It would be too small for Margaret's large frame. It must be one of the Caswell-Jones's. It is clear Polly Caswell-Jones has a great many things to hide, but she is not a mastermind, bright and all as she is. There is still the weight of conscience resting on her shoulders. But still, we cannot rule her out as a suspect just yet. Like her mother, she has thrown some more light on Thomas's strange behaviour — is that a tactic, to take attention away from herself? She is quick to defend her mother — and her grandmother — but eager to throw some other guests under the bus.

There is a lot to think about. The smoke from my cigarette swirls in grey circles up towards the grumbling plasterwork of Zeus in the centre of the room's ceiling. Swathed in shadows, I doubt myself for a moment, remembering the last time I was in this room. Back then, the peach walls were illuminated by a hot July sunshine, the sounds of Kate swimming

*with the children filtering through the window. I had slipped away from
the heat to rest before that night's garden party. It had been the highlight
of the expat summer season, and 1947 was one when we wanted to
laugh and dance under the playful glint of Ursa Minor. Matilda was
coming down from her nap and crossed paths with her son outside the
drawing room door.*

'Going for a dip, Mother?' said Jonty.

*'Don't try that small-talk on me. I know what you did,' Matilda
replied.*

'Not this again. If you think I didn't do everything for Will—'

*'Not that. I know what you did to Catherine. If it comes down to it, I
will support her and the children.'*

*At their mention, the children appeared, screeching with joviality. I
heard Flora and Thomas splash water across the floor. The siblings
reverted to their childlike ways when back together for the holidays.
'Where's Lizzie?' Flora asked her father and grandmother, revealing to
both that I had been within earshot the whole time. I feigned a nap on
the gold-rimmed edge of the sofa, but I'm sure they suspected otherwise.
They left us in there, me and Flora, now a teenager but still very much a
child.*

'Where do you think the secret passageway is?' asked Flora.

'Is there one? I suppose the tunnel between the mooring and the—'

*'That's not a secret, not if we all know about it. I mean a tunnel up
to the attic or some sort of secret room accessed through a cupboard. This
villa is very old, I'm sure the people who lived through the past four
centuries had things to hide.'*

*That was the last time I was invited to Villa Janus. Flora's words
float back to me as I look out on the jet black of the lake. The lights that
twinkle across the water are diminished from earlier, signalling the late
hour, as I hear a familiar footstep on the other side of the drawing-room
door. Time to interview my third suspect, Ludlow Lansdowne de Groot.*

EPISODE 3

Ludlow Lansdowne de Groot

ELIZABETH:

With ten suspects still to interview, I am now faced with my own lust ... another cardinal sin. We're getting through them here, aren't we? Jonty's sloth, Polly's wrath at her father ... and now lust. I am not the only one hiding a secret here, but I need to keep this one hidden, or I might end up putting it in my ear. Now, you and I both know it is statistically very likely that Jonathan was murdered for someone's financial gain, which places his family squarely in the frame, but there is of course space for another. Finance-fondling, silver-supporting, bank-note beloved Ludlow. Jonty's best friend and business advisor, godfather to his son, simoleon swain. Of course, he's wearing a shirt and tie, his adherence to formality only hinted at as his chin-length hair lays unlaquered, hanging attrac-tively about his patrician face.

I will be economical with his entry in my notebook. Just the bare facts, presented as if we were relative strangers. If anyone discovered my journal and gleaned that I knew more than I had let on about Ludlow Lansdowne de Groot, I would be in trouble ... Personal journals seem to be at risk here, as has been demonstrated by Polly's art notebook. I cannot be too careful.

LUDLOW:

So, you are here to try to repair your reputation?

ELIZABETH:

I'm here because Catherine called.

LUDLOW:

What was it that you called her in Florence? A bird-beaked old hag?

ELIZABETH:

I was drunk.

LUDLOW:

I'm a little drunk now, I must confess. That's what happens when you leave it until one in the morning to interview me.

ELIZABETH:

Is Sally in bed?

LUDLOW:

My wife does her drinking in private, with a sleeping draught. She won't be coming back down. Nearly everyone is in bed.

ELIZABETH:

(A sharp whisper) Don't . . . not now . . . not here.

LUDLOW:

You don't usually object like that.

ELIZABETH:

I'm here on business, Ludlow. Will you just – just answer my questions?

LUDLOW:

I just did, Sally is in bed, that is the answer to your question. You are frazzled, aren't you, Liz?

ELIZABETH:

(Sharply) Don't . . . not here.

LUDLOW:

Right. In that case, I'll play your little game here. Who do I think killed Jonty? Well, I think he killed himself in a way. All those years of living extravagantly have caught up with him. God knows what sort of damage was done to him in that bloody prisoner-of-war camp. He had a heart attack. End of story. Perhaps it was a *good* thing that he died, anyone ever consider that? Look, I don't want you to tell anyone, but poor Jonty, well, he was finished. The company faced bankruptcy, without modernising the company, negotiating better prices . . . Combined with some very ill-thought-out investments, Jonty used some chap in Mayfair instead of my own advisor. The Caswell-Joneses haven't tuppence to their name. With Jonty gone, so too goes much of the debt. As the new heir, with death duties, Thomas will most likely be unable to save the

estate but will just about keep the family afloat. If Jonty's death is
found to be murder, it will certainly complicate matters for
Thomas. There will be an investigation, surely here and in England.
Things will be held up, you can't transfer bank shares, et cetera,
without a verified death certificate. It could take months. Why
Catherine is insisting there's more to it – well, if I were you, that's
what I would be looking into.

ELIZABETH:

Why did you turn your back on Jonty at lunch? Were you rowing
with him?

LUDLOW:

The last time I saw Jonty Caswell-Jones, he was as healthy as ever.
A conversation between two very old friends, no matter how
heated, would not have been enough to push him over the precipice. Or if it was, then it could have happened anytime – if the
bloody doorbell rang.

ELIZABETH:

He was as healthy as ever, in your opinion, and yet you think his
weak heart might have killed him . . . It doesn't quite add up,
Ludlow. But you admit you did argue with him?

LUDLOW:

Yes, Liz, but good Lord, I did not murder Jonty Caswell-Jones.

ELIZABETH:

Tell me about this morning.

LUDLOW:

All right, detective. There's not much to tell. I slept late. I was
exhausted from the past few days' travelling on the train. When I
woke up, a little after eight, I think, Sally was already gone. She
often disappears first thing for a walk, so I wasn't surprised. I rolled
over and got stuck into Frankie's thesis.

ELIZABETH:

Thomas's pal?

LUDLOW:

The very same. His signature tome, *Notes from a Man Gone Mad*. Title doesn't make any sense, but his arguments are very sensible really. Good writer. I read damn near half the thing, until Catherine started to rap around to get us down for the gift exchange. She had been up very late last night, preparing lunch for today – she was cranky. Anywho, I hadn't a *clue* about any gifts, but there was no sign of Sally. Instead, I sat out on the balcony for a cigarette and to admire the view. There really is nothing like Como on Christmas morning. The water was a shocking green—

ELIZABETH:

All right, Byron, what time was this?

LUDLOW:

About nine. Well, when I was out there, who did I see out for a stroll over beside the boathouse, but Jonty and Matilda. Well . . . stroll might be the wrong word – Jonty was about six feet ahead of the old battle-axe, gesticulating wildly. From my seat I could see he had gone damn near puce. Hands to his head. For a fellow with a dickie heart, it can't have been good for him. She had the usual stance, hands caught behind her back, inspecting the footpath. The old weapon seemed calm, unlike Jonty. I even heard him shouting, 'Mother, I can't do—' . . . but didn't catch what it was that he wasn't able to do . . .

ELIZABETH:

Did you see anything else?

LUDLOW:

Little Flora was out for a dip, with Peter, Thomas, the dancer chap – what's his name? – Nikolai Ivanov. Margaret was there with the bloody towels for them all. Even Frankie was watching them, albeit with a cigarette in hand. I damned kicked myself, I would have liked a dip to stir the senses. Nothing like it, you know, on

Christmas morning. We used to always take the plunge in Blighty. Anyway, Catherine comes out and ushers them all into that damnable crèche. She spots me and tells me to get a move on. By the time I pull my breeches on and get down, they're back in their civvies, wet hair dripping on the floor. Matilda and Jonty were back, Jonty impatiently tapping the floor . . . Matilda the perfect embodiment of Christmas spirit, reaching into her green velvet sack.

ELIZABETH:

Where was Polly?

LUDLOW:

Oh, yes, she had turned up by then, too, dry as a scarecrow's tongue, in her robe.

ELIZABETH:

So, everyone was there?

LUDLOW:

Let's see, yes, I think – oh, no, perhaps . . .

ELIZABETH:

What is it? Who was missing?

LUDLOW:

I don't recall seeing Sally until we sat down for breakfast. She arrived late with the gifts. Yes, now I remember, Matilda made some remark about her not being there.

ELIZABETH:

What gifts were exchanged?

LUDLOW:

I wasn't paying much attention, to be honest. There were lots of oranges, boxes of chocolates – you know, the usual sort of thing. I couldn't help but see how *agitated* Jonty was. Scratching at his head, not able to stand still. I thought the fellow was going to jump out the window. So, I sidestepped the frippery, caught my good silk dressing gown on a sprig of holly and asked him whatever was the matter. No one else seemed to have noticed, but I have known Jonty my whole life. He denied anything was wrong. But his demeanour changed after that, now he knew I had observed him. He made a very concerted effort to relax, partake in the festivities. That's when I began to get worried.

ELIZABETH:

Why?

LUDLOW:

Well, the *effort* he put in to keeping the stiff upper lip. He was a man on the brink, I tell you.

ELIZABETH:

Did you share your thoughts with anyone?

LUDLOW:

What was I going to say? I did look in on Catherine, but she was distracted, pots of steaming water *every*where . . . I decided to speak with her after lunch.

ELIZABETH:

Did you ask Sally where she had been?

LUDLOW:

Out for an early walk as I'd suspected. Took a look over some accounts down by the lake. Says the fresh air helps get the cogs cranking. There's some inconsistencies in her own business . . .

ELIZABETH:

About the tax? I think you told me when we were in Verona last September.

LUDLOW:

Yes . . . just after I came back from York. We thought it was resolved – I explained the whole thing to you at the time, Liz. We have found no way around paying such a huge tax bill.

ELIZABETH:

Who is Sally's accountant?

LUDLOW:

She is rather private about these things . . . poor old Jonty let me see the picture a bit more.

ELIZABETH:

Who is the accountant?

LUDLOW:

Well, it was Peter Smythson Senior, but now it's changed to a Mayfair outfit.

ELIZABETH:

I see, so what did you do between the gift exchange and lunch?

LUDLOW:

Not very much, lunch was at one, so let me see. I dressed and went down to the library, read some more of Frankie's book . . . then I went down for a cocktail, oh, about twelve-thirty? Thomas has something of a gift for these exotic fandangled things, but they are quite delicious. Negroni is the classic Italian—

ELIZABETH:

Did you notice anything suspicious?

LUDLOW:

Catherine and the girls were slaving away. Thomas and Matilda were getting along terrifically. Polly is the favourite there, so I was a tad surprised to see that. Not that it was suspicious, but this situation makes everything . . . worthy of consideration. I passed the drawing room on the way to the loo and saw Frankie deep in conversation with Flora . . . it was quite obvious he was trying to reel her in – dangerous stuff for a child of almost eighteen. He seemed to be giving her a palm reading. And that chap is not the slickest of chaps. I can't imagine he'd do terribly well with other women, but then Flora is young, inexperienced . . .

ELIZABETH:

The daughters, they must be in high demand, amongst the young men here. Who is Polly's admirer?

LUDLOW:

Hmm, Peter maybe . . . Frankie, too, I'm sure. And Ivanov tried to dance with her last night, too.

ELIZABETH:

How was lunch? Catherine said you turned your back to Jonty's end of the table.

LUDLOW:

Gosh, she noticed that? Doesn't miss a thing, does she? It wasn't borne out of malice or anything . . . Matilda continued to nit-pick at Jonty over dinner. Where was the soup? Why were they serving themselves? It was interminable. And Polly had . . . well, she brought up a strange bit of conversation with me. I was keen no one else could overhear, you know. I tried to stop her from talking about it at all, but she insisted . . .

ELIZABETH:

About?

LUDLOW:

William. *(Slight hesitation here)* She started asking *why* didn't we lay a place for him – apparently some locals do that for their dead. Then she started asking Jonty to tell her about their time in the POW camp, egging Matilda on to recount the story of his birth, too. Matilda obliged initially, but there was a shift in the air . . . Jonty began to turn puce again. I couldn't bear to witness it, so I turned away.

ELIZABETH:

Why did she do that?

LUDLOW:

Polly? She seems not quite herself. Everyone says just how much she looks like William. It must be difficult being haunted by the face of a dead man, a man she can barely remember. Matilda always held her on a pedestal just because of it. I suppose it became a bit of an obsession for her.

ELIZABETH:

We have now moved into the kitchen and Ludlow begins to search for a glass. The remains of Catherine's dessert are stuck to the large rectangular tray, the kitchen countertop laden with dirty plates and used glasses. Pools of red and orange gunk sit in the heavy wine glasses. Ludlow pulls loose the cork from the limoncello with his teeth; this is the real Ludlow. The Ludlow I know well.

The scullery is even worse. After searching in vain for a clean glass, Ludlow sits on the kitchen bench and drinks straight from the bottle. This element, his uncouth manner, it gives the interview a complexity. It has thrown me. Right now, it is rather difficult to think straight. I need a coffee but dare not disturb the precarious arrangement of dirty dishes that might alert the other guests to mine and Ludlow's presence here.

It is warmer here than anywhere else in the villa; I learned that when I was last invited as a guest. A memory flashes once more. A fiery citrus liqueur to breathe life back into a body refreshed from a dip in the lake.

Ludlow's hand is reaching out for my belt, pulling me back from the past. It is as if he is reeling me in to his broad body. Over the years I have learned the importance of staying impartial. But at this moment I am afraid you must be impartial for me. You don't know him as I do. If I was honest with myself, I should never have accepted Catherine's request to investigate, knowing he would be here. I'm no longer certain she is my prime suspect. Of all the people likely to kill Jonty, Ludlow is the most likely. Despite his jaunty demeanour, knowing him as I do, I can't shake the unease I feel here, alone with him. As much as I long to melt into his arms, my sense of how dangerous he is, well, it stops me. Perhaps it was a mistake, but I am in blood; stepped in so far that, should I wade no more, returning were as tedious as go o'er.

ELIZABETH:

Stop it, Ludlow. I'm here to work. Polly said you and Sally were arguing when you arrived last night. That she was frazzled.

LUDLOW:

(Disappointed groan) It was a long journey.

ELIZABETH:

Why are your cases still at the bottom of the stairs?

LUDLOW:

Catherine is economising . . . clearly. They were too heavy to carry up the stairs. Why on earth they haven't arranged a single bit of help is beyond me. It has resulted in Sally coming down to fish out her clothes as if playing a sort of dress-up lucky dip. It's quite humiliating, really, for them and us. Look here, all of these overflowing ashtrays. It's disgusting.

ELIZABETH:

Surely the men could have helped carry them? Surely *you* could have carried them?

LUDLOW:

I shouldn't expect Thomas to lift a finger to help anyone. That skier chap and Jonty did their best with Sally's primary toilette case and a few other pieces. And no, I won't be lugging our luggage up all those stairs myself. Catherine should know this is not how to treat guests. Tell me, Elizabeth, why are you so certain I argued with Jonty?

ELIZABETH:

I expect you row with Jonty every time you see him, but Catherine told me you and that writer chap were missing just before the body was found.

LUDLOW:

Yes, I think I saw him laying into Polly on the patio . . . he is quite *intense.*

ELIZABETH:

She does not look well, that girl. What were you rowing about?

LUDLOW:

I didn't see that Scottish chap anywhere. Francis, I think his name is. But if you really want to know . . . I was just having a few words with my oldest friend. Jonty had decided to sell off some of the art from the estate. A friend of mine at Christie's mentioned it. I had to find out if it was true. First batch included two Sargent portraits. It would be just like him, so short-sighted, to steal the children's inheritance from under them.

ELIZABETH:

But they were broke, you just said that. Isn't it the sensible idea? Why do you care so much about paintings?

LUDLOW:

Thomas is my godson. It's my duty to look after his best interests. There are ways of going about things – if he had just let me help him . . . I still think Jonty popped his clogs naturally, but there might be something else to look into . . . something unusual.

ELIZABETH:

Go on.

LUDLOW:

The Ivanov chap. I know Matilda has known him since before Stalin started to shave, but some of his associates have been proving troublesome to Jonty in London. Last year, there was a terrific drought all down the east coast of Colombia, the plants were withering. That area supplies about three-quarters of all the company's coffee for the year, so he had to rig up an irrigation system. Jonty either couldn't or wouldn't go to the banks for the finance, and instead opted to borrow from some pal of Ivanov's. Now, the system worked, and the past two years the crop has been a bounteous one, but there wasn't enough profit to repay the interest. I managed to help with a bridging loan, but—

ELIZABETH:

You do seem to know an awful lot about Jonty's business.

LUDLOW:

He . . . his approach was scattergun. He needed all the help he could get. Before the war he was methodical. Careful, with an attention to detail. Now . . . well, he bumbled along from one disaster to another, selling off assets, burning creditors, sending a century-old company on a one-track road to financial ruin. This financier friend of Ivanov was not much better than a back-street loan shark.

ELIZABETH:

What about his accountant, financial advisors?

LUDLOW:

Well, that's another area where things get tricky. His accountant is his old neighbour, Peter Smythson Senior – same as Sally's.

ELIZABETH:

Young Peter's father?

LUDLOW:

The very same. Now, Peter Junior, he might be an Olympic skier, but the chap is bright as a button, read maths at Cambridge. Quite unlike old Peter who's as unstable as a cemetery water table. From what I can see, Smythson & Associates has totally taken their eyes off the ball, leaving Jonty open to multiple accounts of tax evasion, fraud, whatever else . . .

ELIZABETH:

What are you trying to say, Ludlow?

LUDLOW:

Do I need to spell it out for you? Whatever happened to the art of nuance and ribaldry? Maybe goodie Peter did in Jonty to get his old boy off the hook. The young fellow is certainly bright enough to pull it off . . . but here we are, back to the question of *how* he was killed. Not a mark on the body, so he must have been poisoned. That could have taken place over months or hours . . .

ELIZABETH:

But if Peter Senior is also Sally's accountant, and her enterprise appears to be flourishing, you can't equate Jonty's failure—

LUDLOW:

Sally . . . needs to keep things malleable . . . but she's very conscientious. Have you considered Peter as a killer?

ELIZABETH:

Let *me* ask the questions. Do you remember, last Easter? Just the two of us . . . that filthy little hovel in Montmartre—

LUDLOW:

In Paris. You had me nailed to the bloody cross—

ELIZABETH:

No need to be so . . . blasphemous. We saw Kate from afar . . . she looked very intimate with—

LUDLOW:

Come here, Liz.

ELIZABETH:

Stop, it's . . . it's not the time. You're rollicking . . .

ELIZABETH:

(Softly whispering) *And that's it. My impartiality has gone for a moment. Kissing Ludlow feels almost more natural than investigating . . . but suddenly, before I can get carried away, the dishes crash around me, like my conscience coming back into play. Or is it you? Trying to get my attention back on the case. Thank you. I knew you would be a useful sidekick. I need all the help I can get.*

ELIZABETH:

Watch out – careful!

LUDLOW:

Out of the way.

(Door opens – enter Margaret)

MARGARET:

What on *earth* is the matter? It's like the last days of Rome in here—

LUDLOW:

(Moving dishes) This bloody house – it's filthy. Will you tell that friend of yours that if she won't have anyone in to help then she'd bloody well better get down here to scrub them herself.

MARGARET:

Oh, what a peculiar shade of lipstick you're wearing Ludlow. Almost identical to Elizabeth's.

(Sound of Elizabeth fixing dishes)

ELIZABETH:

Ah, you don't think – oh no, how ridiculous. Ludlow pulled my glass of limoncello off me, moments after I applied my lipstick.

MARGARET:

If you expect me to believe—

LUDLOW:

It's almost two in the morning, Margaret, what are you doing down here?

MARGARET:

I'm just getting a glass of water. You know, I thought you had more sense, Elizabeth.

LUDLOW:

You're one to talk, Maggie. What was it Catherine wrote you a cheque for last week, an astrology manual? Well, you didn't predict this—

ELIZABETH:

Please, Ludlow, if we could just get to finish our interview.

MARGARET:

I'm going, don't you worry. I'll leave you to get on with your *interview* . . .

ELIZABETH:

Who's that second glass for, Margaret?

MARGARET:

Poor Catherine, she's not able to sleep. I've a little draught to help her. I hope for her sake that you can get to the bottom of this. Young Flora is sobbing herself to sleep in the room next to her mother, it's most tragic.

(Exit Margaret. Door closes)

ELIZABETH:

(Sharp whispering) What are you doing? That's just wonderful, now Margaret has this over me.

LUDLOW:

Margaret has plenty to hide herself. That's why she doesn't want you here.

ELIZABETH:

Do you think *she* could have killed him?

LUDLOW:

Margaret has *always* been jealous of Jonty. She's quite the green-eyed monster. Jealous that he took Catherine away from her – they were such close friends as children, by all accounts. Margaret may not look like a killer, with her miniature Babyshams and sickly-sweet perfume . . . but she has a very colourful track record. You know she drove into a wall, just to get Catherine's attention? Back in September, the evening before Catherine and Jonty were due to leave for South America. It was Catherine's first time to volunteer for the trip in years. Sally and I were called up to their house for lunch. We clocked Margaret's red tank of a car on the gravel when we arrived and dreaded the entire affair. Matilda had caught a marvellous hare for us. Can you imagine, at her age? Anyway, the whole way through lunch, Margaret diverted the conversation to herself, her new wallpaper, her latest shopping sprees. It was *very* bizarre. It was as if we had an excitable, self-centred toddler at the table. Eventually Catherine asked her to stop – to listen to Sally's story – something about meeting some hotshot Massachusetts congressman. Margaret did as she was told . . . but sprinkled pepper onto Kate's wine . . . scraped butter onto the tablecloth – Banquo's ghost had better table manners. Next, she just got up from the table, walked away. Catherine ignored her . . . she knew well what she was after. Attention. We all tried to enjoy our pudding, when suddenly there was a huge revving of an engine – followed by a jolly big smack into the garden wall! Well, there was no talk of Catherine going to Buenos Aires after that. I believe Margaret was shut up in the loony bin—

ELIZABETH:

(Admonishing) Ludlow—

LUDLOW:

And she's only just been let out. This is her first trip abroad since, according to Thomas. Margaret has always hated Jonty and, in my opinion, she has the unfortunate state of mind to be capable of killing him—

ELIZABETH:

She was an auxiliary nurse during the war . . . good Lord, she worked on the cardiac unit at St Francis's.

LUDLOW:

And she always wins those Women's Institute cake decorating competitions . . .

ELIZABETH:

Your point being . . .?

LUDLOW:

She knows how to set out a scene! There's a chance Catherine knows this is the case but can't bear to accuse her best friend. Why else might she ask you to keep it in the family? *(Pause)* Look. What's that out there?

ELIZABETH:

Where?

LUDLOW:

Out on the lake, you see it? There's a boat there, someone is on it.

ELIZABETH:

Peter Smythson; I believe he enjoys sailing in the evening.

LUDLOW:

I can't see an athlete like Peter missing his sleep—

(Scream in the distance)

ELIZABETH:

Crikey, let's go!

LUDLOW:

That's out on the patio . . . this way.

ELIZABETH:

As I trail behind Ludlow, the dark shadows of the villa seem to mock me. The hollow entrance hall is deadened without the candlelight. Margaret will, of course, tell Kate what she has seen. I need to either convince her against it or uncover something compelling enough to keep her quiet. But either way, my reputation is shot. This opportunity to redeem myself . . . it was poorly judged to come in the first place, and to interview Ludlow, as I have done, alone during the middle of the night. I will return Catherine's cheque in the morning, but still offer my services. Are we sure Jonty was murdered? No, but given the certainty of his wife, I am suspicious enough to believe it could happen. The shine of Ludlow's shoes reflects a solitary lamp lighting the back porch. Black patent. Ludlow

*was a connoisseur of footwear, and would never usually wear this shoe
with anything other than a dinner jacket . . . Where are his other shoes?
Still stuck in his case that he refuses to bring up to his own room?*

*Ludlow stands to do rather well from Jonty's will, don't you think?
He seems to know the company inside out. This business about sticking
up for Thomas and the children . . . never have I known him, in the two
years of our entanglement, to particularly care about the Caswell-Jones
children. He has been a poor choice of lover, I understand that, but the
initial familiarity, the coincidence of our meeting, is what led to that first
buttery kiss. I had been forced to take a secretarial job; after the disas-
trous Conte case, my work all dried up. On those meagre secretarial
wages, I missed fine meals and the luxury of a spare pair of nylons. I
was not prepared for a return to wartime frugality so soon. Ludlow
provided an alternative. So now here I am . . . at sincere risk of my
objectivity failing due to impecunious precariousness.*

*As we approach the patio, the moonlight reveals the shapes of two
figures in Peter's boat. So much for Flora crying herself to sleep.*

LUDLOW:

(Bellowing) Flora, Thomas, what in the name of God? Do you realise how dangerous it is, sailing in the middle of night, in the depths
of winter? Do you want your mother and sister to have no family
left at all?

FLORA:

Oh, calm down, you pair of ninnies! Did my screeching wake you?
This water is bloody cold, a whole tranche of it landed in the
boat . . . Gosh, those sailing lessons didn't count for much.

ELIZABETH:

What are you doing? Out here, in the middle of the night?

THOMAS:

(Coolly) Getting some fresh air. It's been a long day.

ELIZABETH:

We all know that's not true. No one gets fresh air in the early hours of the morning.

THOMAS:

Nosy bloody parker Elizabeth Chalice. Here on the authority of whom? A grieving, hysterical widow—

LUDLOW:

Stop that, Thomas.

FLORA:

It's so cold, can we go inside? Just tell them, Thomas, there's nothing wrong with it.

THOMAS:

(Hissing) I *knew* I shouldn't have brought you. *(More calmly)* We were meeting a messenger. In Bellagio. We slipped out when you were speaking with mother.

ELIZABETH:

What is so important that it can't wait until morning?

THOMAS:

It's a copy of father's British will.

ELIZABETH:

But I was under the impression Argento was bringing that here himself.

THOMAS:

(Bitterly) Yes, Elizabeth. No one told me. Argento had already left with it. But apparently he should be here soon.

ELIZABETH:

I look up at the villa from the patio, the moonlight washing a mellifluous glare across the sandstone wall. Lights are on in two rooms, both over the Orangery. Sally and Kate are in those rooms. I see a shadow cross the window of the room on the right. It had been a suicide mission for the children to go out in the middle of the night. Now I have many questions for Thomas to answer. But I do not find their foolhardiness suspicious, for youth is free from the hang-ups and neuroses life washes up on our shores, don't you think? It is well and truly the middle of the night . . . the day of Santo Stefano has only just begun. So far, I have heard from three suspects, with three separate motives.

Ludlow Lansdowne de Groot. Jonty's best friend . . . When he spoke of concern for his friend, all I could hear was the rattle of silver. Ludlow would do anything for money, his greed is unsurpassed.

Now, that leaves us with just nine more suspects, each with their own motive for killing our victim.

My thoughts now are with Jonty. Such a blue-eyed chap, his bones chilled in the midwinter air at the funeral home. Why is Thomas so keen to get his hands on the will? If Jonty died just this afternoon, where has the messenger come from? We must prepare ourselves – I need your attention to detail here, for there will be many more questions asked and answered as we work our way through these twelve motives for murder.

EPISODE 4
MATILDA CASWELL-JONES

ELIZABETH:

This morning, orange streaks cracked through the dark sky as dawn broke across Lake Como. The daily renewal of life this Boxing Day, heralded by sunrise, lifted my tired spirits. There is nothing like watching the dawn break from Villa Janus. I am thrilled to be here to see it again. I shuffled out of my bedroom, facing to the west, to the central upstairs balcony to watch the sky brighten. So much has happened in the past twelve hours, I needed to think.

After interrogating three suspects, I am no closer to knowing who killed Jonty Caswell-Jones. To tell the truth, I am still not even certain it was murder at all. But my instinct pulls at me. From the description of the events, I do agree with Ludlow's observations — it seems to me that Jonty must have been poisoned, for each of the first three interviewees did not describe any violent injuries to the body. There is something strange, something dangerous going on, and I need to proceed with caution. Each of the Caswell-Jones women has lied to me about their role in the death of Jonty. His wife, Kate, Catherine to you, behaved strangely when she found his body. She saw there was no pulse, tried to resuscitate him, but how hard did she try? And she's a trained nurse. She also failed to mention his heart condition. Elder daughter Polly admits that her father had given her an ultimatum, but what for? Even the youngest, Flora, is not as innocent as she portrays — escaping in the middle of the night to meet a messenger. Then, of course, there is the matter of my own precarious situation with Ludlow Lansdowne de Groot, a childhood friend of the victim. The Brits throughout this part of Italy all know one another. By not declaring our affair to Kate, I am putting my professional expertise in jeopardy. How can I properly investigate my own lover? The truth is, I fear Ludlow is the worst sort of person, and I have been trying to disentangle myself for the past few months.

But for now, I must speak with Jonty's mother, Matilda, to understand exactly what happened here yesterday. There's nothing that gets past that woman, not really. I have now taken up residence back in the drawing room, my notebook at hand. Are you ready to begin? I must be *sharp and straightforward with her . . . unlike the rest of her family, I will not pander to her. I have good success with surprising my interviewees by not following a traditional line of questioning. You'll see what I mean. She is a tough old nut, is Matilda Caswell-Jones. Let's crack her . . . It's plain she was once a great beauty and her perfectly blue eyes dart around the room, as observant as ever, accentuated by a turquoise cashmere twinset. She's fiddling with the black pearl necklace – is the old dear nervous?*

ELIZABETH:

Good morning, Matilda. Now – I'm sorry to skip the niceties, but I must get straight to it. Jonty wasn't your favourite son, was he? And everyone knew it.

MATILDA:

Very well, Elizabeth. Yes, quite. Favouritism was no problem in my day. But that doesn't mean I wished him to die.

ELIZABETH:

Why did you favour William, your other son?

MATILDA:

He was my firstborn, but I don't see what it has to do with this—

ELIZABETH:

Background information. To give me a full picture of the family and the various dynamics.

MATILDA:

Very well. I love Jonty, of course I do, it's a terrible tragedy to bury not one but two children. But William was the eldest. I will be honest with you. When he was born, it was such a special time. I enjoyed being a mother far more than I had thought I would. But then Jonathan arrived so soon after, and I suppose I felt I had been robbed of the time I had with my baby, by this imposter, this creature. My whole pregnancy was beset by troubles – I was so sick. And then when he was young, we went through two or three nannies. They kept getting ill, or married, and, well . . . I resented Jonty. Alas, he was but a babe, and wasn't to blame for the fact of his own birth . . . As time went by, I learned to accept the pair; they were firm friends. The two looked so similar, people often mistook them for twins. But look closely enough and you could tell the difference. One good, one not so good. I know a mother shouldn't say these things . . . but that's how it was. Jonty was always looking to lead William astray, or send him off on some wild goose chase. To me, Jonty always seemed to be hanging off William's coat-tails, holding him back, that was until he found Ludlow in Stowe . . .

When the war began, I couldn't imagine they would be *injured*, let alone killed. They were such strong boys. Invincible in my mind. I was glad when I learned they were in the same camp; it gave me some comfort at such a difficult time. But then William died . . . I used to think that the wrong son came home from the war, God forgive me for saying . . . One would imagine that what with Jonty being the only son left, it might change things between us, herald the dawn of a new relationship. But the truth was, I couldn't forgive Jonty for coming home at all. William was something special . . . erm, a natural businessman,– the family business wouldn't be failing with *him* at the helm. He was charismatic enough to win over just about anyone in an argument. Jonty . . . is different.

ELIZABETH:

You had no other children?

MATILDA:

There were times I thought we would be blessed again, but it didn't happen. I would have loved a daughter. Catherine, well, she isn't what I expected. But Polly, *she* is the daughter I never had. She has William's eyes. Although no one remembers those beautiful eyes of William's now. Eyes are the window to the soul . . . they tell us so much. William's eyes have long been forgotten by many . . . and Jonty's, too, now.

ELIZABETH:

Surely Kate remembers her husband's eyes?

MATILDA:

(Uncertain) Oh, yes, I'm sure she does. You'll have to forgive an old woman like me, it is easy to tire.

ELIZABETH:

Where will you go now Jonty is dead?

MATILDA:

I don't intend on *going* anywhere. What a strange question to ask, Elizabeth. I have an allowance from the estate of my late husband.

ELIZABETH:

What was your husband's name? When did he die?

MATILDA:

Robert died forty years ago, in 1912. The children were so small. But he was significantly older than me. A chap in his seventies was not much use to small boys.

ELIZABETH:

How did he die?

MATILDA:

He just dropped dead, as they say, playing cards at his club. Nothing could be done for him – just like that.

ELIZABETH:

How old were you at the time? Did you never consider remarrying?

MATILDA:

I was widowed at forty-three. That's considered a young woman, these days. I did more than consider: I was engaged at one point, secretly, but it was a love match. I had found the right husband the first time. This affair, it was more impetuous. In the end, he broke it off. Swore he couldn't break his mother's heart by rejecting his betrothed.

ELIZABETH:

And who was he?

MATILDA:

(Sharply) What does that matter? It has *nothing* to do with Jonty's death. If you want to speak of broken engagements, I hope you interview *Sally* soon.

ELIZABETH:

Ludlow's wife? Sally Lansdowne de Groot. Yes, I intend to speak to her in my investigations.

MATILDA:

She was nearly Jonty's wife, didn't you know? They knew one another as tiny children. Sally was a beautiful child, and I would have been *happy* for her to match with either of my boys . . . Although to give you some *background* . . . there were questions about where her family made their money, but, oh boy, there was a damned lot of it. Money, that is. And did my boys need to marry money! The estate may be two centuries old, but nothing keeps accruing like the debts over it. Then you see Jonty slaving away at the coffee company. If Catherine had brought money with her, well, who's to say, maybe his heart wouldn't have suffered years of stress and strain?

ELIZABETH:

Was your late husband involved in running the company before Jonty?

MATILDA:

Yes, Robert had a shrewd business sense. He loved that company; his own grandfather founded it. Commerce was always viewed as lesser, of course, but Robert's grandfather was *more* than a green-grocer. Old Caswell-Jones was a financier and spotted an opportunity in coffee. Robert told me he paid his staff well but didn't get too involved. Caswell-Jones coffee was drunk by the royalty of Europe, it was Marie Antoinette's cake accompaniment. They say she shared a cup at the foot of the guillotine with her executioner. It saddens me how diminished our name has become; our coffee is now simply chosen by office girls and car mechanics. No offence intended, Elizabeth.

ELIZABETH:

(Whispering to reader) *Something in her* tone *tells me offence is exactly what she intends.*

MATILDA:

Anyway, this is all ancient history. I can't see what the history of the business has to do with—

ELIZABETH:

Yes, of course, well, let us get back to the matter in hand. Jonty. What sort of father was he?

MATILDA:

One who abdicated his duty almost completely, leaving his son bankrupt and his daughters unlikely to secure any sort of decent husband. Catherine is not much better. In the old days, parents paid attention to these things. I suppose life was shorter, people died terribly often – so care had to be taken. My late husband and I always considered how best to provide for the children throughout their infancy and all the way into adulthood. Jonty, however, he seemed to have very much lost touch with reality this past year. You know, I called at the house on Carlyle Square. It was the week before Royal Ascot. I went to retrieve a special fan I had left there. The staff had diminished to just Cleavers, an old caretaker. No one to even prepare a cup of tea for one! I was quite embarrassed, as I had invited a friend to visit me there. In the end I just let Sephie Smythson's knock at the door go unanswered, rather than have her in. There was no food in the scullery . . . And yet Jonty had been staying there all summer with Flora!

ELIZABETH:

So you were surprised to find the house empty?

MATILDA:

Shocked. Lucky I had the Overseas Club nearby to dine, or else I should have starved!

ELIZABETH:

Why do you think it was locked up? Had you expected it to be open?

MATILDA:

(Cautious) Hmmm, you know, I suppose I must have mixed up my dates. Easy to get absent-minded at my age, you know.

ELIZABETH:

You don't really seem absent-minded, Matilda. You're not the type. And you certainly don't seem like the type to fall asleep at the dinner table. Had you been drugged? Were you feeling unwell? It was quite strange behaviour, wasn't it?

MATILDA:

You mean yesterday? Good Lord, how do you know about that? I am most frightfully embarrassed. I can't quite believe . . . I am only sixty-nine years old, not ready for the rubbish heap quite yet. I had a headache and asked Catherine for some painkillers. She warned me to take just a little bit; I didn't realise how strong it was . . . until I heard Margaret tugging at me. My good cream silk scarf was stained red from the wine that soaked into it. Maggie is a good sort, though, she helped carry me up the stairs to bed. I can't remember much else until the undertaker arrived. I had a peculiar feeling when they told me Jonty was dead; I was conscious of it, but it was as if my body had turned to stone. I could not feel with my heart. But my mind was in overdrive.

ELIZABETH:

Take me back to dinner, who helped Margaret carry you upstairs?

MATILDA:

Oh, Ludlow . . . I think Thomas and perhaps Nikolai? They will confirm – my memory is hazy . . . But I knew, when they told me Jonty was dead. I immediately knew it was murder.

ELIZABETH:

Why are you so sure?

MATILDA:

I can't explain it, I have no logical reason, but I've always had a highly developed intuition. It is really just a gut reaction. Catherine seems certain he was. I, eh . . . I am glad that you came to help us sort this all out, Elizabeth. It's a *shame* that we hadn't had you here in so long. Then when this . . . Jonty . . . it would make the pain so much harder to bear to know people were talking about us. The children have their whole lives ahead of them, we wouldn't want to mar their names with something like this.

ELIZABETH:

So, what do you think we should do with the killer, once we have found them?

MATILDA:

I believe we have two options. I will either use my connections to contact the Italian minister for justice, and have the arrest made at the very highest level – no need to involve the locals. Or, well, we save them from such a fate. In the case of my grandchildren, or Catherine, that a momentary lapse in judgement—

ELIZABETH:

Spare them from the consequences? From my investigations so far, it is my belief that Jonty was poisoned, in a carefully planned and methodical way. It was no heat-of-the-moment thing. You must really suspect your own family?

MATILDA:

When you live as long as I have, you begin to realise that almost anything can happen.

ELIZABETH:

Who, in particular, do you suspect murdered Jonty?

MATILDA:

Oh, it could have been any of them, really. You and I both know how *easy* it is to make a mistake, to ruin your life by doing something when you've not fully considered all of the consequences.

ELIZABETH:

There isn't always time to, but this is no minor transgression—

MATILDA:

You *are* glad that I had Catherine call you, after that business with that child . . . I know you need a chance to build back your reputation and, of course, the cooling of your friendship with Catherine.

ELIZABETH:

Well . . . I don't quite follow, Mrs Caswell-Jones. How do you expect I could build back up my reputation and also keep this affair private? Not that I did anything wrong with Marcello Conte.

MATILDA:

The child died, Elizabeth, because you *insisted* on marking those bank notes.

ELIZABETH:

That was not my decision. His mother *insisted* on it. She hated that some gangsters had taken her child . . . she despised them so much that she could not bear the thought that they would just get away with it, without any come-back. I relive that night in my mind, desperately searching for another way, any way at all to avoid that. I should have talked her out of it. I know that her secretary or maid or someone claimed it was my fault . . . and I have let people think that, because whatever inconvenience it has caused me is nothing in comparison to the agony Adele Conte feels at the loss of her son.

MATILDA:

Now, now, Elizabeth. We both know you're finished unless you set the record straight, which you won't do because underneath it all, you are a decent girl. Now, this way, you will get all of the kudos, because we will be naming a killer. The man who killed Jonty Caswell-Jones. I have just the person in mind.

ELIZABETH:

What?

MATILDA:

Do not act innocent with me, Elizabeth. You know exactly what I mean.

ELIZABETH:

You want to *frame* someone? Who? This is illegal—

MATILDA:

You've just agreed to an investigation outside the law . . . it's not a case of framing anyone, merely saving a young person from a doomed existence.

ELIZABETH:

I haven't agreed to any such thing.

MATILDA:

But you will. Because that way, you can come forward as the detective *extraordinaire*. The clever lady who solved the *unsolvable* crime. Without even a body to analyse. The British newspapers will run your victorious image . . . putting to bed once and for all the very idea that you might have led to the death of a child. No more clerking in a tiny attic for insufferable people. No, *returned* to the lauded position of the cleverest investigator in Italy, Britain, wherever you wish! That's right, I've had my eye on you for a while now, Elizabeth Chalice. You've fallen a great deal, and this is your opportunity to rise back to the level that I fully believe you deserve to live in.

ELIZABETH:

You've planned this whole thing, haven't you? Who is it that you're trying to frame for murder? Is it Sally?

MATILDA:

No, I haven't planned this all, actually. I wouldn't go so far as to kill my own son; one is not such a terrible mother as that. And no, I do not mean Sally – but wouldn't that be fun? I have earmarked this individual as a problem for some time now. He's snuck into my confidence, completely undeserving of the opportunity. He led Jonty down some terribly questionable paths.

ELIZABETH:

Answer me, who is it?

(Knock at the door. Door opens. Enter Flora)

FLORA:

Granny, there's a chap here from the village to see you. Says it's urgent.

MATILDA:

Now, Elizabeth if you'll excuse me.

ELIZABETH:

(Firmly) We are not finished here, Matilda.

MATILDA:

I don't expect we are . . . do let me know when you wish to sit down again.

(Exit Matilda. Door closes)

ELIZABETH:

Who on earth could be calling on Matilda from the village? The sun has broken out into its full, resplendent glory across the meniscus line of

Lake Como. The vivid ochre washes with a pinky-purple, giving way to the full light of the winter sun. I'm looking for Matilda, not to spy, per se, but I am keen to see who this mystery visitor is. Ah ... there she is. I must say, I am impressed at how quickly the old bag of bones moves. In the shadow of the steps at the front of the villa, she stands in hearty laughter with a bedraggled local chap. He has the appearance of a shepherd all right, and hands over a large muslin, full of what I presume to be cheese, to Matilda. The transaction concluded, Matilda is now picking her steps further down to the servants' entrance of the kitchen. What is she up to? All that guff about returning to the standard she expects me to be at ... She loves a bit of drama.

I always expected Matilda to be a challenging interview. She is a wily woman, a social climber with a nose for getting her own way. But seeking to frame an innocent man? It is scandalous. It reminds me of the poisonous side to the Caswell-Jones family. It is dispiriting, seeking the truth from a collection of people to whom lying is as natural as sleeping with their eyes shut. But I am glad of the opportunity to bring the truth to light. Jonty is not the only victim here. The killer aside, he leaves behind family and friends who will mourn him – it is my duty to proceed gently. I must remember that, when dealing with this family. Privately, I am still not convinced about the family's reasons for calling me to this investigation. Does Catherine want it kept within the family? Or does she want something else from me entirely?

Matilda seems to think it was the Conte case, my alleged failings, that explains why Catherine no longer invited me here ... But I felt things between us chill long before that. It was as if she couldn't bear to look at me. Perhaps I just reminded her of the war. That's one reason I left England; the whole place just reminded me of the Blitz ... of Charlie. Matilda pretends to be everyone's friend, but I wouldn't be surprised if secretly SHE had me cast as a persona non grata. Back to the case at hand. Taking out my notebook, I see that I've already used half of the pages, and I have not yet interviewed half the suspects. Now, Matilda has returned ... Here we go again.

ELIZABETH:

Who was that? Calling you away?

MATILDA:

Oh nothing, just a local merchant come to drop off some cheese for Christmas. He's the only person I would buy cheese from! Delicious.

ELIZABETH:

Very well. So tell me. Who are you trying to frame?

MATILDA:

Given your reluctance on this matter . . . I think I will make you wait before saying who. Can't a woman enjoy a Boxing Day breakfast without being troubled? We will come back to the matter. I'm not giving up that easily.

ELIZABETH:

I'm sure you appreciate the tight timeline I am working on. Tell me, how did you meet Robert Caswell-Jones, your husband? You're Finnish originally, yes?

MATILDA:

Correct. I was born as Matilda Alexandra Sofia Emilia Paikkala in Helsinki. My parents sent me to boarding school in England, aged seven. I met Robert at a friend's shooting party, and that is it. My family . . . I had a significant dowry—

ELIZABETH:

Oil, I believe, your family fortune is derived from?

MATILDA:

No, that would be *Norway*. We mined for zinc and cobalt. My father wanted an English daughter. And an English family. He was obsessed with the traditions, the clothes, the manners – he could not be content with who he really was.

ELIZABETH:

You're a bit like that yourself, aren't you? What would Mr Freud say . . . a Narcissus?

MATILDA:

Did you bring me here to insult me or interview me? Now, if this is what you consider—

ELIZABETH:

I apologise. Tell me, are you glad that Thomas's friend Frankie is here? I believe he took the place of someone else at late notice.

MATILDA:

Where did you get that idea?

ELIZABETH:

The seating plan for lunch yesterday, Frankie's place name was different to all of the others. His was scribbled in black pen, everyone else had a gold-edged card. His was plain white.

MATILDA:

Well deduced. We expected Argento until we heard his mother was ill. Catherine thought it an idea to invite another guest to keep the numbers up. But Argento is still coming, of course.

ELIZABETH:

Tell me about Argento, I don't recall him.

MATILDA:

You don't recall him because he was invisible when you were here.

ELIZABETH:

Ah, he worked for the family.

MATILDA:

Not quite. Argento di Silva was the letting agent who brokered the rent of this villa back in the twenties, for my late husband. He was involved in many legal matters . . . he was a lawyer, but suffice it to say that in latter years he had fallen from his high position to working as Jonty's valet-cum-butler. These days, he would usually coordinate the staff, the food, the luggage – I'm sure Catherine has explained this all already . . . He was just like a member of the family; he would sit at the table with us.

ELIZABETH:

So, you liked him?

MATILDA:

He is *very* handsome. At one stage he would have been at the pinnacle of Milanese society, you know, before he was involved in some poorly thought-out actions during the war.

ELIZABETH:

What did he do?

MATILDA:

He never said, but I doubt he had much choice in the matter – I'm sure he was simply a puppet. After the war his licence to practise law was revoked and he turned to coordinating, well, the family's travel, food, accommodation, that sort of thing. He's terribly nice, but very shy and quiet, unless someone has been wronged, in which case he fights for the underdog fiercely.

ELIZABETH:

I look forward to meeting him. Whenever he arrives. So, Francis Heath . . . your latest guest, tell me what you know of him.

MATILDA:

Frankie Heath. What a strange fellow he is. He goes around telling us all he doesn't like Thomas, yet here he is, Thomas's guest, and they stay up all night playing cards like two young boys. He comes from sadness; there was quite the family tragedy. His mother and three sisters died in a car accident a few years ago. I think Catherine feels sorry for him and lets him into the house somewhat in the manner of a wet dog. The way he is with Thomas, it reminds me of Ludlow and Jonty, how they were as boys. Thomas is no wallflower, of course, but there is a definite lack of finesse about him that is present in Frankie. He acts like the epitome of deep thinking, as if he's Cicero reincarnated, but it is all superficial. Velvet jackets on Bond Street, that sort of thing. Rather flashy. This miserable philosopher pose is just that: an act of sullen rebellion. He is terribly, terribly clever, though. The way he cuts through the guff. But it's dangerous to go on like that, open up rifts and expose truths that are sometimes better left in the shadows.

ELIZABETH:

Would you like him for a match with Flora or Polly?

MATILDA:

Good Lord, no. Frankie would be a decent match for someone – but not my granddaughters. There is that iciness underneath the surface with Frankie. A disconnect from reality . . . He removes himself from situations . . . I think his wife would be a very lonely one. And Flora is a wild girl, she will need someone very straight and suave to bring her to task, if time does not do that. And to think she was such a quiet child, until she was a teenager. You know, Catherine was warned that she already has a bad name in society. But hopefully that does not stick beyond the schoolyard. Polly will need to live with passion, therefore she requires a husband of great fortune and position in society. You know that's why I think the artistic leanings will help secure her as an interesting wife. I imagine that a potential husband will think, 'Oh my, she is a beautiful, quirky creature, so rare – life could never possibly be dull with her as a wife.'

ELIZABETH:

Now you say that, do you remember a few years ago – in fact, the last time I was staying here. It was July, the hottest in over twenty years?

MATILDA:

I don't remember the last time you were here, but I do remember telling Catherine not to invite you anymore. Margaret hadn't been here either . . . I never thought I would say it, but I did rather miss her.

ELIZABETH:

I'm not talking about me here, Matilda. So, that summer, I was reading in the drawing room; the children had been out swimming in the lake. Jonty asked if you were going for a dip, and you were very short with him. I remember he had done something terrible, according to you. What was it?

MATILDA:

My, my, what a nosy parker you are, Elizabeth, spying on your own friends – unless there was some crime you were trying to detect?

ELIZABETH:

I just happened to overhear, Matilda; there's a great deal of difference between that and intentionally eavesdropping.

MATILDA:

Jonty blundered his way through life making mistake after mistake. If I tried to take note of each and every instance, I'd scarcely have time to breathe.

ELIZABETH:

Yes, but this transgression must have been a great one. You left the next day, a full week earlier than planned.

MATILDA:

If I remember correctly, Elizabeth, I left with Polly. She had gained a place in the Chorley Summer Art Academy and a girl of seventeen could hardly be expected to traipse across Europe on her own. Catherine had been planning to take her home to England, but then asked me if I would consider it. Polly often told me that I was like a mother to her. Catherine didn't see her as a person back then, you know, just a child who needs to be dressed, washed, fed and sent to school.

ELIZABETH:

So, you support her artistic endeavours?

MATILDA:

She's rather talented, you know. And she has such range; she possesses the same gift for capturing light as Turner, and her portraits sing of the Old Masters. At the moment, it's all so derivative really. But she is so very young. She needs time and space to grow and blossom, she needs time to discover her own style.

ELIZABETH:

So, you wanted her to leave York and be a painter?

MATILDA:

Jolly well no. I don't know where she got the idea that she doesn't need to study art, that she just needs to *be* art. There is only a year left in that university course – she has plenty of time to paint outside of lectures and what have you. Given that it's not a practical course, it is up to her to get the work done, but she has the rest of her life to embrace her artistic tendencies.

ELIZABETH:

From what I've heard, her *art* would not be acceptable to all potential husbands and their families.

MATILDA:

Oh, you mean those terrible male appendages? That's all just a phase, you know. Even Salvador Dalí has more to him than the lewdness of his works. There is some meaning underneath the surrealism. Polly just means to shock. I do hope she learns how to tone it down when appropriate. But there is more to life than marriage. I made a good match, as they say, and spent much of my life miserable and widowed. I don't believe that is all life is about, and certainly not for my granddaughter.

ELIZABETH:

Let me get this straight, Matilda, because I'm having a tough time wrapping my head around it. You, Matilda Caswell-Jones, the woman so concerned with appearances that you've hired a private detective to investigate your son's death lest the police get involved, lest your grandchildren's reputation be tainted with the hint of murder or scandal – this same woman welcomes and accepts her granddaughter's lewd sketches as art?

MATILDA:

Yes. Elizabeth, you are sometimes a bit slow to realise the nuance of things, both about people, and situations. In life, nothing is black and white.

ELIZABETH:

What's the matter with Polly? She does look dreadfully unwell.

MATILDA:

(Sharply) Nothing's the matter with Polly, nothing a good spell of home-cooked meals won't solve.

ELIZABETH:

Who will cook for Polly? As you've said yourself, Catherine has not arranged much domestic help for this week, and I know she's not a great chef herself.

MATILDA:

I can cook, you know. In Finland, when I was a girl, my parents helped the maids cook and prepare the midsummer feast. I made beetroot gravadlax by hand. Now, I have given you quite enough of my time. Continue asking your stupid little questions, and when you have finally come round to my way of thinking, come back and let me know. Picture it, Elizabeth Chalice on the front pages of *La Stampa*, even *The Times*, the *New York Herald Tribune* . . .

ELIZABETH:

Unfortunately, you're overestimating the newsworthiness of Jonty's death. I'm never going to comply with your terrible scheme and without you telling me who you intend to frame . . . there's nothing I can do either way—

MATILDA:

Goodbye, Elizabeth. Do take care not to leave a stain on the silk headrest, your hair could do with a good wash. *(Cackling)*

(Door closes)

ELIZABETH:

She really could not have cared much for her son; did you notice, she didn't express any regret at his death whatsoever? Who is the poor devil she wants to frame? She seems to quite like Frankie and even though she didn't mention him, I can see she cares a great deal for Nikolai. That leaves Ludlow, Thomas or this Argento chap. Whoever it is, he must have quite the hold over Matilda. What secrets does a woman of that age need to guard so tightly? For Matilda, a woman who cares so deeply about how the outside world perceives her, I'd wager it is a matter of her honour. She has plenty of money herself, but not enough to provide for both sons. Matilda has been received by the cream of society and has the love of her grandchildren. I wonder if the person she wants to frame poses a threat to all of that. Why else would she want them out of the picture? In my time investigating crimes, I have seen individuals go to great lengths in order to keep their secrets hidden. But Matilda is not a sophisticated villain. It's foolish of her to think we might succeed in framing anyone. Even in Italy, the accused is tried in open court – there always has to be evidence. Evidence. The word sits heavily on me. We need to revisit the scene of the crime. Let's head to Jonty's study, where Catherine found his body.

(Elizabeth walking)

ELIZABETH:

*The house is still quite quiet. I suppose what reason have they to rise?
Anyone who has ever stayed in a house recently visited by Death will
know of the reluctance to get in the way. There comes a place in an investigation where science and facts don't quite offer the full picture. The
malevolence here is almost tangible, and whilst I have no particular spir-
itual inclinations, I can feel the ill will against Jonty. I can't explain this
sense I have. I felt it too, with the Conte case. The feeling of evil. Now I
know, this isn't any ordinary death – this is a murder. Now, I'm going to
have to be your eyes. What might we find? What did I miss earlier?*

(Elizabeth opens the door)

ELIZABETH:

It's a fine mess here, on Jonty's desk.

(She sniffs)

ELIZABETH:

*A dribble of Scotch – wait, no, there's a distinct lack of peatiness. Could
it be Irish whiskey?*

(Rustling through papers)

ELIZABETH:

*Advice from suppliers, shipping invoices, blah, blah, letters from Avonlea,
the family's Berkshire estate. Oh. What do we have here? An envelope
sealed with a lipstick kiss. Just like we did in the war. It's a purple sort
of red, far darker than would suit an English complexion – perhaps a
match for olive skin? Can't seem to find any letter, though . . . What
sallow-skinned beauty was sending Jonty love letters? Gosh, what—?
There's a loose needle here on the chair. That's all I need, I've just gone
and laddered my stockings. Where's Catherine's chequebook.*
    'Elizabeth C – £500'.
    *That's strange, why would she return the chequebook to Jonty's desk
after writing the cheque for me? Catherine's obviously had a good going
over this desk, too – no doubt she's seen everything here already. I knew*

I should have come earlier in the investigation, but I couldn't imagine I'd find anything the police hadn't already found. And, of course, interviewing Catherine as soon as possible was paramount to me in those first few hours. Now that feels like days ago.

(Opens drawer)

ELIZABETH:

Now, what is in here, under these old train timetables? Here we go. I do love a brown envelope. A bank draft, for 800 guineas, left blank. What could someone like Jonty, in fine money troubles, have to do with filling in bank drafts?

(Shuffles drawers)

ELIZABETH:

A catalogue of this year's debuts – not like Jonty to care about society matters, but I suppose you never know where someone's interests lie. A sewing kit – perfect, I need to put a stitch in the bottom of this hem. Ah, here we have something else. Something a bit more interesting.
'Financials, Year Ending 1952'.
Will take that with me to digest.

(Knock on the door)

CATHERINE:

Elizabeth, is that you in there? *(The door opens and Catherine appears)* What have you got there?

ELIZABETH:

Yes. Just taking another look through Jonty's desk. I never did get a chance to do a good examination.

CATHERINE:

Right-o. Anyway, would you like to come down to the kitchen for some Boxing Day breakfast? I know it's been a long night and you've not eaten much. Come back to all this when you've had a chance to regroup.

ELIZABETH:

Very well, thank you. I'll be there in a minute, just let me finish this page of notes.

(The door closes)

ELIZABETH:

Breakfast my foot. More like 'stop poking around in there'. Catherine should be busy grieving her husband, but she clearly does not want me in the office. Even if she loved him, that's not to say she didn't kill him. Well, we've still got eight more suspects to go. And I only seem to be stumbling across more questions, and fewer answers . . . but we've no time to waste. Oh no, I've caught my stocking on a loose upholstery tack in this chair – I don't even think I have another pair. How inconvenient. The trials of a lady detective. Now, let us see who else had a motive for murdering Jonty Caswell-Jones.

EPISODE 5
Flora Caswell-Jones

ELIZABETH:

The scene from last night was quite something. Washed up on the Como shore outside Villa Janus, Thomas and Flora Caswell-Jones. Two greenhorn pirates, squealing to the splash of the cold winter water. I am yet to explore the full interfamily dynamic in my quest to solve who killed Jonty Caswell-Jones. So far, I have interviewed wife Catherine, mother Matilda, eldest daughter Polly and alleged best friend Ludlow Lansdowne de Groot. My unfortunate entanglement with Ludlow now known to another suspect, my own impartiality is certain to be called into question.

The victim's mother Matilda, even when acting as though her memory was failing her, immediately sought to use the death of her son to blacken the reputation of one of her own guests. Who is it she wants to frame? Matilda would never have successfully framed someone herself, so she knew she couldn't set anyone up for murder without me being complicit and, dear reader, I have not sunk so low as to accept such an offer. I will be satisfied to bring this matter to a private conclusion and find the killer. I am not so egotistical as to require the notoriety of a big case. I am satisfied with my lot. I don't need to be the world-famous detective at the price of framing an innocent man.

Of Jonty's three children, I intended to scrutinise Thomas, but with time of the essence, it makes sense to interview Flora while she's here in front of me at Boxing Day breakfast. Jaunty as her demeanour may be, it is vital to examine her situation carefully. I need to present my findings to the family at the earliest opportunity before my own secrets are strewn across the lake for all to see. She has inherited her grandmother's Scandinavian looks – a shock of blonde hair complements the blue of her eyes. The pink of her lipstick is a shade too bright if you ask me ... but she's nibbling it off; she seems nervous. Her cream turtleneck dress must be her mother's. Why is she trying to look older than her years?

ELIZABETH:

So, are you quite rested from last night's exploits? Why did you take such a risk, going out across the lake in the middle of the night?

FLORA:

Life is full of risk. And the lake is perfectly calm at night. Peter is always saying how soothing he finds it.

ELIZABETH:

So, you just went with Thomas for the thrill of it?

FLORA:

I wanted to make sure Thomas didn't drown. He drank a lot of Scotch yesterday afternoon after we found father.

ELIZABETH:

We? I thought your mother was on her own? Did you find Jonty?

FLORA:

She was the first to see him, but I was there, too – I'm sure she didn't see me. He looked so calm, you know, like a stunned bird fallen from flight. The most relaxed he had looked in months.

ELIZABETH:

Tell me what happened.

FLORA:

I followed my mother – that lemon cake was taking an age . . . I just wanted to get the lunch finished and go to play cards with Thomas. I'm learning to count up to three decks for twenty-one, you know. Plan is to go to Monte Carlo and make enough—

ELIZABETH:

What happened when you followed her, Flora?

FLORA:

I was about six steps behind her. She didn't scream or anything, she just opened the door and said, 'Jonty – will you come along—?' before letting out a big gasp. I suppose he looked so natural, maybe she thought he was asleep at first! After all, Granny had just been slumbering at the dinner table after too much wine. Anyway, Mother immediately said, 'He's been killed.' Which I thought was a strange way to put it, seeing as she didn't *scream* or anything. I let out a shout without meaning to. She hadn't expected me to be there . . . She didn't try to resuscitate him, you know – odd.

ELIZABETH:

(To the reader – whispering) *Does my memory serve me correctly? Catherine explicitly told me she shouted for help and her children came running. Remember she told us how she tried to resuscitate him? Flora, here, however, tells me Catherine did no such thing . . . How long was she alone with her husband's body and who can I believe? I think we'll need to pry a little further.*

ELIZABETH:

What did she do next?

FLORA:

Had a root around his desk, said she was looking for the number of the police station, but there was one little notebook she put into her pocket . . . A little black one just like yours – I've never seen mother behave so strangely. People do bizarre things when they've had a shock . . . but, something about her . . . it wasn't right.

ELIZABETH:

Flora, are you trying to say you think your mother is responsible, that she might have killed your father?

FLORA:

Oh, *no*, I don't mean that, it's just . . . I don't know, things have been quite odd around here. Shortly before you arrived – maybe it was eight o'clock – Thomas told me that Father told him he had cut Mother out of the will. Meaning the estate goes to Thomas, with an allowance for me, Polly and Granny. I mean, Granny has her own money, but still.

ELIZABETH:

That's a lot for a child to think about.

FLORA:

I'm not a child! I'm seventeen next week – old enough to get married.

ELIZABETH:

Ah, marriage. Is that already on your mind? And have you any candidates? Any of the guests, perhaps?

FLORA:

Don't be *silly*. I mean, I am using the opportunity to practise my flirting skills, but I wouldn't consider a match with anyone here. Oh gosh, *(pause)* just to think, Father won't be there to walk me down the aisle when the time does come.

ELIZABETH:

Oh yes, he is gone for good now. But it means you are free to marry as you wish. Catherine won't object.

FLORA:

(Sobbing) What are you insinuating, Elizabeth? You don't really think I would have hurt him, do you? I *loved* him.

ELIZABETH:

I'm sorry. I'm so sorry. You poor thing. It must be tough, I have to ask these questions, you know! It is just important that you tell me everything you know. Did you spend much time with your father, you know, just the two of you? Were you good friends?

FLORA:

Not really. But you know, he did let me go to the casino with him, if we were ever staying in Mayfair, just the two of us. Called me his good-luck charm, although I resent that. I was the *brains* of the operation. They jolly well don't like to see me coming. I've never lost a hand of blackjack. Do you believe that?

ELIZABETH:

Despite how charmingly you say it, I don't believe it. Where did you go? How did you get in?

FLORA:

A little bit of make-up and no one asked any questions. Here.

(Flora unzips her bag and removes a pack of playing cards)

ELIZABETH:

It's hardly the time for playing cards, is it? But, that said, I do find doing something with my hands helps my brain think through things. Speaking with Flora is reminding me of the folly of youth. She's so sure of herself, so confident, but not yet aware of the darker side to life. This is her first taste of loss, the first time something has gone badly for her. And I wonder if there's some part of her young heart that's impure enough to kill her father. A chap would be the only reason, unless she's found herself in with a bad crowd. Let's push her a little more.

FLORA:

Elizabeth, you are the house.

ELIZABETH:

Just a few hands, okay? I have lots of people to interview today.

(Elizabeth shuffles and deals the cards)

FLORA:

What was your question? Ah, yes, where did Father and I go. We went mostly to the Mayfair Club. They don't mind girls going in. Well, it's a lady's house. Huge place off Regent's Street, three rooms dedicated to gambling. Two beautiful parlours for cards, roulette, poker. Then down in the basement, it was deliciously filthy. They had cockfights. Chaps fighting one another. Fellows betting on the throw of a coin. Father didn't like me to go down there . . . But a young girl gets curious, you know?

I don't know why you need to know all this, though. I can't see how it could possibly be connected to this – you know, what's going on here – but there *was* a bit of a *to do* with a boxer chap Father had sponsored.

He used to take me to the club when I was home from school occasionally at the start of the year – Easter, that sort of thing. But then in the summer we went far more often, sometimes as often as a few times a week. Father always seemed to leave with wads of cash, so I was certain he had the same lucky streak as me. The cream of London and wealthy men from the four corners of the world seemed to go there, thriving on its exclusivity and debauchery all wrapped up in one Regency-address bow. It had a respectable front with a darker centre – a bit like Father, I suppose. I just loved spending time with him. It was a secret just for the two of us. Anyway, eyes on the game, Elizabeth.

ELIZABETH:

I can't believe it. I jolly well shuffled there.

FLORA:

Blackjack!

ELIZABETH:

Knave, two, queen – bust.

FLORA:

Another hand.

(Elizabeth shuffles)

ELIZABETH:

Who ran this illegal club?

FLORA:

Golly, I'm not sure how *illegal* it was; the Attorney General lost a hand of poker to Father there once. Anyway. As I mentioned, downstairs, there was boxing. Gruesome stuff to be honest, nothing the Marquess of Queensbury would have agreed to. It was the start of August when Daddy really, I suppose, lost the run of things.

ELIZABETH:

King of hearts. Queen of diamonds

FLORA:

Jolly well stick. Let's see you.

ELIZABETH:

Ten, seven, five.

FLORA:

You're bust!

ELIZABETH:

I'm not very good at twenty-one.

FLORA:

I'm lucky, I told you. I can't lose. Go again.

ELIZABETH:

This is the last time.

(Elizabeth shuffles)

ELIZABETH:

Ah, do you see? This card game of Flora's – it's working well as a distraction technique – I have a feeling she's enjoying telling this story, while also winning twenty-one . . . I'd better ask her about the boxer fellow.

ELIZABETH:

What do you know about the boxer fellow your father sponsored?

FLORA:

Enough. We went to the club every night Mother wasn't in the house. Father stopped trying to stop me from following him downstairs. At first, he was cautious about exposing me to the more depraved areas of the club . . . but at some point, he was so lost in that world, I don't think he took proper notice of *what* I was doing. Of course, part of me was concerned to see his . . . decline, but I figured, he is the adult, I am the child, and if he doesn't mind . . . then I don't. And you know, during the war, seventeen-year-old nurses and the like were exposed to rather a lot. Must we all be so uptight? And I didn't see banknotes anywhere, only the woman who ran it all, and her red notebook, scrawling out his debts. No matter how engrossed he became, he kept me away from that red book at all costs. Anyway, you asked about the boxer. It got very bad after he got an idea that this particular boxer chap, Joe, was a winner. That he was the ticket back to glory. So, he arranged for massages, sent a new coach, all sorts of exercise contraptions, to get behind Joe. And it worked for a while, you know. We were back in the black, Father was in great form – started taking note that it wasn't a respectable place to be bringing his teenage daughter. Essentially, he sought to restore respectability to things. But after a few weeks, well, it all went south again. Joe got a terrible going over from an Italian chap – Monto, they called him. Broken jaw, smashed collar bone . . . it was terrible stuff. They let that go on for far too long until some chap, a doctor, interceded for them to stop. At one point, I thought the crowd would just let him get beaten to death, to die there in the ring. After seeing that, I completely understood the term *baying for blood*.

(Elizabeth deals the cards)

ELIZABETH:

Here you go. Two, three.

FLORA:

Hit me up.

ELIZABETH:

Knave of spades.

FLORA:

Hmmm. I'd better stick there.

ELIZABETH:

House has ten, two is twelve. I'll go again.

FLORA:

Bust.

ELIZABETH:

Ten. Jolly well done. Three in a row.

FLORA:

Told you. I can't lose.

ELIZABETH:

Pride comes before a fall. Did he survive? Joe, this fighter chap.

FLORA:

Barely, I believe. A few weeks later, the first of September, we were packing up. I was headed back to school, Father was leaving on his trip to South America. Anyway, I was up in my room, right up in the attic, of course. Have you been to our home in Carlyle Square? It was a warm evening, I had my window open, I could hear everything. There was a woman who arrived at the door. She managed to get Father out there. She told my father that she had no money to feed the children . . . could he spare this and that. Poor woman, she spoke wonderful English, she sounded educated. What an awful situation for her. I think she might have been the wife of Joe, the boxer.

Father must have given the woman some small change, whatever was in his pocket, and promised to send more. But he obviously forgot to send anything before he left. I happened to be back again the next weekend – the house was all shut up then. I just wanted to collect a stole for Polly. Anyway, there was the woman again. She recognised me – she must have been to some of the fights herself and seen me there. So she asks me, you know, for the money. But she's not nice anymore. This time she jolly well bared her teeth, so to speak. Threatened to reveal the underground club to the police, the newspapers, everything. It wasn't so much the loss of the club, but if all of those important people knew it was the indiscretion of the Caswell-Joneses that had led to its closure, Father would have been ruined. It would have been devastating for our family. So I gave her what I had left in my purse, half a crown, and promised to contact Father. But he was halfway across the Atlantic. I stayed at the house and it was another week before I got in touch with him. He did not want to deal with this woman's blackmail. He told me not to give her another penny. And that was it, really; I never heard from the woman again. I don't know what became of her. I did try to go to the club alone that night to find out more . . . but they wouldn't admit me without Father.

ELIZABETH:

Shouldn't you have been staying at school?

FLORA:

Oh yes, of course I should. But I forged a note from Mother, set the whole thing up and took myself down to Carlyle Square for a while. I must say it was a great deal trickier staying in the house when it was all shut up like that, no food anywhere. I managed about three days; by then Mother had figured out the whole scheme. The school were pretty unhappy but—

ELIZABETH:

Who were you there with?

FLORA:

I, eh, I never said . . . I wasn't . . . I was there alone.

ELIZABETH:

I doubt that very much. You ought to be very careful, I hope you realise that.

FLORA:

I'm not Polly – I, eh—

ELIZABETH:

Peter is in love with you, yes?

FLORA:

He is just wonderful, you know, and I—

ELIZABETH:

He's almost thirty, Flora. Do your parents know?

FLORA:

Mother suspects. But I managed to put her off the scent, otherwise she'd never have invited him here.

ELIZABETH:

Would your grandmother approve?

FLORA:

Granny just likes Peter as if he were some sort of exotic item to collect. If he hadn't the Olympic medals . . .

ELIZABETH:

She wouldn't be keen on the match, would she?

FLORA:

Of course not. None of them understand. It doesn't matter a jot the colour of his skin. I've known Peter my entire life. During the war, he stayed with us. As the only child, he's in line for a decent inheritance. His family's Berkshire house, some land. His father might not be a good accountant but he has enough to keep away destitution. Anyway, I couldn't care less about that. Our . . . friendship did change about a year ago. It was last Christmas, when he was here – well, half of us came down with a dreadful flu. The very worst one could have, all aches and pains and chills. Peter nursed the entire Caswell-Jones family. I suppose it let us have more time alone together. With everyone else in bed, ill.

ELIZABETH:

In bed . . .

FLORA:

Not like that, Elizabeth. Just time to read together. Time to talk. Of course, I realised how hard things would be for him, but had no idea how horrid people could be. Peter is as English as the rest of us. You know the reason he's so athletic is so he can defend himself? He had a jolly good beating when he started school and decided that he just had to become the strongest one there. He was damned contorted by the whole thing. I know he probably thought of me as little Flora when I was growing up, but for the last few years I am sure he could see I was coming of age. You mightn't believe it, but I've seen rather a lot in my seventeen years, Elizabeth. Enough to know how girls get ruined.

ELIZABETH:

Did your father know about Peter?

FLORA:

Father was more himself with me than with anyone else. Allowing me to the Mayfair Club, well, it engendered a sort of secret society between us. Father knew; he sort of ignored Peter's visits during the summer. Ignored, you know, why he was there . . . to see me. Then one evening, we were walking to supper in Piccadilly. He told me that he knew I was in love with Peter, but I couldn't marry him. That I could enjoy the summer with him, but after that it had to come to an end. That I needed to focus on my studies, get to university like Polly. When he found out that Peter was coming to Lake Como this Christmas, well, there was a jolly row with Granny. But I don't think he told her why he was so opposed to Peter's visit all of a sudden. Anyway, before you go thinking of me as a suspect, I know Father would have come round eventually. He had a good heart. I didn't kill him because he was trying to keep me and Peter apart.

ELIZABETH:

I don't know what to say, Flora.

FLORA:

Say something bloody nice to me! We all know about you, your history. I thought you would understand.

ELIZABETH:

What do you mean?

FLORA:

You're a good-time gal. A goer. A party girl. Plenty of suitors.

ELIZABETH:

How dare you—

FLORA:

That's why Mother stopped having you here, you know? Nothing to do with that missing person's case. She'd heard you'd had an affair with the Ambassador.

ELIZABETH:

How on—

FLORA:

I overheard her on the telephone. Yes, it was during the mid-term break that year. We were all at home in Berkshire planning the Christmas gathering when she got the call. Marnie Beresford must have instructed her to cut all ties with you, because I saw her scratch Elizabeth Chalice from the list herself. Here, let me get you a drink.

(Flora makes some noise rattling around the room)

FLORA:

Damn. There's no ice. Back in a second.

ELIZABETH:

I know Flora is just fetching ice to put an end to the interview, but what she's told me has thrown me. This is the problem with interviewing people you know. While there are some advantages . . . there are so many disadvantages, too.

So, what have we learnt from Flora? Of course it boils down to a chap, as I expected. Peter Smythson. I can feel a prick of sweat across my forehead – I do need a drink. Flora is only a child. She lashed out at me, but what she hit me with hurt. Of course that's why I was cut. James Beresford, the Ambassador . . . I have not thought about him in a while.

James introduced me to absinthe when we got talking on a hot July night. I had just finished a week of investigating an unfaithful husband

and wasn't ready to switch from being a nocturnal creature yet. He had the poor café owner rig up a drip for the green liqueur, and thus introduced me to the Green Fairy . . . Something about that drink, well, it let us lose our inhibitions. It was never about the sex but recapturing a feeling. I don't like to admit it, but it was about recapturing the excitement of the war. Peace-time was a slow-burning contentment, but fearing death at any moment had opened a part of ourselves that danced passionately at any opportunity, that sucked up the joy from the moment. The Italians lived that way more than us . . . I know what you're thinking, but for the record, James was young to be an ambassador at thirty – the incumbent died suddenly and they let him at it.

I shouldn't have to explain myself to you, reader. But the expatriate community here is of course very small. The Ambassador and his wife sat at the very pinnacle, along with Princess Heloise of Belgium. No one wanted to upset Marnie.

I had not realised his wife found out about the tryst. She had stayed in Rome in the summer of 1948. James was spending some time in Milan, spearheading a diplomatic campaign to improve banking relations between Britain and Italy. The Italian economy was on its knees. Things were still settling after the war, there were a lot of open wounds and the banking programme was meant to kick-start it. I recall Ludlow had some involvement, and I have made a note to revisit that with him if we have the opportunity. James died when his plane crashed over the Alps. He died too young. He was a good man. I am not proud of my affair, but life is for the living to enjoy. I wasn't invited to Villa Janus for Christmas that year . . . Perhaps Flora is right. Catherine wanted to take the moral high ground, so didn't invite me.

(Flora sets down a glass in front of Elizabeth and one for herself)

ELIZABETH:

Flora, did you hear of James's accident? Poor James. The Ambassador? It was the most horrific thing.

FLORA:

It's why I still prefer to come by land, to be honest. Gives me an excuse to stop in Paris.

ELIZABETH:

Did they ever stay here, the Beresfords?

FLORA:

Not that I recall, although Marnie still calls on Mother at Carlyle Square.

ELIZABETH:

Before I move on to another line of questioning, you mentioned that you don't believe what your father got up to at the club has anything to do with his death. Is that correct?

FLORA:

Yes, why would it? Anything at the club . . . it tended to get sorted *at* the club. It wouldn't follow him here . . . all the way to Como.

ELIZABETH:

Tell me, why did you come here with just your mother, during the summer?

FLORA:

Who told you that?

ELIZABETH:

She is hesitating but before she can answer, a sharp knock cracks at the door. It is Nikolai, the dancer.

NIKOLAI:

I am sorry to interrupt, but you must come. Eh, how do I say this . . .? Elizabeth, there has been another murder.

ELIZABETH:

Good Lord! Flora, you stay here.

FLORA:

(Shocked) No, but—

ELIZABETH:

Stay where you are!

ELIZABETH:

Reader, I can confirm that we do have a second dead body, but is it murder? It's dark as night here in the unlit corridor, but we haven't far to go. Flora, of course, will soon follow us – and then here, in the formal peach drawing room, sits Matilda Caswell-Jones, reposing in an armchair. Still as a mannequin, apart from one thin line of blood from the side of her nose. I didn't get to look at Jonty, but from what I have heard, it seems like they may have died in the same way. Two murders in twenty-four hours. A killer is at large.

NIKOLAI:

I went to get you first. I just got up, went into the kitchen for a coffee and came up here. That's when I found her in the drawing room. I don't think the family knows yet . . . I came in here to read my book, I asked if she had a light. I could see the blonde curls of her hair from the door. I checked her pulse already, she is dead.

ELIZABETH:

Thank you, Nikolai.

(Elizabeth examines the body, stepping around it slowly)

ELIZABETH:

She still feels warm. I saw her myself less than an hour ago. We had better tell the family.

NIKOLAI:

I think you should call the police first.

ELIZABETH:

Would you give me a few minutes here alone, please? Don't tell them yet, don't call the police, just wait five minutes, okay? Then I will need to speak to you.

NIKOLAI:

(Frantic) All right, all right, I will tell you all I know, okay? You'll find me on the veranda.

ELIZABETH:

What do you think then, is this another murder? Matilda was almost seventy . . . but she was healthy. Well . . . healthy-ish. She did pass out during lunch yesterday. This line of blood from her nose is . . . strange. And there's a slight asymmetry about her face. It is consistent with a stroke; that would explain her passing out yesterday, too. But she didn't seem to be confused about things and she had no other symptoms indicating a bleed on the brain. But then again, my medical training doesn't quite make me an expert in neurological matters. Her face, which was contorted with blackmail in our earlier interview, is now so calm. Her perfectly powdered skin is the picture of serenity. It feels like a breach of privacy to inspect someone at such close quarters.

The room is well ordered. On Matilda's lap is a copy of Frankie's book; from what I've noticed, he has gifted signed first editions to all the guests. Now, to the job at hand. Quite literally. Our victim's hands are lightly joined together. I open them to take up the book. Inside the cover, let's see, is there an inscription? No, it's just signed 'Francis'. The publisher is based in Edinburgh too. Ah, but inside there is a note within the pages. 'Matilda – the grandest grandmother of all – Frankie.' Her perfume is cloying at this distance, heavy with notes of oud and patchouli, an oriental scent, uncommon, for sure. It feels as if she could be still here, but the thought brings a shiver across my shoulders. It is my mind playing tricks on me. If anyone would lurk around to haunt the living, it is Matilda, but I work quickly.

If I had a camera, I would take some pictures. Instead, I sit down and sketch this all down, so I can come back to it later. The tourist handbook I flipped through last night is still on the table, but otherwise the room looks neater. The ashtrays have been emptied and the sideboard cleared of empty glasses. Who tidied up, I wonder? I replicate the way Matilda's feet sit. There is something not quite right about it. It seems unnatural to set one ankle bone on top of the other so sharply. It seems to me as

*though someone has rearranged her feet. This is no accident. The drawer
of the side table is empty. I'm certain Catherine sifted through other
papers in that drawer before she took out the chequebook. I lift the
receiver of the telephone; it won't connect. But Nikolai is right, I must
call the police directly. It is now my duty to protect the family's lives
more than their reputation. How can I keep all these people safe from a
killer?*

(Knock at the door)

CATHERINE:

Elizabeth, are you in there?

FLORA:

Granny? Is she here?

ELIZABETH:

Coming!

(Elizabeth opens the door, comes out and shuts the door behind her.)

ELIZABETH:

(In the corridor) I'm afraid there's been another death. It's Matilda—

FLORA:

What? Granny?! You can't be serious . . . open this bloody door—

CATHERINE:

What happened?

ELIZABETH:

I think you'll agree it's best if we call the authorities now—

CATHERINE:

No, no. Goddamn woman, open the door! Matilda expressly did
not want the police involved, and no—

THOMAS:

I say, what's going on here?

FLORA:

It's Granny, Thomas . . . she's dead.

THOMAS:

Old dear, always had to upstage us. She probably did herself in—

CATHERINE:

(Voice firm but with a quiver) Thomas, stop that. Elizabeth, you must investigate this, of course . . . But please, let us see her.

ELIZABETH:

Very well. I shall open the door, but *nobody* may go in. The crime scene was not preserved after Jonty's death. Now we have another body, I am certain both Jonty and Matilda were murdered, and that killer is still here amongst us. I need to collect evidence. Catherine, the telephone is not working, can you go down to the village and alert the authorities? There is a killer at work here. I'm no longer willing to keep this whole mess quiet.

CATHERINE:

Oh all right, all right, I suppose I wouldn't want anyone else to get hurt . . . but it will be hours before anyone gets here. Just open the door.

(Elizabeth opens the door)

FLORA:

Oh, Granny! But she . . . she looks so still. It's not fair, why did somebody have to go after her?

THOMAS:

Are you sure she's dead?

ELIZABETH:

Certain, she has no pulse.

(Crying)

CATHERINE:

Thomas, you go down to the village and let the Polizia know, will you?

THOMAS:

Fine, I could do with some fresh air. This place has the scent of death and desperation.

ELIZABETH:

I thought, Catherine, that you would go yourself. I have not yet interviewed Thomas.

CATHERINE:

Me? But they shan't take any notice of me . . . And I have to prepare something for everyone to eat. No, Elizabeth, I won't be going.

ELIZABETH:

Very well, but please, someone just go.

ELIZABETH:

They may have been on edge last night, but the Caswell-Joneses have completely lost control of themselves. The grief seems genuine, and I am forced to take in the anguish, the flushed face of young Polly, Catherine's tears. Either they are highly skilled at dramatics or Matilda's death is a real shock to them – except, of course, Catherine's odd comment about needing to prepare lunch, but sometimes grief does strange things to us all. But Thomas . . . he has maintained his reserve, taking in the unravelling of his female relations. I can almost hear the cogs of his mind clicking along, calculating the cost benefit to his share of the estate now his grandmother is dead. How much was her life worth to him in the end, I wonder?

THOMAS:

Hold onto your knickers, Liz, although that's easier said than done . . .

FLORA:

Excuse my brother's vileness, Elizabeth. Poor old Granny, she actually looks so peaceful, for once. You don't really think . . .? I suppose it *is* jolly suspicious.

ELIZABETH:

I need to seal this room – here, there is a key. I'm going to lock this door until the Polizia arrive. It may be some time; there's no sense in holding up my interviews.

(Elizabeth locks the door)

ELIZABETH:

But before I go, I have to ask, Catherine, where were you just now? Did you see anything out of the ordinary?

CATHERINE:

As a matter of fact, I did see something strange this morning. I was tidying the kitchen, getting things ready . . . And Matilda, well, she came in with a smelly cheese, wrapped in muslin. Inside is a full round of Bitto. I have never seen Matilda source food like that. I wonder what she was up to.

ELIZABETH:

Yes, she mentioned the cheese earlier. Very well, Catherine, keep it available for me to inspect. I will continue my interviews here in Jonty's study. I'll leave the door open, now I can keep an eye on the door to the drawing room *and* be in earshot of the kitchen and front door. Polly, will you ask Nikolai to join me? He's on the veranda.

FLORA:

Fine. What a terrible tragedy it is, poor Granny. She might have been old, but she wasn't ready to die.

ELIZABETH:

I apologise if I seem abrupt, but time is absolutely of the essence and I must keep a track of things right away. I do hope you understand.

EPISODE 6

Nikolai Ivanove

ELIZABETH:

I wish I hadn't said that I would leave the door open, because I would jolly well love to shut out any sound of this terrible bunch of Caswell-Joneses. Jonty's study is a rather large room, so I'm taking advantage of the sofa and small table beside the fireplace. The ashes are still warm! How interesting. Why would someone have lit any sort of fire in here? Ah ... yes, to dispose of some unfortunate documents. They've done so quite successfully, as I poke around with a bit of kindling ... it's all gone to ash. Pages and pages of documents burned. Jolly wonderful. Do you have any clue who killed Jonty yet? I certainly don't. Oh, hang on a minute, it's probably useless, but I can see a corner of a letter ... It's the very bottom, it's signed Jonty.

This is terrible handwriting, not at all like the letters from Jonty that Kate used to show me during the war. I can just about make out the last line. 'I have still not got over the shock of seeing you, but I do beg that if anything happens to me, for the sake of my children, and their inheritance, you will not say a word.'

But why would he have the letter he had written? Unless he never had the chance to send it. This can't possibly be a coincidence, although it does seem that a large number of papers were burned. Someone knew something about Jonty and he didn't want it to get out. He seemed concerned for his safety – was it just worry about his weak heart? Or was he watching his back?

Imagine not being able to relax around one's own family. Matilda was fixated on framing someone. If that person had got wind of her plan, it would certainly make him a prime suspect in her killing. It was a chap she was out to frame. Was it a mistake to allow Thomas to inform the authorities? And why was the telephone not working? Catherine hadn't seemed to bat an eyelid at that, although rural telecommunications can be extremely poor. I must speak to all of the guests here at Villa Janus by the end of the day, to understand whose motives are the strongest as quickly as possible. Who knows if we might have another victim on our hands before too long?

Flora's illicit romance with Peter Smythson and Jonty's gambling debts have done nothing to rule out Jonty's youngest daughter. I had not thought of her, a mere child on the cusp of womanhood, capable of such a despicable deed, but I was not satisfied with her innocence. She seems to know much more than I gave her credit for.

Matilda appears to have been killed in the same way as her son. Poisoning in such a way indicates the killer is probably the same person. Poisoners are overwhelmingly women. Less physical strength and a tendency to avoid conflict and the emotional pain of the moment of death . . . However, I am suspicious of Nikolai. His figure is lean, a dancer's body in a black polo neck. The darkness of his hair is accentuated with the fairness of his skin. In my experience the person who finds a body can never be discounted. Especially as he was Matilda's guest here at Villa Janus. Did she have a reason to bring him here? Did he have a reason to accept her invitation? I want Matilda to be examined by a coroner at the earliest opportunity to confirm my suspicions.

(Knock at the door)

ELIZABETH:

Come in, Nikolai.

NIKOLAI:

You have called the police?

ELIZABETH:

Telephone is down. Thomas has been sent down to the village to notify the Polizia. Tell me again, what were you doing before you found the body?

NIKOLAI:

I was up to eat. I have been up since four this morning. I rise early, to pray, read and study.

ELIZABETH:

I didn't realise you were religious.

NIKOLAI:

I haven't always been, but life takes you down strange paths, doesn't it?

ELIZABETH:

I suppose. Where is your room?

NIKOLAI:

I am up in the cheap seats, the old servants' quarters. It was the butler's room, so it has, in fact, a cosy little sitting room.

ELIZABETH:

Have you a window?

NIKOLAI:

Oh yes, I am in the top-right corner of the house. It is like a lookout spot, views over the lake down to the jetty, and the road from the village that goes over the hill.

ELIZABETH:

I see. Let's hope Thomas can get the police to come, in that case, lest he has to travel ten miles away from our crime scene. So, Nikolai, tell me . . . are you still a communist?

NIKOLAI:

No. Why do you ask, woman who seems to know it all? I defected from Stalin's Russia a few years before the war. I am not a communist.

ELIZABETH:

How on earth did you meet Matilda?

NIKOLAI:

I think it was the autumn of 1937. I started to smell a rat with how things were going in Leningrad. I had decided that I would not go back. I had managed to get a small part in a ballet – you would have thought the director wanted a dancer trained at the Bolshoi Ballet, but no. Anyway, there was this party after the final night, all of the opera donors were invited to meet the dancers, and *she* picked me out of the crowd. She thought I was the lead dancer, and when she heard my accent, she was *very* excited. She was quite the connoisseur of the arts, you know?

Matilda invited me to her house, in Carlyle Square. Eventually, I told her the truth . . . I knew I had to. She didn't seem to mind. She kindly spoke to her ballet connections about getting me into some rather better roles. She called up the director of Vic Wells Ballet. He came over, and it was settled within a few days. I have never been so grateful for someone to help like that. While I was never considered for a lead role, I was dancing, so I didn't care. But life wasn't that blissfull for long, since the authorities started to home in on foreigners that winter. But my mother, she was English, so I managed to become naturalised – a British citizen.

ELIZABETH:

But you've held onto your accent well. How did your mother go to Russia?

NIKOLAI:

She was a lady's maid. To the Duchess of Cairnryan. They were friends with the Romanovs . . . She met my father . . . he rescued her just in time, you know, from the revolution. Look, I am sorry that Jonty is dead, but we were not close. I had no reason to harm him. What else is there left to say?

ELIZABETH:

Who do you think killed him?

NIKOLAI:

Did someone kill him? Catherine has this idea in her head . . . I try to keep my distance from them, you know. It is Matilda who insists I'm invited. I don't have anywhere better to go, so I come. Frankie is not too bad. He has a very cutting wit. Thomas doesn't have any real friends, but Frankie is at least up front about this. So who do I think killed Jonty? If I'm honest, no one. But if I have to pick, I think Thomas. He is a psychopath. He tells me all the time how impatient he is, that he has to wait for his father to die to start living his own life, to make the estate his own.

ELIZABETH:

What does he want to do with it?

NIKOLAI:

Crazy things that don't even make sense. He wanted to sell off chunks to the neighbours – Peter Smythson's father. They want to change all the land to some new crop. I'm not a farmer, I don't know the ins and outs. Write down in your notebook to ask Peter about that. Thomas is a *strange* guy. That said, I wouldn't rule out Sally. You know, Ludlow's wife? I hear her screaming at Ludlow that she will kill him blah, blah. That she will have him poisoned if he's not careful.

ELIZABETH:

You can hear into their room?

NIKOLAI:

Yes, I can. Sally and Ludlow are staying in the Marble Room. That was originally the room of the master of the villa. Barone Luca. He wanted his butler to have privacy, up in the attic, but he wanted his demands to be met. So the Marble Room is directly under the attic. There is an audio trick, where a long tube carries the sound upstairs. The sound travels from the room very clearly when you put your ear to the receiver.

ELIZABETH:

Good Lord, how clever. Are Sally and Ludlow aware of this fact? What does the receiver look like?

NIKOLAI:

I don't even think Catherine and Jonty know. It is just a speaker in the wall. I think there must have been some way to muffle it. I'm sure Barone Luca didn't want the butler to hear everything that went on there.

ELIZABETH:

I don't suppose there's much of that sort of thing where Ludlow and Sally are concerned—

NIKOLAI:

Quite wrong! Ms Elizabeth – or is that Mrs Elizabeth? Anyway, they are still good lovers, if that's what you're trying to ask. Unfortunately, I know it all too well now.

ELIZABETH:

No, that's not what I'm trying to ask. But I mean, really, that often? You've only been here two nights.

NIKOLAI:

Well, most people say an apple a day keeps the doctor away, for Sally it is a banana—

ELIZABETH:

(Chokes with laughter) Crikey. Oh, Nikolai. Well, apart from that, what did you hear?

NIKOLAI:

Ludlow, he is *quite* the unstable character. Did you know that Sally was once engaged to Jonty?

ELIZABETH:

I did. Why do you think Ludlow is unstable?

NIKOLAI:

He seems to think that Thomas is his son, not his godson.

ELIZABETH:

Good Lord.

NIKOLAI:

What, you didn't know that?

ELIZABETH:

This interview is not about what I do or do not know. Now, tell me, what did you hear and why is Ludlow unstable?

NIKOLIA:

Ms Elizabeth, I don't think you *did* know that. You are not the only one asking questions. Anyway. He works in finance, yes? I don't think his affairs are going very well. But Sally, well, her business is *flourishing*. He was asking her to increase his allowance, so that will tell you how he is in her pocket. So anyway, the first night, Christmas Eve, they arrive late, everyone else is about to start dinner when they get here. Then there's no way to get the bags upstairs, but a few of us help with one. Sally was very agitated about the luggage, very concerned with what might be in there. The woman was definitely hiding something. Anyway, I forgot my cigarettes, so I go back up to the room – and, boy, it is really firing off between the two of them. They were travelling from Paris, yes? Well, there was a problem there with the bags, too. Sally was shouting, 'You can't even get that right!' Ludlow called her all sorts of names, too. What I think she was looking for was a bottle of wine. A bottle of Sauternes, I believe. Now the sound from that room is good, but not perfect, so I can't be sure. I didn't hear how the argument ended, because Frankie turned up at my door. I didn't want him coming in and hearing the sounds from below.

ELIZABETH:

You had accused him of theft earlier, hadn't you?

NIKOLAI:

I wish I had said nothing. There is . . . something going on there. She mentioned she had left her bottle of wine by her bag, that it was missing. Then I saw the label, realised it was her wine. But when I accused Francis of taking the wine, she denied it! Even though I had already seen it. I don't know why she would lie . . . she has something to hide. That wine would have cost a lot of money, she had said.

ELIZABETH:

So he turns up at your door – what did Frankie want?

NIKOLAI:

He was looking for Thomas. Thomas usually stays in my room. But after he arrived just as it was getting dark, I heard Catherine say she wanted to keep an eye on him, so he was down the corridor this time instead. Those rooms are smaller, but more comfortable. The rest of the family prefers to stay there. He was not happy about the arrangement, but she said something to him that I didn't hear. Then he was compliant, and Thomas is *not* known for his compliance. Now that I think of it, if you are convinced it was murder, who is to say Thomas and his mother didn't cook up the plan together? Keep your eyes open, Elizabeth.

ELIZABETH:

Do you believe that Ludlow is Thomas's father?

NIKOLAI:

Does it matter what I believe? He either is, or he is not. Maybe it wasn't just Sally and Jonty who had a romance.

(The telephone rings)

ELIZABETH:

I thought the phones were down.

(She picks up the receiver)

ELIZABETH:

Hello, Villa Janus?

(Pause for reply on the other end of the line)

ELIZABETH:

What a terrible Italian accent . . . you're all right, we all speak English here. You'd like to speak to Catherine Caswell-Jones, you say? I shall fetch her now. Where are you calling from? . . . Ah . . . the British Ambassador. You're speaking to Elizabeth Chalice here.

(To Nikolai) Nikolai, will you tell Catherine it's the British Embassy?
(To the Ambassador) Yes, Ambassador, we will fetch her now.

(Pause for response on the other end of the line)

ELIZABETH:

Yes, you are speaking to THE Elizabeth Chalice. That's me.

(Pause again)

ELIZABETH:

(Confused) No . . . I am not a former investigator. I am an investigator. What are you talking about? *What* must be true?

(Pause again)

ELIZABETH:

Bad news travels fast. Yes, we've had two murders here. Who told you—?

(Nikolai returns with Catherine)

CATHERINE:

Thank you, Elizabeth. Do you mind giving me some privacy, please?

ELIZABETH:

Of course. Nikolai, let's continue this interview on the veranda.

(Elizabeth and Nikolai walk to the veranda)

NIKOLAI:

What was that about?

ELIZABETH:

Oh, just some diplomatic Christmas messages.

(Open doors to veranda)

NIKOLAI:

Oh, there is no ashtray here, do you mind if I go get it?

ELIZABETH:

Please.

(Nikolai exits)

ELIZABETH:

What on earth was that phone call about? That weasel from the consulate . . . who informed them? Catherine and Matilda wanted me to come here to keep the investigation private. I have failed that task, haven't I? Who could possibly have told them if the phone lines were down? It has to be Thomas – perhaps he has just got down to the village and the news has already spread. But so quickly? Unless . . . the chap Thomas went to meet at midnight . . . seeking a will . . . the ex-pat community is so close. But . . . you're right. That is impossible as Matilda has only just died.

Hold on. Unless Thomas planned to kill his grandmother . . . that is the only way he would have been certain of two deaths. I have myself twisted in a jolly good tangle, don't I? I still haven't a main suspect for Jonty's murder. Now we have Matilda, lying in repose pending the arrival of the police. If things don't start coming together soon, I'm not sure how I'm going to be able to help this family . . . And I'm starting to wonder if I do want to help them at all . . . I need to spend some time with my notebook to tie things together. A quick recap would help, I think. And I need to get that wretched thought of Ludlow and Sally off my mind. He loves money more than he loves me; there's no way he would leave her. And if I'm honest, I'm better off without him. Aren't I?

So. Let's think. Jonty's wife, Catherine: the marriage seemed to be in acceptable order for one that had weathered the war and two decades. There seems to be an issue around ordering the house, and in my line of work I have seen wives killing their husbands for less. Can it be true that Ludlow fathered her eldest son? When we nursed together during the war, she really seemed to hate him . . . She did not like her mother-in-law, but I sense a mutual admiration between the two women had developed over the years.

Then on to Polly, Jonty's eldest daughter. A would-be artist, clearly with health trouble. She did not have a good relationship with her father.

In fact, he had her pinned to the collar with a choice between university and finding a husband. There's the matter of her damaged notebook ...

Ludlow claims to be Jonty's best friend, but he is not a good man – I have my own personal experience there. He is in financial trouble, and was likely taking advantage of Jonty's financial ineptitude.

Let's not forget that old battleaxe, Matilda Caswell-Jones. She seemed so enlivened at the opportunity to frame someone for the murder of her son. She hadn't wanted him home from the war. He was the runt of the litter in her eyes. Who had she wanted to frame? Who would have killed her?

The youngest daughter, little Flora, what a sweetheart. She reminds me of myself at that age. On a treacherous path with Peter Smythson. Folly comes so easy to youth, and passions are so easily flared. Jonty always seemed like such a calm-tempered chap, not the sort to rule his daughter's lives with an iron fist. The large gambling debts accumulated were a great cause for concern. Could Catherine have found out about this? Even Thomas, as heir to the estate, would likely be angry that his father was burning through his inheritance.

Now we have Nikolai, eavesdropping on his neighbours. He is no fool, I'm certain he knows of my affair with Ludlow and made a point of flaunting Ludlow and Sally's passion in front of me. Six suspects, six motives ... some more convincing than others ... I fear I have just scratched the surface of the foul goings on in the Caswell-Jones family. How about you, are you certain who the killer is? If not, let's continue our quest for the truth.

(Nikolai returns and sets down the ashtray)

NIKOLAI:

Here's the ashtray.

ELIZABETH:

Thank you.

(They light a cigarette)

ELIZABETH:

Did you ever socialise with Jonty and Catherine?

NIKOLAI:

I was never invited to socialise with them. Catherine, she is a social climber, you know. Just like Matilda. A fake, a fraud. I come here for the view and the food. Stop for some girls in Milan on the way back.

ELIZABETH:

Charming.

NIKOLAI:

I did see Jonty occasionally, in this club I visit. During the summer he was there almost every night, but the last few months, when he was travelling, I did not see him. I still go myself – and they ask after him there. They are keen for him to return. Spend some money.

ELIZABETH:

The Mayfair Card Club.

NIKOLAI:

Ah yes, of course. You've spoken to Flora. His little charm for the summer. When I saw them together the first time, she looked so young, but with the red lipstick . . . well, it made her look like a common prostitute. And that's how it would have appeared to the other guests there. Even *their* eyebrows were raised at her age. I was certain they were in the wrong place, there by mistake. I was careful to hide myself. You see, although I am a British citizen, the world is harsh for anyone with the hint of red. I did not want to get busted in there. I watched their descent into the seventh circle of hell.

ELIZABETH:

And you ensured your friends in the club made money off his situation.

NIKOLAI:

I'm not his babysitter. I told him to be careful, but you say that to a gambler and see what reaction they give you. What you really want to find out about is Margaret. Margaret Horton.

ELIZABETH:

Who? Oh, of course. Margaret. There are *so* many people here – she, to me anyway, is the most easily forgotten. Good Lord, what business would she have in such a den of iniquity? I'd be less surprised if Princess Margaret were there, having heard some of the important people who spent time there.

NIKOLAI:

She was blackmailing Jonty. Said that she would tell Catherine about the debts. So not only did he owe the Mayfair Club, but he was paying blackmail money to Margaret. I saw her one night. It was a horrible wet week, I happened to be leaving the club just after Jonty and Flora. I hung back, anxious they would not see me. But with the umbrellas – the night was dark, it was hard to see anyone.

But there was a moment, a particularly heavy downpour. I stepped into a doorway, on Carlyle Square. There was Margaret, waiting for them outside their residence. It mustn't have been the first time; she seemed angry, like she had been waiting there. I made my way closer and stood in the phone box outside their house. The rain eased off, and I could hear her. Her voice, it was shrill. She was threatening to tell Catherine if he didn't write her a cheque then and there. So, he went into the house, leaving Flora on the doorstep with Margaret. She wasn't too happy with Flora, either, but Flora didn't care. She threatened to tell Catherine that Margaret was blackmailing her father . . . but obviously realised that would be the undoing of him. The housemaid, I believe, from the house next door came out to look, and that shut them up. Jonty came back with the cheque. I waited until Margaret was down the street and the door was closed. I followed her. She went back to the

Mayfair Club! I can only conclude that she has debts there herself, that's how she first saw him, and that's why she needed money. Her dislike for him was a bonus.

Now I can't imagine Catherine would have been too happy about this. If she found out. Ludlow told me some crazy story over our drinks on Christmas Eve that Margaret drove into a wall up in Berkshire, for Catherine's attention. I don't know why that woman bothers Ludlow so much – or why he bothers her. But how do you know Jonty didn't poison himself? All those debts and threats . . . life would have been difficult.

ELIZABETH:

I'm not ruling anything out. Did you ever see Margaret there? Actually in the club?

NIKOLAI:

It's hard to remember back to the summer. But, I mean, there were other rooms, small ones, more respectable for a woman like that to play – I don't know – bridge or gin rummy or something.

ELIZABETH:

Hmmm. Now, back to the present. How did Jonty seem to you in the days before he died?

NIKOLAI:

Well, given all that had been going on back then, he was remarkably calm. I had not seen him in months. The management at the Mayfair Club wanted him to repay the debts, so I thought perhaps he has been in hiding over the autumn. He was already here when I arrived on the twenty-third. As I said, we were never close, but he welcomed me with a warm brandy, asked me into his study. We were the only ones here that night. We had a light discussion and he played Toscanini's *Eroica*, a new record he had. It had just been performed in America two weeks before, can you believe that? He was a man in high spirits, that is for sure. He told me that his luck had changed, that he had some big news to tell everyone. That he was waiting until after Christmas dinner. He asked me to come to Bellagio with him after Christmas, said he wanted to buy a new boat.

ELIZABETH:

Why did you not mention this before?

NIKOLAI:

I am sorry – discovering Matilda's body must have thrown it all from my mind. It is just coming to me now.

ELIZABETH:

Why did he need a new boat?

NIKOLAI:

I think he wanted it. It sounded like he had made a big deal, come into some money from somewhere.

ELIZABETH:

Where do you think he got the money? I was under the impression finances were tight.

NIKOLAI:

Even if they were that would not have mattered to Jonty. He was addicted to spending. He might not have been gambling at the club, but a person like that is gambling somewhere, on something. He was the worst sort of gambler. You know, sometimes I would watch him play roulette, and he would even mix up the numbers. Say he chose red twenty-six, if that came up, he wouldn't realise he had won. I think that's why he had Flora . . . maybe it was his vision. So I think he probably just took money from his company or won on a bet – anything could have happened with him.

ELIZABETH:

You saw quite a lot of him during the summer then.

NIKOLAI:

Ah, he was the fool of the place. The butt of the jokes, you know?
But I knew Matilda would want me to keep an eye out for him.

ELIZABETH:

Matilda. She preferred you to her own son, didn't she?

NIKOLAI:

Why is this relevant? We are talking about finances—

ELIZABETH:

It's you that Matilda invited to the opera, even to Royal Ascot, in
the place of her son. That must have annoyed Jonty.

NIKOLAI:

I don't think he was very skilled at studying the form, as you say.
But he would bet on anything. But what do you want me to say?
Yes, she was a . . . an admirer of mine. Matilda liked to collect
people. Scratch beneath the surface and there was little in the way
of real affection. I'm sure Jonty knew his own mother well enough
to see that.

ELIZABETH:

Do you think you'll be left anything in her will?

NIKOLAI:

I had not thought of that so soon; I do have some common
decency.

ELIZABETH:

Because Matilda's estate in and of itself is rather valuable. She
entered the marriage with almost forty thousand pounds of a
dowry. I remember she explained it to me before; she even
explained that in her family, prenuptial contracts were the standard.
But she retained interest in the fortune she brought, and essentially
retained ownership of it throughout her marriage. You must have
wondered about it, all these years?

NIKOLAI:

You're just like everyone else. Oh, he must be after the money or the will. There are times when I asked myself, 'Nikolai, is that what's going on here?' And I can answer no, I was not after her money. We all like being around wealthy people; it is a thing to behold, to see people living a life of such ease. For anyone who must earn a living and knows anything about the struggles of the average person. You are eking out a living as a secretary, aren't you? When you compare what you earn in a month – well, Catherine probably spends more on a bottle of wine. It was not the pounds in the bank that interested me. But the things that wealth brought. Opening nights here, an interesting garden party on Green Square there. Sitting on a veranda like this, with the smell of the lake. Instead of some disgusting alleyway that stinks of piss. You came here, with Catherine, for years. Are you going to tell me you didn't enjoy the ease of it all? Even knowing things were paid for – no one was going to try to force you to pay three shillings for a plate of peas.

ELIZABETH:

You have quite a way of putting things, Nikolai. But wouldn't you prefer to have the money yourself, and decide where to go? After all the days and hours and evenings you have spent as a fading charm on the arm of a woman who probably never even asked the name of your mother?

NIKOLAI:

You and I are very similar, Elizabeth. In this house, there is the family. There's Sally and Ludlow, even Peter. Then there is Frankie, Margaret, Argento – he's coming, have you heard? Then there is you and me. None of us would be here without them. Drawn together like this. If you are so certain it is murder, and if you really want to know my thoughts on who killed Jonty, it is them. One of their own. Because when you don't need to fight every day to live life, it takes far less to drive you to murder.

ELIZABETH:

You hardly need to fight every day of your life for survival.

NIKOLAI:

Not now, I don't, but I did, in the war, every day was a fight for life.

ELIZABETH:

It was difficult for us all. Now, coming back to you. You can't earn much as a dance teacher. That must make you bitter.

NIKOLAI:

I make enough. I say the same to you. I make extra with private lessons for little Anna Pavlovas. Referred by Matilda. You see what I mean? Just being in the vicinity of people with money is beneficial. But I can live my own life, too, you know.

(Knock on the door)

CATHERINE:

All done with my phone call now if you want to go back in?

ELIZABETH:

I think we are fine here. Everything okay, I hope?

CATHERINE:

Thomas has gone and put his foot in it, I'm afraid. He was trying to get in touch with Argento, our friend and lawyer.

ELIZABETH:

Why would he call the *embassy* looking for Argento? And wasn't Argento already on his way?

CATHERINE:

Jonty's will, it was stored there. He had wanted to make some changes so had a new will drawn up a few weeks back. Anyway, we knew Argento was coming . . . yes, of course, he told us all already – I think Thomas just wanted to inform him of the change of circumstances . . . We now know Argento has left Milan and should be here very shortly. I still have Matilda's cheese if you want to examine it, though I can't imagine there's anything the matter. But you know, it does look just delicious. Margaret is salivating – she's volunteered to check it's not poisoned!

ELIZABETH:

No one should touch that cheese until I get there. I will join you in the kitchen when we are finished here.

(Exit Catherine)

NIKOLAI:

She is very jolly for someone who has lost her husband and mother-in-law in twenty-four hours.

ELIZABETH:

She always was good in a crisis. I remember during the war, the bleaker things got, the brighter Catherine became. Although even I can see she is particularly chirpy today.

NIKOLAI:

I know many women would be happy to be free from a mother-in-law like Matilda.

ELIZABETH:

From what I've seen this weekend, it appears to me they had reached some new understanding recently. Something has changed; Catherine has been very much the lady of the house. In previous years, I really remember how imposing Matilda was. Not so, anymore. Now, Nikolai, I think we will leave this here. I am so far satisfied with your answers. I must speak with the others.

NIKOLAI:

Before you leave, Elizabeth, one more thing. You really must be careful. Even if there isn't a killer in the house, these people are dangerous.

ELIZABETH:

But Nikolai, you've spent so much time saying you don't believe it's murder at all.

NIKOLAI:

You're the professional here, Elizabeth, not me. Use your best judgement.

ELIZABETH:

We don't have much time. Thomas has been gone for over an hour now, the Polizia should be here soon. Nikolai has impressed me. I admit I had allowed his gruff and aloof demeanour to cast him as an immediate adversary, but his information is decidedly useful. Of all the suspects, I found him the most refreshing to interview, so reasoned and tempered his answers were. But I can see he is playing the role of impartial reporter and I could tell he was lying about Matilda's will. Nikolai would not have stayed around for so long simply for the feeling of ease he described. He would need cold, hard cash. He is hiding something, I just can't put my finger on what it might be.

From the left of the lake I hear the low growl of not one, but two vehicle engines. The Rigoletto figures of the Polizia in the first, navy car. Behind that, obscured by the exhaust of the police car, is a red Ferrari with a white roof. The sound of the engine guzzling up oxygen grows as the sports car gains in pace and overtakes the police car. The red car is speeding across the narrow bridge, scattering gravel as it swerves into position beside the villa. Argento, I presume, pushes back his hair, as silver as the mist that rose on the lake this morning. He is certainly beating the officers, taking the steps to the veranda two at a time, a large brown envelope in hand. He is acquainted with the villa – and all of a sudden I find myself holding a pocket mirror to reapply my lipstick. I told you I used to behave badly here. Reader, I feel like being badly behaved again.

EPISODE 7

Thomas Caswell-Jones

ELIZABETH:

Oh, there you are. I am in a state of undress. I didn't want you to come across me like this, but I suppose all good detectives need a fatal flaw. So, the chap with the will has arrived, the famous Argento, and here I am in my room looking for a clean pair of nylons.

Oh, but he is a handsome thing . . . silver hair to his shoulders, the most evenly tanned skin, not that jaundice yellow some people go in the winter . . . and quite the chest. The way he took those steps up from the road – two at a time! Matilda's comments about my greasy-looking hair are unfortunately entirely accurate, so I'm twisting a wonderfully colourful scarf into a band, a pop of lipstick, there we go. I know what you're thinking – what about Ludlow? Well, he is old news, I don't owe him a damn thing. And, oh yes, the two murders that I'm investigat- ing . . . requiescat in pace, Jonty and Matilda. Well, look, I need to put myself right. I shall get to the bottom of it, but I can look good doing so. Can't I?

And they won't start reading the will until Thomas is back anyway . . . I do like to be admired – don't we all? Maybe Argento will be too sad to notice me, if his mother is sick. Gosh, perhaps she's even gone and died? Strange background, this fellow; he used to be the fami- ly's lawyer but was disbarred after some wartime misconduct. Now he cooks and cleans for the family, but sits with them for dinner, which is a peculiar set-up.

Secrets, eh? We all have them.

Damn, I only have one black and one tan stocking . . . Hmmm, that's either bare legs or two pairs of holey black ones on top of each other, so there's no flesh on show . . . Oh, you don't care about this situation . . . why am I thinking of – yes, that's it. Polly had a tear in her nylons in the same location. Just here under my left knee – where I pulled a thread sitting at Jonty's desk. She must have been there, too . . .

I found a tear in my previous pair. Do I have time to put a few stitches in this frock? How lucky to have found a sewing kit. It's just one of those cheap ones. I wonder what Jonty was doing with it.

(Pause)

ELIZABETH:

Oh, one of the needles is missing, the tiniest one that no one can ever thread. At least, I don't believe anyone here is such a skilled seamstress that they could. Can you? You probably don't do much about sewing at all, do you?

(Pause)

ELIZABETH:

Hang on a minute. Could it be . . . ? What if the poison was administered at the tip of the needle, pressed through his flesh into the bloodstream? It's possible, isn't it? I have been thinking that perhaps he was injected with the poison somewhere like the inside of his mouth or ear, that the killer used a small syringe. I still can't rule that out, but the prick from such a small needle would be imperceptible to the naked eye . . .

It certainly points towards a female killer, doesn't it? Excuse my stereotyping, but I've never seen a man pick up a sewing kit. Though they sell these kits in any newsagents across the world. Reader, if my suspicions are correct, I think we might have found our murder weapon . . . I think it's quite likely that Jonty Caswell-Jones was killed by poisoning on the needletip. I wonder, is it the same poison used by Amazonian hunters? They apply it to the tip of an arrow, and as soon as the poison breaks the skin, the victim's body is paralysed. Something the size of a human would take two or three minutes . . . paralysing every muscle in the body. Poor Jonty, the chap would have been conscious the entire time as his body shut down. His lungs paralysed, his brain and heart would have become starved of oxygen. His heart went into cardiac arrest and ceased to function, leaving our ultimate cause of death as a lack of oxygen in the blood. The only upside is that perhaps Jonty's dickie heart arrested more quickly than one might have expected, but it is still a terrible fate. I wonder what he thought about, in those horrific few moments. He must have seen his killer leave the room.

Charlie told me about it once. Not that he had a habit of breaking the Official Secrets Act, but there were times during the war when he had been so disturbed by something, by what one human can do to

another, that he had to tell someone. He explained how curare worked,
I'm almost certain that's what was on the needletip. Without more
evidence, I can't be certain.

But why did the killer leave the sewing kit behind? It is rather sloppy,
I must say.

While the killer may be female, if my hunch about the sewing kit is
correct, son and heir Thomas Caswell-Jones will be my next interviewee;
I've not managed to nail down the fellow, but by all accounts he is quite
the Mad Hatter. Of everyone here, his is the strongest motive – he is the
heir to the entire family estate.

Now, Matilda – who is it she wanted to frame? Any ideas yet?
Nikolai? She died, unfortunately for us all, without revealing who the
victim of her scheme would be. The old dear passed in much the same
way as her son, leaving a perfectly still corpse reading a copy of our
Scottish philosopher's treatise. Any doubts I may have had about Jonty's
death being suspicious did fade away when I found her. That reminds
me, I have six more suspects to speak to, including the author of
Matilda's book, Frankie Heath. After Thomas and Frankie, I'll need to
track down Catherine's friend Margaret. She's an ordinary sort of
woman, but everyone is a suspect until I can rule them out. And from
what I've heard, she has behaved rather strangely towards Catherine
and Jonty of late. Then, once I'm finished with Margaret, that leaves
Ludlow's wife: businesswoman Sally, former fiancée to our victim, Jonty.
Two more suspects include former lawyer Argento, even though he wasn't
here at the time – but you'll soon see why I want to interview him, and
family friend, the Olympic skier Peter Smythson.

The chilling fact remains that there is a killer on the loose in this
house. I'm aware that I'm probably top of the list for this individual.
You'll need to pay close attention to anyone who seems on edge. Someone
who has killed twice has passed the point of no return and will surely
not hesitate to do so again. I'm all of a sudden quite conscious of being
alone in my room, here at the end of an empty corridor. I'm in one of the
great rooms, not the comfortable corridor assigned to the family. It is
terribly cold without any heating, but I have views over the lake and

into the hills. The villa is enclosed on three sides by the steep mountain; in summertime arching olive groves are visible. Even in the half-light, I see the cliff-like hills are a muddy slush.

(Loud bang)

ELIZABETH:

Good Lord! The wind is picking up – these damned shutters.

(She shutters the window)

ELIZABETH:

The sky looks angry, with thick grey cumulus clouds, settling down for a jolly good snowstorm by the looks of things. Right, time to get downstairs. Oh, there you are, foxy. A little stole to keep the draught away. All in all, I don't look too shabby now, with a fresh black dress on. That reminds me, Flora said she snuck back into the family house in Carlyle Square to get a stole for Polly; in September she'd hardly need it. Why was it so important?

Where's my journal? Ah, there we have it. Are you ready to face this awful bunch and discover who the killer is? And don't worry, I'm not ruling out the potential that there's more than one in on it.

(She closes the door and walks down the corridor)

ELIZABETH:

Sally? Is that you? Are you going somewhere?

SALLY:

You bloody bet I am. I need to be back in London for New Year's Eve. Princess Margaret has invited us to a ball at Kensington Palace – not a chance I'll be missing that.

ELIZABETH:

The Polizia are downstairs. I'm sure they'll want to speak with you, as well as me.

SALLY:

Oh, wake up, Elizabeth. I'm terribly sorry poor Jonty died, but what motive have I? Sure, we had a silly fling as teenagers, but that's it, and what would I gain from his murder all these years later? Now, if you'll excuse me—

ELIZABETH:

All I ask of you is to stay until after lunch, okay? Then I can rule you out as a suspect. You might have possibly seen something useful. Here, let me help—

SALLY:

STOP! *(Calmer)* I mean, no, no, thank you, Elizabeth. This bag is rather light! Not a trifle too heavy at all. Look, it's started snowing. If we don't leave, we will be snowed in. May I ask, you've already spoken to Ludlow, yes? How was he?

ELIZABETH:

Reader, do you think she knows?

ELIZABETH:

Um, well. All of my interviews are confidential . . . I wouldn't like to . . .

SALLY:

Oh, I don't mean about the *murder*. He is having an affair. I'm sure of it. Last week Gales sent me a receipt for a fur stole, one I do not own. There have been other things, too—

ELIZABETH:

Hang on, did you say *murder*, singular? Have you not heard?

SALLY:

Heard what? I've been up here packing all morning.

ELIZABETH:

(Whisper) *Reader, I think I've distracted her. For a woman in her forties, she hasn't a line on her face, nor a grey amongst the striking red*

hair. I think she's even wearing a Dior suit – that belt. I will watch her
reaction to the news closely.

ELIZABETH:

There's been another murder since . . . Matilda.

SALLY:

Good Lord, are you sure? She's, well, she's no spring chicken.

ELIZABETH:

Certain.

SALLY:

My, my. The poor dear. We used to be rather close, you know. She
used to say I was the daughter she never had.

ELIZABETH:

Forgive me for asking but why did you call off the engagement?

SALLY:

I didn't. Jonty did. He'd met Catherine. He spent a summer in
London, working in the father's coffee company – he was quite the
whizz at the books back then. And they met in the Serpentine
Gallery. I'm sure Catherine can tell you the rest. We were due to be
married on the first of September, and he wrote to me in the last
week of August, the cad. Married Catherine before the month was
out.

ELIZABETH:

How did you come to marry Ludlow?

SALLY:

It . . . was complicated. We three were all very close as children, you
know? I knew them both terribly well. When things didn't work out
with Jonty, well, Ludlow pursued me. That's the only way I could
describe it. I felt like the hare being chased by a hound. I had the
idea of being someone's wife in my head . . . so I went along with it.
We had a small wedding. Daddy did drink a full bottle of Jameson

whiskey before the wedding breakfast was served . . . but I've always been proud of my roots.

ELIZABETH:

Who do you think killed Jonty and Matilda?

SALLY:

Catherine! She'll certainly be happier. Just last night, I was down in the kitchen. I heard her say that the wrong Caswell-Jones died . . . in the war. She was whispering away to Margaret . . .

(From downstairs)

FLORA:

ELIZABETH! Are you up here? The Polizia chap wants to talk to you.

ELIZABETH:

(Shouting) Coming along now, Flora! *(To Sally)* Don't leave, Sally. Not until I've had a chance to talk to you. I have something to tell you about Ludlow.

SALLY:

An hour. I'll wait an hour. Look, out the big window there. The snow is bucketing down. So beautiful, it's a shame we can't sit and enjoy the view.

ELIZABETH:

(Walking down the stairs ahead of Sally) (Whispering) *Blimey, that was close. Do you think she knows about Ludlow and me? Could she have harboured such ill feeling towards Jonty after he jilted her, enough to kill him thirty years later? Surely she would have had a chance before now. I have to confess, I will need your unbiased opinion when I interview Sally. Goodness knows why own motives may play a part . . . Now, to the matter at hand.*

ELIZABETH:

Argento, I believe.

ARGENTO:

Elizabeth Chalice, I believe. I follow your cases.

ELIZABETH:

Oh, it's been quite a while since I've heard that. Where are the Polizia officers?

ARGENTO:

In Jonty's office. I believe you have the key to the drawing room, where Mrs Caswell-Jones's body is?

ELIZABETH:

Very well. The family has been expecting you. I hear your mother is unwell—

ARGENTO:

It is still very bad. Praise the Lord she will not suffer much more.

ELIZABETH:

Ah. Here are the police. Hold on, give me a moment while I speak to them. I might have to translate for you, too – you don't speak fluent Italian, do you, reader? (Pause) *They're asking me to unlock the door – which is rich, seeing as they're only now treating this and Jonty's death as murder. Ah . . . yes. They're telling me they're going to collect the evidence, dust for fingerprints and then talk to me. Luckily someone – and by someone I mean you and me, reader – has been conducting full interviews . . . And now they're giving me instructions. Asking me to gather everyone in the dining room so they can take prints. Where were they when Jonty dropped dead, hmm?*

ELIZABETH:

(To Argento) Did you hear that? Can you help me gather everyone in the dining room?

ARGENTO:

Of course. I have something they all want to see – Jonty's will.

ELIZABETH:

Is it juicy? You know, any big surprises?

ELIZABETH:

Stay professional, Elizabeth, for goodness' sake!

ARGENTO:

(Shocked at the insinuation!) Eh, I have not yet broken the seal! Anyway, *I* will gather everyone.

ELIZABETH:

Great. I will tell Kate, I believe she's in the kitchen.

ELIZABETH:

Good Lord, woman, you're leading a double-murder investigation here ... there will be time for fun; there is undoubtedly that telling glint in Argento's eye ... but attend to the inquiry at hand. People always underestimate me, and in this case I am allowing the two Polizia officers to underestimate me deliberately. If I do not object and go along with their requests, they will shoot off home to their Santo Stefano dinner. Meanwhile, I will uncover who the real killer is. I have two main candidates in mind, do you know who they are? But, you're right, let's not be foolish, there is real danger in Villa Janus. I may well require the services of these officers. Catherine and Matilda may have wanted this kept quiet, but there's only so much one can conceal. If it comes to a trial ...

(Opens the kitchen door)

CATHERINE:

Elizabeth. Have they arrived? Argento and the Polizia? Is Thomas with them? Here. Have some coffee and panettone. You must be starved.

ELIZABETH:

Thomas is *not* with them. The officer Esposito, quite a round-bellied chap, wants to take everyone's fingerprints if you don't mind heading up to the dining room.

CATHERINE:

Oh gosh, it's filthy up there. Fine, fine, I'm going. The cheese is out there. And they'll have to wait for Thomas before reading the will . . .

(Exit Catherine)

ELIZABETH:

Kate seems quite distracted this morning. First, she tries to stop me from looking in Jonty's office, now she's more worried about the dining room being messy . . . She is distracted . . . but what is bothering her? Other than the murders, of course. Hang on a minute, something looks out of place here. It was dark when I was here last night . . . but this vase of dried poppies has certainly been disturbed. Such an ugly flower now. What's this? Jonty's wallet, on the windowsill by the vase. It seems like a strange place for it to be. It would be remiss not to take a look, eh?

Some banknotes, thirty pounds sterling, ten American dollars, some lira. Library card for the British Library. Membership to the Phil University club. Two betting receipts, one for the George VI Chase at Kempton . . . starting in a few hours. Good Lord, the fellow has put a thousand pounds on a complete outsider! Barnacle, at a hundred to one. That's not your average bookie to place such a large bet. Best keep a close eye on this race. I wonder if it had something to do with the big news he wanted to tell everyone later . . . It's starting in less than . . . four hours! And here's another slip, for ten bob on the favourite. I am no stranger to the racecourse, so I have seen gamblers offset a risky bet with a sure thing so as not to lose both, even if there is a huge inequity in the stakes.

That's almost everything . . . now just one last card . . . Thomson Travel Insurance. Which has reminded me . . . I must check what sort of life insurance policy Jonty would have had. For, of course, that might provide anyone with a pretty good motive, don't you think?

(Footsteps on kitchen tiles)

ARGENTO:

Elizabeth, are you coming?

ELIZABETH:

Oh, yes, gosh, that was quick. I just need to check one final thing and I'll join you.

ARGENTO:

I will be waiting . . .

ELIZABETH:

Did you hear the fire there? Ladies, I am girding my loins. Now where on earth is this bloody cheese? Ah, here we go. Wrapped up in a muslin cloth, we have a large white cream rind – so far, standard-issue cheese. It seems a shame to do anything, but really better to check there's nothing in it. Oh gosh, what if it is poisoned . . .? Perhaps that's what killed Matilda? Ah, no. This round of cheese is perfect, so Matilda hasn't even had a slice. It couldn't be this that poisoned her.

(She chops the cheese)

ELIZABETH:

(With her mouth full) *Mmmm, a lovely soft, creamy sheep's milk cheese. I do not blame Matilda for ordering straight from the manufacturer . . . Oh. What do we have here? Hmmm, the cheese is dense but not as solid as metal . . . I keep cutting. My, my, I'm glad you are with me for this discovery, I can't quite believe it. There's a ruddy great slab of gold bullion right in the heart of this fromage. You old dog, Matilda Caswell-Jones. What on earth were you smuggling gold within a cheese for? I can't leave it here. I best take it back to my room. I've left some large hunks of cheese. I think I will just about get away with having removed some. I can tell Kate I just needed to cut it into pieces to check there was nothing there.*

(Quiet creak)

ELIZABETH:

What is that noise? It sounds like someone has just come in the back door. I can just about spy into the kitchen from here. There he is. Back at last. Thomas. One of my prime suspects. He looks absolutely drenched.

ELIZABETH:

Thomas? What on earth? You're soaked to the skin.

THOMAS:

What are you doing lurking in the dark, Elizabeth? Where's Mother? Has Argento come?

ELIZABETH:

Yes, they're both in the drawing room. What on earth?

THOMAS:

Fell into the lake, long story . . . *(Urgently)* I've got to see them now.

(Runs out of the room)

ELIZABETH:

He didn't see the gold bar. And yes, I'm more concerned with this than with why Thomas is soaking wet. I did notice that his cashmere jumper was once yellow but is now a mucky brown. I'll have to work quickly to hide the gold. That said, however, I did spot something strange on Thomas. There's something above his ear that looked like blood. Was it just to do with a fall, or is there more to it?

(Sound of rummaging)

ELIZABETH:

This will do, a fine big chamber pot. I can't imagine there'll be call for one. Nice and tucked away. Right-o, best head to the dining room. Someone has rearranged these pots and pans recently, there's a thick layer of dust on one side, but on the left is all—What have we here? A little crystal bowl, one of the expensive set, not like these heavy old pots. It's a tiny glass vial. Hang on, we seem to have a tag. Curare. I knew it! This is the poison used to kill Jonty. It just has to be. And the way the killer has it sitting here at the back of the cupboard, instead of dumping it outside, in the lake. They must not be finished with it yet. Who else are they planning to kill? Let me tell you about this, reader. What a nasty death! Used at the correct dosage, curare paralyses the victim. Though it can be beneficial too, you know. After the war, I went back to St Thomas's for a spell, and a famous doctor was demonstrating its benefits to relax the stomach muscles of a patient requiring an appendectomy. He spoke at length about it. Now, let's leave that bottle back in there, careful not to touch it.

(Sound of Elizabeth walking up the stairs)

ELIZABETH:

I'd also better get a bowl of water and some rags for everyone to wash their hands after being inked. I've learned the hard way the damage fingerprint ink can do to a good silk blouse. Here we go.

Ah. Jonty's wallet, still on the windowsill beside the unlocked door. I'll stick it in my pocket. If nothing else, it will remind me to ask Flora about it. If I'm honest, I really am rather shocked that Jonty found a bookie to take a bet that big. One-hundred thousand is an impossibly large payout. Perhaps it was his last-ditch attempt to drum up finance for the business. But more likely, it was the desperate action of a thoroughly addicted gambler right at the end of his rope. If this horse wins, would any bookie really pay out? If so, this betting slip is jolly well motive enough to kill – such a vast sum of money.

(Elizabeth opens the dining-room door)

ELIZABETH:

Here they all are, our suspects. The skinny officer is pressing Polly's palm onto the card to record her prints. I finally feel like this investigation has moved up a notch, now we have found the poison. The sight of the Polizia uniforms will inevitably put the murderer under more stress. There is a closeness in the air, no one seems to be talking to anyone else. It feels like a control room during a classified operation. The winds continue to lift outside. The snow has turned to hail, pelting rivulets against the wall outside. The atmosphere is reflecting the mind of the guests. Even Catherine, fastidious to the point of fussiness, has allowed her standards to slip.

The window shutters are half closed from want of someone to open them. The table is only half cleared from yesterday's dinner, with dirty glasses and used side plates mounted in a pile at the opposite end. Someone in this room is responsible for the death of one, and possibly two, people – time to double down on our killer.

ELIZABETH:

Here we go, soap and water.

CATHERINE:

You are clever. I feel like Lady Macbeth trying to wipe this ink off!

POLLY:

Ouch, my wrist! No need to hold it down so firmly. Margaret, will you tell him, please?

MARGARET:

Delicatamente, per favore. Right, who's next? Frankie?

FRANCIS:

This is farcical, but I'm your guest, Catherine, of course I'll oblige.

ELIZABETH:

Did Thomas come in here?

CATHERINE:

He's gone up to change. Silly boy took the boat along to the village and got himself drenched when he hit a rock, and a jolly great wave crashed in on top of him.

PETER:

(From the other side of the room) What a damned stupid thing to do, any-one could have seen from that sky this morning a storm was on the way.

LUDLOW:

Let him be, Peter, it must be hard to think straight – his father has just died.

SALLY:

How long will this take? If we leave now, we will just about make the train to Milan.

LUDLOW:

Yes, Catherine, you have our fingerprints, you'll easily rule us out. Jonty and Matilda were dear friends of ours—

SALLY:

You can't really keep us here any longer—

FRANCIS:

Did you see that? The thunder and lightning are right on top of us—

(Loud crashes of thunder, screams)

CATHERINE:

Calm down! It's going further away. Are all the windows shuttered on the outside? I do not want to be responsible for broken bloody windows, too.

(Peals of thunder)

POLLY:

The lights, it's so dark in here I can barely see a thing – there it is again, more lightning.

CATHERINE:

It's moving along, calm down, everybody. Now, there are some candles here somewhere.

(Sound of rummaging)

CATHERINE:

Here. Can you believe it's so dark here for the middle of the day?

(Sound of matches)

(Door opens)

ARGENTO:

I'm afraid *no one* is going *anywhere*. The lightning has struck the bridge. The hillside to the back of the house is completely impass-able – such a steep slope. And now Thomas informs us the engine of the boat is flooded. We are all stuck here. Until the storm is over.

SALLY:

(Growing frustrated) Are you a civil engineer? Let me see. I refuse to stay a minute longer. Someone take a look at fixing that boat. We shall certainly miss our flight – it is the last one from Milan to London this week. Oh, Ludlow, *say* something—

ELIZABETH:

(Stern) Enough. That's *enough*, everyone. Let's just remember what has happened in the past twenty-four hours. The weather is impos-sible – Sally, Ludlow, you aren't going anywhere. We will need to survey the bridge once the storm lifts, but for now, here we are. First of all, has everyone had something to eat and drink? It's just past midday – Catherine, perhaps you could bring up some sort of snack: cheese and bread or something? It's important for us all to keep our strength up and our minds alert. In my investigations, I have already spoken to six of you, I want to interview the other half now. Hard as it may be, it is time to accept that there is a killer amongst us. For your own safety, I suggest we stay together for the duration of the storm. If you need to use the washroom or fetch something from your room, go in pairs. Flora, Polly, will you help your mother to bring up some food?

ARGENTO:

I will do that, don't worry—

ELIZABETH:

No, Argento, I want you to ensure no one leaves the villa.

MARGARET:

I don't see why we need to be babysat—

ELIZABETH:

Please, Margaret, our hosts have invited me here to investigate this terrible crime, and I intend to get to the bottom of it. Now, I am going to speak to Thomas. The Caswell-Jones ladies will source some snacks, and everyone else is to stay here with Officer—What does your name badge say? Officer Rossi. Now, there we are. I'm off to find the other chap. Sally, I'll interview you once I've found Thomas.

FRANKIE:

Aye, I can't believe you've not spoken with the prime suspect yet.

LUDLOW:

Keep your opinions to yourself, Jock.

FRANKIE:

Who are you calling . . .? You great lumbering idiot, it's no wonder—

(Sounds of an argument as Elizabeth and the Caswell-Jones women leave)

CATHERINE:

Let's hope they don't all kill one another, eh? Will you go easy on my boy, please, Elizabeth? All that guff about prime suspects – he is only twenty-one.

POLLY:

He's been murdering things since childhood; age is of no relevance when it comes to Thomas.

ELIZABETH:

I will remain impartial, don't worry. Kate, I've sliced through Matilda's cheese – nothing suspicious other than how delicious it was. You might serve that. I'll come back downstairs once I've located your son.

(The Caswell-Jones women walk off)

ELIZABETH:

What a pack of hounds, eh? Like rats in a cage. Perhaps they'll have eaten one another up by the time I get back – that poor officer. Now, where is this other one? That's strange … Matilda remains in repose in this drawing room, but there's no sign of our lead officer.

ELIZABETH:

Hullo?

(Elizabeth hits the receiver on the telephone)

ELIZABETH:

Telephone's gone again. No surprise.

THOMAS:

Cigarette?

ELIZABETH:

(Surprised) Good Lord! You frightened me.

THOMAS:

Sorry, I didn't mean to frighten you.

ELIZABETH:

Oh, quite, I didn't hear you come in over the din from the drawing room. What are you doing in here?

THOMAS:

Oh, I was just passing and saw you had the door open. So *spooky*, isn't it?

ELIZABETH:

I suppose. No matter how long I do this job, I'll never get used to seeing a dead body. So still like that. Now. You're all changed. It is time we sat down together, Thomas.

THOMAS:

I suppose it is. I don't know about you, but I prefer not to have my conversations in the same room as my deceased relatives.

ELIZABETH:

Let's go into your father's study.

(They cross the hallway)

ELIZABETH:

Looks like you had a lucky escape.

THOMAS:

It's too early to say. The murderer is still at large, apparently.

ELIZABETH:

I meant from the storm.

THOMAS:

Yes, it turned up out of nowhere, really.

ELIZABETH:

So now do you believe your father was killed?

THOMAS:

Please – you take the comfortable seat here, the green one.

ELIZABETH:

I'm quite fine here on the sofa. Answer my question.

THOMAS:

Do I think Father was murdered? I mean, I think it's more likely Granny was murdered, and Father's death was just a distraction. Either he cottoned on to the plan, or who knows, maybe he really had a heart attack? I don't believe anyone had a decent reason to kill that half-wit. Granny, on the other hand, now *there's* someone quite evil.

ELIZABETH:

Evil? That is rather a strong word?

THOMAS:

She was rather a strong woman. After Father warned us about his dickie heart, we all knew to be careful and not pounce out at him.

Yet Granny took no heed of Father's warnings, unlike the rest of us, and she tore strips off him yesterday morning. The same old line, the wrong man came home from the war, he would never replace his brother . . . On and on. I overheard them when we had our morning dip. He had serious money troubles, I'm sure you've figured that out by now. Granny had a big old allowance, yet she wouldn't lend him a penny. Then there's Polly. My sister is her pet, but it is a poisoned chalice. Granny forces her into all sorts of things. Latin classes, volunteer work with all of the 'wonderful charities' she's a patron of. Runs her bloody ragged, it's no surprise she's failing university. But something strange has been going on with them over the last few weeks, it's like . . . Polly has had the soul sucked out of her . . . I'm not sure what's going on exactly, but I am certain that old Granny Caswell-Jones was at the heart of it. Polly doesn't talk to me, of course; she's said nothing of the matter to me. But why would she? She detests me.

Then there's Nikolai. Granny is responsible for fishing him out of Russia, of course, but she's never let him forget it. She likes to collect people, but it comes with a price. She loves them to feel *indebted* to her. In this case, rather literally, I suspect. I saw him give her money on a few occasions, big envelopes. I wouldn't be surprised if the old dingbat was blackmailing him. And then, I'm sure you know, Granny's a royal pain in Mother's backside—

ELIZABETH:

Hmmm. You know, I've heard some interesting stories about you, Thomas. It takes a lot to quench the life from another living being, something you have a track record in doing.

THOMAS:

That bloody wolfhound; my sister Polly told you I killed him, did she? Well, I did. But what she didn't tell you . . . a few weeks before the beast really went after me, bit straight through the tendons in my leg. Look, you can still see the scar. The damage was such that I had to stop playing rugby. You know how important sport is in a school like that? I spent the year out of everything, was called a cripple, lame. So, yes, in hindsight it was a dreadful thing to do, but I was a child, an angry child.

ELIZABETH:

That does look nasty. But nasty enough to kill? And what about this horse-riding accident, when you were twelve?

THOMAS:

Poor Echo Frawley. I told him his mare wouldn't make the ditch . . . It must have been six foot across. I shouted for him to follow me up to the fence . . . But he— I suppose he was showing off. She didn't make the jump, Echo fell off and twisted his neck. Quite a thing for a boy to see. I knew he was dead, though. So I brought him back with me . . . Why are you dredging up all of this? I didn't kill my father. Polly told you all this, didn't she? Well, she has plenty to hide herself. I came up to my room for a pack of cigarettes, Granny giving out about dressing for dinner and all that. Ludlow was traipsing along behind Polly. It was dark up there, and they couldn't see me. He was whispering something and then handed her a bundle of cash. 'Get the job done,' he said loudly.

ELIZABETH:

What job do you think he wanted her to do?

THOMAS:

Oh god, who knows, Ludlow is always looking out for us, I'm sure she got herself into some trouble. *(Angry)* Don't you see, she's trying to put your attention onto me? With all these tall tales. When really she is the one hiding something.

ELIZABETH:

You seem to get angry easily. And you threw tea on a secretary? Scalded her? Is that a tall tale too?

THOMAS:

Another bloody fantasy. Jeanine tripped over the lamp with a tray full of tea. Someone has been trying to frame me, have they? Convince you that I'm a psychopath? A chap who has killed before and would kill again? I'm not buying it. Why would you?

ELIZABETH:

I'm just asking the questions. Tell me, Thomas, you stand to inherit the entire estate, including the business, yes?

THOMAS:

I believe so. Ludlow says I shan't be able to keep both houses, death duties being as much as they are. The company is nothing but a tonne of debts. So, if you think choosing which of our family heirlooms to sell off, and still remaining in debt, is a lucky lot in life, I would so hate to see what unlucky would be.

ELIZABETH:

Do you do everything that Ludlow tells you? Is he the boss of you?

THOMAS:

Ha-ha, Elizabeth, nice try, but you're not going to get me all riled up. Anyway, I'm tired after the morning's activity, and I didn't really sleep last night.

ELIZABETH:

Why did you take the boat this morning?

THOMAS:

There were no cars here. Well, there was Frankie's, but it's not working. Usually Argento would be here to ferry us to the village and Bellagio. I figured taking the boat around the lake and up the inlet would be far quicker than walking. I forgot to check the engine – damned thing gave up before I reached Bellagio. Eventually a shepherd came within earshot and I convinced him to find some diesel, but I was hours waiting. Then by the time I alerted the Polizia, *ufficiale* Esposito was not keen to see me – and when I got back to the villa, the winds were picking up. Good Lord, I nearly drowned within twenty feet of the damned place.

ELIZABETH:

Horrifying, Thomas. So, were you close to your father?

THOMAS:

Not really. Don't remember much from before the war, and the fellow who came back was so distant . . . He acts as if he were a perfect stranger. He's never had much of an interest in me or Polly. Flora, yes, he loved little Flora. But it often feels as if I had no father, so yes, I'm willing to take counsel from Ludlow if he's good enough to offer it. I'm a banker, but I deal mostly in currency – all these layers of intricacies with wills and estates are new to me. All I know is there's a bloody great mess to work out.

ELIZABETH:

And you trust Argento, a disgraced lawyer, cook, man of odd jobs, to handle these layers of intricacies?

THOMAS:

Gosh, no, we have a firm in London to do that. I'm not even sure what sort of will Argento has or why it was in the British Consulate, but of course I'm damned keen to know what it says. Grandmother had a hand in that. Argento is a very clever chap. He may not do things by the book, but he knows the law inside out.

ELIZABETH:

Why would your grandmother have had a hand in your father's will?

THOMAS:

She was like that, you know? A terrible puppeteer. She could have made him create a new will or something horrid like that. I wouldn't put anything past her. Anyway, neither of us is a lawyer. Have you anything else to ask me? I must be getting back.

ELIZABETH:

Fair enough. Tell me, why did you invite Frankie here?

THOMAS:

Frankie? He is hilarious, don't you think? He's a bloody comedian, and I felt this year we would need to lift the mood somewhat. He cuts a bit close to the bone sometimes, but I'd rather that than some insipid brown-nose like Margaret.

ELIZABETH:

I can't say I've seen much of Frankie's funny side in action just yet . . . And have you any girlfriends?

THOMAS:

What? Where . . .? Um, no. I'm travelling with the bank and haven't had the chance. Are you looking? You're not bad for a forty-year-old—

ELIZABETH:

(Harshly) My, my, Thomas, you are quite wrong! Good thing I am not easily offended. I am not forty, I am mid-thirties. But you do like an older woman?

THOMAS:

Ah, so you know? Someone must have seen us the other night and told you. Not my proudest moment . . . But Christmas, it's just, you know, some light entertainment. You fancy a spin, Elizabeth? That smile of yours is hiding rather a lot, I gather.

ELIZABETH:

(A flirtatious admonishment) I appreciate the compliment, my boy.

THOMAS:

You'd appreciate rather a bit more than that, I think.

ELIZABETH:

(Firmly) Now, now. Be a good chap and don't look at me like that. We have business to attend to—

(Knock at the door)

POLLY:

Oh, am I interrupting?

ELIZABETH:

We're just about finished here . . .

THOMAS:

What is it, sis? Someone drunk all of the sherry?

POLLY:

There's been a bit of an incident, we need your medical skills, Elizabeth. Mother said you were neater at stitching a wound—

ELIZABETH:

I haven't done that for many years . . . but I'm happy to help. What happened?

POLLY:

Just a little fracas between Peter and Nikolai. Tensions are running high in that dining room. Nikolai doesn't speak Italian and doesn't trust Margaret to translate . . . Sally is determined to leave . . . I think it would be useful to have you with us all. Argento wants to read the will any moment now.

ELIZABETH:

Right-o. I'll be along in a minute.

THOMAS:

Oh goodie, it sounds like great fun watching them squirm.

(Exit Polly)

THOMAS:

(Softly) Oh and, Elizabeth, you are welcome to finish this off later on, if you wish to come to my room.

ELIZABETH:

That reminds me. I have something written here in my notebook. About accommodation. Why did you give Nikolai your room?

THOMAS:

That bloody notebook of yours. Key to the whole investigation, isn't it? Eh, *I* didn't. Mother swapped our rooms. She apparently wanted me under her watchful eye this year. Shame. One can do almost anything up there without anyone hearing a peep.

ELIZABETH:

That reminds me, do you have any idea what happened to Polly's notebook?

THOMAS:

I do, actually. Mother couldn't start the range in the kitchen and tore out a few pages to get it going. I don't think she realised it was Polly's notebook until after. Keep a close eye on her, she is up to something, I tell you. But keep me out of this. Up until recently they've had rather a strained relationship and I wouldn't want to be accused of opening up old wounds at a time like this. Even though I know you love rubbing salt in to see if you can draw more blood.

ELIZABETH:

Right, that'll be all for now. Goodbye, Thomas.

(*Door shuts*)

ELIZABETH:

What a petulant young man . . . His cockiness is so off-putting, but when answering questions about the death of his father and grandmother, well, the fellow was far too calm and collected. I may well need to revisit our chat when his guard is down. The pup might think he has me fooled, but I wager he would not want dear old Ludlow to find out he was canoodling with his wife . . . Even if Polly hadn't told me of her brother's dalliance with Sally, Thomas himself would have given the game away. Sometimes it's worth shooting in the dark and seeing what secrets they will give up so willingly . . .

Did Catherine really not mean to put the pages from Polly's notebook in the fire? Perhaps it was an honest mistake, which has driven her to overcompensate in commiserating with her over its damage ... Or perhaps there's more to it than meets the eye.

That reminds me, I've done a good job of keeping my distance from Ludlow, but Margaret has caught my eye a few times. I best not delay in interviewing her next. I am so looking forward to getting to know her better ... discover what secrets she has been hiding behind that rather stern exterior. But first, let's hear what Jonty's will sounds like, shall we?

EPISODE 8

Margaret Horton

ELIZABETH:

There is a wireless in Jonty's untidy study. I may be here to investigate his murder, but I haven't forgotten today's racing schedule. Besides, you and I both know it might have a crucial part to play in what has transpired this Christmas weekend . . .

(Elizabeth fiddles with the dial)

ELIZABETH:

Living in Italy, I do so miss the plumes of hot breath from the horses as they warm up around the parade ring on a cold December day. The George VI Chase is outclassed only by Cheltenham, and I am just dying to hear who the winner is. For I fear Jonty's death is linked to today's race. My suspects are waiting to read the will – but for now, I just want to catch . . . There we go.

RADIO ANNOUNCER:

This is the BBC World Service. As the country gears up for a bumper sporting day, please stay tuned for regular updates. *(Breaks up)*

ELIZABETH:

This bloody storm is really taking hold.

RADIO ANNOUNCER:

There have been some last-minute changes to the starting line ahead of this afternoon's George VI Chase at Kempton Park. The favourite, Day of Reckoning, is out of the running due to a sprained ankle, with others including Ian Morella's Chance Encounter and Wild One also pulled from the race at the last moment.

ELIZABETH:

Crikey. That sounds jolly suspicious, doesn't it? And here . . .

(Sound of rustling paper)

ELIZABETH:

. . . we have Jonty's betting slip – a huge bet of one thousand pounds for an outsider with odds of a hundred to one. Most likely this will prove worthless, but if the horse wins? Well, then this six by four square of copy paper is worth a small fortune. If the favourites won't run . . . well, our outsider stands a far greater chance of success. I am surprised the race is still going ahead, with such clear *interference. Oh well, we shall have to come back to hear the result later. I suppose you're all dying to hear Jonty's will being read? Let's go.*

(Elizabeth turns off the radio and leaves the office)

(Elizabeth walking. Clattering and banging from the storm)

(Sounds of the crowd in the dining room)

ARGENTO:

Elizabeth, good, we are about to begin. Now to say first, I am not here as a lawyer, merely as a – well, I hope you would say, a good family friend. Jonty had left a copy of this will with the British Consulate, and he had another copy at home in Berkshire. I will begin: *(Reading) I, Jonathan Caswell-Jones, make this my last and final will and testament dated this third day of December 1953.*

I appoint Margaret Horton and . . . Ludlow Lansdowne de Groot as trustees to administer the trust, apportioning an annual income of twenty thousand pounds to each of my children, Thomas, Flora and Mary.

FRANKIE:

Who's Mary?

ELIZABETH:

(Whispering sharply) It's Polly's birth name – do be quiet, Francis.

ARGENTO:

Please – no interruptions. *(Reading) To my daughter, Mary. I bequeath the entire family art collection from Carlyle Square, and our*

Berkshire estate, including two Sargent portraits, Rembrandt's landscape and the Modigliani, on the condition that it not be sold in her lifetime.

THOMAS:

(Furious!) He bloody can't do that . . . they were mine—

ARGENTO:

(Sternly) Please. Do *not* interrupt me. *(Reading) To my wife Catherine, should she survive me, I bequeath my entire property portfolio and their contents, with the exception of the aforementioned art collection, including Avonlea, Berkshire; 8 Carlyle Square and Acerca de Via Cesare Battisti, Milan.*

THOMAS:

No, this isn't the right will, it just can't be—

POLLY:

Do sit down, Thomas. Father was right to cut you out, you—

THOMAS:

Shut your face, sister dearest, if you think I'll let you take those pictures—

CATHERINE:

That is enough, both of you. Let Argento continue.

ARGENTO:

Where was I? Yes. *(Reading) To my godson Peter Smythson, of Beauparc, Berkshire, I bequeath my financial portfolio, including all stocks, shares and funds outside the aforementioned trust. Any other assets I bequeath to my youngest daughter, Flora.*

(Turning of pages)

ARGENTO:

Yes. That's it. That's all there is.

THOMAS:

(Outraged) I don't trust the paper that's written on – third of December! I bet this is your doing, you scheming little—

CATHERINE:

Leave your sister alone – it is only right Polly, the artist, inherits Jonty's pictures! Thomas, will you *please* calm down. You are embarrassing yourself. You're embarrassing all of us. Your father has left you a considerable allowance. What were you expecting – every single item in the entire estate? This isn't *Pride and Prejudice*, you know, there's no entail.

THOMAS:

He has denied me my birthright! The old fool couldn't even be relied upon to do that right.

SALLY:

What about the company? Who'll take that?

THOMAS:

(In a mock-Italian accent) All other assets go to Flora. *(In his usual accent)* Why are you even here? This should be family only.

(Smash of glass in the background, in the drawing room)

THOMAS:

What on earth?

CATHERINE:

It's the storm, Thomas. Now, that's enough. You should remember from when your uncle died that probate is a terribly long and drawn-out process. If you really have an issue with it, object! Shouting and threatening us isn't going to change the facts. Now, where did that glass break—

LUDLOW:

Your brother-in-law left a simple will transferring all assets to Jonty, not carving things up like this. Don't you worry, my boy, this won't stand up a jot in court. And a trust that will pay out £60,000 every year – hardly! Where will the money come from? We will get this well and truly sorted.

(Knock on the door)

ELIZABETH:

Ah, Esposito. He's back. He's beckoning me to the doorway, clearly aware of the tension in this room. I'm glad for the breather. Hold on, let me hear what he has to say, and I'll report right back to you.

Yes. Hmm. Hmm. Okay, so Esposito says one of the windows in the drawing room is bust and the snow is getting to Matilda's body! We must move her somewhere else. To preserve what we can of the evidence. This really is the worst kind of murder investigation, and I must say, after that will, it's only going to get a lot more muddled.

ELIZABETH:

I'm sorry to interrupt, everyone. Esposito has informed me that we must move Matilda's body – the drawing-room window has broken open.

LUDLOW:

Nikolai, Peter, let us do this, the family do not need to be involved.

CATHERINE:

Where will we put her? The coldest place in the house has to be the basement.

POLLY:

Poor Granny, she'd hate to be manhandled like that.

CATHERINE:

You look exhausted, Polly. Elizabeth, can you please let us leave this room, at least to move somewhere more comfortable?

ELIZABETH:

Absolutely not. There is a killer here. If you are to move around the house at all, you must stay with a partner. Ludlow, Nikolai, Peter – if you go move the body, I will continue with my interviews. Now, who do I need? Margaret, time for our interview. Let's move into the study.

MARGARET:

Fine. I'll join you in a minute.

ELIZABETH:

And what do you think of the will? Why did he change it? It is terribly suspicious that he made the amendments so close to his murder ...Yes, Thomas hasn't been handed the keys of the castle right away, nor has he been cut out completely. Ludlow did have a good point: how will a trust pay out those large sums to the children? The gesture of giving the art to Polly – a last-minute attempt to reconcile with his daughter after his displeasure at her paintings? Remember when she was so distraught about losing her notebook? That seems so long ago ...

Was there anything of value in the bequest to Peter Smythson, all of his stocks, shares and savings? It would take some time to find out, but perhaps I could contact his bank in London ... or Catherine could. After all, she is set to inherit the house and a large allowance. Not that anyone is getting a penny anytime soon; Ludlow and Thomas will of course object to the will in court. What did the previous will say? All and everything to Thomas ...? If we could only get our hands on that copy. Honestly, once again, as with everything in this investigation, the will has just created more questions than answers. But you know whose will no one is talking about? Yes, Matilda's.

Here comes Margaret. She is such an unassuming woman, decked out in her lilac dress suit and small cream handbag. Blackmail is a dirty old business, but it's often delivered by someone as apparently clean as Margaret. As we've heard from Nikolai, she was blackmailing our victim in the summertime. But I can't imagine Margaret would extend herself to double murder. Remember, she discovered me with Ludlow last night. Well, I think I have one secret over her, too. It's not something I wanted to use to barter with her ... but it's not always possible to play clean, is it?

ELIZABETH:

Why do you think Matilda fell asleep at Christmas lunch yesterday?

MARGARET:

What an odd opening question, Elizabeth. Frightful business with the will, there's plenty for you to go on there. And I thought he was flat broke! Now, Matilda. The old dear passed out from one too many Sauternes. Really, Elizabeth, if this is what you call detective work—

ELIZABETH:

The Sauternes was all drunk on Christmas Eve, I believe.

MARGARET:

Well, sherry, whatever, wine, she just drank too much on an empty stomach.

ELIZABETH:

Do you think it could have been more than alcohol? Could she have been sedated?

MARGARET:

No, well— I mean, potentially, who knows? I didn't really dwell on it too much – it didn't seem unusual to me, and besides, soon after we all had something much more pressing on our minds, don't you think, Elizabeth? This business with poor Jonty happened immediately after Matilda's little nap.

ELIZABETH:

When Matilda passed out, did you leave the table?

MARGARET:

(Hesitant) Briefly. I went to my room, to get smelling salts. I ran straight back to help her up to her own bed.

ELIZABETH:

Where is your room?

MARGARET:

It's an old servant's room at the back of the kitchen, it is a damn sight warmer than upstairs when there's no one to light a fire. Listen, I know Jonty and I didn't always see eye to eye, but he was Catherine's husband and I wouldn't have wanted to hurt him.

ELIZABETH:

But you were blackmailing him.

MARGARET:

(Shocked) Good gracious, how—? *(Resigned)* Okay. Yes. But why on earth he would bring a child like Flora to a casino with him . . . it was quite ridiculous. Someone had to stop it . . . It's no secret the family were headed for rough times financially. On the one hand, Catherine was scrimping and cutting corners wherever she could. On the other, Jonty was blowing hundreds of pounds every week in the Mayfair Club. I was trying to help.

ELIZABETH:

Why were you there at the club in the first place? Or did you go looking for Jonty?

MARGARET:

There are no laws against meeting for a game of bridge. The Mayfair Club is a hundred years old, a wholly upstanding organisation. That was before the management began to allow the unsavoury aspects downstairs. I never saw anything myself, but one couldn't be oblivious to the reports.

ELIZABETH:

Not wholly innocent, though, eh, Margaret? Surely you were compounding the problem by extorting money from him.

MARGARET:

Not for my own gain, good gracious, I wasn't pocketing the money—

ELIZABETH:

You do live on a meagre allowance, though. What is it, about three thousand pounds?

MARGARET:

Really, Elizabeth, how dare you? That is my business. I don't seek to humiliate you in all of this . . . so please tread carefully.

ELIZABETH:

Are you threatening to blackmail *me* now? To maintain Margaret Horton's standards of decency?

MARGARET:

Do shut up a moment, Elizabeth, and let me tell you the bloody story. I've been a member of that club for almost thirty years. When I joined, I went along with my aunt, to play bridge. The temperance movement was gaining traction and she wanted me to keep away from the glittering nightclubs of which I'm sure *you're* acquainted. We played our bridge, and drank tea and minded our business when the rest of the city vibrated with the sound of jazz and the tinkling of champagne coupes. The club kept going throughout the thirties and into the war, and it was a tonic to go there when I was on leave.

In recent years, there has been a distinct lowering of moral standards, but I have been assured by one of the croupiers, also a Thomas, who is as old as the hills, that this is a temporary thing. So, I continue to go, entering the top-floor suite through the respectable doors of 56 Grosvenor Street. The other *guests*, as I suppose you'd call them, enter through the back, at Brook's Mews. Anyway, one evening I was leaving and I was shocked to find Flora in floods of tears at the mews. That's the direction I take home. Of course, I was certain she had escaped there with some pals from school, she is such a wild girl, but then she explained to me that *Jonty* had brought her there! That she was his good-luck charm, but that she had failed him as he had lost a bet of thirty thousand pounds! Can you imagine!? Putting all that pressure on a child.

Anyway, I didn't want to embarrass the chap by blazing in there, so I waited outside with Flora until he appeared. It wasn't long, of course; he'd lost his shirt and was in no mood to continue the party. The sight of Jonty and Flora was just deplorable. That he would inflict this on his daughter . . . well, it beggared belief.

ELIZABETH:

When was this?

MARGARET:

Back in July, I believe. Perhaps August. It was damned hot, nearly balmy for us to be standing about on the street like that. So, anyway, I told Jonty he had a week to settle his affairs with the club or I would tell Catherine. I am godmother not just to Flora, but to Thomas and Polly, too, and had a moral obligation to make sure their inheritance was not squandered. Plus, Jonty seemed completely out of control, unable to make any sort of reasoned decision. The very fact he was there with Flora—

ELIZABETH:

So, what happened?

MARGARET:

He came to see me, explained how he needed to win big on a boxing match that was coming up – typical talk of a gambler. He was so enlivened, so much fresher than I'd seen him in months, so I gave him another week. He didn't show up a week later to explain how he'd got on, so I knew he'd fallen off the wagon. Bear in mind that Jonty and I were never that close – in fact, I think it's safe to say I've always disliked him – and here I was, holding an awful secret from my best friend. I was lost as to what the best course of action was.

But then my hand was forced. Somebody saw me with Flora and Jonty that first night, a woman, I'm not sure whether she was Italian or from somewhere else along the Mediterranean. She claimed to be the wife of a boxer called Joe, who in essence had been—

ELIZABETH:

—sponsored by Jonty Caswell-Jones.

MARGARET:

Indeed. Well, after he was badly injured the wife asked me to intervene, explained her plight, her starving children. I didn't know her
from Adam, of course, but she was clearly a bright and intelligent
woman. That intelligence coupled with her apparent desperation
really scared me. Because a clever woman is someone to watch, a
desperate woman is someone to fear. I knew I had to let Catherine
know. So, I wrote her a letter, explained everything.

ELIZABETH:

How did she react?

MARGARET:

That's the thing. She never had the chance to read it. Flora had
been playing truant and the school discovered this, so Catherine
was in London retrieving the little madam. The letter must have
arrived in Berkshire the day she was in London, and someone
destroyed it. Of course, I did not realise that she didn't know until a
few weeks later.

ELIZABETH:

Weren't you surprised that she didn't reply?

MARGARET:

I was surprised, but then I assumed she was mired in a marital
dispute. Anyway, she invited me to lunch shortly before they were
due to leave for South America. That's when I realised she hadn't
read the letter, because if she had, there's no way she would have
been going ahead with the trip.

Things were terribly fragile with Jonty. All through lunch with
that joyless couple Ludlow and Sally, I tried to get her attention. In
the end, I had to drive into the wall to get a few moments alone
with her. It's terrible, really, that I have such a reputation as a, well,
busybody I'm afraid, that my own friend would not even talk to me

privately. I explained the whole scheme to her, and well, she didn't really seem to care. Spoke about how he could do whatever he wanted with his money, that it was none of her business – and that Flora had already told her! She can't have had the full picture, though, because she seemed to think Flora was only there once or twice. I thought Catherine would have been horrified at the thought of her daughter in such a place. Did she mention any of this to you?

ELIZABETH:

No, it didn't come up once.

MARGARET:

You see, I can't understand why this wouldn't bother her. Anyway, I can't help but think Jonty's murder is somehow related to this woman and her husband, the boxer.

ELIZABETH:

Hang on a minute, Margaret, just take me back a moment. Tell me, are you absolutely certain that the evening you visited the family's house on Carlyle Square was dry and warm?

MARGARET:

It was a long and hot summer, Elizabeth, I barely remember seeing it rain once. What does the weather have to do with it?

ELIZABETH:

Just checking. I need to get my facts straight. Did you ever see the woman again?

MARGARET:

She came to me one more time, caught me unawares as I walked home from a dreadfully boring game of bridge. The last two weeks in August are always a drag with so many people off in the country and town so quiet.

ELIZABETH:

How do you suppose Jonty's murder was connected to her?

MARGARET:

Argento.

ELIZABETH:

What about him?

MARGARET:

I think he cooked the whole thing up. He is this sort of shady lawyer, who's been disbarred for some secret reason we don't know anything about. Jonty is clearly inept financially, and Argento has full access to his accounts to book travel and what have you – plus, he knew that Jonty was the most terrific gambler!

ELIZABETH:

That wasn't widely known?

MARGARET:

Oh no, not at all. You see, his brother William was the worst sort of gambler, would bet on the toss of a coin, he had awful trouble in his youth. Anyway, Argento . . . I do remember many years ago he mentioned he had a cousin in London, a woman who was an English teacher. When I asked him about this cousin earlier, he acted very strangely and denied he even had any such cousin. Why would he do such a thing? Because . . . the cousin is married to Joe, our boxer fellow!

ELIZABETH:

By all accounts this Joe did really have a terrible time of it; Flora told me it was an extremely bloody fight, the chap almost died. Are you suggesting this was part of the scheme?

MARGARET:

That I can't tell you for sure. This cousin of Argento's might not have had anything to do with the boxer—

ELIZABETH:

Argento wasn't even here when Jonty died.

MARGARET:

How do you know he wasn't hiding in the attic? That he didn't escape to the village after the fact and appear so visibly afterwards?

ELIZABETH:

It's something I am considering, but I must say it seems incredibly unlikely. Now, Margaret, tell me about how Jonty and Catherine met each other.

MARGARET:

But I am telling you who the killer is now! What point is there in dragging up ancient history?

ELIZABETH:

Humour me.

MARGARET:

Right. You're making a mistake. Wasting everyone's time. But, well, if you must know, I suppose they must have met in the twenties . . . I believe they were introduced at Peter Smythson's wedding to Abigail. Peter Senior that is, the father of the Peter Smythson we have staying here with us. Anyway, back then everyone was quite surprised at how big the wedding was – you know, some terrible people were angry that his bride was not white. Peter and Abigail married for love, but we all knew the match wouldn't have been accepted without the backing of her large fortune. I believe Catherine met Abigail during their volunteer work for the Red Cross. She didn't have many friends in London and was worried at filling her side of a big wedding. Jonty was a terribly quiet chap, and were it not for the fact that Abigail sat Catherine beside Jonty, I don't believe they would ever have started talking. Of course, Peter's family and friends all knew one another already . . .

ELIZABETH:

Were you there, that day? You're Catherine's cousin, yes?

MARGARET:

Yes, our mothers were sisters. So, I went to chaperone Catherine, a duty I took seriously, but I really did not see Jonty as much of a risk. I was sitting beside a family friend who explained how Sally had broken things off and how heartbroken he was. Somehow Catherine and Jonty obviously got on rather well, and they even had a dance at the end of the night. They parted ways without much fanfare, so when Catherine told me she had met Jonty again for a walk in Hyde Park . . . I was surprised.

First, I thought perhaps she just wants some security. Her own father had passed away, and between the death duties and poor investments her brother had made, her allowance had dwindled . . . It still maintained a reasonable lifestyle but not anywhere near the same level that she was used to. Even as the younger son, Jonty had a very big allowance. But you know Catherine – you met her during the war – her head wouldn't be turned too much by things like that. She is a beacon for lost causes. Has such a terribly big heart.

ELIZABETH:

She often sat reading to the dying officers when she was off duty.

MARGARET:

There you go. She has compassion. That's why I'm sure Jonty never wanted his blackmailer, that Italian lady, the wife of Joe, to speak with Catherine. She would have been horrified at what Jonty had put this woman through. Catherine would have kicked him out, I'm sure. You know, back in their youth, Jonty was a heartbroken waif of a thing, almost a ghost, after Sally ended their engagement. I imagine it was that sadness about Jonty that attracted Catherine to him in the first place – she wanted to repair him . . .

ELIZABETH:

Wait a minute – I thought *Jonty* broke things off with Sally?

MARGARET:

Oh. That wasn't the tale I heard . . . but gosh, it's so long ago now. The match was made – between Catherine and Jonty, that is – and they married a few months later. They appeared to be happy. The children came along in quick-smart succession; they really seemed to bring him out of his shell. He was a terrific father when called upon. Then, before we knew it, we were at war. That's when things . . . well, went a bit sour between them. Some strange business about their living quarters – I'm almost certain Matilda stuck her nose in about it.

ELIZABETH:

How do you mean, things went sour?

MARGARET:

They bickered . . . when they did see each other . . . which was rare, with Jonty stationed in Aldershot and Catherine the other side of the country. When he came home from the camp, Catherine did not know what to expect – we were all wary of this creature; we'd heard terrible things about . . . things were never the same between them. I think she did try, you know, to lift things. And he tried to be a good father, but there was a new awkwardness that had grown like weeds between the Caswell-Joneses. Then came the long trips to South America, the stints in London. Another reason why I was so surprised when she wrote to invite me to lunch with them before she left for South America – she had never been, and apparently had decided this was the year.

ELIZABETH:

Do you think she could have killed Jonty?

MARGARET:

I very much doubt it, even if she really downright despised the fellow, she loves her children far too much to deprive them of a father – and that's the most important thing to keep in mind.

ELIZABETH:

How about Matilda? They had a fractured relationship?

MARGARET:

Catherine was doomed from the outset when it came to Matilda, because she wasn't Sally. Why the old crone had such affection for Sally I'll never know. As a rule, Matilda was not good with other women. Her own mother died when she was a child, and she had no sisters or aunts. She was spoiled and used to getting her own way; she believed she knew what was best for William and Jonty. On the surface, Polly and Catherine are cordial – all in the name of the family, of course, to give a good outward appearance – but, really, Matilda had done a *great* job of poisoning Polly against her mother.

ELIZABETH:

Poisoned how?

MARGARET:

Giving her money to do things Catherine had forbidden. Supporting Polly's application to York when Catherine wanted Polly to take up the place she was offered at Cambridge. Matilda sought to claim Polly as her own, because even after William died in the war, Matilda had little interest in Jonty. If I'm honest, I'm glad Matilda is dead – the woman was nothing but souring the blood of the Caswell-Joneses.

ELIZABETH:

Right. That's helpful information, thank you, Margaret. Let's talk about something else. Fooling the world, let's say. Does Catherine know where you spent 1947?

MARGARET:

What on earth do you mean? I was volunteering on the Orkney Islands—

ELIZABETH:

I can't believe that Catherine's bought that all these years. Did you have a false address, to intercept her letters? I can't quite imagine Catherine writing to Her Majesty's Prison, Holloway, for some reason.

MARGARET:

Elizabeth, how on earth—?

ELIZABETH:

Don't worry, I don't plan to tell anybody, if you help me with my investigation.

MARGARET:

How did you know?

ELIZABETH:

I realised years ago, of course; in fact, the first time we met, I think it was '48? I knew it was you.

MARGARET:

How on earth?

ELIZABETH:

Betty Cheadle ring a bell?

MARGARET:

Good God. That woman. I feel sick even hearing her name.

ELIZABETH:

How did she come to . . . recruit you into her service?

MARGARET:

That year was the worst of my life. The conditions in there . . . you think it was bad on outside, well, it was ten times worse in Holloway. Like something from Charles Dickens. The food was worse than during the war. But the women . . . I wasn't the only mark Betty had used. And no one else had given her up either. There were four or five of us, all fooled by Betty. Strangely, that group helped me get through the year – we were all in the same boat. Betty found me at Hugo's. I . . . well, I was penniless and there was this Italian café, where people used to sit outside. I used to— God, I am so ashamed to remember those days. I used to pluck out half-smoked cigarettes from the ashtray . . . I thought I was subtle about it, but Betty noticed. She sat down, ordered me a coffee. It was so easy, you know? She would do the dirty work, the actual pickpocketing . . . but would drop the items into my bag. I still had some decent clothes, looked like a woman of means, so it would not arouse suspicion if I was searched. But my luck ran out after a bobby searched me and found a chap's pocket watch and wallet. I didn't even know there was so much cash in it until they opened it. Don't look at me like that, I was desperate.

ELIZABETH:

I'm not looking at you like anything. What happened then?

MARGARET:

You obviously know the answer . . . Well, I was charged . . . the judge was not very lenient, so off I went to Holloway. You won't tell Catherine, will you?

ELIZABETH:

I'm sure she would not want *anything* to do with a convicted felon. Especially given all the effort she's going to to keep these murders 'in the family', as she says. So, I won't say anything as long as you don't hinder my investigation. Why didn't you just get a job?

MARGARET:

Oh, I hated work. And no one in my family has ever needed to earn their money. We hadn't been wealthy by any means, but we always maintained appearances. Mother made sure I was immaculately turned out, knew how to repair all my clothes. After my mother died, well there was nothing left. No allowance. I was left penniless. But I had standards to maintain, such big overheads. I didn't want Catherine to find out, you know what they are like about monet.

Anyway, I would have had to leave my apartment in St John's Wood had I not begun to work for Betty. But how on earth could you have found out about it?

ELIZABETH:

After the war, before I came out here, I went back to St Thomas's to nurse for a while. In palliative care. I nursed Betty. On her death-bed, she confessed to me about the scheme she had run. As the days dragged on, it was a terrible end for her, from lung cancer. So, I told her stories from the war, hardly knowing if she could hear me or not. I mentioned a friend of a friend, a woman called Big Margaret, on account of her height. And she knew your name. It took me a while, but I remember Thomas and the children called you that, when they were small. And I knew for *sure* when Betty mentioned Kate and the family.

MARGARET:

You never said it . . . all these years.

ELIZABETH:

We all make mistakes, Margaret. I wasn't going to mention that to Kate. But Jonty knew, too, didn't he?

MARGARET:

He . . . never said anything.

ELIZABETH:

But he could have, and that's why you killed him, isn't it?

MARGARET:

Please, Elizabeth, you have to believe me. My spell in that hell-hole . . . I would never risk going back there again.

ELIZABETH:

I'm inclined to believe you . . . but why did you not shop Betty?

MARGARET:

She knew about Kate . . . saw us having lunch one day. She thought
I had been with a mark, insisted I turn over what I had taken. Then,
when I was arrested, she threatened to go after them, to hurt the
children, snatch the girls away and . . . put them to work. *(Crying)* I
could never have done that. I'm their godmother, you know.

ELIZABETH:

There, there, Margaret. I know, it can be a challenge to drag up
these old histories of ours.

MARGARET:

You know, Elizabeth, I've never spoken about this with anyone
before. It is a relief in some ways, but it really doesn't have anything
to do with what's gone on here. Tell me, as we are sharing secrets,
how did you come to kiss that dirty old dog? *(Laughing)*

ELIZABETH:

It's terribly moving, Margaret, I can only imagine how difficult it
has been to hide, all day everyday. And if you did learn your lesson,
then I commend you. You want to know my dirty secret? Well,
Ludlow and I shared the train from Paris to Milan a few years ago.

MARGARET:

Years? My, you are a bold girl. Go on . . .

ELIZABETH:

You know I used to love the time I spent at Villa Janus . . . so we
recounted our memories. He piled on the usual compliments . . .
and by the time we arrived in Milano Centrale, well, let's say the
spark was lit. He was actually on the way here, but I was not invited
that year. He'd managed to tack on some time in Milan and came
to seek me out! Yes, there had been other passing amusements, but,
I'm afraid to admit, no one was a cut on my Charlie.

Ludlow . . . he just reminded me of him. Charlie was tall like
that, with a broad chest and long hair. I let myself think it was his
freckled shoulders lying tangled in my sheets . . . I've no doubt that

it's all just a matter of convenience to him. I was weak when this affair started, I hadn't worked in months and in fact was only going back to Milan for a few weeks with a plan to move somewhere else. But I'm stronger now, and I can see as clear as day what a ruthless old fellow he is.

MARGARET:

You know, it's very possible he could be in on things with Argento. He is most vocal about his praise for the man – part of the reason why they kept inviting him back all the time and handed over their affairs to such a 'capable' fellow.

ELIZABETH:

Margaret, for the last time, I'm not keen on your theory about Argento. There are too many holes for it to make sense. Please – don't push it any more. Now. Tell me about your godchildren. Polly aside, did they like their granny?

MARGARET:

Oh, all right. But do make sure you take a damned close look at the fellow. And also, please scrutinise that Nikolai chap. You know, this whole thing is a great excuse for Catherine to clear the decks with all these hangers on the family accumulated. Nikolai, Francis, Sally, all of those . . . nobodies.

Anyway, I see the way Nikolai looks at Polly, looks at Flora. He has a hunger in his eyes – well, you know . . . He's managed to maintain his composure suspiciously well, in my book. He's never married. And all that business with him and Matilda . . . I hope Catherine gets rid of the fellow for once and all after this.

ELIZABETH:

What business with Matilda? Her getting him a job in the ballet?

MARGARET:

Oh, that's a jolly good cover story for both of them. But it's rather deeper than that. Matilda was Finnish, Nikolai was Russian. Of neighbouring countries. Matilda's family were successful merchants in Helsinki, but also held lead and zinc mines. They owned acres and acres of land all along the Russian border. All I'm saying is, there is more to that relationship than they led us to believe.

ELIZABETH:

Do sit down, Margaret. *(Shock)* Oh, wow! And there was light! The electricity is back. Thank God for that. *(Disappointed)* Oh – no, it's gone again.

MARGARET:

And with it, this suspect. This has dragged on far too long, Elizabeth. I'm tired and need to rest. I'll be in my room if you need anything.

ELIZABETH:

Well, while I've never known Margaret well, I'm glad that news of Betty came back to me at just the right moment. I have a feeling she won't be bothering me about Ludlow now. But no ... I think I rather like Margaret. There's more to her than meets the eye.

EPISODE 9

Peter Smythson

ELIZABETH:

How many killers does it take to break the Caswell-Joneses? That is the question. How many murderers do we have? The snowstorm rages on around Villa Janus. With the bridge crumbled by lightning, we are essentially stranded at the lakeside villa, backed by an almost vertical hillside. The gloom in Villa Janus is soupy, the air strangling our twelve suspects of oxygen. The killer is amongst us. It has now been almost a day since Jonty was murdered – I'm observing our suspects for signs of fatigue, exhaustion of the adrenal glands . . . With the body of our second victim, Jonty's sixty-nine-year-old mother Matilda, resting in the basement . . . we wait.

Did the same person kill Jonty and Matilda? Were both of them murdered? Did both mother and son die accidentally, of natural causes? Jonty did have a weak heart, and Matilda was approaching her seventh decade. Have you got any ideas? Honestly, it has been the most exhausting day since I arrived here last night. Maybe Thomas was right, the real target was Matilda, and Jonty either discovered the plan or was an incidental complication. You've heard from eight of our suspects; now, let's continue our probing of this most scheming of families. Olympic skier Peter Smythson was born three villages away and grew up with the Caswell-Jones children. Is he one of them? Or is he one of us? Let's find out.

It's almost two o'clock, and I'm damned near starving . . . parched with thirst. Not like you, I'm sure, burping in your pyjamas, stretched out trying to solve this mystery. Well, spare a thought for your bloody detective, at the coal face of it all. Sorry. Look – I could just do with a cigarette, and this bunch is getting on my nerves. Maybe it's the lack of food causing sensory hallucinations, but it seems to me there is the most delicious smell of chocolate coming from the kitchen. Remember, eight down – four more suspects to go. Let's get on with it.

ELIZABETH:

Sally, you are clever to get the range going down here. What a delicious smell.

SALLY:

I can't bloody mope around, can I? I did invent twenty bestselling kitchen gadgets, you know. Need to keep the strength up to get out of this place when this bloody storm dies down. We'll have missed our train, so here, have a cup.

(Slurping)

ELIZABETH:

This is very good, Sally.

SALLY:

But there'll be another train. It was always going to be the most terrific rush to get back to London for the New Year's Eve ball in Kensington Palace, I'm not sure why on earth I agreed. But men do strange things to us, isn't that right, Elizabeth?

ELIZABETH:

Reader, I think this is a rhetorical question.

ELIZABETH:

Oh – Peter, there you are. Can we sit down together? Need to go over what happened, things you might have seen, that sort of thing.

PETER:

Well, I was just . . . oh go on, all right.

SALLY:

Rather you than me.

ELIZABETH:

You're next, Sally. Hang on a minute, why are you both alone rambling around? Didn't I advise you to be cautious and always travel in pairs. There have been two dead bodies—

PETER:

I came down here with Sally, we had a few things to discuss. Business things. For my father.

ELIZABETH:

So be it. Let's return to Jonty's study.

ELIZABETH:

Can you hear that? Whatever should I call you, my listeners? Sisters in sleuthing? Hawkshaw Henrys? The storm . . . I've never seen thunder and lightning turn to snow before . . . perhaps it's something to do with our position on the lake . . . But the air is as cold as a mortuary, the gloom dark and far-reaching. Here I have Peter Smythson, still wearing his sailing shirt, although it is not a brilliant white, but an old grey top, flanked with navy stripes. He looks exhausted.

PETER:

Ah, let's get this fire going again, it's bloody freezing.

ELIZABETH:

The drawing-room fireplace is inclined to smoke when it's windy, let's hope this chimney has been swept recently. Now. Please sit down.

PETER:

I'm seated.

ELIZABETH:

What's this business of taking the boat out in the middle of the night?

PETER:

I like to take in the night air.

ELIZABETH:

You don't need to take a boat halfway across Lake Como to do that.

PETER:

But the water . . . often, it is so still . . . and dark . . . it's comforting. Like a womb. It helps me to think.

ELIZABETH:

About?

PETER:

Oh, just the usual. Life, and what we're all doing here. There are certain places where the stillness is richer, deeper, purer than anywhere else on the planet. The summit of a mountain is one. When all you can see is the clouds above you – sometimes below you and the sky all about. The middle of the lake is another. It's so dark it's almost as if we were in an underground cave. The human condition is one that needs examining, probing. Recently, these past few months, I've started to see things in a new light, things have changed for me.

ELIZABETH:

Good Lord, I expected this guff from Francis, not you, too. What is it that has changed for you?

PETER:

Oh, it's not important now. But it's in those moments that I think about the future. I picture my life as I want it to be, and am at one with what already is and what has passed. To be in a moment, but not of a moment, is a very precious thing.

ELIZABETH:

Well, let's be of the moment of Jonty's murder, eh? Did he ever go out on the boat with you during your time at Villa Janus?

PETER:

No. Well, I often invited him . . . in fact, I hoped he would come out on New Year's Eve, but that's not going to happen now. Poor old Jonty. He was my godfather, you know? Wasn't a terribly good one, but he was a kind old soul. Bought me my first set of skis. If he hadn't, I probably wouldn't have badgered my parents to take me skiing and, well, wouldn't be where I am today.

ELIZABETH:

And what about Catherine?

PETER:

Things would have turned out all right for Jonty if it wasn't for her.

ELIZABETH:

Why do you say that?

PETER:

You see how she is, such a busybody, interfering in everyone's business . . . why? Just to make up for her own unhappiness.

ELIZABETH:

You're quite the armchair psychiatrist today, Peter.

PETER:

She has to control everything around her. Even this joke about there being no staff. What's the point? To make us all miserable and uncomfortable and remember we're all here at her majestic grace.

ELIZABETH:

How much do you estimate that Jonty left you in his will?

PETER:

Honestly, I'd be surprised if there was a single penny left once the debts are settled.

ELIZABETH:

There's been talk of these debts, but I'm not sure there are any. Your father was Jonty's accountant, wasn't he? So, you'd have a very clear idea of what that actual balance looked like.

PETER:

I am a skier, Mrs Chalice, I do not share my father's head for numbers. He runs a professional outfit, not some leering loan sharks.

ELIZABETH:

Call me Elizabeth, please. Right, didn't mean to quite go for the jugular there, Peter, but I don't mean to mess around here. We're dealing with a double murder, and the killer is very much here with us. Thomas seemed surprised at his inheritance. Then when Argento read the will, we learned that you were in line for a windfall too. Did you know he had made a new will?

PETER:

I had no idea I was in Jonty's will, until Thomas mentioned it just after the murder. When Argento began to read, and it was clear Thomas was surprised, I did wonder, but you can't really miss what you never had, can you, Elizabeth?

ELIZABETH:

What do you mean?

PETER:

Oh nothing, nothing. Look, I'm not bragging here, but I don't need any money. Between my father's allowance and the prize money . . . let's just say I don't want for anything.

ELIZABETH:

Apart from Flora. Tell me, why are you leading on a child?

PETER:

(Cough) Yes, she told me that you knew about us. Flora is not a child. She will turn eighteen in three months' time. And I'm not leading her on – you know, I was just going to ask for Jonty's permission to marry her. I would prefer it if she was older, but she is terribly mature, you know.

ELIZABETH:

Really? Mature is not how I would describe her. She's running away from boarding school, following her father to a casino. Is that why she was so keen on you – her own father was such a poor character? That's often the case with girls who go after older men.

PETER:

You're hardly one to pry into the relationships of others.

ELIZABETH:

Oh, I see what you're inferring. Well, let me tell you, that's exactly why I am in a position to have insights on the relationships of others.

PETER:

Oh, so tell me, Elizabeth, what is your insight into the marriage of Sally and Ludlow? I saw you, you know, last night. I was bringing the boat in and could see through the kitchen window. Not very subtle, if I do say so. But it just serves to remind me of how morally bankrupt you are.

ELIZABETH:

I don't really care what you think, Peter. I'm here to find out who killed Jonty, and you've not done a good enough job of convincing me it wasn't you.

PETER:

I don't have to convince you, or anyone else for that matter. Flora knows it wasn't me . . . in fact, I hope we can wrap this up quickly, so I can keep an eye on her . . .

ELIZABETH:

You haven't seen each other in weeks, isn't that correct? Weren't you worried she would have gone off you? Perhaps taken a shine to a chap her own age? Where were you again, South America?

PETER:

Yes, I was in the Andes – nowhere near the coffee plantations, if that's what you're getting at.

ELIZABETH:

Oh, I didn't think you went near the coffee plantations. The little dollies you got for Flora were Peruvian, yes? But what a terribly long way to go! But what puzzled me is why an Olympic skier would travel almost as far away as is possible, right as it's coming into prime snow season on the Alps, especially with the Winter Olympics just down the road the year after next. And with the Russians sending along their athletes, the competition is certain to be fierce. What were you doing in South America, Peter?

PETER:

Any good athlete knows it's important to gain experience in a lot of different conditions and settings. The Andes resorts have such high settings – new slopes, new paths – it's imperative for me as an athlete to ski on runs I haven't already been down dozens of times, or mountains that I don't know.

ELIZABETH:

If we accept that as true . . .

(Fire extinguishes)

ELIZABETH:

Oh no, that's just wonderful . . .

PETER:

It was bound to go any minute . . . Here, the fire will come back to life with a bit of a prod.

ELIZABETH:

It's a hugely long journey – how many days were you travelling to the East Coast?

PETER:

It was the best part of a week from the Andes to Buenos Aires, and I did make use of one of the resort owners' planes for part of the route. It would have been almost impossible to get up to São Paulo from that direction, so I tracked down to Buenos Aires, and from there took a ship up the coast. We were three weeks at sea before reaching Lisbon. I took the train to Paris, spent a few days there, then the final leg to Milan, and here we are. It was a long journey, but I've always wanted to see the world. And I am deathly serious about Flora – I was just getting it out of my system . . . I suppose that's what you could call it.

ELIZABETH:

And were you welcome in first class during your journey?

PETER:

If you're asking did porters ask to see my ticket more than anyone else; if elderly guests tried to have me removed or if the colour of my skin bothered other travellers . . . the answer is yes. People have begun to forget the lessons of the war already . . . I can't remotely see what that has to do with anything here.

ELIZABETH:

Have you ever been treated differently here, at Villa Janus?

PETER:

Good Lord, no, I've known the family since I was born – Jonty is my godfather.

ELIZABETH:

What about by Francis Heath? I hear there was an incident with him and Nikolai over a bottle of dessert wine last night?

PETER:

Oh that. Quite right you are. But it wasn't actually about the wine . . . Francis has the dullest sort of common humour. I know Thomas likes the chap, but I can't stand him. That accent just rings through my ears. Anyway. He commented that Polly looked like a busted pup, or some other disgusting slur – I mean, who does he think he is? Then he tried to tell me what he would do to Catherine . . . awful stuff.

ELIZABETH:

I didn't take you for such a prude—

PETER:

There are certain standards of common decency.

ELIZABETH:

I accept that, okay. What happened?

PETER:

I just warned him that if he didn't keep his smutty comments to himself I would take him outside and give him a good thrashing. He asked me to repeat myself and the wine spilled.

ELIZABETH:

And what happened with Nikolai?

PETER:

Did something happen with Nikolai? I, eh, oh that. He took me the wrong way is all. I mentioned how Matilda expected us to all pay the piper with our unusual jobs or quirky characteristics. He got too hung up on the word 'pay' and thought I was saying he didn't contribute . . . Really, he was terribly sensitive and made this big deal of nothing.

ELIZABETH:

Where was Jonty during these disturbances? How did he seem?

PETER:

He was there, with us all. Very chatty, he looked jolly – he had on a brand-new dinner jacket. The Italians use a lighter wool blend, and it sits more easily on the skin. He looked to me like the picture of health. He had a good suntan from his own time in South America. I saw a few terse words with Catherine, but it would be strange if there wasn't, you know, with them hosting us all. He kept joking about his heart. Not to give him a fright, that sort of thing.

ELIZABETH:

Did you cross paths with Jonty when you were away?

PETER:

No, no, it's a darned big place, you know, Elizabeth. He was in Brazil, visiting plantations – the other side of the continent!

ELIZABETH:

What dates were you away? Just for my record.

PETER:

Oh, I'm not totally sure, but I left London at the beginning— was it the fifth of September? Spent October and November in the Andes and arrived in Milan two nights ago. I'll need to check the exact dates for you.

ELIZABETH:

I see, just let me make a note of that. Are they your cigarettes there? On the sideboard?

PETER:

This packet of Conquer? No, I don't know whose they are. Here you go.

ELIZABETH:

Thank you. Dying for one. Now, what did you make of Flora's visits to the Mayfair Club?

(Sound of cigarette lighting, Elizabeth inhaling)

PETER:

I suppose she's entitled to her fun . . .

(Elizabeth faints)

PETER:

(Faintly) Elizabeth, Elizabeth. Are you okay?

ELIZABETH:

Oh my, this is awful. I am, eurgh, I'm here on the floor. How did that happen?

PETER:

Can you hear me Elizabeth? I'm going to get help.

ELIZABETH:

(Breathy, she is exhausted) *I shall just lie here, on the cold floor. That's it. Ahh. My heart is still racing, I can see the little star chaps. I feel quite nauseous. Oh, deep breaths, Elizabeth. Now. Deep breaths. Beginning to feel normal. What on earth caused me to faint? I was feeling completely fine. But I fainted ... After what, that bloody cigarette? It did not taste all that strong as cigarettes go ... I wonder who they belong to. I don't believe Jonty smoked. Was that Nikolai's brand?*

Then again, I don't suppose I slept terribly well. I struggle to relax when residing somewhere there has been a violent death ... And where there is a murderer free to roam around ...

I don't quite have my head on straight, my feet feel a little strange. I see they've tangled up at the ankle, almost like how Matilda's feet were tangled. Was it Peter's doing? I do hope he's not going to return with an accomplice to bundle me into a suitcase and throw me to the bottom of the lake. Oh, don't be stupid, Elizabeth. You know, I thought I was working on a shortlist of potential killers – but it's as if those people have faded from my memory. Here she is now, Nurse Kate.

CATHERINE:

Elizabeth, oh Elizabeth! Are you quite all right?

PETER:

She just keeled over, as soon as she took a few puffs.

CATHERINE:

No wonder, you haven't eaten a damned thing today and it's almost lunchtime. I am so sorry. Will you get her a glass of water, please, Peter? And ask one of my girls to find a kettle – we need to give her a cup of sweet tea. And get some bread and cheese.

PETER:

Right-o.

ELIZABETH:

I am quite better now, Kate, thank you.

CATHERINE:

Here, let me help you up to the seat. What happened?

ELIZABETH:

Just as Peter said, had a few puffs of a cigarette, haven't eaten much today so it just knocked me. I'm quite fine now, just a bruised ego lingering.

CATHERINE:

You little lamb. I know you're here to investigate, and you are a clever thing. But you don't need to put on this show of bravado . . .

ELIZABETH:

I appreciate your concern, Kate, but with due respect it would take more to throw me off course.

CATHERINE:

You always were a lightweight. Do you remember VE night? You'd passed out by nine in the evening. All that cherry wine.

ELIZABETH:

When I woke up at three or four, your beds were still empty. I walked down to the village, and there was old Roger, with his gramophone out in the middle of the street. It was another lifetime, wasn't it?

CATHERINE:

I've missed you around here, Elizabeth. All I'm saying is, I'm your friend, you can nose out this horrid killer, but you can still be yourself—

ELIZABETH:

I don't intend on being anyone else, Kate. How is everyone?

CATHERINE:

I think it's finally hit the girls, you know, what's actually happened to them. Flora's asleep in my bed. Thomas has rooted out some backgammon boards and cards, and they've nestled up with Nikolai in the old butler's quarters. Much calmer now we are all away from that dining room. It's like the storm is calming us . . . we've all been so highly strung these past twenty-four hours . . . it's not sustainable.

PETER:

Here we go: water, some focaccia, and some cheese and tomatoes. Polly put the kettle on! I've always wanted to say that.

CATHERINE:

Ah, Peter, well done.

ELIZABETH:

Thank you, Peter, I'm feeling quite back to myself. Kate, if you don't mind.

CATHERINE:

Right-o, yes. Come up to my room when you've finished, we've a glorious fire going – and now, there'll be tea!

(Door closes)

PETER:

My God, who does she think she's fooling with that act? You'd think you were here to find out who took a slice of the apple tart, not find her husband's killer.

ELIZABETH:

Grief does funny things to people. She's probably putting on a show for the girls. Tell me, Peter, what do *you* think happened to Jonty?

PETER:

I think Nikolai killed him, poisoned him. I fear there's something going on between Polly and Nikolai. Matilda might have been fond of her pet Russian but would absolutely object to a match with her favourite grandchild. Jonty wouldn't have disobeyed Matilda. Nikolai is penniless, desperate, and whether he actually loves her or not . . . no one here knows a damned thing about him really, not about his past.

ELIZABETH:

He has lived in Britain for years, though; I mean, it's not like he arrived last week—

PETER:

My suspicions were confirmed when I went down to fetch your water. Polly came in from the storm, with no coat on or anything. She then went into the pantry – it's tiny, less than four foot by three foot – where he was. I heard them whispering. I pretended like I had just arrived, but I could smell vomit from Polly – I wonder if she's ill, she seems so exhausted these days. It's not the first time – as far back as the end of the summer I've had my suspicions. Once, when I was visiting Flora at Carlyle Square, Nikolai and Polly turned up together. She didn't know that Flora was there . . . They were obviously looking for something, because they weren't there for very long . . . But out of everyone here, they are the only two that I can just . . . sense something isn't right.

ELIZABETH:

Surely Polly would have confided in her only sister?

PETER:

Ah, they're not close like that. Polly is as good as – or should I say *was* as good as – Matilda's daughter. Flora is still Catherine's baby . . . as much as they didn't like that, they have accepted those roles.

ELIZABETH:

But Polly loved her grandmother, why would she kill her?

PETER:

Did she really love her? Or was she forced into that role by a rail-roading battleaxe?

ELIZABETH:

How is your own relationship with your father?

PETER:

That's none of your business.

ELIZABETH:

That answers that question.

PETER:

You think you're so clever, don't you, to make all these judgements and assumptions about other people? So confident you can figure everyone out. Well, you will never figure me out. You know when you came here yesterday you reminded me of someone, and it's just dawned on me, it's him. My father. He thinks he can poke his nose into everyone's business, convinced finances can tell the story of a person's life.

ELIZABETH:

What about your mother, she doesn't poke her nose into your life?

PETER:

Oh, yes, she does, but at least she's up front about it. Of course, she's trying to find me the perfect wife. The fairer and richer the better, according to her. She thinks that at least that way, our children will pass.

ELIZABETH:

Does that matter to you?

PETER:

We all have to play the hand we are dealt. Oh, but my mother doesn't mean harm; she saw how I had to fight twice as hard as anyone else, and just wants an easier life for them. Her mother was born a slave in Alabama. Escaped north . . . found love with my grandfather. He was a Yankee, free for three generations, so they had built up some money. But he was smart – who would have thought they could go from slave to millionaire in a generation? My mother inherited his intelligence – she can run rings around my father. Mother and Father are loving and balanced. Unlike the

Caswell-Joneses. I've known them my whole life, of course, but I see how twisted things are. They might look perfect on the outside, but ... underneath it is a complete tangle of lies. Catherine with her chirpiness. Don't you think that's bordering on ... some sort of mania? To bounce around in such a manner.

(Knock at the door)

CATHERINE:

(Frantic!) Quick, Elizabeth, I need your help. There's been an accident. There's so much blood. I ... I can't stop the bleeding.

ELIZABETH:

Good Lord, I'm sorry, Peter. Thank you for your honesty. I think we had best leave it there.

(Elizabeth running down the steps)

ELIZABETH:

(Breathless) *Blast it, I am still a little weak from my episode earlier, so I'd better walk to Kate's crisis. I was not expecting to keel over like that ... but perhaps Kate is right, I need to let my guard down somewhat ... After all, we are friends – even if there is a killer on the loose. I have never had such a strong reaction to a cigarette, even a terribly strong one ... could it be that it was poisoned? I know they are starting to say smoking is no good for you ... but to cause such a strong reaction ... My body feels poisoned. Hmmm. But this snack and the water are helping to slow my heart rate to normal again – I feel the danger has passed.*

And just when I was getting somewhere with Peter, could you feel it? He was talking himself in circles, getting closer to the truth. His rant about Catherine was not about her directly, but about some other force in his life wielding too much influence. I don't know about you lot, but I do not believe his reasons for travelling halfway across the planet, instead of training for the Olympics. What on earth was he doing in South America? Somehow, I feel that it may have been connected to Jonty, to the coffee company, even though he said it wasn't. Catherine certainly has some questions to answer on what has come out in these past interviews.

Once I've seen to this accident, I think I will need to lie down before I interview our final three suspects, Sally, Argento and Francis. I do not quite feel like myself . . . Whatever can it be? I am not expecting, in case that's what you're wondering; the mathematics would not balance on that front. But if my head was not already swimming . . . here I smell the metallic tang of freshly spilled blood.

ELIZABETH:

Where's she bleeding from?

CATHERINE:

Here, I think just here at her temple.

ELIZABETH:

I haven't worked as a nurse in so long . . . But why is there so much blood? Where is the light? Closer, Polly.

CATHERINE:

Yes, it's a nasty laceration to the scalp all right.

ELIZABETH:

Hence all the blood. Sally, what happened, we need you to tell us?

CATHERINE:

I've been trying, she just keeps bleeding – I don't know why.

LUDLOW:

She's bleeding because she's a haemophiliac.

CATHERINE:

Ludlow, where on earth have you been? I sent Polly to fetch you . . .

LUDLOW:

The tail wagging the dog again, my dear? These kitchen gadgets are terribly dangerous.

CATHERINE:

Elizabeth, I'm worried at how much blood she's losing. If we can't stem the bleeding, she'll bleed to death. Keep the pressure on.

PETER:

(Interrupting) Elizabeth – I think our only chance is to see if I can fix the boat. It is treacherous out there, but I might be able to get out to Bellagio on it and call for help.

ELIZABETH:

Peter, thank you. Yes – you must go now. You of all people shouldn't be put off by some snowflakes.

CATHERINE:

Ludlow, come here, apply as much pressure as you can, my arms are tiring. Peter – will you please hurry?

ELIZABETH:

As you can see, I rather have my hands full here . . . I think we are dealing with an attempted murder . . . unless we stop Sally bleeding to death we will have three murders to solve. Let me at least try to save her first!

EPISODE 10

Francis Heath

ELIZABETH:

Oh, there you are. Sorry I'm not as chatty as normal. Poor Sally. Catherine's with her now, in her bedroom, beside the fire. Barely any pulse at all ... but the bleeding has slowed a bit. Truth be told, with no medical supplies or blood for a transfusion ... it's unlikely we can save her. Peter has been working on the boat; he's going to take it out, see if he can make it to Bellagio for help ... but God knows if it will even make the journey there and back in this storm. Why would I let him go, you might wonder, given that he is still a suspect? Wouldn't the killer relish the opportunity to escape from the villa? I suppose I'm gambling on his being absolutely lovestruck for Flora. If he did murder Jonty, and I don't think he did, it would be because he objected to their match. To not return would paint him as guilty and Flora would never speak to him again – it would all be for nothing. But, it is a risk ...

(Wind raging outside)

ELIZABETH:

Can you hear that? The ruddy storm is still going ... albeit a bit less than earlier. Argento and the police officers are out on the bridge, trying to get the thing opened again. I'm just in the subterranean kitchen of Villa Janus, boiling a pot of water to make some spaghetti to feed our suspects ... Margaret was here somewhere, where on earth has she gone?

My body has entered a state of alarm ... I need some time and space to consider the chaos that has enveloped this investigation. As you know, I have narrowed down our twelve suspects to two. Although I have three more to interview, Sally will hardly be fit to be questioned, the poor thing. Francis Heath, our Scottish philosopher, has been almost invisible over the past few hours ... I can't imagine he had much skin in the game. But I need to rule him out. Writers are often the best observers ... I'm hopeful he can fill in some of the gaps.

(Distracted) *Now, where is the oregano? You would imagine the herbs would be easily accessed here ...*

(Focused again) *And then there's Argento ... Jonty's lawyer. That makes up my twelve suspects, each with their own deadly motive, big or small, for murder.*

And a little basil, marjoram, sugar is my secret ingredient for pasta sauce ...

(Sound of footsteps)

LUDLOW:

There you are. I was looking for you. Can't you clean up this mess?

ELIZABETH:

Clean up? Do you realise how much blood there was? Look where we wrung out the mop in the drain outside, will you? It is like a slaughterhouse. How is she?

LUDLOW:

It won't be long. I thought you'd come to see me sooner. Don't you see, now we can be together properly? Seeing you here, in command, taking charge of the whole group ... well, it is another side to you that I have not seen in many years. You are a professional, Elizabeth, a beautiful, bright—

ELIZABETH:

Stop it, Ludlow, I'm not really in the mood. And someone might see.

LUDLOW:

Oh, go on ... Should I have brought some mistletoe?

ELIZABETH:

Stop it.

LUDLOW:

All right. I say, where did that lemon cake come from? I thought we had eaten it all.

ELIZABETH:

Is that all you can think about? In your gob or in your trousers?

LUDLOW:

That's hardly any way to treat a fellow, after doing something like this for you.

ELIZABETH:

(Horrified) Wait, what do you mean? You did this? You . . . tried to kill Sally?

LUDLOW:

Yes. When she's dead, we can get married. I know that's what you want, that's what all ladies want, isn't it? To be respectable? To get married? To have a ring on your finger? Some people would do anything to get a ring from me. And Sally is too clever to wrangle through the divorce courts. This way, it will only be written off as one of three deaths.

ELIZABETH:

(Disgusted) You are *sick*, why on earth would you want to . . . to kill your wife?

LUDLOW:

All I did was give her a push . . . the water on the floor did the rest. Do keep your voice down, Elizabeth, for Christ's sake, someone might hear you. I thought this is what you *wanted*.

ELIZABETH:

What I *wanted*? What is wrong with you? I rather hope someone does hear you . . . For who will believe that you – up until now a seemingly gentle person – could be so twisted?

LUDLOW:

It's not like I shot her in the head. If anything, it was more like a happy accident.

ELIZABETH:

I can't keep this a secret, you know. I am a detective.

LUDLOW:

(Threateningly) You're going to have to.

ELIZABETH:

(Hissing back) Let go of me. In case you forgot, I am still married. Until I see Charlie's body, I will never marry someone else. You are more stupid than I imagined, to think this . . . this thing between us was anything more than a distraction . . . What a terrible group of people you are, the lot of you, you're all horrible people . . . Don't you realise how precious life is? For all her flaws, Sally loved you.

LUDLOW:

I'll say we were in it together. Margaret saw us together; she'll probably even confirm it if I pay her enough. You'll have questions to answer. Like why did you accept this job at all? When you knew your lover and his wife would be here . . . unless you planned to make a move against her? That looks incriminating, doesn't it? It's all very easy to construct, you know. Besides, it's not like anyone has particularly *warmed* to you being here, is it? Who are they going to believe? You, the one they kicked out of their house for years, or me, their long-time family friend? Jonty's very best friend . . .

ELIZABETH:

(Coolly) Did you . . . did you kill Jonty?

LUDLOW:

Don't be ridiculous. I had *nothing* to do with Jonty or his old dear. Now you had better pull yourself together. Sally's death will be put down as a tragic accident – with water all over the floor, she tripped and cut her head on a sharp corner. End of story. No one else – no one other than you – is even really suspicious.

ELIZABETH:

Of course they are suspicious, Ludlow, Sally would be the third death in less than twenty-four hours.

LUDLOW:

You're either with me or against me, Elizabeth. And . . . don't you see I love you? I did this because I love you.

MARGARET:

(Coldly, but with some humour) My, my, Elizabeth, you do know how to pick them.

LUDLOW:

(Worried) Margaret – how long have you been—?

MARGARET:

Oh, long enough. What do you say, Elizabeth? Shall we call the police officers down here to arrest him?

LUDLOW:

(Snarling) Don't try to out-manoeuvre me, Margaret. No one will believe a word you say, or will you drive into another wall until they pay attention to you?

ELIZABETH:

I can't stay and listen to this, I have a job to do. Even if you did give Sally a shove, I don't believe you had it in you to do over Jonty and Matilda.

LUDLOW:

Do over? Are you an American now? Aren't you even grateful?

ELIZABETH:

I'll be grateful if you stay out of my way. Let go of the door.

(Elizabeth slams the door)

ELIZABETH:

(Sounds of her steps audible throughout) *Eurgh, he has me over a barrel! If I try to have him arrested, he will tell everyone about our affair, and if I don't . . . well, I am not doing my job for Catherine. Who am I kidding, I'm going to have to tell them eventually. Well, at least he can't go anywhere. His body language . . . something about him . . . I'm not convinced he had it in him. But I couldn't possibly confront him on my own anyway, he could easily overpower me. No, I'll let him think he's off the hook, and if more things point to his guilt . . . I will recruit someone to help arrest him.*

I must remain calm and aloof. With Sally unwell, I need to speak with our three final suspects immediately. But first, Jonty's financial papers. The corridors are dark in the late-afternoon murk, the winds creaking the hallway shutters as I go up to my room. I wish I had heeded my own advice about walking around alone . . . the absence of human noises disturbs me. Within these four walls lies the deceased Matilda Caswell-Jones, the dying Sally Lansdowne de Groot and her attacker, at least one killer, me and a house full of suspects who can't be ruled out . . . not yet. Our two police officers are seeking a way to escape this damned villa. What a shame one can't ski up a hill . . .

That is what I feel like I am doing, just as I figure out one piece of the puzzle, the story shifts with an extra perspective, taking me further from the truth.

Well, I've made it back to my room. What is that . . . ? There is some-thing different, a smell. It's perfume, the last hint . . . of Matilda. The oudiness of it takes me back to staring into her dead, grey eyes this morning. I would imagine her spirit stayed around to see what happened next . . . (whispering) *but I must admit I am not all that brave in the face of a haunting.*

(Speaking normally) *I don't always have much of a head for numbers. But I can just about tell red from black. Before I interview Francis, I had better make myself acquainted with Jonty's folder entitled 'Financials'. Let's head to his study.*

(Slight pause)

(Sounds of paper rustling)

ELIZABETH:

Here we are, looks like company accounts. What do we have? Wages, hmm, that doesn't seem to be very much. I wonder how many people are actually employed by the company. This is only enough to pay one manager and two labourers, perhaps. Wilson's Packaging seems fine, Humberside Transport, The Times advertising. I'm no business analyst, but this appears to be more or less in order ...

Currency transactions ... sterling to cruzeiro – that's Brazil, I believe. Peso ... must be the Argentinian peso ... and the dollar. Let's see, banknotes were issued from sterling to dollars in the amounts of fifteen hundred, two thousand and seven thousand last year. For an international organisation that does seem like a modest amount. I am unsure of what the South American currencies work out as in pounds sterling. I can either ask Peter, or Ludlow, potentially even Thomas, but which of the three can I really trust?

The final bill from the Majestic Ruby, that seems to be Jonty's final crossing across the Atlantic. Cigars, laundry, service, tip, wines ... everything is itemised here. It seems like he had a jolly good time on that ship, which reminds me, I must speak to Argento about my next trip if he's such a good travel agent. He would have good advice on how to get to Egypt. But back to Jonty's bill. Good Lord, what an outrageous amount to spend on a telegraph ... to just one address. 34 Young Street, Edinburgh. Where did I that address before? (Pause for thought) *That's it. Francis's book ... the author's preferred Christmas gift is his own work. Here it is ... Yes ... There we go, on the back page. Why did Jonty send such a long telegraph to Francis's publisher from the ship? Time to speak to the chap.*

(Brief pause)

ELIZABETH:

There is a name for the hairstyle he wears, brushed forward into a cone. On my last visit to London, the Tottenham Court Road was populated by similarly attired fellows. Teddy boys. A yellow suit with black stitching is most striking, but for the day this has become, he is rather overdressed.

ELIZABETH:

So, Francis. Where did you buy the bottle of Sauternes?

FRANCIS:

Was Nikolai asking you about this? What a bloody nuisance. Why does he care so much about other people's affairs? I didn't buy it anywhere. It was a gift.

ELIZABETH:

From?

FRANCIS:

My driver.

ELIZABETH:

You have a driver? Where, here in Italy?

FRANCIS:

No, in Edinburgh. I often like to get out of the city, up into the Highlands, for inspiration. I've no inclination to have my own car, it's just easier to call the old boy up and organise it.

ELIZABETH:

Not many drivers would know a good bottle from a bad bottle.

FRANCIS:

He doesn't have a clue about wine, but he has a good memory. I was talking about it over the summer and, well, he remembered it. Anyway, I thought we were going to talk about the three horrible murders that have happened. Have you solved it yet?

ELIZABETH:

Sally's not dead yet.

FRANCIS:

No, but they're getting ready to open the pearly gates for her, right?

ELIZABETH:

You're enjoying this, aren't you?

FRANCIS:

Enjoying an over-privileged, dysfunctional and highly toxic group of people who call themselves a family coming apart at the seams? What's to enjoy about that? *(Chuckles)*

ELIZABETH:

You don't really mean that. I saw how you made Thomas eat the bread and cheese when he came in from the boat this morning. Watched you get a hankie for Polly. You've been lurking in the background like a helpful little owl, haven't you? You've loved every minute of it.

FRANCIS:

Hardly, I—

ELIZABETH:

Because despite what is en vogue in the world of philosophy, or how jolly trendy it might seem to be cool and detached, you're most likely a decent sort of fellow who happens to have a big mouth.

FRANCIS:

I don't think I'm that self-aware, so I'll trust you on that, Elizabeth. Mind if I smoke?

ELIZABETH:

Not at all . . . There are matches on the mantelpiece. Behind the holly.

ELIZABETH:

I don't believe him for a second about that bottle of wine! What a ridiculous story. To think that a taxi driver would have the money to pay for or the inclination to locate an expensive vintage. So he stole it from Sally, after searching through her bags. But then he drank it in front of her. And she denied he had stolen it. Her reluctance to incriminate him confirms something: what is the connection between Francis and Sally? The motives for theft are almost as complicated as the motives for murder. The belief that no one will notice, however, that your victim has so much that they couldn't possibly miss the item, seems to trump reason. It did for Francis. But there is more to it. Sally confirmed something to him through her lack of reaction. Now, are they even his cigarettes?

ELIZABETH:

Out of interest, Francis, what brand are they?

FRANCIS:

Player's. Go on, you know you want one.

ELIZABETH:

No, thanks. Now. Where did you go after the main course yesterday?

FRANCIS:

Eh, when Jonty was killed? I was sitting wondering where dessert was like everyone else.

ELIZABETH:

No, you certainly weren't. You had left the table, so where did you go? With a female of your own age? With whom it's likely there are some romantic feelings – am I right?

FRANCIS:

With young Mary Caswell-Jones? I don't think so.

ELIZABETH:

Why did you use that name, Mary, instead of Polly?

FRANCIS:

To help remember it, Elizabeth. You told me Mary Caswell-Jones was Polly's real name, remember? That's what you do when you want to remember something, repeat it over a few times. Well, *I* wasn't having any sort of affair with anyone here.

ELIZABETH:

The way you phrased that – with the emphasis on the 'I' . . . you're thinking of who else is having an affair here . . . you knew Thomas had been seeing Sally, didn't you?

FRANCIS:

(Coolly) Was he? Oh, that's why . . .

ELIZABETH:

What is it?

FRANCIS:

Nothing. I don't know if I would believe Thomas and Sally . . . But Thomas doesn't know how to keep his mouth shut. You can imagine the detail he likes to boast about. But for the record, I have no interest in either of his sisters. It's true, I did leave the table. I knew Catherine was struggling – all those courses. I just went down to the kitchen every so often to help out with the chopping, prepping, that sort of thing. It's meditative, that sort of drudgery. And Catherine didn't mind me smoking. So I went down . . . eh, I don't know why I'm telling you this.

ELIZABETH:

Essentially, you're a decent human who has grown extremely tired of the prolonged stress engendered by this current case, and your desire to elucidate a conclusion outweighs your loyalty to your friend . . . or something like that?

FRANCIS:

Aye. Anyway, all the hard work was done, I thought; the porchetta, the pasta, the primi and secondi, wrapped up. Didn't know what was taking her so long . . . so I went downstairs to the kitchen. But she wasn't there. The sugar on the lemon cake was starting to burn. I checked the clock; it was twenty past three – she must have left it in for an hour. So, I had a look outside the back door; no sign of Catherine, but I did see your precious Polly, or should I say I heard her, down on the deck to the boathouse. She was telling someone to *(in Polly's accent)* 'Get off', that it wasn't 'the time or the place'. There was a scuffling noise, so I went back inside in case they saw me.

ELIZABETH:

Who was she with?

FRANCIS:

I never got to see. Next thing you know, I heard Catherine scream.

ELIZABETH:

You mean Flora. You heard Flora scream.

FRANCIS:

Whatever – Flora. It is pretty difficult to distinguish one woman's scream from another, isn't it?

ELIZABETH:

You seem to have considered this.

FRANCIS:

I have, only because the others were talking about it. And I realised it is difficult to distinguish the two.

ELIZABETH:

Quite right. Has there been much speculation about who the killer is amongst the other guests?

FRANCIS:

I mean, everyone was giving Ludlow a wide berth when we were all shut up in the dining room. There was some sort of disagreement between him and Thomas.

ELIZABETH:

Was this before or after Argento read the will?

FRANCIS:

Before, of course. But good Lord, that will. I mean, it seems very suspicious that it was changed so soon before his . . .

ELIZABETH:

Let us come back to that. Isn't it true that Jonty forbade you from coming here?

FRANKIE:

Thomas wouldn't listen to his father even if that was true. Why do you say that? I'm not that bad an influence on his son.

ELIZABETH:

Well, Thomas used to stay in the private and comfortable butler's room, until his parents found out about the two of you. You are in a relationship with the victim's son.

FRANCIS:

Maybe so, but that doesn't mean I killed the man.

ELIZABETH:

But your lover's father wanted him to settle down, find a decent girl and get ready to line up another heir to the estate. Why else would he hold onto the Deb Guide of 1953 and, in fact, write Thomas's name on it? But then he uncovered your relationship and realised the first step would be getting rid of you. He sent a lengthy telegraph to your publisher in Edinburgh. He was angry enough to send it while sailing across the Atlantic. Such a communication would cost an inordinate amount of money, even for someone wealthy like Jonty.

FRANCIS:

Yes, he seems to follow the Marquess of Queensbury's school of parenting. And I dislike violence as much as Wilde. My publisher has no problem . . . with me. And Thomas didn't care what his father thought. It's the 1950s, for Christ's sake.

ELIZABETH:

You have my sympathies. However, it's still illegal, and a convicted criminal is banned from working in certain regulated industries, such as finance. Jonty was willing to sacrifice his son's happiness to protect the family name. So he drafted a new will, isn't that correct? So when Jonty saw you arrive on Christmas Eve, he was quite beside himself with rage, knowing you could ruin all the plans he had laid out. That's the reason why you followed him into his study on Christmas Day, isn't it? To have it out with him, knowing full well that he had immense heart trouble, that a single raised voice would be enough to kill him.

FRANCIS:

A chap that at risk of death ought not to visit a train station or a grocery market if a loud holler is all it would take. I very much doubt a jury would accept that as a murder weapon. Anyway, so what? I did go after him, after he humiliated me on Christmas Eve, telling everyone, 'Oh that's not a half-decent bottle of wine' . . . that it was stolen from the cellar . . . digs at me all night. So I went to him yesterday, to discuss the matter plainly. I'm not stupid, Elizabeth. I always did expect Thomas would find himself a pretty wee lass for propriety's sake. I knew that the old will had a condition that he must be married to inherit all as it stands. That Thomas would advance into the bright light of day, into the world of the ordinary person, as the shadows overgrew me. I am black on the inside. He is white, he is day, I am night.

But then I heard that Jonty had banned me from seeing him, had him posted abroad for that very reason, all of this . . . interference. And that's what bothered me, you know. We are all here to make our own path . . . Thomas can't stand up to him. They're both blinded by the same weaknesses and biases. It takes an outsider to call time on it. I decided to lay it out to him: that until Thomas decided otherwise, I would be there. A good friend, company in the night. Yes, I was angry Jonty called my publisher. They may be understanding, but there's plenty who are not.

ELIZABETH:

Do you care what people think of you?

FRANCIS:

I don't worry about myself . . . but I need to fight for my ideas, to ensure they reach as large an audience as possible. I am merely a vehicle to deliver the theories. Newspapers, critics, they all might decide not to discuss the ideas; I don't want to become the story. But I suppose now this bloody series of murders will become the story.

ELIZABETH:

It's not living very authentically, is it? And notoriety leads to more book sales, surely?

FRANCIS:

The ideas are authentic, oh, that they are . . . but I am just the person to deliver them.

ELIZABETH:

Well, why don't you marry a nice wee lass, too, then? Settle down into the bright light of day, as you put it?

FRANCIS:

You're beginning to focus on the rhetoric of the argument here, Elizabeth. I called him out for ruining his son's happiness, for denying him the chance to be himself . . . he got angry, briefly, for a minute, but his anger wasn't directed at me. It was directed at my situation, because it was one he had known himself. Poor chap broke down, explained how he went so far out of his way to put Thomas on the straight and narrow, tried to separate us . . . all of that because he knew the pain of living in the shadows. He told me he had married Catherine to perpetuate the Caswell-Jones line . . . but hid his true self. That's why he goes off travelling so much – or should I say, why he went off travelling. To South America. He can be himself that far away from home, if you know what I mean. Oh, do take that look off your face, Elizabeth, you're hardly an old prude.

ELIZABETH:

But why would he seek to cast his son into the same false life he had experienced?

FRANCIS:

I don't have any children, so I couldn't tell you. We had our discussion, he was embarrassed that he had broken down, but I still felt— How can I describe . . .? The burden of his relief at having told me . . .

ELIZABETH:

About South America—?

FRANCIS:

No, that is only my supposition, but I expect it to be true. Jonty was a man who carried his secret heavily. After he uttered those words – his confession, if you like – the last beat of winter sun streamed across his desk and it was as if his body grew taller, as if a heavy backpack had been removed. I swore not to tell Thomas, a promise that I intend to honour even now. But despite the lightness following his revelation, I watched his eyes . . . and there remained a sadness. Of something he could not tell. There was something else he was hiding . . . and I wish he had managed to free himself of it before he died.

ELIZABETH:

How long did all of this take?

FRANCIS:

I couldn't have been in there more than ten minutes before Catherine knocked on the door. She was surprised to see me. I suspect she understood what had been said between us. She asked me to go and whip some cream whilst she spoke to her husband. She said once the cream was whipped, I should call everyone to sit down again. So off I went, back to the kitchen, trying to get my head around what it meant for Thomas and me. Jonty could hardly continue to object to our seeing one another, especially if Thomas agreed to marry one day.

ELIZABETH:

Did Catherine come back to the kitchen before you heard her scream?

FRANCIS:

No, I was in there. Have you any idea how long it takes to whip cream for twelve puddings?

ELIZABETH:

Eleven puddings. There were just eleven of you yesterday.

FRANCIS:

No, we had twelve plates for everything –oh, wait. Argento. Yes, there was an empty plate. Catherine was convinced he was just about to arrive, and that he must be catered for. She was antsy about that all afternoon, even sending me to check the bridge for any sign of him. But he never came.

ELIZABETH:

Did you eavesdrop on Catherine and Jonty before you went down to whip the cream?

FRANCIS:

Och, I tried, but she'd been careful to close the door fully and his desk is the other side of the room – and the crowd next door were boisterous, all that booze.

ELIZABETH:

Okay. Thank you for your honesty. I've heard enough. Will you help me, please? Will you tell Sally to come and speak to me?

FRANCIS:

So you don't have to go outside and mess up your hair in the wind? You're not the only one paying attention here. Aye, I will, Elizabeth Chalice.

ELIZABETH:

One more thing, Frankie. Did you not know Thomas was having that . . . flirtation with Sally Lansdowne de Groot?

FRANCIS:

Oh that. Silly twit seems to have a penchant for toying with the affections of old dears. I do hope she doesn't get too fond of him.

ELIZABETH:

Wait, Apollo, before you go, who do you think killed Jonty?

FRANCIS:

No one. Or any one of them. But you know what? I'm glad he's dead. Not for us, but that man was swathed so deep in secrets, at least he is free of them now. Goodbye, Elizabeth.

ELIZABETH:

Francis and Catherine. One of them is lying, but who? Francis must have been furious at Jonty for contacting his publisher. I am sure Frankie's spiel about his publisher being understanding is not true. My husband Charlie— I shall tell you what happened to him another time, but I will tell you this: Charlie read a great deal of philosophical and religious texts, and Philosopher's Press Publishing was not what one might describe as liberal. They will certainly drop Frankie. Funny that he lied to me about their reaction. He does not want to be considered a suspect because of it. But he has been put through so much by the Caswell-Joneses. That, along with Jonty seeking to surgically remove Frankie from his son's life, are both strong motives for murder, don't you think? And was Frankie really not bothered by Thomas's dalliance with Sally?

Or do we believe Catherine, the long-standing wife? Did she know her husband's secret? Had she accepted him, complicit from the start, or just been surprised to discover such a thing? Theirs did not seem to be a warm match . . . but one of convenience, still. And why would Catherine not mention that Francis was with Jonty so soon before he died? By Frankie's account, Catherine could have easily killed her husband, then remained there to scream. But then, her daughter did claim to follow her into the study when she found the body. Again, strange that mother and daughter would have different accounts of the very same moment.

Oh, it is a long afternoon. What I would not give for a fresh, unpoisoned packet of cigarettes as I sit to work out the motives of our two final suspects, Sally and Argento. Come back to me later, and we'll see if we have a third death to investigate.

EPISODE 11

Sally Lansdowne de Groot

ELIZABETH:

Ordinarily I would spend the days post-Christmas enjoying the local delicacies, snoozing by the fire and taking a break from the busy office where I clerk. I suspect this bears a closer resemblance to your situation than my own at present. Murderers tend to pick inconvenient times and places to do their work, in order to maximise their chances of evasion.

The veil between this world and the next thins in the night. They say the soul slips from the body of the dying once the sun sets. As darkness climbs the brow of the hills overlooking Villa Janus, I am getting more and more eager to find our killer. I do not want to spend the night here with a murderer on the loose. The scent of Matilda in my room ... Something makes me think these departed Caswell-Joneses may not have completely left the villa. It pains me to think of their deaths. Their souls were torn violently from this world. The soul of a killer has a sort of blackness about it. I can see this all across Europe, in Italy or in England, the half-shadow that lurks over the shoulders of the men who killed others in the war.

Death touched us all with those stinging black tendrils, and here it is, returned to what should be a place of sanctuary. A place of retreat. There is darkness about each of the ten suspects I have interviewed. With two left, who do you think has the strongest motive for murder? Yes, I'm speaking to you again. Did you think you were just here to listen and go about your own business? Your deductions can help me, believe it or not.

As we approach the end of the investigation, I feel it is useful to split our suspects into two broad groups. Family and friends. Statistically, it is far more likely for a murderer to be a relative of his or her victim. Five of our suspects were related to Jonty. We have Jonty's wife, Catherine; his banker son, Thomas; daughters Polly the artist and schoolgirl Flora; and his mother, Finnish heiress Matilda, who herself was murdered earlier this morning. I'm certain this second murder was unplanned but considered necessary by the killer to cover their tracks.

And then we have the friends of the Caswell-Jones family. I use the term pejoratively, of course, for I have found little sign of true friendship as I've interviewed this group of seven. Nikolai Ivanov is a strange addition to the party. Invited by Matilda, the former ballet star from Russia is ignored by the other family members. But I believe he holds the key to the family's painful past. Time will tell us more. I am not quite finished with him, I think. The woman Catherine selected as godmother for all three of her children, the matronly Margaret Horton: barely able to conceal her dislike for Jonty, she had him over a barrel in more than one way. Peter Smythson is connected to the family as a neighbour, and as the admirer of Jonty's youngest daughter Flora. The Olympic athlete's erratic behaviour worries me, too. And what do I think of Francis Heath, close friend of Thomas Caswell-Jones? Jonty just ruined his career by revealing his sexuality to his conservative publishers.

Ludlow Lansdowne de Groot calls himself the victim's best friend, although he was surely exploiting Jonty financially. Which leaves our final two suspects, Argento di Silva and Sally. Now ... Argento can't quite be considered a friend of the family, as a paid member of staff. How confusing. He also seems to act as Jonty's butler in organising travel for the family. We certainly need to dig a little deeper there, wouldn't you say?

But now, we turn our attention to Sally, Jonty's oldest friend and wife of Ludlow. She did break off an engagement to marry our victim's best friend. But do we know that for certain? Couldn't Jonty have ended it? And is that ancient history in the complicated rat-run of Jonty's life or a deadly issue?

Now, Ludlow's claims that he tried to kill his wife to be with me ... It just doesn't seem true. You might have wondered why I did not intervene, ask the Italians to arrest him ... It's simply because I can't imagine him actually doing it. Ever since I have known him, he has refused to get his hands dirty. He even refused to light the fire in my apartment. He likes to act as a marauding gangster, but in fact he has no substance to support that affectation. I do not believe he really tried to kill his wife.

Oh dear ... Sally ... she does look frightened, with a two-inch gash to her temple. Here we go. Let's be gentle.

ELIZABETH:

We will take things slowly, Sally, don't worry. If you need to stop or slow down, just let me know.

CATHERINE:

Perhaps I should stay with her. Do we really need to do this now?

ELIZABETH:

I need to interview Sally alone, but do stay nearby in case we need you. Don't worry, Sally, this won't take long.

CATHERINE:

Right, don't tax her too much, she has had a serious head injury. I'll be in Flora's room, next door.

ELIZABETH:

Is that okay, Sally?

SALLY:

(Weakly, with a slight slur) Yes, I suppose.

(Catherine closes the door)

ELIZABETH:

Are you in much pain? We thought you were going to die.

SALLY:

Peter's medicine has helped.

ELIZABETH:

Do you know Peter is a drug addict? Strange, really, for an Olympic athlete.

SALLY:

Damned convenient if you have a bad fall like me. Oh, let me sit up a bit. Well, he used to pick and choose it; for the last Olympics he managed to wean himself off the majority before being tested . . . but I don't think he will be capable this time. And have you seen him exert himself? He's not terribly fit at all. That's why he goes out there at midnight. To take the drugs.

ELIZABETH:

Ah, yes, his sailing trips under the cover of darkness. He must be desperate for privacy. How well do you know his family?

SALLY:

His father, Peter Senior, is my accountant, and I was born halfway between Avonlea and the Smythson home. I've known the family longer than anyone else in this villa, now that Jonty and Matilda are dead. But what is the matter at hand for us to discuss?

ELIZABETH:

I'd like to ask you about what happened to you this evening.

SALLY:

Terribly silly of me – an accident, the floor was so slippy, I had been sipping the Montepulciano . . . I don't know, I just found myself flat out on the ground.

ELIZABETH:

Do you honestly mean that? That you just slipped and gashed your head open like that? How many glasses of wine did you drink?

SALLY:

I am ashamed to admit . . . I had been drinking most of the day, really. It's been so tense, I just needed a release.

ELIZABETH:

You seemed very fresh earlier – you know, when you were *insisting* on leaving.

SALLY:

Oh, I'm used to putting on a good show. Ludlow will tell you that.

ELIZABETH:

It's not the first time he's done something like this, is it?

SALLY:

What are you suggesting, Elizabeth? *(Momentary pause)* Oh dear,
you don't really think Ludlow would do something . . .? Ha-ha.
Good Lord, Elizabeth, I thought you had a bit more sense than
that. Let me tell you a secret about Ludlow. Like me, he knows how
to put on a good show too. In his case, he plays the role of this
wolfhound . . . but in fact, he's very meek. You'd only need to look
at the chap's investment choices to see how risk-averse he is. No, I
would never let him get away with that sort of thing. Ouch.

ELIZABETH:

Are you okay? Is it pounding?

SALLY:

I'm fine, just a bit of a thud. If I suspected for a moment that someone was after me, I would not by lying here, I can tell you that
much.

ELIZABETH:

Do you think Ludlow could have killed his best friend, or Matilda?

SALLY:

I've been thinking of that since it happened. Ludlow had fallen out
with the family, you know. I was surprised Ludlow accepted the
invitation . . . so I thought it had all blown over. He'd never kill his
best friend. Not intentionally. If he wanted anyone dead, he would
have paid someone to do the hands-on work. But – and I'm sure it
won't surprise you – the disagreement was over financial matters. I
had hoped it would have been all resolved before we arrived here,
but they did have an argument on Christmas Eve. We arrived terribly late. No help. Frost in our room. Jonty was never the best host,
you know. Matilda would have had open fires roaring in all the
bedrooms, local chaps to help with the luggage and a full twelve-
course meal. That was Catherine's doing, of course. She insisted
that this year she would not play second fiddle to Matilda. That
times were changing; we would all want something more casual.

What a load of tosh. But where was I? I am rambling. It's just hard to keep on the same train of thought—

ELIZABETH:

Take your time, you've probably been concussed. I am sorry to put you through this now, but I knew I had better speak to you when it's all still fresh. Ludlow lent Jonty some money, was it?

SALLY:

Oh no, Jonty had lent twenty thousand pounds to Ludlow. You asked if Ludlow could have done this to me. He wishes. The balance of power between us is quite the opposite. For a stockbroker, he's useless with managing his own cash. I've quite the upper hand financially. There was something going on with some gambling club. Ludlow is always complaining about money.

ELIZABETH:

Right, okay. That explains a few things. Now, I know you're tired, but I will be quick. Let me throw all of my questions at you.

SALLY:

Yes, that sounds about right, I've heard this is how you do it. From Catherine. You know she was just preparing me.

ELIZABETH:

Is that so? Now, tell me, what were you rowing about with Ludlow? When you arrived.

SALLY:

We were rowing? Who told you that? I don't recall that . . . But you know how stressful travel is, and then arriving in here with such a cold reception . . . Ludlow and I tend to keep our disagreements private.

ELIZABETH:

Tell me, did you know that your room is fitted with a microphone that sends sounds through a tube up to a room for the butler upstairs?

SALLY:

How interesting, I didn't know that. But I'm not surprised. Ludlow told me there's all sorts of hidden things in Villa Janus. The hint is in the name. There's a vent down in the kitchen where you can hear most of the conversation in the dining room, too. All to help the myriad staff who used to serve here, I'm sure. Who is up in that room there now? Thomas likes it up there; he says it's as if he's sailing a ship.

ELIZABETH:

Usually, yes, but this week it is Nikolai. Aren't you worried about being overheard?

SALLY:

I'm not guilty of anything, so why would I worry? In fact, I'm glad we were overheard. A woman my age . . . never mind. Are we nearly finished? My head is getting sore.

ELIZABETH:

Bear with me. Who did you sit beside for Christmas lunch?

SALLY:

Jonty and, um, Thomas.

ELIZABETH:

Witnesses have said Ludlow turned his back on the table throughout lunch. What was the disagreement about?

SALLY:

Did they? I didn't notice that . . . Jonty and Ludlow spoke on the telephone an awful lot, you know, so I think perhaps they were just more interested in the other guests – they didn't need to speak to each other. But yes, their financial disagreement – the business about the loan wasn't wholly resolved.

ELIZABETH:

And sitting to your . . . left was Thomas. Are you close with Thomas?

SALLY:

Close? What . . . *(Coldly)* Oh. Someone was lurking in the shadows.

ELIZABETH:

Polly told me. But you should really be more careful.

SALLY:

We're not all experts, you know. Look, no one died, did they? Oops,
I didn't mean—

ELIZABETH:

What were you retrieving from your suitcase – the large one that
hadn't been carried upstairs – on Christmas Eve, before the
dinner?

SALLY:

From my suitcase? Hmm . . . oh yes, a book. I had finished what I
was reading on the train and wanted to get to Mr Heath's work
before meeting him for the first time. Not very interesting, I'm
afraid.

ELIZABETH:

You were looking for the bottle of wine, weren't you? The bottle of
wine that Thomas had given to you during your own private gift
exchange. I presume it happened a little like this, but correct me if
I am wrong. You met on the landing, when Thomas went up to his
room, he gave you this extravagant bottle of wine. Not one for
sentimentality, you warned Thomas that you would give the wine
to the host. So you toddle downstairs to say hello to everyone,
leaving the wine with the rest of your bags in the entrance hall.
Where Francis finds it, and takes it. Nikolai is close by and sees
him do it, so there is even a witness. Nikolai didn't realise until he
knocked it with his elbow. When it fell on the floor Nikolai saw the
label. Sauternes. He accused Frankie of stealing from you, right
there, in front of everyone. But you pretended it was just a coincidence, didn't you? That he hadn't taken it at all? Why did you do
that, Sally? Because Thomas had given it to you as a love token

and you didn't want that to get out, or to encourage him, isn't that correct?

SALLY:

That bloody bottle of wine must be cursed. I didn't make a fuss at dinner because why would I? It was an expensive bottle of wine, but what difference does it really make to me? I have plenty of money and had plenty of other gifts.

ELIZABETH:

You knew about Thomas's relationship with Francis, didn't you?

SALLY:

Oh dear. Don't forget you were young once and had secrets, too, Elizabeth. I suppose I did know, but I didn't want to acknowledge it to myself. Their strange set up. In fact, I thought that perhaps Frankie had got wind of our dalliance and that he was looking through my bags for proof . . . of our affair. Either that or the fellow was flat broke and wanted a drink! It's nothing, really, a total diversion. And there is nothing of note between Thomas and me either, for the record. A passing flirtation . . . you might call it. A kiss here and there when no one is looking. Really, I should be better behaved at my age. I tell you, I've jolly well learned my lesson now. It wasn't worth all of this trouble!

ELIZABETH:

But why was Nikolai so bothered about the wine?

SALLY:

I barely know the chap, Elizabeth. But I think he views himself as the scales of justice – eager to enforce law and order.

ELIZABETH:

Hmm. And what does your husband think of your affair with Thomas? Tell me, Ludlow is clearly very passionate about ensuring the best for his godson. Does that bother you?

SALLY:

What? Why would that bother me? We have no children, something I know one should pretend to be very down about, but I was pleased. Thomas has fulfilled that role for my husband.

ELIZABETH:

It's not the first time you've disappointed the Caswell-Joneses, though, is it? Matilda was very disappointed that you didn't marry Jonty. Margaret seems to think that you ended things with him, but what actually happened?

SALLY:

Oh that! You're actually considering that as a genuine line of inquiry? It was *years* ago, Elizabeth. What about Nikolai, the flat-broke Russian ballerina? Or Polly's huge family argument about bloody university? You really think a three-week fling thirty years ago is motive enough for me to murder him? One of my oldest friends? Jonty, William and I all grew up together. In those days our nannies would take us to this wonderful little pond, to sail boats or watch the water lilies bloom. It was the picture of perfection, really, I doubt anyone could have a nicer childhood.

But as the boys grew, William's favour with Matilda really became very obvious. Once their father died, Matilda almost forgot altogether about Jonty. She would even leave him in school when she took Will out for day trips here and there. It was heartbreaking to see. He was a very sullen chap, so when we were seventeen, I said it, you know, to make him feel better. Asked if he would marry me. The idea really got him excited. But he took it too seriously . . . And suddenly, things began to move rather quickly, although my mother still wanted me to debut with the other ladies. Everyone seemed dead set on it being the right thing, apart from me. And then, because it had been me suggesting it . . . well, it was rather difficult to step back. Let's just say I learned a lesson about trying to be nice. It doesn't really pay off. After that, well, I was never that nice again.

ELIZABETH:

Yes, okay, thank you, Sally. Well, you do look jolly pale, I think it's time to leave it there and let you rest—

SALLY:

What is it, Elizabeth? I can see your face; something has clicked in that terrific little brain of yours. Oh, I do feel exhausted.

ELIZABETH:

Reader, I have just seen something worth noting. But I don't want Sally to realise that I've seen it. She's having a big yawn, so I'll tell you what she has beside her. It's Frankie's book, and on the front page it's signed, but it's not just signed, there's an inscription here. It is dark and rather hard to make out. 'Sumptuous Sally,' is about all I can see. Hmm. Who signed it though, the author, or someone else? Oh quick, back to it.

ELIZABETH:

Ha, no, I mean, my eyes are a little tired, it's been a long day. That's all. But let me ask you one last thing. Is your marriage, um, all right? Do you think he could have—

SALLY:

I already told you I know he's having an affair. That bill for a fur stole. But the strangest thing, they charged for two of the exact same item. Either the exacting Mr Gales of Mayfair made a mistake or he has two girls on the go. *(Laughing)*

ELIZABETH:

Thank you, Sally, that has been most helpful . . . Let me feel your head . . . Yes, you're a little warm but fine. I will leave you to rest. Can I get you anything? Are you thirsty?

SALLY:

(Dismissive) Quite all right, Catherine is taking great care of me. I'll get a good night's rest and we will be on the road in the morning. *(Coldly)* I'm sure you'll have solved the case by then. Good evening, Elizabeth.

(Door closes)

ELIZABETH:

I jolly well hope to confront our killer this evening, for I don't think I could suffer another sleepless night with a murderer on the prowl. I must find Flora . . . I need to run something by her. Have you figured it out yet? What do you think then, did Sally really have an accident? Or was she so drunk she didn't realise someone had shoved her. Ludlow is pathetic, to claim an attack like that. Of course, he just wanted to use it to force my hand. All that talk about getting married.

Sally really spoke in vino veritas, *didn't she? I did have more questions to ask her, but it wasn't worth putting her through any more right then – she was looking very wan. I don't think she does suspect my dalliance with her husband . . . but she's quite right. Her little dig about how she isn't an expert at having an affairs . . . I'm sure she was aiming at me. She could be referring to James Beresford, or one of the other dogs I've taken for a walk. She was quite right about Ludlow as a wolfhound. Underneath it, he is nothing but a weak little weasel.*

As the storm diminishes the last dregs of afternoon light, it won't be long until nightfall. Matilda's body will be turning as cold as the waters of Lake Como down in the wine cellar. I can still smell her perfume in my room, the sickly-sweet smell. How did it come to be there? When I nursed the dying soldiers during the war some said that the hearing was the last sense to go, but I think smell *is so evocative. There is something otherworldly about the stench of Matilda's perfume in my room. It is a sight too close to the odour of human decomposition. That's too close to reality for you, especially after the large lunch of Christmas leftovers you may have just enjoyed, isn't it? I imagine you're shouting at the speaker. Well, mix another negroni, everything is going to happen rather quickly from here on—*

CATHERINE:

Who are you talking to Elizabeth?

ELIZABETH:

Oh, I didn't see you . . . standing in the shadows there.

CATHERINE:

Sorry to frighten you. How is Sally?

ELIZABETH:

Tired. She's resting. Where has Flora gone?

CATHERINE:

It won't be long until we are surrounded by the pitch-black night. So how are you getting on? Have you earned my five hundred pounds yet, and found my husband's murderer?

ELIZABETH:

I am very close, I just need to make some final investigations with Argento—

CATHERINE:

But he wasn't even here. What on earth—?

ELIZABETH:

Just a few minor details. Now, if you don't mind . . . where is Flora?

CATHERINE:

I'd like to know who you suspect to be the killer, please. My three children are in this villa, and they are currently in danger. I need to know.

ELIZABETH:

Oh, I'm not quite ready to say—

CATHERINE:

Answer me. This is no joke, Elizabeth. You might live recklessly, but I have children to protect. Friends I am responsible for. I will not have another body to answer for.

ELIZABETH:

If you're referring to what happened to the Conte boy . . .

CATHERINE:

Yes, you've never quite explained it to me.

ELIZABETH:

How many times must I repeat myself? The kidnappers asked for unmarked notes . . . but Mrs Conte couldn't bear the thought that they would get away with taking their boy. When she took the money out of the bank, she included a batch of marked lira . . . the kidnappers must have seen it . . . or, you know, kidnappings can get messy . . . it sometimes can be easier to . . . put an end to things . . .

CATHERINE:

The papers made out like it had been your fault . . .

ELIZABETH:

Well, I wasn't going to make things worse for Mrs Conte . . .

CATHERINE:

How very noble of you, Elizabeth. Now, to the matter at hand . . . who is it then? Who killed Jonty?

ELIZABETH:

Okay. If you have to push me, I think it might have been a man, but I am not willing to say any more . . . Okay?

CATHERINE:

Ludlow. He's the killer. It would all make sense. Or Nikolai? He seems a troubled sort. Peter is one of our oldest family friends, I doubt he would—

ELIZABETH:

I will explain it all very shortly, but please, will you tell me where Flora is?

CATHERINE:

In her bedroom, she's in her bedroom, okay? Come back to me, I have something else to tell you.

(Elizabeth's footsteps)

ELIZABETH:

Talk about putting one on the spot. Are you shocked to hear me say it's a man? Do you agree? The truth is I'm not certain, not yet, but I had to put her off the scent. But I am guessing that the fellows are currently the most dangerous in the villa. And that's all Catherine needs to concern herself with now. Safety.

(Elizabeth's footsteps. Knock on the door)

ELIZABETH:

Flora, can I come in? It's Elizabeth. Hello?

(Door creaks open. Wind howling through the window)

ELIZABETH:

Good God, it is freezing in here—

FLORA:

Shut the door. Is Mother still out there?

ELIZABETH:

What the—? Where are you going?

(Slams window shut)

FLORA:

I thought she would never leave. I'm getting out of this hell hole before I'm forced to watch any more of my family members die.

ELIZABETH:

Yes, but don't jump out the window, good God, he won't be able to catch you in that boat, and if you end up in the water you'll freeze.

FLORA:

I wasn't going to jump out the window, I was just looking out there. And don't think about trying to stop me—

ELIZABETH:

I wouldn't dream of coming between a seventeen-year-old runaway and a chap in his thirties. I was young once, too, you know. But you do know that Peter is addicted to opiates, don't you?

FLORA:

Peter is a lot of things, but he's not a killer and he's *not* a drug addict. He has old injuries that need to be treated. How did you know?

ELIZABETH:

You've been out in the boat with him at night, haven't you? I saw your Peregrine cardigan drying by the fire in the study after it had got wet. Peter was too keen to offer to take the boat out. I knew he had a plan. I knew you'd agree to go with him, away from the villa and all of this, the storm, the murders – well, it is the perfect distraction . . .

FLORA:

He really has gone for help, but he will be back soon. Do not interfere, please. You can see how dysfunctional my family is. Peter and I can start afresh. We deserve that. We've been trapped in this ridiculous Caswell-Jones drama for too long.

ELIZABETH:

What about Polly, your mother? Don't you think it's a little unfair to run out on them at this time?

FLORA:

Oh, they'll all survive.

ELIZABETH:

Oh, you're young, I suppose. You have a clean slate, really, decades of opportunities and potential and memories to make. And you know, people afford you a lot of slack when it comes to the first taste of life, loves.

FLORA:

Nobody has afforded me any slack; in fact, they just want to tie me up like a dog on a leash.

ELIZABETH:

But there is safety in that . . . I remember, it can all feel, well, rather intimidating, this great long canon of humanity, of freedom.

FLORA:

(Suspicious) I suppose. What do you want anyway, coming in here to tell me that youth is wasted on the young?

ELIZABETH:

Do sit down a minute, please, Flora. I have a waterproof mackintosh in my room, you can take it if you want. But you know . . . I would love a game of cards. Do you have that pack of playing cards around here?

FLORA:

It's hardly the time for cards, Elizabeth, but I will take you up on the offer of the mackintosh. This is worse bloody weather than in England.

ELIZABETH:

Humour me. We both need a break.

FLORA:

You are ridiculous. But fine, since Peter isn't back yet and the last thing I want to do is be near the rest of my family . . . I need something to take my mind off my worry, too – I am praying he makes it back safely. What shall we play? Switch?

ELIZABETH:

Twenty-one. Your favourite. Infallible Flora.

FLORA:

I'll deal. Here you go. Nine, ace.

ELIZABETH:

I'll stick, thanks.

FLORA:

Okay, for the house, queen of hearts, ace, twenty-one.

ELIZABETH:

Let me deal now. So, Flora, where will you both go? Don't worry, I shan't do anything to stop you – it's not my place. I just wanted to make sure you had someone to talk to . . . if you had any concerns . . . You've kept it all from your mother, from Polly?

FLORA:

Very well. To my father's pensione in Milan. It's empty, for the moment. Those two crones wouldn't understand. Nobody does. Well, go *on*, deal them to me.

ELIZABETH:

Here you go. Two, queen of hearts.

FLORA:

Hmmm, hit me.

ELIZABETH:

Ace of spades. Where after Milan?

FLORA:

It's your turn. The apartment in Milan – go on, lay it out.

ELIZABETH:

Very well, jack of clubs. Ace of hearts. That's twenty-one.

FLORA:

I don't believe it – how on earth? You do know—

ELIZABETH:

Yes, yes, that you've never lost a hand of cards before. Well, let me tell you this, Flora: in this life, you've been lucky enough to be dealt a clear run of good luck. Born to a loving family, a privileged position in society, pretty, intelligent. But your luck can sometime run out. I'm not telling you this to scare you . . . I have nothing but the best hopes for you. But it's time that you stop relying on good luck. Once upon a time, I was like you. I can't *tell* you how much you remind me of myself at your age. I married young. Too young, in fact. I was your age when I skipped down the aisle at St Clement's. Oranges and lemons. I was too young to know that a great love is damning. Because it damns you to the before, which you are currently in, and the after, when you're no longer in the midst of that great love. Nothing in your life will ever feel like this again – and the curse of it all is that you'll know exactly what you are missing. Sometimes love dies when two people outgrow one another or are cleft apart by the reaper's scythe.

FLORA:

Like you and Charlie—

ELIZABETH:

No, Flora. We don't know that Charlie is dead. I am not going to stop you from doing whatever you want. But my point is, you have a choice . . . even if you are happy and Peter jolly well takes care of you, which I expect he intends to do, to the best of his ability. A great love is a precious thing, it can never last forever. Once it's gone, you'll only have the memories to sustain you. Be careful, my child.

FLORA:

I will be.

ELIZABETH:

Just quickly, why did you go all the way to London to get Polly's stole?

FLORA:

Why, oh, well because I wanted to borrow it; not that strange is it?

ELIZABETH:

Perhaps, I forget how important these matters can be to a young lady.

FLORA:

It is beautiful, and was in a brand new box. Lucky thing.

ELIZABETH:

Okay, well, here's my address. I'm not far from where your father's apartment is, if you do need anything. Now, before I let you go, I have one more nugget of information I need from you. Margaret told me about this business with the boxer's wife. But she insists the weather was warm . . . Bear with me . . . However, Nikolai seems certain it was raining, that he waited in a phone box because the downpour was so heavy . . . which was it?

FLORA:

I don't recall it ever raining . . . Father and I always enjoyed strolling home afterwards, recounting the evening, but we would not have walked if it was wet. But I do remember one evening, it was raining. Could . . .

ELIZABETH:

What? What is it?

FLORA:

It was the first night to rain in months, I went to bed to fall asleep to the sound. When I woke up the next day, father had told me it hadrainedluck, thathe'dhadagiftofsomemoney. Itdidn'tmakesense—

ELIZABETH:

Could your father have been gambling someone else's money?

FLORA:

Well, he did run up large debts at the club. He was so concerned about being able to pay.

ELIZABETH:

Well, that doesn't quite add up. You see, from what I can tell of your father, his estate had plenty of money. Even if he was gambling the amounts you mentioned, he would still have had plenty of other . . . resources. So why was he getting so worried about it?

FLORA:

Who was he playing for then?

ELIZABETH:

Did you ever see Ludlow at the club?

FLORA:

No, he's a stockbroker . . . he's banned from gambling . . . or meant to be adhering to some code of honour . . . oh my, you think he was gambling Ludlow's money, don't you? And he lost it all . . . Do you think the beast killed Daddy?

ELIZABETH:

It's not that straightforward. But thank you, you've been very help-ful, my child. See those lights out there? That must be Peter now.

FLORA:

Thank you, Elizabeth, and tell me, please be honest with me, are you quite sure Peter didn't kill Daddy, or Granny? Or even Auntie Sally?

ELIZABETH:

Sally is doing well. But yes, I'm quite sure. Trust your own heart. Now, remember what I told you, okay? And you know where I am. And for goodness' sake, child, do not let yourself get into trouble.

FLORA:

Will you keep Mother occupied? I can go down the back stairs, past your room, and out that way.

ELIZABETH:

Fine, but before you go. What do you know about this betting slip?

(Elizabeth takes out Jonty's wallet and shows Flora the betting slip)

FLORA:

What on earth . . . that's for today's race. Did the horse win?

ELIZABETH:

No, but look at the stake, it's enormous. Why did he make this bet?

FLORA:

If you haven't figured that out by now, my father was a gambler. I thought he had used up his credit at the Mayfair Club, but my guess is they chalked this up for them. Now, I must go!

(Whispers) Bye! Good luck!

ELIZABETH:

Don't look at me like that, what did you expect? Someone has to have a happy ending. I'm a sucker for a love story. She's been spoilt for so long but deserves some happiness. Strangely, I think it will work out for the best. Flora needs to learn the lessons of running away. Peter needs the responsibility of having her as a young wife in order to bring him back to himself. It really is time to take stock . . . Catherine is in her room with Sally. Funny, the two never seemed to get on before now . . . but situations like these can cause strange happenings between the most normal of us all. Shall we see what they might be discussing? This might be the closest we can get to being a fly on the wall.

(Sound slightly muffled behind door)

CATHERINE:

I do think that old battleaxe is lucky she wasn't murdered a long time ago . . . Some of the stories I've heard from their childhood. Elizabeth is soft on Matilda because she knows *I* wouldn't have invited her here.

SALLY:

I don't know how you tolerated either of them, to be honest.
Elizabeth still looks to me like a fox in the headlights . . . She must
be out of her depth—

CATHERINE:

Now, now, let's just watch her methods unfold . . . Let's see if she's
worth a penny of what I'm paying her. I am getting quite famished
– has your appetite returned?

(Footsteps to the door, door opens)

CATHERINE:

What are you doing there, Elizabeth? Did you find Flora? Where
on earth has the child got to?

ELIZABETH:

Yes. She went to speak with Polly.

CATHERINE:

Has hell frozen over, too? Never have I seen a set of sisters so
distant . . . Anyway, how do you propose we manage supper?

ELIZABETH:

As long as we all stay in pairs, I think we shall be safe. You stay with
Sally. I'll recruit an assistant to bring some up to you.

(Door closes)

ELIZABETH:

*Right, come with me down these stairs. Here's my room. At the end of
the corridor, which is helpful, as it allows me to see who is going up
and down the back stairs. I'm six doors away from Catherine's room.
Flora has taken my jacket; that is a relief. I feel like I've helped her.
But she probably just thinks I'm a raving old bag. I know I would
have at her age. There is that smell again, in my room, that oudy
Matilda smell, her perfume, it's sickeningly sweet. Someone is playing
with me . . . This is a despicable group of liars, although some*

deceptions are unavoidable in life. Unearthing everyone's secrets is a dirty business. Wait, do you hear that? Sounds from Jonty's study. It's probably the wireless.

RADIO ANNOUNCER:

And finally, there was little competition for Galloway Braes at the King George VI Chase this afternoon at Kempton Park. Bert Morrow took him home, trained by Alec Kirkpatrick. It's the mare's first victory in the Christmas festival. A smaller field than intended with a few last-minute non-runners.

ELIZABETH:

Of course, the outsider wouldn't win that race. But the killer almost had me believe that Jonty put on a huge bet. The slip was false, of course, planted there by the murderer after they knew it would be me investigating. You didn't fall for that, did you? No bookmaker would have filled out a ticket for such a large bet. That rather changes things, doesn't it?

So, let's take stock of where we are at. We've now interviewed eleven potential suspects in the murder of Jonty Caswell-Jones. All but Argento, who wasn't here, he claims, so couldn't really be a suspect anyway. But we shouldn't believe that for a minute . . . One of those interviewed, the mother of the victim, Matilda Caswell-Jones, was found dead. I've agreed to let the victim's daughter, Flora, and her lover, Peter, leave the house to run away together. I appreciate not all detectives would allow suspects to abscond from the scene, but I don't believe either were involved in the deaths and I think she deserves a chance to get away, after all Catherine and Jonty have put her through. Don't you? Do you judge me?

Now from what I can see, in fact, the family have plenty of money, but I will need to look again. We've learned that Francis Heath is the lover of the victim's son and heir, Thomas Caswell-Jones. Francis insists that Jonty himself was a homosexual . . . in which case we must take another look at Catherine. Her turning up right behind me out in the landing . . . it was rather unnerving, as if she had been standing there in

*the dark. A final piece of the puzzle is the life insurance policy for Jonty.
I have not asked her directly, for I do not want to arouse additional
suspicion.*

(Creak on the stairs)

(Knock at the door)

ELIZABETH:

(Whispering) *Oh no. It is very dark in here . . . but I am quite in the
shadows. Oh, it is Polly, come to my room, with Matilda's perfume
bottle . . . she is trying to spook me. Now she is looking through my bag!
The little vixen . . . Wait, of course,* she *is the girl Ludlow is having an
affair with. The penny must just have dropped for her, too, and she's in
here looking for something . . . evidence perhaps. Well, she shan't find any.*
(Frantic whisper!) *Oh, quick, she's looking over here. I'd better be quiet.
Come back when I find Argento, and we can interview our twelfth and
final suspect.*

EPISODE 12

ARGENTO DI SILVA

ELIZABETH:

Dear reader, welcome back to this, the final interview with our twelfth suspect. Only eleven of the suspects are still alive, of course, now that Jonty's mother Matilda is sipping sherry with him on the other side. Deception runs in the blood of the Caswell-Joneses, and the secrets we have uncovered here are numbered enough to do any other family for a lifetime. And the level of detail to that treachery ... Eldest daughter Polly spraying the perfume of her deceased grandmother in my room to unnerve me. When I was a friend of the family, I came to this villa often. I knew Polly well, and often sat for hours to allow her sketch and draw me. But even a young woman like her is intent on disturbing my investigation however she can. Why would she do so? I can't quite imagine her as a killer, but as I unfortunately know first-hand, people often kill for reasons that make little sense.

Our final interview, this time with Argento di Silva. The family's butler, friend and disgraced former lawyer. Even the law-abiding can push past the boundaries of immoral behaviour, and a certified maverick is all the more lethal. Could this man be responsible for the death of his employer? It has been a long day, and I feel as though I have lived many weeks in the short time since I arrived at Villa Janus last night. My body and mind need nourishment, but I must dampen down those needs and proceed, as I look for one more motive. As you know – or at least you must take my word for it – our Argento really is a handsome devil, so I'd better not let myself get carried away.

ELIZABETH:

So, you were in Milan when Jonty died?

ARGENTO:

Yes, I was sorry to let down Catherine and Jonty . . . but my mother, she was sick – is sick; really, she is dying. I had to say my goodbyes.

ELIZABETH:

What's the matter with her?

ARGENTO:

She has a tumour; it has spread all over the body. She is without hope.

ELIZABETH:

I am sorry to hear that. Where in Milan does she live?

ARGENTO:

Eh, Strada Nuovo, the new apartments there. You live there, too, don't you?

ELIZABETH:

Yes, it's quite lovely there. Now tell me, were you in Villa Janus this week, before Jonty and Catherine arrived for their Christmas festivities?

ARGENTO:

Yes, I always come to open up the place at the start of December. I know Jonty and Catherine were travelling and expected that people might be arriving earlier in December. I would usually stay here to greet them . . . but not this time.

ELIZABETH:

So when did you leave?

ARGENTO:

I got the call from my mother's nurse – you know, to come and say goodbye – early on the twenty-second. Just before Jonty arrived. I had to leave a note, you know, to explain it – my absence. Otherwise they would have thought it unusual, worried about me.

ELIZABETH:

What did you do with the key to the villa?

ARGENTO:

I left it with *ufficiale* Rossi, his house is on the road, he would see Jonty arrive. Jonty called me once he had arrived and settled in. He was very understanding, told me not to come back.

ELIZABETH:

And your mother is still alive? Why did you leave her deathbed?

ARGENTO:

Well, when I heard Jonty died I had to come. You know, I was glad of the distraction . . . watching your mother die, well, it is difficult. The family here needed help with the arrangements, and I was asked to collect a document from the British Consulate.

ELIZABETH:

Who asked you?

ARGENTO:

Polly. Or was it Flora? I think the older one. She called me with the news that her father was murdered.

ELIZABETH:

What time was this?

ARGENTO:

Ah, I don't know for sure . . . The bells from the duomo were ringing six o'clock, I think. She sounded very upset, but organised. Yes, that's how I knew it was the elder daughter. The little one, Flora, she is more Italian than she is English, with all of the drama. Polly was very specific that I was to contact the secretary to collect the will. I could not get through to him, that was the delay. I would have come sooner.

ELIZABETH:

Didn't you think it was strange she would request the will in the same phone call to tell you her father had died?

ARGENTO:

Well, I, eh, not really – you know, I was in Milan anyway. I see why she wanted it straight away. I was just saving a later trip for them all, you see.

ELIZABETH:

It's only about sixty-five miles away, not the world's longest journey. Couldn't you have come immediately, to help the family, and gone back for the will once the shock had settled down?

ARGENTO:

Ah, yes, you know, maybe I could have, but time is of the essence, Polly told me. She was particularly anxious to see the will. And my mother . . . I had hoped to get back in time to see her. But that's not to be; with all that has happened here, I couldn't possibly leave. My family are not wealthy, there will be no big inheritance from my mother, so I have to keep my job here . . . with the family. Otherwise I would be working as a labourer, or as a shepherd or something.

ELIZABETH:

So, you manage the family's travel. And what else? It seems you do rather a lot for them. Isn't it rather difficult to make travel arrangements for the family from here, in Italy?

ARGENTO:

Not when you have a telephone – everything can be done with a good telephone!

ELIZABETH:

But the telephone line here is terrible, it's dropped at least twice since I arrived last night.

ARGENTO:

The lines are vulnerable in the bad weather in December because they must travel over or under the bridge. But I plan for that, you know, if I need to make a call, I can travel to Bellagio, the police station in the village. Then, if I need someone to collect tickets, currency, this sort of thing, I can arrange a local courier. And the rest of the year, I am in Milan, so this is not a problem.

ELIZABETH:

Where do you find these couriers?

ARGENTO:

I only use people who can be vouched for, but many Italians have left northern Italy since the end of the war, you know? There are plenty of my friends and neighbours who have moved abroad, to America, to England. Like Joe, he is married to my first cousin, who I have known all my life. It is a very trustworthy set-up I have.

ELIZABETH:

Joe is your courier in London, yes? What is your cousin's name?

ARGENTO:

My cousin's husband, yes. She is an Italian teacher. Why she went for Joe, I don't know. They don't earn much—

ELIZABETH:

London is an expensive city.

ARGENTO:

Yes, but there are enough rich people willing to pay for private tuition. Do you mind if I close these shutters?

ELIZABETH:

Em, no, I suppose it's good to keep the heat in.

ELIZABETH:

Quick – while he's yanking at the shutters there, let me have a minute alone with you. What a peculiar fellow Argento di Silva is. He is quite the dish, up close, although there is a peculiar smell, an earthy smell. Like he's been down in the cellar . . . Someplace under the villa. There had always been talk about these passageways, surely Argento would know this house inside out? If so, then he could well have been here at the time of the murder. I can't conclusively rule him out at this stage.

But first I'd better get a handle on what he actually did for Jonty. I didn't know Jonty terribly well – we just met a handful of times during my earlier stays here at Villa Janus – but he struck me as a wholly good sort of fellow. Now of course we know he had many secrets. But why would he want a disgraced lawyer to work for him? This I must get to the bottom of. Had Jonty criminal intentions? I understand well-organised criminals tend to recruit from the ranks of professionals who have been struck off from accountancy and law. The gang who took the Conte child . . . oh, to think of it . . . nobody was ever caught apart from Tamino, their accountant. All that expertise with none of the morals, is that what Jonty wanted Argento for? Perhaps I am overthinking it. He may just have wanted to give a break to a fellow war veteran. Jonty didn't have many friends . . . It seems Argento fulfilled the role of friend and companion along with the other hodgepodge. What's that you say? Oh yes, that is another possibility – perhaps they were lovers!

ARGENTO:

Anyway – you ask any of the family, there has never been a ticket or currency gone missing.

ELIZABETH:

I'm sure that is the case, Mr Di Silva. Now, as well as arranging travel, you also cook and provide legal advice? That's a lot of roles to fulfil, how do you like life as a gentleman's servant?

ARGENTO:

(Sharply) I am not a servant, I just . . . facilitate the Caswell-Joneses. I was involved in cooking when I was in the army. I don't love doing it, but it needs to be done.

ELIZABETH:

Still, it is quite a fall from the position of a lawyer, isn't it?

ARGENTO:

Perhaps, for someone who is shallow and places too much emphasis on job titles, positions, that sort of thing. Are you like that, Mrs Chalice?

ELIZABETH:

Not at all. Now, I know this might be uncomfortable, but how did you come to be banned from practising law after the war?

ARGENTO:

I broke it, that's all I want to say on the matter. I acted illegally, and then – no more lawyering for me.

ELIZABETH:

Was it a violent crime?

ARGENTO:

(Angry now) This is insufferable. Stop it. I did not murder Jonty if that's what you're getting at. Why on earth would I? Catherine will not need me to work for her anymore. Without Jonty . . . there will be no job.

ELIZABETH:

She doesn't like you, does she? Why is that?

ARGENTO:

She never has liked me. I don't know why.

ELIZABETH:

Most wives don't like their husband's lover.

ARGENTO:

Me? What on earth . . . you're not suggesting? That I was Jonty's lover? Ha-ha. Elizabeth, you have the wrong end of the— how do you say? I am getting my English idioms confused. Jonty and Catherine might not have seen much of each other, but I could see they loved one another, their family, their children. And I am not interested in men, neither was Jonty. I am interested in women.

ELIZABETH:

So you didn't know he also enjoyed the company of men?

ARGENTO:

I am not going to get into the secrets of my employer, Mrs Chalice.

ELIZABETH:

Don't you rather think that keeping secrets got Jonty murdered? If I am to have the full picture, you must tell me what you know.

ARGENTO:

I never saw anything for sure, you know. But I did wonder. And now that you say it . . . *(momentary pause)* well, maybe I am not surprised. But you know, I never saw a thing.

ELIZABETH:

What made you wonder?

ARGENTO:

He read a lot of Oscar Wilde.

ELIZABETH:

Good God, you can't really be serious? That doesn't mean anything.

ARGENTO:

Well, there was something else. When I called to the family in London, there was a dickie bow in Jonty's bag. I never saw him wear one, in all my years with the family. It must have belonged to some young fellow. I don't know. That's it – I don't recall a single other thing. Can we move on to another topic?

ELIZABETH:

Do you think anyone here may have been, let's say, entangled with Jonty?

ARGENTO:

Absolutely not, he told me everything . . . apart from that. So there's no way he would have taken the risk of being exposed. I told you, I didn't even know for certain that that was the case until you brought it up. He was a very discreet, quiet and gentle man.

ELIZABETH:

All right. Now, let's move on to another topic. You mentioned Flora is always causing drama, why do you say that?

ARGENTO:

Oh, you know, she is just hungry for life . . . A couple of months ago, I visited Jonty in London – August, I think it was. I try to visit the family at home once a year, get an idea of the trips they want to plan, buy currency, that sort of thing. Jonty wrote to me to come early, that he needed me to help him with something. Anyway, Flora, well, she . . . tried to kiss me one of the evenings. Her father walked in . . . I was so shocked it took me longer than I thought to push her away. Thank God Jonty had seen her in the mirror as he was walking in and he believed me, but she is *dangerous*. She is barely a woman yet, and me, more than twice her age. She really is quite stupid. It turns out she had been gambling with that lady . . . Margaret had been sneaking her into the Mayfair Club. We found out one night that we went there. Jonty did like to gamble, maybe a bit too much. He had got into the habit of bringing Flora with him at the start of the summer, but we found his line of credit had been cut off – the women had run it out. Jonty was very angry . . . but I don't know how hard he tried to stop it, you know? He told her not to go back, but he still gave her money to go shopping. He was not fully engaged with life at the time. You know, he was very worried about money, worried the business would fail, but he showed me the accounts; they looked to be in order.

ELIZABETH:

Did Flora ever come across your cousin, Joe?

ARGENTO:

Ah yes, another big drama! Joe is a big guy, he likes to fight. And he was taking on people in the club . . . Flora was betting big on him, according to my cousin, and then she got an infatuation with him – it was all such a mess, writing him letters. I was glad to be there because Jonty couldn't have managed on his own.

ELIZABETH:

I see. You know, when I interviewed Flora, she told me that it was Jonty who had brought her to the club every time, that he had insisted she was his lucky charm—

ARGENTO:

The child is delusional—

ELIZABETH:

That Jonty had sponsored a prize fighter, called Joe, who was seriously injured in a fight, and then his wife came to blackmail Jonty for money to feed her family. Was any of that true?

ARGENTO:

She said what? That my cousin would try to blackmail anyone . . . I mean, it is crazy. See, I told you she is dangerous – dangerous enough, she could have tried to kill her father . . .

ELIZABETH:

Her account was verified by Margaret.

ARGENTO:

Of course it was, they managed to keep the whole thing from Catherine. She would never have forgiven her for getting Flora involved in that situation.

ELIZABETH:

And also by Nikolai Ivanov.

ARGENTO:

Nikolai . . . oh yes, the Russian. What did he say?

ELIZABETH:

That he witnessed Margaret blackmailing Jonty one night after the casino.

ARGENTO:

Hmm. Well, you know that didn't happen. Jonty was approached by a Russian in the club, to give him more credit . . . but of course he turned it down. But I wonder if . . . No. It couldn't be . . .

ELIZABETH:

You think Flora had something to do with Jonty's death?

ARGENTO:

Well, no, wait, you know . . . why would Nikolai say that? If it never happened. Nikolai was in need of money . . . I overheard him ask Matilda for some cash. It was a total chance, really, that we were all there. Jonty had invited me to London during the summer. We were having lunch with Jonty in the Overseas Club, beside Green Park. Jonty had gone to the bathroom when we arrived, but I saw Matilda and Nikolai at the other end of the dining room. I didn't want to rush over until Jonty came back, but he took a while. It was after two and the room began to clear out, and the sound carried a bit too much. He said sorry to ask, but you know, can you help, sort of thing. Her face was perplexed, even angry for a moment, but eventually her expression relaxed. She must have said yes. Then Jonty came back in, we greeted them, and they left.

ELIZABETH:

Was Jonty a member there?

ARGENTO:

Yes, why—?

ELIZABETH:

And so was Matilda?

ARGENTO:

Yes.

ELIZABETH:

Well then, what's the surprise? It seems highly likely they would meet one another there. How did he greet Matilda?

ARGENTO:

Yes, I suppose you're right. Sorry, it has been a tiresome couple of days for me. They barely spoke ordinarily, but Matilda made a big effort that day – you know, because people were watching. They didn't see much of each other, to be honest. Oh, I am just so thirsty, and I need a cigarette – you mind if we take a break?

ELIZABETH:

No problem, could you spare a cigarette?

ARGENTO:

I'll go get my pack – they are in the dining room. I'll get some water, too.

ELIZABETH:

That scheming little liar ... I can't believe Flora duped me ... and to think, she's now sailing across Lake Como. I was so swept up in that bloody love story – acting like her fairy godmother, giving her a mackintosh and every-thing. I feel such a fool. Well, I'm not going to let anyone else make an idiot of me. Did you suspect her? Girls of that age are so foolish ... she reminded me of myself so much. I can't imagine she would have pulled it off on her own. Peter and even Nikolai must have been in on it with her. All that acting about how dreadful everything was ... the little minx knew what she was up to all along.

I must admit, I feel quite ill at the thought of allowing the pair to leave ... Well, who am I kidding? I didn't just allow it, I encouraged it! I must speak to Nikolai when I've finished with Argento.

It is now completely dark outside. Just when I thought I was close to solving this crime ... I notice my own smell of perspiration. It has been a long twenty-four hours. My body and brain are being held together with the fear of spending the night with the killer.

(Clink of wine glasses)

ARGENTO:

You looked like you needed a drink. Here.

(Argento pours wine)

ELIZABETH:

Oh my, are you trying to get me drunk?

ARGENTO:

Here. Let me light it for you.

ELIZABETH:

Thank you. Oh, that's nice. What are you doing there?

ARGENTO:

Have you missed this?

(Christmas music starts playing on the record player)

ELIZABETH:

Oh my, yes, it has . . . been a long day. Is that Christmas music playing in the background? I haven't heard music here all weekend.

ARGENTO:

This was . . . is my mother's favourite song.

ELIZABETH:

You wish you were with her now, don't you?

ARGENTO:

Ah, my sisters are there . . . she knows I was there . . . Who knows how long her death will drag out for? We watched my father die last year. For weeks, he slowly declined; he did not want to die. It was awful at the end; he was fighting to live, you know? I can't watch that again. My sisters . . . they are there for my mother now.

ELIZABETH:

I have been there, at the moment of death. I know it is rarely peaceful.

ARGENTO:

Let us talk of something else. About your life. Was your husband a good man?

ELIZABETH:

Oh, well, I don't really want to get into it—

ARGENTO:

It would do you good to talk about him. I can see it.

ELIZABETH:

We don't have time. Here I see in my notebook I still have to ask—

ARGENTO:

Tell me about your wedding day. I think it might help me take my mind off my mother, you know?

ELIZABETH:

Oh all right. Well, it was nearly half my lifetime ago, the sixth of April, 1939.

ARGENTO:

What was his name?

ELIZABETH:

Charlie Chalice – you'd never forget that. He was a doctor, in St Thomas's, and we met the previous summer. I had just finished my first year at King's College and was working as an auxiliary nurse . . . scholarship only goes so far. We met on the TB ward. The patients were wheeled out to these little shacks in the hospital grounds to get as much fresh air as possible. They were young men and women . . . Anyway, Dr Chalice was always so careful to spend time and talk to them. Even when the older consultants wanted him to hurry up, he stayed after his shift. Which was really unthinkable, you know, at that time. We got chatting walking between the hospital and the shacks. And then . . . he asked me to the hospital ball that October. Took my dance card from my handbag and scribbled his name in after every single one. Well, I wasn't too popular with the other nurses after that; I wasn't even trained.

But by then I was back at university. He was so unlike the other doctors, any other fellows at all. All he wanted me to be was myself.

We stayed up till midnight, reading Sherlock Holmes and smoking dozens of cigarettes by the cosiest of fires in a charming little house in Westminster. The war was looming, but we didn't know what it would mean, you know? We had no children, so I went back to the nursing corps, Charlie went off to the RAF. We saw each other as much as we could, but he was in an elite team, so it was rare. He wrote, but eventually the letters stopped – it was around the end of 1944. I got the notice. Missing, presumed dead. They never found his body, and I didn't even know where he had been or what had happened to him. Then I passed a fellow from his regiment one day, waiting for the Tube in Aldwych. I begged him to come with me for a coffee. He agreed, but of course he couldn't tell me anything at all about what had happened to Charlie. He was in rag order himself; I could see my probing was painful to him. All he said was that some of the regiment were still alive, under assumed identities in an Italian POW camp.

ARGENTO:

That's how you came to Italy. You thought he was still alive.

ELIZABETH:

I *still think* he's alive. Charlie was so clever . . . if he had had the chance, he would have made it. He is a doctor, a highly skilled operative. I just feel it somewhere, that he is still breathing. Anyway, I don't know why I told you that . . . But it is quite time enough to get back on track, I—

ARGENTO:

You clearly love him very much. And that's why you do what you do with men. Charlie is on such a pedestal that to you everyone else is no better than a dog in the street. Where would you have been today, if it wasn't for this investigation?

ELIZABETH:

Truth is, I hadn't any plans. You know, there's supper at the British Bankers' Club. I do tend to miss England at this time of year.

ARGENTO:

Christmas in Italy is beautiful, the food, always the scent of sage and orange, the warmth of the donkey's breath in the cold air in the crèche in Bellagio . . . I would never leave it.

ELIZABETH:

It is something special all right. Now, we ought to get back to business. Where are the police officers?

ARGENTO:

They are rebuilding the bridge. Or trying to – that fat one hasn't shifted anything heavier than a panna cotta in many years.

ELIZABETH:

That's not a bad thing, that they are still here. I must speak with them soon – you know we will need a hand in arresting the killer.

ARGENTO:

You know who it is then?

ELIZABETH:

I'm quite certain. But until I have learned all there is to know, I will keep an open mind. Did you know Matilda well? Did she ask you to help her, too?

ARGENTO:

I liked Matilda. She reminded me of Mama, you know? She was definitely the boss when she was here. Always wanted a huge meal, extravagant decorations – everything over the top. Apart from this year. And the local people, they loved her, she was so generous.

ELIZABETH:

Tell me about the farmer who brought her cheese this morning. Inside, I can scarcely believe it . . . there was—

ARGENTO:

A bar of gold bullion. Marco is an open-minded, progressive type of farmer. And Matilda . . . she was always thinking of interesting gifts for her grandchildren. Each of those bars—

ELIZABETH:

There's more than one?

ARGENTO:

There's three. One for each of the Caswell-Jones children. She told me that she wanted to secure their inheritance . . . She was quite the woman, you know, not to be trifled with, so when she came to me with the idea last year, I obliged. And then Polly called me to say Jonty had died . . . I suspected that Matilda had had some idea that it would happen – that it was all part of her absurd plan. But it was rather clever, really; if anyone found the cheese, a customs officer, they would expect it to be rather weighty.

ELIZABETH:

Where are the other two?

ARGENTO:

Flora and Polly have theirs because as soon as I arrived Thomas asked me about the cheese. His had been . . . tampered with. By you, I assume?

ELIZABETH:

Yes, I did examine it . . . But I left it in the pantry, in a pot.

ARGENTO:

I helped Thomas search the whole area. It is not there now.

ELIZABETH:

No one has mentioned it in any of the interviews.

ARGENTO:

Why would they? Each of them thought they were the only one to get some gold. Plus, it hardly seems important.

ELIZABETH:

Have you seen a copy of Matilda's will?

ARGENTO:

She died intestate, I think, unless the family solicitor in London has a copy of it.

ELIZABETH:

Jonty changed his will very recently; do you know why he did that? Would this London firm have a copy of the previous will?

ARGENTO:

Jonty thought Thomas was . . . dangerous, that he couldn't be trusted as heir, that Ludlow was controlling the boy. He wanted his daughters to be looked after.

ELIZABETH:

They weren't in line to receive anything in the previous will?

ARGENTO:

A small allowance, but nothing near what has been granted to them now.

ELIZABETH:

But why would Jonty make Ludlow and Margaret the executors, if one was in debt to him, and the other was blackmailing him? It doesn't make sense.

ARGENTO:

I suppose it depends who you believe. Do you think I could have killed him?

ELIZABETH:

What would your motive be?

ARGENTO:

You didn't see me written into the will, so it wouldn't be for financial gain. More likely jealousy. Perhaps I am madly in love with Catherine, or one of the daughters? Or revenge . . . because he did

me some great injury many years ago? There are only so many
motives to go around.

ELIZABETH:

Almost everything boils down to three things: money, sex or power.

ARGENTO:

My three favourite things.

ELIZABETH:

As motives go, you had more to lose with Jonty's death than gain.
You've obviously been struck off for some petty criminal reason – who
else is going to give you a job? And that's why I believe everything that
you've said . . . because you are a man with nothing left to lose.

ARGENTO:

A man with nothing left to lose is liable to do almost anything,
though.

ELIZABETH:

Perhaps. Now . . . tell me. How did Jonty get on with Polly, his
eldest daughter? You know her rather well, don't you?

ARGENTO:

Polly, where did . . . ah, you think she and I? Am I an old dog,
ha-ha?

ELIZABETH:

Not everything boils down to sex . . .

ARGENTO:

She barely spoke to her father. Or even her mother, for that matter.

ELIZABETH:

Pass me the ashtray, thank you. I'm exhausted with this act, it's all
so tiresome. Tell me, how did you get back inside the villa, to set up
the trap that killed Jonty? *(Pause)* Wait, where are you going?

(Argento shuts the door)

ARGENTO:

Oh, nowhere. We are not going anywhere.

ELIZABETH:

Everyone knows I'm interviewing you in here. Pass me another cigarette, will you?

ARGENTO:

You're not scared of me.

ELIZABETH:

Not particularly. What do you plan to do to me? Answer my question about Jonty.

ARGENTO:

What would you like me to do to you?

ELIZABETH:

Eh, after your ridiculous comments, I'm jolly well happy enough to sit it out, thanks.

ARGENTO:

When I arrived, I saw the way you looked at me. And I knew that it is your weakness – your release. Your appetite for passion . . . ha-ha. And I did not kill Jonty. Not personally anyway. I bet you could do with a release, couldn't you, my dear?

(Exaggerated moment of silence)

ELIZABETH:

If you will excuse me, I just need to use the loo.

ELIZABETH:

All right, reader, are you there? It is terribly convenient that there is a WC in this study. But I do not want him to hear me. Oh, how I would like to explore Signore di Silva . . . Those broad shoulders . . . Phew. Okay. Deep breath, Elizabeth. Now is not the time. I'm right to pull it together, aren't I? You don't want to see me go back in there and drop my knickers? Oh GOD. Yes. Okay, moment of inner turmoil quashed. I almost forgot I was here to investigate a murder for a moment. He is so easy to talk to ... I wonder why Catherine doesn't like him. Now, if you'll excuse me, I do actually have to use the bathroom. Can you go and see what the others are up to in the kitchen?

(Meanwhile, in the kitchen ...)

LUDLOW:

You have absolutely no right to do this to me, no proof, nothing. Get your hands off me.

CATHERINE:

Elizabeth said she shortlisted the suspects, and you're one of three. Officer, please proceed, I'm sure this man killed my husband. As the officer says, Ludlow, your prints are all over Jonty's desk.

LUDLOW:

My prints are all over his things in there because I was his *friend*, I had been helping him review his finances. I'm sure I wasn't the only one.

NIKOLAI:

Eh, I think we should wait for Elizabeth, you know, for the full picture.

CATHERINE:

You! You were second on her list of suspects.

NIKOLAI:

I would never lay a hand on the fellow. He was harmless. I had nothing against him.

CATHERINE:

But Ludlow, when did you go into Jonty's study?

LUDLOW:

Oh, I don't know. I've been in there so many times over the years. I don't recall having been in there once on this trip, as we arrived so late, but—

POLLY:

Liar! That's a new desk in there, the ceiling leaked all over the old one and Argento arranged for a new one.

CATHERINE:

Where is Argento?

POLLY:

He's gone off with our lady detective, to show her the wine cellar and the access to the hill.

CATHERINE:

Elizabeth has gone out in the dark? Really? Officer, can you please proceed . . . Arrest him.

LUDLOW:

Get your bloody hands off me.

CATHERINE:

Put him in the pantry for the time being.

LUDLOW:

Get my wife down here now!

CATHERINE:

Your wife is in bed, resting. I always knew things would come to no good between you two. You were such a parasite—

LUDLOW:

I was the parasite? Jonty never had an original thought for himself, never made a single friend. Who here, apart from me, would actually call himself his friend? *No one.* He didn't have any. Call Elizabeth back here *now* and she will tell you who the real killer is.

(Back in the interior study)

ELIZABETH:

Reader, did you hear anything interesting? Now . . . let's get back to our final interview, shall we?

ELIZABETH:

Now, where were we?

ARGENTO:

Another glass of wine?

ELIZABETH:

No, no, thank you. I just have a few more queries. Now, tell me, where is the washing done?

ARGENTO:

Oh, it is sent out, to a woman in the village.

ELIZABETH:

But it hasn't been sent out yet, yes?

ARGENTO:

I'm sure it is all still in everyone's rooms, I can't see why—

ELIZABETH:

The family went for a Christmas Day swim yesterday morning. Flora, Peter, Thomas, Nikolai. Margaret was there with the towels for them all. And Frankie watched. I can't see them dragging sodden towels upstairs – where would they have been left?

ARGENTO:

Eh, you had better ask Catherine, I think they are left out in one of the washing shacks.

ELIZABETH:

Can you show me? Good chap.

ARGENTO:

All right, come along.

(Argento walks ahead, opens the door and shuts it after himself quickly)

(Elizabeth tries the door frantically)

ELIZABETH:

(Shouts) What the . . . ARGENTO. Did you lock this? Hello? Let me out! Can anyone hear me?

ELIZABETH:

Oh no, are you there? Damn shame you can't help me get out of this one. I really hadn't thought Argento was our man. I still don't, but his locking me up like this . . . it is concerning. I mean, I say concerning . . . but I am . . . what if they are all in on this, and they mean to kill me next?

Perhaps the killer has instructed him to keep me in here? I feel cheap for sharing Charlie's memory with Argento. He did it on purpose, to make me lose track . . . to help me settle down. Well, you know, there is no point in panicking. I had better sit down and get out my notebook. Let's take a look.

Phew – Elizabeth, breathe! Okay. If we remember why we are all here . . . the death of Jonty Caswell-Jones is looming over us. If nothing else, this time trapped in here will let me get my head around everything. All their conflicting stories, lies here and there, or forgotten truths . . . Who should we believe, and how do we get around piecing it all together?

He was a good man, was Jonty. Do you recall any of our suspects speaking of him being violent? Or cruel? Or abusing those lesser than him? No, because he didn't. He was a victim long before he was murdered. It is in this room where his life was extinguished most violently. The fire has gone out completely, and outside the last fringes of light are receding away from the water's surface. There must be something . . . ah, a lamp. This desk is covered in dust from the fingerprints. I shall put on a set of gloves to examine it more closely in case I missed anything earlier. I might as well put this time to good use. Papers, tickets, receipts. No, nothing new. Ah, the windows, of course. But they are shuttered. Locked up. And the winds are so high – I doubt anyone could hear—

ELIZABETH:

Hello?

(Wind slams window shut)

ELIZABETH:

Dammit. Be patient, Elizabeth. The clue, there must be something in here.

(Rustling through drawers)

ELIZABETH:

What's this? Here, just beside the light switch? 'Maggiordomo' – *ah, it's for the butler. This must reach the butler's room.*

ELIZABETH:

(Into speaker) Hello? Hello? Can anyone hear me?

ARGENTO:

(Down speaker) Ah, you found it more quickly than I thought. But no – only I can hear you! Why don't you sit down, relax and enjoy the rest of the wine? *(Laughing)*

ELIZABETH:

They will just hear me banging on the door!

ARGENTO:

Please, bang the door. They will not hear. How do you know they are not the reason you are in there?

ELIZABETH:

That dirty, rotten blighter ... Oh, I can't talk to you anymore. I need to work out a way to leave this room. Argento is not working alone, I'm certain of it. He is under orders from the killer, and I must review my notes. You too? Okay. This wine is actually terrible. Join me later, when we will uncover who, from our twelve suspects, committed this awful murder.

(Christmas music playing out in the background)

EPISODE 13

The Denouement

ELIZABETH:

Oh, you're back! About bloody time! Do you know how long I have been locked in Jonty's study? There has to be a key here somewhere, I'm sure I saw one. That blighter Argento . . . he's up in one of the bedrooms laughing at me. We've heard all of our twelve suspects and their big and small motives for murder. The mantlepiece, people always leave things lurking – what's this behind the mirror, a picture? (Gasp) *The two brothers, Jonty and William. Christmas 1941 is scrawled on the back. They are smiling – they had made it home together, the entire Caswell-Jones family together. I recognise the deep bay window of the family home in Little Bedford. I was wretchedly jealous of Catherine that year. My husband hadn't made it home, and she told me all about their wonderful time together. The resemblance between the two is incredible. I shall tuck this into my pocket. Jonty kept this hidden behind the mirror, the only family picture in the entire villa. He must really have missed William. Now, as I keep looking for the spare key, let's go back over our progress in the investigation to date. It's time to solve this for once and all.*

It is now twenty-four hours since the body of Jonty Caswell-Jones was discovered by his wife, on the perfectly still waters on the edge of Lake Como. So whodunnit, do you think, reader? Could it be the fed-up wife, the rail-roaded daughter, an opportunistic old friend, the petulant child, the impecunious son, an embittered old lady?

(Sound of the storm)

ELIZABETH:

Hang on, there is quite a commotion outside, although it's hard to hear with this wind. I've finally opened the shutter.

(Sound of the shutter opening)

ELIZABETH:

Oh my! It's the small yacht! It's sinking, with Peter and Flora wet as two river rats on the lake's edge. Our two lovers haven't made it away . . . (Sarcastic) *Oh, that is a shame. The little mare. And there's Catherine . . . They are all looking up at me now.*

CATHERINE:

(Shouting from outside) Are you quite ready to tell us who the killer is, Elizabeth? Before anyone else tries to get away?

ELIZABETH:

(Whispering to reader) *Just in time, here is the key, shoved behind the mirror over the fireplace. It is Villa Janus, isn't it? Janus was the god of doors, gates and transitions. Pretty ironic, really, as I'm locked in here … From what I can remember of my grammar school classics, Janus represented the middle ground between concrete and abstract dualities such as life and death or the beginning and the end. Well, let's hope Janus is on our side. I'm trying this lock now.* (A sigh of relief) *Ah, the door works. Let us leave this study. Hang on, I can hear breathing on the other side, let's take a peek. Oh, look who it is … Argento, my gaoler. What's that on his trousers? It looks like dust. And there's that musty smell again. He's come down from the butler's apartment. Is it safe to go out, I wonder …? Well, only one way to find out.*

ARGENTO:

Well done, my lady detective.

ELIZABETH:

Good God, what on earth … where? Why did you lock me up in there?

ARGENTO:

Ah, we just needed you out of the way … I never got to use that hidden microphone before … it was most fun. Now, if you please follow me down to the dining room. Catherine would like you to present your findings. I'm presuming you have some?

ELIZABETH:

And Flora … Peter … The old mare would not let her daughter be happy?

ARGENTO:

Thomas saw them; he didn't want to let his sister drown. Here we are.

ELIZABETH:

I need a drink of water after being stuck in there.

ARGENTO:

I will get some for you.

ELIZABETH:

I need the WC too. I won't be a minute.

ARGENTO:

I, eh, ok.

ELIZABETH:

Are you there? I really won't be a minute, but we need to see if that vial of curare is still there. Can you feel it? We are getting close to the end, now if I can just get down to the scullery without being seen. Good, I see our star-crossed lovers are trailing into the dining room, that will keep them busy.

(Rummaging around)

ELIZABETH:

Gone. The killer's moved the poison. Have they dumped it into the lake or is it ready to prick someone else? Best get back up to the room before anyone notices where I am. And the glass of water.

(Runs taps)

ELIZABETH:

Argento is in on it of course. That's why he locked me in at the end, to get rid of the curare bottle without me seeing. Time to call out our killer.

(Door opens)

ELIZABETH:

(Whispering) *Here we are indeed. Are you quite ready for this? It's what is called in the industry the denouement. They are all here now, our eleven suspects, with the twelfth dead in the cellar. Old Matilda. I'd say she would love to be here for this. No one looks happy, that's for sure . . . Even poor Sally has made it down from her sick bed for this final moment. Let us begin. Reader, it is time to conclude our investigation into the deaths of Jonty and Matilda Caswell-Jones.*

CATHERINE:

Ah, Elizabeth. We are ready for you. Ready for this nightmare to end.

ELIZABETH:

In the past, I came to Villa Janus as a guest, but then the invitations stopped. Why was that?

CATHERINE:

I hardly think it's the time to discuss—

ELIZABETH:

Our business here is uncovering the truth. You might answer?

CATHERINE:

Oh, very well—

THOMAS:

For God's sake, let's crack on before we die of old age—

CATHERINE:

Quiet. We just outgrew you, Elizabeth. Nothing more sinister than that. Everytime you came, whilst we did enjoy your company – I mean, we do enjoy your company, but – it just brought us back to the war. To that horrible ward where we watched the youngest and fittest of fellows . . . expire. You were obsessed with Charlie. Matilda thought you were a wet blanket . . . and I am sorry to say, I agreed. You have since regained some of your vim, and I know that mind of yours is so clever, so it was clear to me that only you could help us sort out this terrible mess.

ELIZABETH:

Thank you. I quite understand. And this afternoon I am not here to be your friend. I have a job to do. To find out who killed Jonty Caswell-Jones. To be murdered, by one of your closest friends or family, well, one can't imagine the terror that ran through the cooling veins of our first victim. He was *indeed* murdered.

In fact, he was poisoned, but then, you don't need to be a detective to know that. He was killed with a poisoned needle. I will give you a full account of the means by which Jonty was killed, but first, let's identify who had the opportunity to put an end to the life of a man who had the best in mind for his family. Let's walk through the details again. There are a number of differing accounts, but I have put it together. Let us return to that fateful Christmas Day, shall we?

The lemon cake was a big feature of the investigation, I must say. All of you seem to have paid particular attention to it. So, what I have learned is that at around four o'clock, Catherine puts the lemon cake back in the oven. She returns to the dining room, sees Jonty is missing, so goes to look for her husband. She notes that Ludlow, Polly and Francis are also out of their seats. Why is Ludlow ignoring his best friend? Where have our missing guests gone? And who is looking after lunch? Why did Jonty go to his study in the first place? Matilda is passed out on the table. But who is looking after her? Yes, Margaret is helping her to come around. Catherine ignores this drama and goes ahead to Jonty's study, followed by Flora. Yes, Catherine. That is a fact you omitted to tell me. You told me you were alone. Why hide this detail? Were you trying to protect yourself, or your daughter? Or was your memory just addled by shock? I did not expect the lies to begin so soon, in our very first interview. But anyway, back to your account.

So, you don't realise he's dead, not right away, confused by Matilda lying in an almost identical position at the lunch table

– you think he must be joking. But as you move closer, it dawns on you. It takes a moment for you to be *absolutely* sure. But as you and I both saw on the battlefields, Catherine, the mask of death is unforgettable and the realisation of what it is, so shocking.

This is the point that has stuck with me all along: how you were so certain your husband was killed. Not just as the day wore on, but instantly, as confirmed by Flora, who had followed you into the office. Something had *prepared* you for his murder. It was almost like you knew in advance.

However, as some of you may know, and one of you knows all too well, the means by which Jonty died does not point to a clear window of opportunity. So, I had to conduct my enquiries under the impression that you ALL had a large window of opportunity to murder Jonty. Even Argento, who was in Milan at the time, could have laid a trap before leaving for the city, by sticking the needle in the chair, with the poisoned end pointing up. But I believe the killer was still cautious and did not want any unintended victim to die by these means.

Now, this leads us to the motive. Each of you has a very clear reason for wanting to end the life of this fellow. Let's remind ourselves of what you each had to hide.

Ludlow, I don't think it's a surprise to anyone here that you've been fleecing your best friend for years. You've been *so* keen to make sure Thomas and the children are well-looked after, you've been trying to convince Thomas to hand over the running of the business to you. He would go along with anything his godfather says. But I don't think you murdered Jonty. No, while you had motive, and I'm sure you've thought about it before, you would have been well aware that any *investigations* would draw attention to your misdeeds.

Let me begin this next part with an apology, Polly. No one could help but notice your pallor, the dusting of purple under your eyes. I wondered if it was something more serious, perhaps the hereditary weakness of the heart. Then I thought a little more about your age, and remembered the last time I'd seen the life so sucked out of an otherwise perfectly healthy young girl . . .

POLLY:

No, Elizabeth, not here, please have—

ELIZABETH:

Now, I hadn't wanted to expose you like this, Polly. That's right, you're expecting a baby, aren't you? By that slight pouch, I would estimate about three or four months gone. But I believe your father knew and had tried to encourage a . . . a . . . surgery. That's what the ultimatum was about, wasn't it? Leave York or get married? Your father wasn't—

CATHERINE:

Elizabeth, please. Polly, this can't be true?

POLLY:

Yes, Mother, I'm afraid I am expecting— *(lost to sobs)*

CATHERINE:

But, three months ago, you were in . . . York. Who could you—? We shall talk about this later, poor child. Elizabeth, I've asked you to investigate. I wanted it kept within the family. You have no right to expose poor Polly.

ELIZABETH:

I'm afraid everything is relevant. We're keeping it within the family for now, but it's about time for everyone to admit their weaknesses . . . The father is in this room. And you've been blackmailing him, haven't you, Polly? Ludlow.

LUDLOW:

You can't be serious, Elizabeth—

ELIZABETH:

But I think it's you. You followed Polly back to her room last night. With wads of cash, the final payoff as such. 'To get the job done,' so Thomas overheard. Polly, you were convinced he would change his mind, and decide to leave Sally for you. But for Mr Lansdowne de Groot, it boiled down to money. You were terrified Sally would sue for divorce. Because the truth is, you're actually flat broke, despite stealing from your best friend . . . Oh, don't worry, Ludlow, don't look so shocked. I know you didn't kill Jonty . . . I've said it already. But this leads me to, eh— As much as it pains me to say, I fear I cannot, in good conscience, continue without revealing—

SALLY:

We all know already, Elizabeth. Polly, I do wish you had exercised slightly finer judgement, but then again you aren't the only one who has been foolish here. You're not the only detective, you know, Elizabeth. I realised it as soon as I saw you and Polly had an identical fur stole, both from the same furriers. I buy my own fur there.

POLLY:

(Spitting) Of course I realised too.

ELIZABETH:

That's why you came into my room to spray your grandmother's perfume, isn't it? You just wanted to spook me . . . to think the place was haunted.

POLLY:

Yes. I'll admit it was quite . . . juvenile of me. But it's rather sickening to see you prancing around here, as if you own the place, as if you're some sort of paragon of virtue, when in fact you're nothing more than a common prostitute yourself—

CATHERINE:

(Sharply) Do watch that tongue, Polly.

ELIZABETH:

I wondered if you knew, Sally, and I do apologise. As I was saying, we are just beginning to scratch the surface of the duplicitousness here. Not one of us is exempt from carrying secrets. And that's why

I admit to my own blunder. Uncovering secrets is not why I am here, and I don't intend to reveal you for the jolly good sake of it. Those of you who I have made promises to, be sure I will honour them. But this whole investigation is into the suspected murder of Jonty Caswell-Jones. I will get to Matilda in time. But I have news for you all. Jonty was not murdered.

(Gasps of shock)

THOMAS:

What on earth do you mean? You've just been yapping on about it being a murder investigation.

ELIZABETH:

The man who died here yesterday, seated at Jonty's chair, might have very closely resembled the younger Caswell-Jones brother. But Jonty really died eight years ago, not too far from where we are right now. You see, when Matilda complained that the wrong brother came home from the war, she wasn't lying. Her favourite son, Will, came home instead. Whatever happened in that camp, we shall never know. But what we do know, Will returned to England as Jonty.

They looked very similar, although Will had a small circle of freckles to the right of his chin. Freckles that were duly noted and incorporated into up-close portraits of the family that Polly had begun in recent months. I wondered why Polly and Catherine would react so strongly to the notebook going missing. Catherine pretended to be concerned for her daughter's sake, but that concern was an act. Because it was she who tore out several portraits of Jonty. Why on earth would she do such a thing? I wondered. There are no recent photographs anywhere in the villa. But these sketches were far more detailed than any photograph could be, a testament to Polly's artistic capability. But the particular pattern of the freckles . . . the slightly squarer jaw. A keen observer could see these were not sketches of Jonty, but of Will. You wanted to keep the identity swap a secret, didn't you, Catherine?

This was the first clue. Then I learned that William was clueless when it came to numbers, and that Jonty was something of a whizz, that was until after the war. You see, Will was never good with numbers, and would be unable to keep accounts to the same basic standard as Jonty had before the war.

Then there is the gambling. The nature of addiction is that one cannot help oneself. And despite managing to assume the life of his brother, Will was a well-documented gambler, and this proclivity to gamble was too great to fight, as he spent the summer frequenting the Mayfair Club, gambling more and more on behalf of his friend, Ludlow. And, of course, he brought Flora with him a few times, not because she was his lucky charm, but because she was *good* with numbers . . . just like her father. Now, the final clue as to 'Jonty's' identity was confirmed to me by Francis, to whom Will broke down and confessed yesterday afternoon; he confessed to being a homosexual.

Now, my next point, Catherine—

(Margaret faints)

POLLY:

Auntie Margaret! Auntie Margaret! Are you okay?

THOMAS:

Get her some air. No wonder, with this ridiculous wild goose chase.

ELIZABETH:

I'm afraid, Margaret, your amateur dramatics are not welcome here. You also deceived me with your corroboration of Flora's account of her father taking her gambling every time. In fact, it was you who took her in search of financial gain. I doubt you would have had the capacity for planning a murder. But while you are innocent of murder, you are not innocent of wrongdoing. And Flora—

FLORA:

Go on, you old bag, tell us what you've unearthed.

ELIZABETH:

I must admit, you, young lady, managed to fool me better than anyone else at Villa Janus. Your account of the summer spent gaming with your father was convincing. I wondered how Jonty would have allowed you to become privy to such a level of vice. I watched how you counted the cards when you insisted we play twenty-one. An admirable skill, but you are all too trusting. No surprise, for a schoolgirl. I removed a couple of the high-value cards from my pack. I planned it to warn you against being too rash in running away with Peter. It confirmed how *young* you really are. So foolish to concoct this tale of blackmail by Argento's cousin – Joe's wife – I wondered what else you'd concocted? And then Argento told me you tried to kiss him in London.

PETER:

Is that true, Flora?

ELIZABETH:

Yes, Peter, it is. You see, you can expect this sort of behaviour from silly young schoolgirls.

FLORA:

I am not—

ELIZABETH:

The man you believed was your father saw that your relationship with Peter would be filled with heartache for the both of you. He thought that assuming the life of his brother would make his life better, he would not need to find a wife for appearances. But it only served to encase him further in secrecy.

He forbade the match, of course. But it was not just his concern for you that made him forbid the match. No. Peter kept some other secrets for your uncle. Although, Peter, you still understood the man to be Jonty; you did not know it was William. You knew that this man was homosexual, however, and on your trips to South America you knew that he shirked the sedentary life of the English husband to experience the passion of life that he craved – in the company of young men. William could not bear to be reminded of this constantly by having Peter as a son-in-law. And if you two were to marry, would his secret not one day run the risk of being revealed to you, Flora, a young woman William had come to think of as his own daughter?

MARGARET:

Oh my lord, is this true?

ELIZABETH:

It's that reaction he wanted to avoid, Margaret. But, Flora, while you are naïve, stupid, sometimes cruel, I know what it takes to commit a crime like this, and you are simply incapable of doing so.

FLORA:

You don't know a thing, Elizabeth—

ELIZABETH:

And Peter. You guarded the confidences of your lover's father well.

CATHERINE:

Flora, do not tell me—

ELIZABETH:

Allow me to continue. Peter, it had been a coincidence that you were both in South America at the same time, on the very same vessel out of Southampton. During the course of the month it took to arrive in São Paolo, you learned a great deal about your godfather, or the man pretending to be him. You were well taken care of in his will because he genuinely liked you, I would wager. He could see reflected in you the frailty of weakness . . . There is no chance you'll be competing in the next Olympics, is there? Does your young lady know why?

PETER:

No, I had not thought it wise to tell her.

FLORA:

Tell me what?

ELIZABETH:

He's dying. Cancer, isn't it? That's why you have the pain relief, the opium. And access to a syringe. I'll get to that in a minute.

FLORA:

Is this true? I ... I thought you had some trouble training ... Oh Peter, you're not ... sick. Tell her, she has it all wrong!

ELIZABETH:

The man posing as Jonty wanted to ensure you were financially looked after. He might not have been your real godfather, but he took on that role seriously. He did not know you are ill, though. Like Thomas, unless the actual Jonathan Caswell-Jones accounted for you in his will, the document you were mentioned in is likely to amount to nothing; you are not due to inherit a thing for keeping his secrets.

FLORA:

Did you know he wasn't really Daddy?

PETER:

No, no, I did not. Look, Flora, I was only trying to help – he seemed so low in himself when we met ... I had no idea it was William. I just introduced him to a few fellows, friends of mine. I realise now it was a mistake ...

FLORA:

If you weren't skiing, what on earth were you doing there?

PETER:

I *was* skiing. I have always wanted to ski in the Andes.

FLORA:

(Angry) How long have you left to live? You would really make me a widow at eighteen?

PETER:

(Angry) A very rich little girl is what I was going to make you . . .

(Rowing continues between the two)

CATHERINE:

Flora, Peter, that is quite enough. Elizabeth has a job to do.

(Elizabeth begins coughing)

ELIZABETH:

Oh, excuse me . . .

(Another argument breaks out)

LUDLOW:

You bloody thief, stealing from Jonty.

NIKOLAI:

Don't drag me down to your level—

LUDLOW:

You did use it against him, putting those loansharks after him. You knew the company was in financial trouble. And you knew he couldn't repay them. By suggesting he get money from there, you effectively sealed his death warrant.

ELIZABETH:

My, my, the gloves have well and truly come off. Flora and Peter have gone from star-crossed lovers to warring enemies for all to see. Speaking of gloves, I am watching Argento's hands. Thankfully, it does not look like he, or anyone else for that matter, is holding a pin. And the others, well, everyone wants to be a detective; they all feel like grilling one another. I should say something about rats in a barrel. The mood is on a knife-edge here. We are all tired, and here is Ludlow deflecting attention from himself by bringing up Jonty's debts. Sealed his death warrant? What a load of absolute tosh. He has resorted to inventing lies here. But I do love the drama of the denouement, don't you?

ELIZABETH:

(Coughing) That's a bit better. What is this commotion?

NIKOLAI:

I warned him, you know, about gambling, using the loansharks. He knew what he was getting himself into. He only came to me because Ludlow wouldn't lend him the money for the irrigation works he needed to do on the plantation.

LUDLOW:

I didn't have it to give him!

ELIZABETH:

Ludlow, I believe you are concocting a web of lies. I've seen the books, Jonty may have been a gambler, that much is obvious. But the company was doing okay, the irrigation must have paid off because 1952 saw the accounts back in the black. The truth is that YOU owed him money, isn't it? He lent you cash because Sally would not give you much of an allowance.

But you alone are not the only one with a financial motive to kill Jonty. Because there's the betting slip. No ordinary bookie would accept such a large stake on an outsider at Kempton Park. Who would accept such a large bet? The Mayfair Club. On credit, so Jonty didn't even need to produce the cash. But the club could apply as a creditor against the estate. You encouraged him, Nikolai. Because you owed them big too. And for your role, the club management agreed to erase your own debt.

In her rush to take cash to pay the local shepherd, Matilda took the wallet from her dead son's study. Rifling through the wallet for lira, she undoubtedly found this slip. What does this tell us? That just before her son was murdered, she saw this outrageous bet. If any doubts were creeping in about killing her own son, this betting slip likely reminded her of all the trouble he brought to the family. But I don't think anyone would have killed Jonty for this alone.

Who else acted strangely in the months leading up to this very memorable Christmas? Fearing for her grandchildren's inheritance,

Matilda recruited Argento to arrange for three bars of gold bullion, each worth fifty thousand pounds, to be hidden – in what? Something as simple as a local cheese.

She arranged for the bullion to be delivered to the shepherd, which he encased in the curd that set into cheese. The perfect way to move extremely large quantities of money across borders. Easy to liquidate. But Matilda didn't mastermind the murder on her own. In fact, she was merely a *whey* – excuse the pun – of hiding some valuables for her grandchildren. When the killer realised how simple it was to just extinguish a life like that . . . well, they decided to use the same method to do away with Matilda. We all saw how difficult a woman she was, bossing about her children and grand-children, belittling the common man, engineering every possible situation to her own preferred outcome. It seems life would just be more straightforward without her here. That's my guess, anyway. We will come back to Matilda in a moment.

Now, Sally – or Sarah, as we know to be your real name—

SALLY:

That's hardly worthy of comment, is it? Polly's real name is Mary.

ELIZABETH:

That business of yours may be moderately successful, but it's not the great enterprise you let us all think it is. The truth is, I believe you were actually financing a portion of the float at the Mayfair Club, isn't that true? Giving the whole business a legitimate means to remove cash from highly illegal gambling activities. It came to me when I was locked in Jonty's study. I was looking through all of the papers again, when I remembered a note from you, to Jonty. An envelope sealed with lipstick. It was an unusual shade of red, so I initially thought perhaps it was from an Italian woman. But given your colouring, I realised it has been in front of me the whole time. Anyway, inside the envelope was a Queen of Hearts, and a note in your handwriting saying *'Don't bet too big against the house – S'*. The funny thing is, you had to have known it was William you were writing to. And he welcomed your attentions to deflect from the deception, pretending to be his brother. He was only too keen to pretend that he was having an affair. And Ludlow—

LUDLOW:

I never went near that dirty, betting place—

ELIZABETH:

You didn't have to, for Will did all your dirty work for you. If anyone scratches under the surface, they will find numerous links between your legitimate enterprise and the Mayfair Club. That's why you were so keen to be back in London for New Year's Eve, isn't it? Both of you knew Will was pretending to be Jonty and you wanted to put thousands of miles between you and the murder. Princess Margaret isn't hosting any ball at Kensington Palace, is she?

And what were you and Ludlow rowing about, Sally? Nikolai overheard quite the barney from his butler's room upstairs. But you two weren't arguing about Jonty. Or the wine. No. You made a bit of a mistake, Sally. You didn't realise that the copy of Francis's book, which had been gifted to you by Thomas, featured an inscription from Thomas on, er, page sixty-nine. You obviously didn't read that far. It clearly outlined Thomas's interests in Sally. I have a note of it here: 'To my most sumptuous Sally, something for your soul, my corporeal companion.'

THOMAS:

I say, Elizabeth, that is quite enough.

ELIZABETH:

But Ludlow did find it, didn't he? In fact, he finished the entire book on Christmas morning. You may have proposed to Jonty out of pity all those years ago, Sally, but you are a long way from being that kind and empathetic girl now. Didn't you realise that Will was spending your husband's money? That, in fact, you were betting against your own house? You'll never be able to recoup those large debts now. And your relationship resembles a house of cards, Ludlow and Sally. Little affairs wherever we look. But all your anger at one another, this game-playing, tells me you are both still in love with each other. Otherwise neither of you would care. I don't believe either of you to be guilty of killing Jonty. You are so entangled in the web of your marriage that you wouldn't possibly commit a murder, with all the complications that would bring. Sally, you are so stressed out about mere travel arrangements, if you were the killer you would have already confessed. Ludlow, you might claim that money is more important than love, but your actions, say otherwise.

Now, Thomas, you do look perplexed! And that is why, I'm afraid, your innocence was confirmed to me. It seems that you are just as bad with numbers as your uncle, despite your job in finance. What a joke! Your godfather Ludlow had a wicked sense of humour when he helped you get that job. But you're nothing more than a good-looking chap in an expensive suit, to wine and dine clients. But ironically, it does always come back to money for you. Your main motive in killing your father would have been financial.

Didn't you say you would have run the business better? That you wanted to get your hands on the estate? In the end, however, I thought your sisters told me this because they were themselves frustrated.

I have no doubt you'll all be tied up in probate on this for years, but to the best of my knowledge, the will read by Argento in the name of Jonty Caswell-Jones is invalid. Unless your uncle made a recent will in his own name with those same stipulations, you are the heir to the estate in its entirety, although it is likely there is some provision for your female relatives. This is the portion of the evening given over to airing your dirty laundry—

CATHERINE:

There's no need to ruin the poor chap, Elizabeth.

ELIZABETH:

And that's why you didn't tell me who was in Jonty's office when you first went up. You might not have been born a Caswell-Jones, Catherine, but you have certainly adopted their obsessions with outward appearances. An obsession shared by Thomas here, who always planned to settle down and marry a girl. You know how to put on an act, Thomas . . . you've been doing it your whole life. So I know you are innocent. And anyway, no one saw you leave the table at Christmas lunch.

POLLY:

So who was in his office? I don't understand—

THOMAS:

Francis was.

POLLY:

What on earth were you doing in there?

THOMAS:

It doesn't even matter, sister, will you just drop it?

POLLY:

Good God, Elizabeth? Don't we deserve to know what happened?

ELIZABETH:

I'm getting there, Polly. Francis Heath. Frankie. When Jonty telephoned your publisher he seriously jeopardised your career. For that particular publisher is favoured by the Church of Scotland and its affiliated organisations. They produce mainly religious texts and will not have been so *understanding* as you said they were. So . . . Jonty hurt you. And you were also the very last person to see him, in his office, at the precise time of his murder.

FRANCIS:

That's not true, Catherine walked into the study—

CATHERINE:

No, I certainly did not.

ELIZABETH:

Please, I do not want any more interruptions. Francis, you have no alibi for this time. So, let's be very clear: you have the motive and the opportunity to commit this murder. But what about the means? How was William, the man pretending to be Jonty, murdered? I did wonder if it had been an accident. Jonty had been warned a heart attack was imminent and could be brought on by loud shouting, stress, that sort of thing. And Matilda was elderly, and although fit, well, it could plausibly be natural causes that killed her.

In fact, neither of these deaths were innocent. I mean, the killer probably thinks that they are terribly clever to have devised such a scheme, to leave a perfect corpse, almost flawless, the very picture of serenity. But underneath this calm exterior, both Jonty and Matilda suffered what must have felt like an agonisingly slow and horrendous death. It took me some time to realise what had caused this, but I am certain that, once the bodies are examined in a post-mortem, the doctor will find a tiny puncture hole, almost invisible to the naked eye. If the examination is not performed in a timely manner, the mark will be lost to decomposition – this our killer knew. Hence why they resorted to committing the crime here, at this remote location over the Christmas break.

Poison: a method preferred by women, and those whose victims are family members. Both Jonty and Matilda were dosed with the toxin curare. Just the tiniest amount. This is a plant extract alkaloid originating from Central and South America. Curare is active only by an injection or a direct wound contamination by poisoned dart or arrow – in this case a simple needle dipped in the poison. Poison that you procured from Jonty's collection of curios. Remember, you told me of how he always brought momentos home from South America over the years. Including arrow heads. Well he must have brought a little jar of curare along the way too. It was all so *easy!*

It was a small thing, really. I found a sewing kit in Jonty's office and took it upstairs to hem this dress. When I opened it, the tiniest needle was gone. No one could possibly have used it for stitching, so I wondered why it was missing. When I put that together with the poison that killed Matilda and Jonty, I realised we have our murder weapon. I had initially thought a syringe was used, but even the smallest syringe these days could leave a mark. This death would be distressing to watch. I wonder, did the killer look them in the eye and tell them why they were doing it? Or did they cowardly avert their eyes? As many of you have said, it was, as it always is, his heart that gave up in the end as he went into cardiac arrest. The killer then burned a bundle of documents – what was in there, we will never know. Apart from the end of one letter, which I will come back to in a moment.

As he remained seated, the killer was someone he trusted enough to let them walk behind him, where they stuck the needle into him – in the back or the scalp I would imagine are the most likely places.

ELIZABETH:

I'm looking round the room for any signs of weakness, waiting for our murderer to step forward. Part of me always hopes at this point, however, that they don't give anything away. For I love playing with them. And the Caswell-Joneses ... the history we have together, and the way they have treated me in the past ... this revenge feels rather sweet. I have a terrible feeling that I've just scratched the surface of their secret lives, and I am glad not to have to pry any further. It is so very tense. I am watching the female suspects especially closely now. Where are your tells? Even a veteran killer would likely begin to show signs of stress ... but they are all worried I'm going to air their dirty laundry. No one is speaking or looking at each other; each of our eleven suspects are staring into the void. They will leave here as different people, that is for sure. And one will leave in handcuffs.

ELIZABETH:

Without examining the body, it is impossible to say. However, once Jonty's mother suffered the same fate, I did have a body to examine. But we will come back to Matilda.

(Pause)

The truth is, Catherine, that you have known all along that Jonty wasn't himself. I realised the deception when you had me locked in that room. I saw Jonty's handwriting in the study. One, from last year's accounts, was messy – squiggly letters all over the place. And another sample, in a letter you had tried to burn along with other documents. A far cry from the beautiful script he had used in the letters to you during the war. I found myself thinking it was as if they had been written by two different people. Then I found the lease to Villa Janus, signed by the real Jonty in 1929, and compared it to his recent correspondence. Then it all came to me: the lack of family photos, the discrepancies in behaviour of the two. They say war changes a man, but it does not change people so much. And how could a wife not know her own husband? Initially, maybe you didn't want to consider the alternative, but Jonty Caswell-Jones didn't come back from Italy in 1945. William did. I gather everyone thought they were twins as children, and to strangers it was difficult to tell the pair apart. William wore his hair short, he was clean-shaven. Jonty had a moustache, parted his hair to one side and wore looking glasses. Like this photo – Christmas 1941. Both brothers together at Avonlea.

CATHERINE:

Where on earth did you find that?

ELIZABETH:

Behind the mirror in the study. Here you have Jonty on the left, and William on the right. Almost identical.

POLLY:

Gosh, they did so look alike. I can't believe this is true – is it really, Mother?

CATHERINE:

(Snidely) Let's listen to Elizabeth. She seems to have it all worked out.

ELIZABETH:

Coming out of a POW camp after so many years, of course one would expect Jonty to look a little different. He was awkward in settling back into his brother's life. I imagined how you might act, Catherine. Put myself in your shoes to see if it was possible you didn't know. It must have seemed that Jonty was a bit shellshocked, a bit forgetful. Eventually it dawned on you. You looked for evidence to support your theory, maybe tested him with queries about your wedding day, when the children were born. Despite his bad head for numbers, William was bright; he pulled off a good bluff. Nonetheless, your suspicions were confirmed. But rather than disrupt the family further, you accepted it. The children had been young the last time they had seen their father; their memories of their early years would be hazy at best. You flipped from being hoodwinked to becoming complicit in the scheme. And what harm would it do, really? A sense of relative peace was maintained. A welcome accord settled across the Caswell-Jones family.

ELIZABETH:

Reader, are you there? How am I getting on? I am rather rusty at a denouement like this … But I think they are all still on their toes. I'm guessing half of it, of course, based on my knowledge of the family, my knowledge of human nature. I expect this is how William managed the great deceit. I have always been listening to the little conversations … wondering why something was not quite right about the family. I have always known there was something at their very core that was rotten. How right I turned out to be? Best keep laying it all out for them.

ELIZABETH:

But why had he done it? William was one of the country's most eligible bachelors and could expect a whirlwind of balls and society belles on his return. There was the estate to run, with one of the country's largest private art collections. He was, after all, of an artistic disposition after studying Classics in Cambridge. But by returning as Jonty, it was a fresh start, with a ready-made family, wife and business. It was also the perfect way to hide being homosexual, without foisting a woman into a false marriage and siring children. In a family like the Caswell-Joneses, Matilda would never have allowed William to be himself, even in his own home. As his own younger brother, William would inherit the estate anyway. He had always been jealous of the apparent peace of Jonty's life. Whether or not you ever confronted him about it, you accepted him.

THOMAS:

Mother, is this true?

CATHERINE:

It is. What was I meant to do? You were all so happy to have Daddy back, and life could go on, I supposed. Yes, it was William, but he assumed all the best bits of your father. There was no way to replace him, but it meant not being widowed at thirty-five. I had always liked William; they were good friends, you know.

THOMAS:

So you went along with a . . . lie?

CATHERINE:

He absolutely loved you all.

FLORA:

So, Daddy really died . . . years ago?

ELIZABETH:

Your father died in the summer of 1945. A wave of dysentery ran through the camp; it had been a hot summer.

FLORA:

Didn't Granny know?

ELIZABETH:

Yes, good question, Flora. Surely your grandmother could recognise her favourite son? Tell William from Jonty? She enjoyed telling me how clearly she remembered the eyes of her sons. But just like Catherine, I gather Matilda initially explained away the inconsistencies . . . But she realised before long. Whether it was an errant birthmark, a missing childhood scar, she knew it was William. But she confronted him about it: 'Reveal yourself to the world!' she would have insisted. By then, Catherine and the children had accepted him back. He had committed fraud! Matilda only loved William when he was the successful elder brother, the toast of society and friend to royalty. She had built up this perfect picture of her first-born son, but the reality was very different. She had been betrayed, and that's where you come in, Polly. Granny's new favourite.

But why did someone kill Matilda, too? And how do you fit into this pretty picture, Nikolai? An early riser, Matilda was so keen to keep your company at the beginning of each day. What a strange friendship. At first, you thought she was an eccentric old dear, collecting an array of interesting characters for dinner parties to illuminate the evening. But Jonty, or as we know now, William playing Jonty, was not happy to see you here. At every occasion he tried to have you cut from the guestlist, or your invitations not sent, but Matilda overruled him. Why is that?

NIKOLAI:

I . . . I will not spill forth someone else's secrets. I will not breach the Official Secrets Act . . .

ELIZABETH:

I found a letter Jonty had written to you that he never got to send. You were at the POW camp, too, weren't you, Nikolai? For why else would the victim hate having him here? A constant reminder—

NIKOLAI:

Yes, I was there. I was there with the two brothers at that camp. But don't think so little of me that you expect I just come along to look for money . . . I never blackmailed anyone. Yes, I knew it was the wrong brother come home, but strange things happen at war. It wasn't bothering me. I have danced in productions across the world, captivating audiences, crown princes, anyone with an appreciation of art and music. Matilda came to many, many of my performances . . . I wanted to be around people who remembered that, not just the wizened old body who came home from that war.

ELIZABETH:

And how does a Russian Bolshoi dancer end up in a camp with two British officers?

NIKOLAI:

I thought you only ask questions that you don't know the answers to? My mother, she is English. It's complicated. I cannot talk any more about the war. But I will tell you this: there was no quarrel between the two brothers . . . In the camp, we all looked on; we were jealous that they had each other. They stayed laughing, joking, when the rest of us could not. They kept each other going, and that bond, it helped the rest of us to get through. Jonty died just two weeks before the camp was evacuated. We knew it was close to the end . . . which made it so much harder. Will argued to get him to a hospital, but it couldn't be done. Then, after they took us from the camp, I found a bed in a lodging house outside Florence. Will was there, but he had the moustache, the glasses. He had *become* Jonty. I knew immediately what they had done. And he knew that I knew. The moment he saw me, he froze, right there in the hot sun; the cigarette fell out of his mouth. The next morning, he was gone. The

next time we saw each other was at the summer fête at Avonlea . . .
I did not realise who Matilda was until he was there. I never spoke
of our time together in the camp, of seeing him that morning in
Florence, disguised as his brother. I never held it over him in any
way. Despite what he might have thought.

THOMAS:

Thank you, Nikolai. Did my . . . father suffer much, at the end?

NIKOLAI:

We had, by then, received health supplies for the outbreak; I'm sure
he would have had painkillers. There was opium there, other
things . . . He died the best death of anyone there, with his brother
by his side. I am very glad this is finally in the open.

ELIZABETH:

Now, Matilda. The cigarettes left in the study that you handed to
me, Nikolai, were the brand Matilda smoked. I did not see anyone
else smoke this particular brand, with its distinctive taste. When I
fainted, I was not just hungry or warm. I was poisoned. Someone
had dipped the cigarettes in nicotine – the extra nicotine would
knock someone out cold. So, whoever planted these cigarettes did
not necessarily intend to kill her, but the intention was certainly to
incapacitate her. This might, of course, explain why it was impossible to rouse her at lunch. Now, why would someone want Matilda
out of the picture at the precise time of her son's death?

It told me that whoever planned the murder of Jonty had
planned it well. And it all makes sense, of course, because the truth
is, this is not the first time our murderer has killed . . . It was a
moonless night in April 1943 when we were returning from the
officers' dance where we were stationed at Lannisterfield. One of
the staff nurses had gone off with a chap . . . A big tall fellow, had
her dancing all night. She refused to come home with us; he had
plied her with gin and she was drunk. It's an old story, isn't it? Well,
she returned to the lodging house, snuck in through the window
over the loo. That's how we thought she had cut herself. She tried

to wash the blood away, hiding her sobs from the landlady. But the truth soon became clear. The chap had raped her, left her in a ditch.

CATHERINE:

That's quite enough, Elizabeth, there's no need to go into such detail.

ELIZABETH:

Oh, but there is. Now, in this instance . . . I can't say you had a bad motive. What he did to that nurse was unthinkable. But I saw the plan come together in your eyes. On the ward you quizzed his ranking officer, joking as if you were seeking details of the chap for a single friend. Who he was, where he would be. All the details you needed to murder the fellow. The next night, by the slightest sliver of the new moon, you ran him over—

CATHERINE:

You were there, too, Elizabeth.

ELIZABETH:

I didn't really believe what you were doing, . . . initially I thought we were going to make a delivery – that we had just happened upon him, that it was all an accident. And then, even after seeing you scheme and plan, when we were in the middle of it all, in the middle of killing this fellow, it just didn't feel real. But you didn't just hit him once, you reversed over him, too, letting on as if you had just lost control of the jeep or hadn't meant to do it. I was a young girl then; you were a married woman in her thirties. That night, I witnessed for myself how you have this special quality, Catherine . . . you can just turn off empathy for another. You use your anger, let it slow burn and build into a terrible force that turns deadly. I've tried to talk to you about that night before, but you never want to go there. That's really why you stopped inviting me, isn't it? And you know, I was rather glad. It is not good to occupy the same space as a killer.

And that's why you brought me here yesterday, isn't it? All these years you've tried to suggest that I am as guilty as you . . . you thought I'd never dare incriminate myself to expose you. Yes, I knew what you did. I never reported it. You thought I wouldn't dare incriminate myself for being in the car with you that night during the war, for knowing what you did and not reporting it. You hoped that would play in your favour – that I would go along with whoever you put forward as the suspect. Polly speaking of Thomas's history of violence. Catherine, you telling me of Ludlow's business endeavours gone wrong. You and Matilda wanted to lay out your own son as a suspect, didn't you?

FLORA:

Mother, is this true? Did you kill . . .?

POLLY:

That's where my sewing kit went – Mother, I can't quite believe you!

THOMAS:

Of course it is true, it makes complete sense. You remember the way she looked at him, as if he were a dog.

ELIZABETH:

It's you, Catherine. You killed the man posing as Jonty. And you killed Matilda, too, once you saw how easy it was to do. She was a loose end, a thorn in your side. With her gone, no one would know what you had done to Jonty. With Matilda dead, you would be free of the whole lie, free to remarry, free to spend your money as you wanted to – all without anyone to answer to. But I do have one question, which might come as news to you all, because Matilda was in on it too, wasn't she? Now why did Matilda want her last son to die?

CATHERINE:

Matilda was as angry about being fooled as me. Although it took her far longer to realise. She brought it up, casually, when we were planning for this Christmas. You know she killed her husband the same way, and got away with it? She was brilliant, although quite the schemer. We weren't really that different, you know; we liked to play up this little feud. She said she was fed up with William moping around the place, and that the children needed their inheritance to move on with their lives. I was sick of looking at him, too – a constant reminder that Jonty had never come home. And there he was, cluttering up the table at Christmas. That was another ingenious manoeuvre: Matilda and I planned out this year's guest list with that in mind, making sure everyone would have a motive for murdering the chap – whether a petty feud or a lifelong rivalry . . . I knew you'd look at every little thing, never letting anyone off the hook until you had *evidence*. She even tried to recruit you into her scheme to frame—

ELIZABETH:

Your own son! Thomas. Despicable.

THOMAS:

Is this true, Mother? *(Angry)* He was still our uncle. What real harm had he done to you, for God's sake?

CATHERINE:

Don't you see, child? He had stolen from me, from us all. Stolen a future full of memories, the chance to love again, the chance to heal from the loss of a father. As it stood, he cast us all into purgatory with him. It was so oppressive – I tried to keep it from you. I have hated him every day of my life for years. Yesterday was the first day of freedom for me. You know, Elizabeth, I am relieved . . . it's all out in the open.

ELIZABETH:

I know you. You've never been happy to hide away your own clever handiwork. That and the fact, of course, that you were worried the children and his business associates would not accept the death as accidental. Given the changes to the will, you knew the death would be scrutinised. This way, by inviting me you could *control* the investigation. You thought you could blackmail me for being your passenger the night you ran over that officer, didn't you? You've always seen me as nothing more than a pawn in your life. You are the very definition of a narcissist. I'm sure they will come up with other names and classifications for criminals like you. Someone who is incapable of feeling empathy. Oh, you might pretend to understand, commiserate, for show. But it's only because that's what's expected of you. Despite what you say, the only person you really care about is yourself. You were so *cocksure* that you'd commited the perfect murder that you wanted to show off, didn't you? It was a test, wasn't it? You wanted to see if *I* could work it out, to test your skills, to show off your handiwork. But you were too haughty to believe I would actually crack it, weren't you? Well let me tell you this, Catherine. I am no fool. But neither are you. Now, it might have been Matilda's idea, but you executed it. After Frankie left, you snuck back into the study. You stood behind him. Were you pointing to something on his desk?

CATHERINE:

He was looking at that debut guide for Thomas.

ELIZABETH:

And you jabbed him with the needle, which, in your haste, you left in the study. You would have seen it all, watched him drown, unable to take a breath. You had to wait there until it was done, though. To rearrange his face, and body, all contorted. So that he would be left as serene as a monk. You left the study, sneaking out by the back stairs, at the exact moment Matilda had fallen asleep at the table. She had planned to make a diversion, but you didn't want to risk it – you worried she might change her mind and expose your plan after all. So you dipped her cigarettes in nicotine.

And the lemon cake, that was very cleverly done, because there were actually two – one underdone, and one overcooked – giving you the perfect alibi. If anyone came into the kitchen, you could show them the cake that best matched your timeline, therefore giving you an alibi that could be tied to physical evidence. After swapping the underdone lemon cake for the cooked one, you marched back to the study, with your daughter behind you. All quite simple, really; with so many people in the house, it was easy to move around, so that no one could really pinpoint where you were.

But you had help from someone else. I knew this person was involved from the very start – Argento, that grand entrance you made in the red car. It was too obvious. You were trying to prove you couldn't have played a part as you weren't here. That was how I knew you had to be involved. The dust on your navy trousers was unusual, a sort of grey colour. I remembered the children talking about all the secret passageways and hidden doors in the villa. I found the one that went between the kitchen, under the house and bridge, and over to the other side of the lake. You were here, watching out for Catherine as she murdered the man posing as her husband. But she got lazy and made you kill Matilda, didn't she? You didn't want any link to Jonty hanging around, did you? You were happy to kill her too. It made sense to you. As a nurse, Catherine would have known how to keep physical evidence to a minimum, apart from that little line of blood. Then, when all was done, you left through the tunnel and made a big show of returning over the bridge and blazing up the stairs.

And it wasn't your first time killing a civilian either, was it? That's what got you disbarred. A bar-house brawl that ended with you jabbing a broken glass into the carotid artery of the man who refused you another drop of drink.

You see, I remember that, too. An old friend of mine, James Beresford, told me all about the lawyer who stood trial for murder. He had been called to the Bar, too, at the time, a young diplomat. It was when the British Ambassador called that it brought it all back to me, you see. It is such a terribly small world. And a convicted murderer could no longer work as a lawyer.

ARGENTO:

Well done, Elizabeth. You can congratulate yourself on solving this terrible crime against this man who lied to us all. The war did strange things to us . . . I will admit I was an angry man, I saw red. That young guy – he was barely out of the school house, and he tried to stop me – a man who had served his country – from having a glass of wine!

ELIZABETH:

And that's why you locked me into the study, isn't it? You knew there was no need to kill anyone else, it was simply time to get rid of the evidence. So, you locked me away, to keep me from seeing what you did with the bottle of curare. But I know it is headed for the dark depths of Lake Como. Gone.

THOMAS:

So, what now, we wave Mother off to prison? Where have those Italian Polizia gone?

ELIZABETH:

Rossi is not going to arrest Catherine. Or Argento. Those officers have been well bribed. That's where your missing block of gold has gone, Thomas. This whole investigation was a farce.

THOMAS:

I shan't let you both go anywhere—

POLLY:

Absolutely not, if you think we won't stand up for our family—

ELIZABETH:

Don't you see, Polly, Thomas, that is why your grandmother and mother planned it all to happen here? It is remote, hard to access. It's Christmas, so many things are closed, there's fewer police and pathologists working. All of the locals, the undertaker, the police officers will be well paid. There will be no evidence of any wrong-doing, no one to arrest them . . . Your mother and Argento will slip off into the night, never to be heard of again, except to draw down her widow's allowance.

CATHERINE:

Well, Elizabeth, you have quite outdone yourself. Identified the killers – and let them go! You see, you have it almost perfectly. And my children, do not worry, I will turn up to see you from time to time. But now, I am free, to live, to love again.

MARGARET:

What about me?

CATHERINE:

Who said that?

ELIZABETH:

Margaret is wondering why you wouldn't ask her to help you. My, my. Margaret, Catherine isn't really a friend of yours. But are you a friend to her? You sent Jonty that poison pen letter, threatening to push him off a cliff. Why? Just because you're so unhappy with your own life, you want everyone else looking over their shoulder, isn't that true?

CATHERINE:

She had the right idea, even if you are a dumpy old mare, Margaret. Now, if you will all excuse me. We have somewhere to be. If you leave now, Sally, I'm sure you'll make your flight home to London. One thing I've learned – and I'm sure you'll agree, Elizabeth – it is very hard to run away from bad things—

NIKOLAI:

You're not the only detective, Elizabeth. I, too, realised Catherine killed her . . . husband . . . I mean, brother-in-law. I contacted the authorities in Milan. They will be sending a full team to investigate. As clever as you've been, Elizabeth, I knew you could not be trusted to fight for real justice. The storm, it is settling into the horizon, I'm sure they will not be so very long.

POLLY:

Mother . . . I feel so . . . betrayed by you. Don't you see the legacy you've given us, to be torn asunder like this? I never *knew* you to be so violent.

CATHERINE:

Life is full of nasty surprises, my dear, which I'm sure you're embarking on your own troubled journey. This is the first time I've felt alive in a very long time . . . And Nikolai, justice doesn't scare me. Here is Argento, a decade after killing that fellow. It doesn't look too bad for me.

POLLY:

Does this mean Thomas gets to keep the art? Granny will be rolling in her grave.

FLORA:

You'll not get a penny then, Peter.

MARGARET:

Am I in line for a small allowance? What if I keep all this a secret, Catherine?

(Sounds of arguing as Elizabeth closes and locks the door)

Elizabeth's Conclusion

ELIZABETH:

Oh my, my. I'd better lock them all in here until the police arrive from Milan. There we have it, the case is solved. Rather convoluted, wasn't it? So many secrets bubbling under the surface . . . Let's sit down and have a drink, shall we? Leave them to argue amongst themselves? Even if there is another bloody murder, I shan't be investigating it.

(Pouring wine into a glass)

ELIZABETH:

Let's go out onto the veranda.

(Elizabeth's steps in the background)

ELIZABETH:

I am terribly sorry to keep the tunnel from you, and a few other tidbits including Sally's letter, but I had to hold something back until the end. Perhaps you worked it out for yourself? It was just too obvious that Argento had been here. And his motive was the key: he was flat broke, and the family was his only way to earn a penny. Catherine has always cared far too much about what other people thought. And she couldn't bear the thought that all of that clever work would go into planning something this complex and no one would ever know. She had such pride. *It's so much easier to investigate a murder when all the suspects care only for themselves.*

(Doors open)

ELIZABETH:

Ah, it is good to breathe out here. The dark cloak of night has settled across Como, the storm has well wound down from earlier. I am jolly glad of this fur stole; even though it is sheltered up here, it is quite cold. Even if it was a gift from a two-timing low-life, I am grateful, you know, for this investigation. It has woken me from the slumber I had found myself in, filing correspondence for dull old bankers in Milan. I may not get the public notoriety, but I will look for more investigating work. There are always husbands who drop their britches and wives who want to know all about it. Speaking of which, I hope never to see Ludlow Lansdowne de Groot again after we leave here. And I am rather glad now that my drawers stayed up. And there is a certain joy to not being too badly behaved, isn't there? What a healthy, clean sense of satisfaction. There we are – the lights of the Milanese murder squad, the headlights of their black Fiats twinkling a reflection onto the murky depths of Lake Como. Well, I might be a little badly behaved, if he's a good-looking detective. And thank you to you, reader, yes, all that mental energy is bound to have assisted me.

All those decades that have passed between 1953 and 2020, those years of consuming television shows and detective novels have helped you a fair deal, I am sure. Did you know it was Catherine? It's well known by now that it's usually the spouse who commits the murder . . . even if she is a seasoned liar. Now, until we meet again, I had better go and reapply my lippy. Goodnight, and thank you for helping me find the most deadly of these twelve motives for murder. I've loved being your detective, Elizabeth Chalice. And let me tell you, this is not the last you've heard of me.

THE END

BONUS SHORT STORY

Jonty's Guest

The shutters of Villa Janus were now open. The midwinter day was so still that the Angelus bell from Bellagio carried over the green of Lake Como, ringing noon. He had been moving soft furnishing over to the verandah all morning.

Placing two glasses on the table, Jonty Caswell-Jones whistled, 'It's a long way to Tipperary'. Armfuls of cushions and blankets would make the wrought iron more comfortable. He hadn't seen his guest in many months. What a stroke of luck that they could have this moment together before the entire Caswell-Jones family arrived for Christmas. It had been a long journey to Como, across the Atlantic, and then by train from Lisbon. He wasn't the same man as the one who had left London. It would take a great effort to maintain the charade.

For now, just like the house with its open windows, he found he could breathe. He had considered not coming to Villa Janus at all. He could have disappeared into the spicy air of La Paz, viewing the colours of life. But he had something to do for his family. This was a promise he would keep.

The Valpolicella washed clean the final vestiges of dust from the bottom of the wine glass as he poured himself a drink. He'd missed them in the cursory rinse, so eager was he to pour a glass. But now he could see the ring of dust on the glass was terrible. It would unhinge his wife, too, no matter how much she'd insisted they could manage without Mrs Balliano and her dusky pink apron.

The place hadn't been let since last Christmas. Once upon a time, that might have appealed to him – having the exclusive use of the villa. But with the lack of other guests over the summer, it meant

Villa Janus was full of dusty cutlery and Como-damp sheets. He couldn't know if his family would take the chill out of the place – their arrival indeed wouldn't herald warm domesticity, more like a post-clear out bonfire.

She may not even arrive before the others. Though by his estimations, she should have been here hours ago. But time was as changeable as the clouds over the green hills. Getting to Villa Janus was a marathon configuration of timetables, transport hubs and fellows to tip.

It was a concern that someone had moved the photographs. If no one had been there since their last festive visit, who displaced them? And when? He stood looking over the verandah edge as the foamy tide shifted the pebbles of the coastline. The middle of the lake retained its green opacity. But at the shore, the surface was clear. He imagined his secret swallowed by that great body of water. Under water, they co-mingle with the secrets of others who had stood on the lakeshore over the years. Millennia of lies and threats and injustices sent to the water's fathomless depths ever since the glacier cleaved its way through.

The present was like the water's edge; it looked as if everything were transparent. But the further into the lake you went, murkiness clouded the truth before any semblance of verity was swallowed by the water's black expansive volume. He worried the hem of the red cashmere knit. It smelled of leather from the belt that had been displayed with it in the boutique on the Porto Nova. Staring down into the water was not good for a man as delicate as he. The stone-grey balustrade came to his knee. It would not be hard to jump into oblivion. Was that why he insisted she come early? So that he wouldn't be alone?

Jonty returned to the wine. Despite the smut on the glass, the winter sun reflected the pink material.

She had arrived.

Read on for a sneak peek of
Fiona Sherlock's new novel

SUPPER FOR SIX

Twenty years later, and murder is on the menu at an unexpected,
exclusive and extravagant dinner party in Mayfair. But this time
Elizabeth Chalice isn't here to be an investigator. She is here as a
guest . . . which may just prove to be far more perilous.

Available in audiobook and ebook in Spring 2022

HODDERstudio

Elizabeth Chalice
7.00pm

It is rather hot up here, in this pokey little attic room. But the view is good, I can see all the way over the chimney tops to Berkeley Square. Not much in the way of creature comforts either, just a single bed, and the ewer and basin to wash my face. The servants' quarters, I suppose. But in my line of work, it's hard to know where your next job is coming from so I'll take what I can. Sybil's house is only a two-minute walk from here, at least. Convenient if she wants me to work on a case nearby. In these cases, where my client is a wealthy woman, I've almost always tasked to find ammunition for a divorce case. But I do hope it's something a bit more interesting than an extra-marital affair.

I am already rather late. Hopefully, she won't be offended in our little supper à deux.

You know, it really can wear you down, investigating other people's lives. Uncovering secrets that no one really wants to hear. But despite my feelings on the matter, I have to put on the lipstick and stand tall. That's what it takes to confirm an adulterer, or uncover a murderer. I must have a certain knack for figuring things out; I get good results for my clients. So, if Lord Anderson has been cheating on his wife, I will find out. But, still, who really knows what she wants me to investigate. Already this year, I've located a lost cat and a misplaced briefcase for a banker. I'm almost sixty, I can't afford to consider these things beneath me. In order to manage, I've learned not to judge anyone, least of all, myself. And there is a certain vindication that I feel, when I've caught out a rotten apple.

It was quite the coincidence, when I ran into Sybil in Hyde Park. Or Lady Anderson, I should say. We've written to one another quite a lot since we first met. I gather the husband travels a lot, I daresay she's a lonely woman. Sometimes the letters go on for twenty pages! In fact, when she passed me in Hyde Park, she had been on her way to post a letter to me. She still gave me the letter. Isn't that odd? I suppose she'd gone to the trouble of writing it. But she asked me there and then to help her investigate something, once she'd gotten over the shock of seeing me. I did specify that I preferred not to work for friends after what happened in Italy, all those years ago. It does one no good to incriminate old friends. But yet she insisted only *I* could possibly help. And my savings are very nearly exhausted – so I couldn't say no. But I can't keep up this sort of work forever. The late nights, the dangerous surroundings, they do hurt.

I first met her about ten years ago, I was working on a case in Paris. I stayed in the top floor apartment, in a pretty little corner of the Boulevard St Germain. Lord and Lady Anderson were newlyweds, staying in the apartment below me. You can imagine I didn't sleep terribly well after they moved in. We met in the boulangerie and struck up a friendship. She was desperate to go out. It was as if she couldn't bear to be in the company of her own husband. We visited every play-house, theatre and club – she was thrilled to watch other performers. She had been a famous singer before they wed. And although she never said as much, I got the feeling that he wouldn't let her get on the stage again. Some outdated belief in what was a proper career for an aristocrat's wife, I'm sure. Not that he would have known, his late father was given the peerage only a few years before that.

As I step out of my apartment, I am hit by the smell of the city on a hot spring day. A torrid mix of melting tar and exhaust fumes, and the rotting fish in the bins there at the back of Luigi's. London is quite an assault on the senses. It feels as if a layer of grime comes to settle on my skin almost immediately after stepping out into the fug.

So I've already started to look into the business of Lord Anderson, in preparation. A good investigator always knows what she's getting herself into – and I certainly do not want Lady Anderson to spring any nasty surprises upon me at our *intimate* dinner.

Lord Anderson, plain old Mr Anderson when I first knew him, well, his father was responsible for introducing the Anderson Ant, of course, allowing millions of families to own a car. The company then diversified into military production, fulfilled all sorts of last-minute top-secret orders – in my research, that part is always a bit vague – and the Queen awards him a peerage. His son is a hard worker too, no wonder Sybil barely sees him. Twelve- or fourteen-hour work days are commonplace. And he plays hard too, a massive fan of the horses and casinos, he's so wealthy that he hasn't to worry about losing anything.

But here's the interesting part, nobody seems to have seen him in *months*. Since last June, in fact. He's undoubtedly not signed into his club, visited his factories, or been seen anywhere at all in England. He has, however, been calling the factories with instructions and is reachable by telephone quite easily. I need to know what Sybil wants – there are so many directions I could begin to look in. What does she want to know from me? And why is it only me who can help?

At that moment, six ambulances are wailing past me ... Six ambulances? I hope it's not another bomb. Then, just as quickly as the sirens stop, indicating they're only just around the corner, they start up again. They're coming back this way!

Surely this means it must only be a drill. What a relief. It terrifies me to think how close to the precipice of disaster life can be.

I am nearly at Sybil's now. From the map, it seems that she's the first house here after the lane. Right on the corner. Bruton Square is such a beautiful place. So elegant, even if it is rather small. The grass is so green it's hard to believe the blades erupt from soil of Central London. It reminds me of the fields I grew up beside. I'm sure all squares have healthy-looking grass. A lot of people don't know Bruton Square is here, they're so distracted by the stuccoed plaster-work of Berkeley Square. I'm no expert in architecture, but Bruton Square is early Victorian flat fronted, and very simple. Although the houses aren't actually very wide. There's the hallway and then it's just a single reception room across –exquisite, high-ceilinged rooms.

The window closest to the street is usually the morning room, and at the back a private sitting room. Upstairs, the room closest to the road is typically the dining room, with a parlour at the back. Kitchen downstairs, bedrooms and servant's quarters upstairs – I can see the half-windows at the top. But it is 1977. The Andersons could well have changed the layout. If it's just the two of us, I suppose we could just have our supper in the kitchen, or even on a little balcony. There . . . I see it. At the back of her house, there is a table and chair set out.

But then I spot her. Another young woman outside. I was so sure Sybil just wanted it to be me and her. If this young woman is staying for dinner, it may be more challenging to get the truth out of Sybil.

CHRISSY:
Hi, oh are you here for Syb— Lady Anderson?

ELIZABETH:
Seems like it, Elizabeth Chalice, pleased to meet you.

CHRISSY:
My husband is meant to be here somewhere too. Sorry, I'm Chrissy Crowley.

(DOOR OPENS)

SYBIL:
Good evening, Chrissy, so wonderful to see you! Thank you for joining me. Ah, Elizabeth Chalice, as I live and breathe.

ELIZABETH:
Pleased to see you, your Ladysh—

SYBIL:
Stop! There'll be none of that here! We're old friends. Come on in. I'm doing a risotto so can't leave it for too long. We're down here. Oh, Chrissy, that bag does look heavy, thank you for picking those items up. Here let me help you carry it. Are you alright to follow on, Elizabeth?

ELIZABETH:

Lead the way, Sybil. My eyes are just getting used to the . . . dark.

As Sybil leads me into the hallway, it's impossible to see what is going on. I was distracted by Chrissy, her thick black hair, and didn't notice the fanlight had been all blocked up.

I thought I was the only one going to be here.

I hope she gets to this job she has for me, there's nothing I detest more than being strung along and ending up with nothing. And what does this Chrissy woman have to do with the business at hand?

How peculiar, the doors to the rooms off this hallway are closed. There's barely a sliver of light from under the doors, but there's quite a scent of patchouli, and thick, expensive perfume.

SYBIL:

Do you need me to come back and get you, Elizabeth? I should have lit a few candles.

ELIZABETH:

It's ok. Here I am.

SYBIL:

(with hesitation) It is rather dark, the builders insist on keeping the light out, I'm so used to it.

ELIZABETH:

(quietly) Eh, I was expecting it to be just the two of us.

SYBIL:

Don't worry, we shall have a moment together. There is a reason I've brought you all together, you see, but I shall explain later. (Loudly) Anyway, follow Chrissy down those steps, to the open plan kitchen. You're very welcome to number 26! We have almost everyone here, let me introduce you. Everyone, this is Elizabeth Chalice, a very special friend of mine, who *loves* travelling. We lived in the same building in Paris a few years ago and stayed in touch ever since. You've already met Chrissy Crawley, the most talented

makeup artist in the West End! And this is Jeremy, her husband.
Jeremy is a musician and an artist too. One has to be impressed by
the height of that mohawk.

JEREMY:

How do, Liz. Nice to meet you.

SYBIL:

Will you pour Elizabeth here a glass of wine? And finally, I'm
delighted to introduce you to my neighbour, Mrs Agapanthus
Langford. If you're looking for any tips for the races, Aggie is the
lady to talk to. Tell us, did you have Red Rum in the National?

AGAPANTHUS:

Of course, I mean it was his third time to win, quite something.
Francois was sure he couldn't do it, which reminds me, where
could my errant husband have gone—

SYVLIA:

It's only just gone seven, I'm sure Francois will be along shortly.

AGAPANTHUS:

Pleased to meet you, Elizabeth. I don't quite know where my
husband could be detained.

ELIZABETH:

Well, there was the strangest convoy of ambulances just now, did
you hear the sirens?

AGAPANTHUS:

Good lord, I hope Francois is ok.

ELIZABETH:

Oh, sorry. I didn't mean to worry you, it looked like an exercise –
nothing more than a drill. They drove down towards the Mall,
stopped very briefly and turned around. I wouldn't worry.

SYBIL:

Yes, Aggie. I read that the Met are doing their best to counter IRA attacks. It probably is just an exercise in preparedness. Elizabeth, you sit in there beside Jeremy. Sorry, I know it's a bit of a squeeze, but I'll explain later. Now, I have to apologise for leading you up the garden path a little, I know you were all expecting a small plate and a chat. I have something very important I wanted to ask you— Oh! The bloody rice.

ELIZABETH:

Just chuck in more white wine, that'll unstick the risotto.

SYBIL:

Back in a minute, I'm just running out to the fridge.

This is not what I was expecting. Perhaps it's not about her husband at all. But how on earth are this bunch of people linked? Agapanthus, what a name! Mother had something to prove by naming a child that. I'm surprised she can breathe, with four rows of pearls tangled around a chiffon pussy-bow blouse. And Francois? I look forward to meeting him. Chrissy is a bright young thing, it's as if she's been dipped in gossamer. Perhaps she is really just a brilliant make-up artist. But how on earth she is married to Jeremy? I've noticed the punks, with their torn tights and badly dyed hair, hanging around Soho. But up close, the construction on his head is quite something to behold. His eyes are ringed with black, it looks like the fellow keeps the hours of a vampire.

Sybil is as healthy as ever. Her yellow maxi dress just reflects her own brilliance. She still has that star quality. Risotto aside, she doesn't look particularly troubled, so either the matter at hand is inconsequential, or she is a very good actress. This dinner party is clearly by design, she obviously wants me to meet these people. So, I had better pay attention.

JEREMY:

My hairdo ain't ideal for this set up, ladies. I tell you what, I'll try not to spike one of you in the eye. If I'm honest, I was expecting we'd be put up in a big fancy ballroom or something. Not rammed into this little table here. I think my old mother has something similar over in Forest Hill. She'd be chuffed to see the Mayfair lot had the same style.

ELIZABETH:

It is just marvellous, Jeremy. The mohawk, I believe it's called?

CHRISSY:

Try not to embarrass me now, Jeremy. I'm sorry, ladies I didn't think anyone else would be here this evening . . .

AGAPANTHUS:

Same here, I just thought, well, we are her neighbours, but we haven't really spent much time here since they moved in. Did you know about the others, Elizabeth?

ELIZABETH:

Eh—

JEREMY:

Sybil's always up to tricks like this, I wouldn't take it personally. Back when I was in the band with her, she'd insist everyone have dinner together. No airs and graces about her.

AGAPANTHUS:

(frustrated) Be that as it may, Elizabeth, you were expecting to be on your own tonight too?

ELIZABETH:

Yes, but I'm sure she has her reasons. Now, how about you tell us about your days in the band, Jeremy?

JEREMY:

Well, I'll let Sybil go into that. But this mohawk. I'll not lie, it takes a while. But once it's in, it's in.

AGAPANTHUS:

You mean you don't wash it? (Coughing)

JEREMY:

Oh, I do wash it, but it takes hours don't it, love? And Chrissy puts in a fresh colour. So, I don't wash it that often. Are you ok?

AGAPANTHUS is coughing uncontrollably

ELIZABETH:

Are you ok, Agapanthus. Can we give her some space?

SYBIL:

Now a lovely bottle of Chablis – Aggie, what's the matter?

I watch as Agapanthus collapses into her chair and rush over to her immediately. Her body has gone entirely limp and lifeless. There's no time to wait.

ELIZABETH:

(Panicked) Ring an ambulance, will you Sybil? I think she's stopped breathing. I think there was something in her wine. I think . . . I think she has been poisoned.

Acknowledgements

This book would not exist without the creativity and professionalism of my editor, Sara Adams. I am eternally grateful for the agenting expertise of Lina Langlee and Julie Fergusson and the North Literary Agency.

Thank you to the whole team at Hodder Studio, especially: Callie Robertson, Ellie Wheeldon, Bea Fitzgerald, Claudette Morris, Lewis Csizmazia and Jenny Platt.

For bringing the audiobook to life, thank you to the actors: George Weightman, Clare Louise Connolly, Tom McCall, Stephanie Lane, Nneka Okoye, Joseph Capp, Ruth Lass, Hannah Barrie.

Thank you to my husband, Macken. It would have been impossible to write a book with a newborn and a toddler, without the amazing support of my mother, Deirdre White. I am forever grateful to Orla and the team at Little Robins, Donna and Kelen for minding Sephie and keeping the show on the road at home. Thank you to Anna Deasy and Eoin Carleton-Keogh for your magic organisational skills.

For contributing facts for this book and helping me hone my craft, thank you to Mary Walsh, Kelley Burke, Nigel Heneghan, Suzannah Dunn, Willie Passmore, Erica Jackson, Evelyn Sherlock, Linda Farrell, Philippa Grant, Nicholas McNicholas, Megan McNicholas, Donnacha Lynch, Les Hanlon and the

Hinterland Festival, Morgan Kavanagh. Thank you to everyone who responded to a random text in their field of expertise, and to all of my friends and family. For their encouragement, thank you to Kathleen Watkins and Gay Byrne, Mary and Walter McNicholas. And to that person who is wondering why they aren't named, I'm sorry, I've forgotten, thank you too!

For teaching me there's no such thing as 'can't' only 'won't', thank you to my dad, John Sherlock. For introducing me to the beauty of the English language, thank you to my grandmother, Monica Sherlock.

ABOUT THE AUTHOR

Fiona Sherlock is an Irish writer living in Bective, Co Meath. A regular contributor to the *Sunday Independent*, she writes murder mystery books and creates games at BespokeMurderMystery.com. She's undertaking an MSt in Creative Writing at Cambridge University. She enjoys midday fires and making elderflower champagne.